MAGNUS CHASE
and the GODS of ASGARD

THE HAMMER OF THOR

Also by Rick Riordan

RICK RIORDAN

MAGNUS CHASE
and the GODS of ASGARD

II

THE HAMMER OF THOR

𝔇ɪsɴᴇʏ•HYPERION

Los Angeles   New York

First Edition, October 2016
1 3 5 7 9 10 8 6 4 2

FAC-020093-16232

Printed in the United States of America

Library of Congress Cataloging-in-Publication Control Number: 2016025920

Rune and symbol art by Michelle Gengaro-Kokmen

ISBN 978-1-4231-6092-2

Reinforced binding

Visit www.DisneyBooks.com

SUSTAINABLE FORESTRY INITIATIVE   Certified Sourcing
www.sfiprogram.org
SFI-00993

THIS LABEL APPLIES TO TEXT STOCK

To J. R. R. Tolkien,
who opened up the world of Norse mythology for me

CONTENTS

MAGNUS CHASE

and the GODS of ASGARD

II

THE HAMMER OF THOR

ONE

Could You Please
Stop Killing My Goat?

LESSON LEARNED: If you take a Valkyrie out for coffee, you'll get stuck with the check and a dead body.

I hadn't seen Samirah al-Abbas in almost six weeks, so when she called out of the blue and said we needed to talk about a matter of life and death, I agreed right away.

(Technically I'm already dead, which means the whole *life-and-death* thing didn't apply, but still . . . Sam sounded anxious.)

She hadn't yet arrived when I got to the Thinking Cup on Newbury Street. The place was packed as usual, so I queued up for coffee. A few seconds later, Sam flew in—literally—right over the heads of the café patrons.

Nobody batted an eye. Regular mortals aren't good at processing magical stuff, which is fortunate, because otherwise Bostonians would spend most of their time running around in a panic from giants, trolls, ogres, and *einherjar* with battle-axes and lattes.

Sam landed next to me in her school uniform—white sneakers, khaki slacks, and a long-sleeve navy shirt with the King Academy logo. A green hijab covered her hair. An ax hung from her belt. I was pretty sure the ax wasn't standard dress code.

As glad as I was to see her, I noted that the skin under her eyes was darker than usual. She was swaying on her feet.

"Hey," I said. "You look terrible."

"Nice to see you, too, Magnus."

"No, I mean . . . not terrible like *different than normal* terrible. Just terrible like exhausted."

"Should I get you a shovel so you can dig that hole a little deeper?"

I raised my hands in surrender. "Where have you been the last month and a half?"

Her shoulders tightened. "My workload this semester has been killing me. I'm tutoring kids after school. Then, as you might remember, there's my part-time job reaping souls of the dead and running top secret missions for Odin."

"You kids today and your busy schedules."

"On top of all that . . . there's flight school."

"Flight school?" We shuffled forward with the line. "Like *airplanes?*"

I knew Sam's goal was to become a professional pilot someday, but I hadn't realized she was already taking lessons. "You can *do* that at sixteen?"

Her eyes sparkled with excitement. "My grandparents could never have afforded it, but the Fadlans have this friend who runs a flight school. They finally convinced Jid and Bibi—"

"Ah." I grinned. "So the lessons were a gift from Amir."

Sam blushed. She's the only teenager I know who has a *betrothed*, and it's cute how flustered she gets when she talks about Amir Fadlan.

"Those lessons were the most thoughtful, the most considerate . . ." She sighed wistfully. "But enough of that. I didn't bring you here to talk about my schedule. We have an informant to meet."

"An informant?"

"This could be the break I've been waiting for. If his information is good—"

Sam's phone buzzed. She fished it out of her pocket, checked the screen, and cursed. "I have to go."

"You just got here."

"Valkyrie business. Possible code three-eight-one: heroic death in progress."

"You're making that up."

"I'm not."

"So . . . what, somebody thinks they're about to die and they text you *'Going down! Need Valkyrie ASAP!'* followed by a bunch of sad-face emojis?"

"I seem to recall taking *your* soul to Valhalla. You didn't text me."

"No, but I'm special."

"Just get a table outside," she said. "Meet my informant. I'll be back as soon as I can."

"I don't even know what your informant looks like."

"You'll recognize him when you see him," Sam promised. "Be brave. Also, get me a scone."

She flew out of the shop like Super Muslima, leaving me to pay for our order.

I got two large coffees and two scones and found a table outside.

Spring had arrived early in Boston. Patches of dirty snow still clung to the curbs like dental plaque, but the cherry trees popped with white and red buds. Flowery pastel clothing displays bloomed in the windows of high-end boutiques. Tourists strolled by enjoying the sunshine.

Sitting outside, comfortable in my freshly laundered jeans, T-shirt, and denim jacket, I realized this would be the first spring in three years that I hadn't been homeless.

Last March, I had been scrounging from Dumpsters. I'd been sleeping under a bridge in the Public Garden, hanging out with my buddies Hearth and Blitz, avoiding the cops and just trying to stay alive.

Then, two months ago, I died fighting a fire giant. I'd woken up in the Hotel Valhalla as one of Odin's *einherji* warriors.

Now I had clean clothes. I took a shower every day. I slept in a comfortable bed every night. I could sit at this café table, eating food I'd actually paid for, and not worry about when the staff would force me to move along.

Since my rebirth, I'd gotten used to a lot of weird stuff. I'd traveled the Nine Worlds meeting Norse gods, elves, dwarves, and a bunch of monsters with names I couldn't pronounce. I'd scored a magical sword that presently hung around my neck in the form of a runestone pendant. I'd even had a mind-melting conversation with my cousin Annabeth about the *Greek* gods who hung out in New York and made *her* life difficult. Apparently North America was lousy with ancient gods. We had a full-blown infestation.

All of that I'd learned to accept.

But being back in Boston on a nice spring day, hanging out like a regular mortal kid?

That felt strange.

I scanned the crowd of pedestrians, looking for Sam's

informant. *You'll recognize him when you see him,* she'd promised. I wondered what kind of information this guy had, and why Sam considered it life-and-death.

My gaze fixed on a storefront at the end of the block. Over the doorway, the brass-and-silver sign still gleamed proudly: BLITZEN'S BEST, but the shop was shuttered. The front door window was papered over on the inside, with a message hastily scrawled in red marker: *Closed for remodeling. Back soon!*

I'd been hoping to ask Samirah about that. I had no idea why my old friend Blitz had abruptly disappeared. One day a few weeks ago, I'd just walked by the shop and found it closed. Since then, there'd been no word from Blitzen or Hearthstone, which wasn't like them.

Thinking about this made me so preoccupied I almost didn't see our informant until he was right on top of me. But Sam was correct: he kind of stood out. It's not every day you see a goat in a trench coat.

A porkpie hat was wedged between his curly horns. A pair of sunglasses perched on his nose. His trench coat kept getting tangled in his back hooves.

Despite his clever disguise, I recognized him. I'd killed and eaten this particular goat on another world, which is the sort of bonding experience you don't forget.

"Otis," I said.

"*Shhh,*" he said. "I'm incognito. Call me . . . *Otis.*"

"I'm not sure that's how *incognito* works, but okay."

Otis, aka Otis, climbed into the chair I'd reserved for Sam. He sat on his back haunches and put his front hooves on the table. "Where is the Valkyrie? Is she incognito, too?" He peered at the nearest pastry bag as if Sam might be hiding inside.

"Samirah had to go reap a soul," I said. "She'll be back soon."

"It must be nice having a purpose in life." Otis sighed. "Well, thank you for the food."

"That's not for—"

Otis snapped up Sam's scone bag and began to eat it, paper and all.

At the table next to us, an older couple glanced at my goat friend and smiled. Maybe their mortal senses perceived him as a cute child or a funny pet dog.

"So." I had a hard time watching Otis devour the pastry, spraying crumbs across the lapels of his trench coat. "You had something to tell us?"

Otis belched. "It's about my master."

"Thor."

Otis flinched. "Yes, him."

If I worked for the thunder god, I too would have flinched when I heard Thor's name. Otis and his brother, Marvin, pulled the god's chariot. They also provided Thor with a never-ending supply of goat meat. Each night, Thor killed and ate them for dinner. Each morning, Thor resurrected them. This is why you should go to college, kids—so when you grow up you do not have to take a job as a magical goat.

"I finally have a lead," Otis said, "on that *certain object* my master is missing."

"You mean his ham—?"

"Don't say it aloud!" Otis warned. "But, yes . . . his *ham*."

I flashed back to January, when I'd first met the thunder god. Good times around the campfire, listening to Thor fart, talk about his favorite TV shows, fart, complain about his missing hammer, which he used to kill giants and stream his favorite TV shows, and fart.

"It's *still* missing?" I asked.

Otis clacked his front hooves on the tabletop. "Well, not *officially*, of course. If the giants knew for certain that Thor was without his you-know-what, they would invade the mortal worlds, destroy everything, and send me into a very deep funk. But unofficially . . . yes. We've been searching for months with no luck. Thor's enemies are getting bolder. They sense weakness. I told my therapist it reminds me of when I was a kid in the goat pen and the bullies were sizing me up." Otis got a faraway look in his yellow slit-pupil eyes. "I think that's when my traumatic stress started."

This was my cue to spend the next several hours talking to Otis about his feelings. Being a terrible person, I just said "I feel your pain" and moved on.

"Otis," I said, "the last time we saw you, we found Thor a nice iron staff to use as a backup weapon. He's not exactly defenseless."

"No, but the staff is not as good as the . . . *ham*. It doesn't inspire the same fear in the giants. Also, Thor gets cranky trying to watch his shows on the staff. The screen is tiny, and the resolution is terrible. I don't like it when Thor is cranky. It makes it hard for me to find my happy space."

A lot about this did not make sense: why Thor would have so much trouble locating his own hammer; how he could possibly have kept its loss a secret from the giants for so long; and the idea that Otis the goat would have a happy space.

"So Thor wants our help," I guessed.

"Not officially."

"Of course not. We'll all have to wear trench coats and glasses."

"That's an excellent idea," Otis said. "Anyway, I told the Valkyrie I would keep her updated since she is in charge of Odin's . . . you know, special missions. This is the first good lead I've gotten to the location of the *certain object*. My source is reliable. He's another goat who goes to the same psychiatrist. He overheard some talk in his barnyard."

"You want us to track down a lead based on barnyard gossip you heard in your psychiatrist's waiting room."

"That would be great." Otis leaned so far forward I was afraid he might fall out of his chair. "But you're going to have to be careful."

It took all my effort not to laugh. I'd played catch-the-lava-ball with fire giants. I'd eagle-skied over the rooftops of Boston. I'd pulled the World Serpent out of Massachusetts Bay and defeated Fenris Wolf with a ball of yarn. Now this goat was telling me to be careful.

"So where is the *ham*?" I asked. "Jotunheim? Niflheim? Thorfartheim?"

"You're teasing." Otis's sunglasses slipped sideways on his snout. "But the *ham* is in a different dangerous location. It's in Provincetown."

"Provincetown," I repeated. "On the tip of Cape Cod."

I had vague memories of the place. My mom had taken me there for a weekend one summer when I was about eight. I remembered beaches, saltwater taffy, lobster rolls, and a bunch of art galleries. The most dangerous thing we'd encountered was a seagull with irritable bowel syndrome.

Otis lowered his voice. "There is a barrow in Provincetown— a *wight's* barrow."

"Is that like a wheelbarrow?"

"No, no. A wight . . ." Otis shuddered. "Well, a wight is a powerful undead creature that likes to collect magical weapons. A wight's tomb is called a—a *barrow.* Sorry, I have a hard time talking about wights. They remind me of my father."

That raised another batch of questions about Otis's childhood, but I decided to leave them for his therapist.

"Are there a lot of lairs of undead Vikings in Provincetown?" I asked.

"Only one, as far as I know. But that's enough. If the *certain object* is there, it will be difficult to retrieve—underground, and guarded by powerful magic. You'll need your friends—the dwarf and the elf."

That would have been great, if I had any idea where those friends were. I hoped Sam knew more than I did.

"Why doesn't Thor go and check this barrow himself?" I asked. "Wait . . . let me guess. He doesn't want to draw attention. Or he wants us to have a chance to be heroes. Or it's hard work and he has some shows to catch up on."

"To be fair," Otis said, "the new season of *Jessica Jones* did just start streaming."

It's not the goat's fault, I told myself. *He does not deserve to be punched.*

"Fine," I said. "When Sam gets here, we'll talk strategy."

"I'm not sure I should wait with you." Otis licked a crumb

off his lapel. "I should have mentioned this earlier, but you see, someone . . . or *something* . . . has been stalking me."

The hairs on my neck tingled. "You think they followed you here?"

"I'm not sure," Otis said. "Hopefully my disguise threw them off."

Oh, great, I thought.

I scanned the street but saw no obvious lurkers. "Did you get a good look at this someone/something?"

"No," Otis admitted. "But Thor has all sorts of enemies who would want to stop us from getting his—his *ham* back. They would not want me sharing information with you, especially this last part. You have to warn Samirah that—"

THUNK.

Living in Valhalla, I was used to deadly weapons flying out of nowhere, but I was still surprised when an ax sprouted from Otis's furry chest.

I lunged across the table to help him. As the son of Frey, god of fertility and health, I can do some pretty awesome first aid magic given enough time. But as soon as I touched Otis, I sensed that it was too late. The ax had pierced his heart.

"Oh, dear." Otis coughed blood. "I'll just . . . die . . . now."

His head lolled backward. His porkpie hat rolled across the pavement. The lady sitting behind us screamed as if just now noticing that Otis was not a cute puppy dog. He was, in fact, a dead goat.

I scanned the rooftops across the street. Judging from the angle of the ax, it must have been thrown from somewhere up there . . . yes. I caught a flicker of movement just as the attacker ducked out of sight—a figure in black wearing some sort of metal helmet.

So much for a leisurely cup of coffee. I yanked the magical pendant from my neck chain and raced after the goat-assassin.

TWO

Your Standard Rooftop Chase Scene with Talking Swords and Ninjas

I SHOULD introduce my sword.

Jack, these are the peeps. Peeps, this is Jack.

His real name is *Sumarbrander*, the Sword of Summer, but Jack prefers *Jack* because reasons. When Jack feels like snoozing, which is most of the time, he hangs out on a chain around my neck in the form of a pendant marked with *fehu*, the rune of Frey:

When I need his help, he turns into a sword and kills things. Sometimes he does this while I wield him. Other times he does this while flying around on his own and singing annoying pop songs. He is magical that way.

As I bounded across Newbury Street, Jack sprang to full form in my hand. His blade—thirty inches of double-edged bone-forged steel—was emblazoned with runes that pulsed in different colors when Jack talked.

"What's going on?" he asked. "Who are we killing?"

Jack claims he doesn't pay attention to my conversations when he is in pendant form. He says he usually has his headphones on. I don't believe this, because Jack doesn't have headphones. Or ears.

"Chasing assassin," I blurted out, dodging a taxi. "Killed goat."

"Right," Jack said. "Same old, same old, then."

I leaped up the side of the Pearson Publishing building. I'd spent the last two months learning to use my einherji powers, so one jump took me to a ledge three stories above the main entrance—no problem, even with a sword in one hand. Then I hop-climbed from window ledge to cornice up the white marble facade, channeling my inner Hulk until I reached the top.

On the far side of the roof, a dark bipedal shape was just disappearing behind a row of chimneys. The goat-killer looked humanoid, which ruled out goat-on-goat homicide, but I'd seen enough of the Nine Worlds to know that humanoid didn't mean human. He could be an elf, a dwarf, a small giant, or even an ax-murderer god. (Please, not an ax-murderer god.)

By the time I reached the chimneys, my quarry had jumped to the roof of the next building. That might not sound impressive, but the next building was a brownstone mansion about fifty feet away across a small parking lot. The goat-killer didn't even have the decency to break his ankles on impact. He somersaulted on the tar and came up running. Then he leaped back across Newbury Street and landed on the steeple of the Church of the Covenant.

"I hate this guy," I said.

"How do you know it's a guy?" Jack asked.

The sword had a point. (Sorry, I keep stumbling into that pun.) The goat-killer's loose black clothes and metal war helmet made it impossible to guess his or her gender, but I decided to keep thinking of him as male for now. Not sure why. I guess I found the idea of a bro goat-assassin more annoying.

I backed up, took a running start, and leaped toward the church.

I'd love to tell you I landed on the steeple, slapped some handcuffs on the killer, and announced, *You're going away for livestock murder!*

Instead . . . well, the Church of the Covenant has these beautiful stained glass windows made by Tiffany in the 1890s. On the left side of the sanctuary, one window has a big crack at the top. My bad.

I hit the church's slanted roof and slid back, grabbing the gutter with my right hand. Spikes of pain shot up my fingernails. I dangled from the ledge, my legs flailing, kicking the beautiful stained glass window right in the Baby Jesus.

On the bright side, swinging precariously from the roof saved my life. Just as I twisted, an ax hurtled from above, slicing the buttons off my denim jacket. A centimeter closer and it would've opened up my chest.

"Hey!" I yelled.

I tend to complain when people try to kill me. Sure, in Valhalla we einherjar are constantly killing each other, and we get resurrected in time for dinner. But outside Valhalla, I was very much killable. If I died in Boston, I would not be getting a cosmic do-over.

The goat-assassin peered down at me from the peak of the roof. Thank the gods, he appeared to be out of throwing axes. Unfortunately, he still had a sword at his side. His leggings and tunic were stitched from black fur. A soot-smeared chain mail coat hung loosely on his chest. His black iron helmet had a chain mail curtain around the base—what we in the Viking business call an *aventail*—completely covering his neck and throat. His features were obscured by a faceplate fashioned to resemble a snarling wolf.

Of course a wolf. Everybody in the Nine Worlds loves wolves. They have wolf shields, wolf helmets, wolf screen savers, wolf pajamas, and wolf-themed birthday parties.

Me, not so much loving the wolves.

"Take a hint, Magnus Chase." The assassin's voice warbled, modulating from soprano to baritone as if going through a special effects machine. "Stay away from Provincetown."

The fingers of my left hand tightened on the hilt of my sword. "Jack, do your thing."

"You sure about that?" Jack asked.

The assassin hissed. For some reason, people are often shocked when they find out my sword can talk.

"I mean," Jack continued, "I know this guy killed Otis, but *everybody* kills Otis. Getting killed is part of Otis's job description."

"Just chop off his head or something!" I yelled.

The assassin, not being an idiot, turned and fled.

"Get him!" I told Jack.

"Why do *I* have to do all the hard work?" Jack complained.

"Because I'm dangling here and you can't be killed!"

"Just because you're right doesn't make this cool."

I flung him overhead. Jack spiraled out of view, flying after the goat-killer while singing his own version of "Shake It Off." (I have never been able to convince him that the line isn't *cheese graters gonna grate, grate, grate, grate, grate*.)

Even with my left hand free, it took me a few seconds to haul myself up to the roof. Somewhere to the north, the clanging of blades echoed off brick buildings. I raced in that direction, leaping over the church's turrets, launching myself across Berkeley Street. I bounced from rooftop to rooftop until I heard Jack yell in the distance, "OW!"

Most people might not run into battle to check on the welfare of their swords, but that's what I did. At the corner of Boylston, I scrambled up the side of a parking garage, got to the roof level, and found Jack fighting for his . . . well, maybe not his life, but at least his dignity.

Jack often bragged that he was the sharpest blade in the Nine Worlds. He could cut through anything and fight a dozen enemies at once. I tended to believe him, since I'd personally seen him take out giants the size of skyscrapers. Yet the goat-killer was having no trouble forcing him back across the roof. The assassin might have been small, but he was strong and quick. His dark iron sword sparked against Jack. Every time the two blades connected, Jack yelped, "Ow! Ow!"

I didn't know if Jack was in real danger, but I had to help. Since I didn't have another weapon and I didn't feel like fighting empty-handed, I ran to the nearest lamppost and ripped it out of the cement.

That sounds like I was showing off. Honestly, I wasn't. The pole was just the handiest weapon-like object I could find—except for a parked Lexus, and I wasn't quite strong enough to wield a luxury automobile.

I charged the goat-killer with my twenty-foot-long jousting light fixture. That got his attention. As he turned toward me, Jack lashed out, opening a deep cut in the assassin's thigh. The goat-killer grunted and stumbled.

That was my chance. I could have taken him down. Instead,

when I was ten feet away, a distant howl cut through the air and froze me in my tracks.

Jeez, Magnus, you're thinking, *it was only a distant howl. What's the big deal?*

I may have mentioned I don't like wolves. When I was fourteen, two of them with glowing blue eyes killed my mother. My recent encounter with Fenris hadn't done anything to increase my appreciation for the species.

This particular howl was *definitely* that of a wolf. It came from somewhere across the Boston Common, reverberating off the high-rises, turning my blood to Freon. It was *exactly* the same sound I'd heard the night of my mother's death—hungry and triumphant, the baying of a monster that had found its prey.

The lamppost slipped from my grip, clanging against the asphalt.

Jack floated to my side. "Uh, *señor* . . . are we still fighting this guy or what?"

The assassin staggered backward. The black fur of his leggings glistened with blood. "And so it begins." His voice sounded even more garbled. "Beware, Magnus. If you go to Provincetown, you will play into your enemy's hands."

I stared at that snarling face mask. I felt like I was fourteen again, alone in the alley behind my apartment the night my mother died. I remembered gazing up at the fire escape from which I had just dropped, hearing the wolves howl from our living room. Then flames exploded from the windows.

"Who—who are you?" I managed.

The assassin let out a guttural laugh. "Wrong question.

The right question: Are you prepared to lose your friends? If not, you should leave Thor's hammer lost."

He backed to the edge of the roof and toppled over.

I ran to the ledge just as a flock of pigeons surged upward, rising in a blue-gray cloud, swirling away over the Back Bay's forest of chimneys. Down below: no movement, no body, no sign of the assassin.

Jack hovered next to me. "I've could've taken him. You just caught me unprepared. I didn't have time to do my stretches."

"Swords don't stretch," I said.

"Oh, excuse me, Mr. Expert on Proper Warm-up Techniques!"

A tuft of pigeon down helicoptered to the ledge and stuck in a smear of the assassin's blood. I picked up the tiny feather and watched red liquid soak into it.

"So what now?" Jack asked. "And what was that wolf howl?"

Ice water trickled down my eustachian tubes, leaving a cold, bitter taste in my mouth. "I don't know," I said. "Whatever it was, it's stopped now."

"Should we go check it out?"

"No! I mean . . . by the time we figured out where the sound came from, we'd be too late to do anything about it. Besides . . ."

I studied the bloody pigeon feather. I wondered how the goat-killer had disappeared so effectively, and what he knew about Thor's missing hammer. His distorted voice reverberated in my mind: *Are you prepared to lose your friends?*

Something about the assassin had seemed very wrong . . . yet very familiar.

"We have to get back to Sam." I grabbed Jack's hilt and exhaustion washed over me.

The downside of having a sword who fights on his own: whatever Jack did, I paid the price as soon as he returned to my hand. I felt bruises spreading across my arms—one for each time Jack had been struck by the other sword. My legs trembled like they'd been doing lunges all morning. A lump of emotion formed in my throat—Jack's shame for letting the goat-killer fight him to a standstill.

"Hey, man," I told him, "at least you cut him. That's more than I did."

"Yeah, well . . ." Jack sounded embarrassed. I knew he didn't like sharing the bad stuff with me. "Maybe you should rest for a minute, *señor*. You're in no shape—"

"I'm all right," I said. "Thanks, Jack. You did good."

I willed him to return to pendant form, then reattached the runestone to my neck chain.

Jack was right about one thing: I needed rest. I felt like crawling inside that nice Lexus and taking a nap, but if the goat-assassin decided to double back to the Thinking Cup, if he caught Sam unaware . . .

I took off across the rooftops, hoping I wasn't too late.

THREE

My Friends Protect Me
by Telling Me Absolutely
Nothing. Thanks, Friends

BACK AT the café, Sam was standing over Otis's body.

Customers walked in and out of the Thinking Cup, making a wide arc around the dead goat. They didn't seem alarmed. Maybe they saw Otis as a passed-out homeless guy. Some of my best friends were passed-out homeless guys. I knew how well they could repel a crowd.

Sam frowned at me. Under her left eye was a new orange bruise. "Why is our informant dead?"

"Long story," I said. "Who hit you?"

"Also a long story."

"Sam—"

She waved aside my concern. "I'm fine. Just please tell me you didn't kill Otis because he ate my scone."

"No. Now if he'd eaten *my* scone—"

"Ha, ha. What happened?"

I was still worried about Sam's eye, but I did my best to explain about the goat-killer. Meanwhile, Otis's form began to dissolve, melting into curls of white vapor like dry ice. Soon there was nothing left but the trench coat, the glasses, the porkpie hat, and the ax that had killed him.

Sam picked up the assassin's weapon. The blade was no

larger than a smartphone, but the edge looked sharp. The dark metal was etched with soot-black runes.

"Giant-forged iron," Sam said. "Enchanted. Perfectly weighted. This is a valuable weapon to leave behind."

"That's nice. I'd hate for Otis to be killed with a shoddy weapon."

Sam ignored me. She'd gotten pretty good at that. "You say the killer wore a wolf helm?"

"Which narrows it down to half the baddies in the Nine Worlds." I gestured at Otis's empty coat. "Where did his body go?"

"Otis? He'll be fine. Magic creatures form from the mist of Ginnungagap. When they die, their bodies eventually dissolve back into that mist. Otis should re-form somewhere close to his master, hopefully in time for Thor to kill him again for dinner."

That struck me as a strange thing to hope for, but not any stranger than the morning I'd just had. Before my knees could buckle, I sat. I sipped my now-cold coffee.

"The goat-killer knew the hammer is missing," I said. "He told me if we went to Provincetown we'd be playing into our enemy's hands. You don't think he meant—"

"Loki?" Sam sat across from me. She tossed the ax on the table. "I'm sure he's involved in this somehow. He always is."

I couldn't blame her for sounding bitter. Sam didn't like talking about the god of deceit and trickery. Aside from the fact he was evil, he was also her dad.

"You heard from him recently?" I asked.

"Just a few dreams." Sam rotated her coffee cup this way

and that like the dial of a safe. "Whispers, warnings. He's been mostly interested in . . . Never mind. Nothing."

"That doesn't sound like nothing."

Sam's gaze was intense and full of heat, like logs in a fireplace just before they ignite. "My dad is trying to wreck my personal life," she said. "That's nothing new. He wants to keep me distracted. My grandparents, Amir . . ." Her voice caught. "It's nothing I can't handle. It doesn't have anything to do with our hammer problem."

"You sure?"

Her expression told me to back off. In times past, if I pressed her too far, she would slam me against a wall and put her arm across my throat. The fact that she hadn't yet choked me unconscious was a sign of our deepening friendship.

"Anyway," Sam said, "Loki couldn't be your goat-killer. He couldn't wield an ax like that."

"Why not? I mean, I know he's technically chained up in Asgardian supermax for murder or whatever, but he doesn't seem to have any problem showing up in my face whenever he feels like it."

"My father can project his image or appear in a dream," Sam said. "With extreme concentration, for a limited time, he can even send out enough of his power to take on a physical form."

"Like when he dated your mom."

Sam again demonstrated her affection for me by not clubbing my brains out. We were having a friendship fest here at the Thinking Cup.

"Yes," she said. "He can get around his imprisonment

in those ways, but he can't manifest solidly enough to wield magic weapons. The gods made sure of that when they put a spell on his bindings. If he could pick up an enchanted blade, he could eventually free himself."

I supposed that made sense in a nonsensical Norse-myth kind of way. I pictured Loki lying spread-eagled in some cave, his hands and feet tied with bonds made from—ugh, I could hardly think about it—the intestines of his own murdered sons. The gods had arranged that. They'd also supposedly set a snake over Loki's head to drip venom in his face for all eternity. Asgardian justice wasn't big on mercy.

"The goat-killer could still be working for Loki," I said. "He could be a giant. He could be—"

"He could be anyone," Sam said. "The way you describe him—how he fought and moved—he sounds like an einherji. Perhaps even a Valkyrie."

My stomach dropped. I imagined it rolling across the pavement and coming to rest next to Otis's porkpie hat. "Somebody from Valhalla. Why would anyone—?"

"I don't know," Sam said. "Whoever it is, he or she doesn't want us following this lead on Thor's hammer. But I don't see that we have any choice. We need to act quickly."

"Why the rush?" I asked. "The hammer's been missing for months. The giants haven't attacked yet."

Something in Sam's eyes reminded me of Ran the sea goddess's nets, the way they swirled in the waves, stirring up drowned spirits. It wasn't a happy memory.

"Magnus," she said, "events are accelerating. My last few missions into Jotunheim . . . the giants are restless. They've summoned huge glamours to hide whatever it is they're up to, but I'm pretty sure whole armies are on the move. They're preparing to invade."

"Invade . . . where?"

The breeze made her hijab flutter around her face. "*Here*, Magnus. And if they come to destroy Midgard . . ."

Despite the warm sunlight, a chill settled over me. Sam had explained how Boston sat at the nexus of Yggdrasil, the World Tree. It was the easiest place to pass between the Nine Worlds. I imagined the shadows of giants falling over Newbury Street, the ground shaking under iron-shod boots the size of panzer tanks.

"The only thing holding them back," Sam said, "is their fear of Thor. That's been true for centuries. They won't launch a full-scale invasion unless they're absolutely sure he is vulnerable. But they're getting bolder. They're starting to suspect the time might be right—"

"Thor's only one god," I said. "What about Odin? Or Tyr? Or my dad, Frey? Can't *they* fight giants?"

As soon as I said it, the idea sounded ridiculous. Odin was unpredictable. When he showed up, he was more interested in giving motivational PowerPoint presentations than fighting. I'd never even met Tyr, the god of bravery and personal combat. As for Frey . . . my dad was the god of summer and fertility. If you wanted flowers to bloom, crops to grow, or a paper cut to heal, he was your guy. Scaring away the hordes of Jotunheim? Maybe not.

"We have to stop the invasion *before* it happens," Sam said. "Which means finding the hammer Mjolnir. You're sure Otis said Provincetown?"

"Yeah. A wight's barrow. That's bad?"

"On a scale of one to ten, it's up there in the high twenties. We'll need Hearthstone and Blitzen."

Despite the circumstances, the possibility of seeing my old buddies lifted my spirits.

"You know where they are?"

Sam hesitated. "I know how to get in contact. They've been hiding in one of Mimir's safe houses."

I tried to process that. Mimir, the disembodied god's head who traded drinks from the well of knowledge for years of servitude, who had ordered Blitz and Hearth to keep an eye on me while I was homeless because I was "important to the fate of the worlds," who ran an inter-world pachinko racket and other shady enterprises—Mimir had a collection of safe houses. I wondered what he was charging my friends for rent.

"Why are Blitz and Hearth in hiding?"

"I should let them explain," Sam said. "They didn't want to worry you."

That was so *not* funny, I laughed. "They disappeared without a word because they didn't want to *worry* me?"

"Look, Magnus, you needed time to train—to settle into Valhalla and get used to your einherji powers. Hearthstone and Blitzen just got a bad omen in the runes. They've been taking precautions, staying out of sight. For this quest, though—"

"A bad omen. Sam, the assassin said I should be prepared to lose my friends."

"I *know*." She picked up her coffee. Her fingers trembled. "We'll be careful, Magnus. But for a wight's tomb . . . rune magic and underground skills could make all the difference.

We'll *need* Hearth and Blitz. I'll contact them this afternoon. Then, I promise, I'll fill you in on everything."

"There's *more?*" Suddenly I felt like I'd been sitting at the Thanksgiving kiddie table for the past six weeks. I'd missed out on all the important conversations among the adults. I didn't like the kiddie table.

"Sam, you don't need to protect me," I said. "I'm already dead. I'm a freaking warrior of Odin who lives in Valhalla. Let me help."

"You will," she promised. "But you *needed* training time, Magnus. When we went after the Sword of Summer, we got lucky. For what comes next . . . you'll need all your skill."

The current of fear in her voice made me shiver.

I hadn't considered us *lucky* when we retrieved the Sword of Summer. We'd come close to dying multiple times. Three of our comrades had sacrificed their lives. We'd barely managed to stop Fenris Wolf and a host of fire giants from ravaging the Nine Worlds. If that was lucky, I did not want to see unlucky.

Sam reached across the table. She took my cranberry orange scone and nibbled off the edge. The icing was the same color as her bruised eye. "I should get back to school. I can't miss another AP physics class. This afternoon I have some fires to put out at home."

I remembered what she'd said about Loki trying to mess up her personal life, and that little hitch of doubt when she'd said Amir's name. "Anything I can help with? Maybe I can stop by Fadlan's Falafel and talk to Amir?"

"No!" Her cheeks flushed. "No, thank you. But definitely not. No."

"So that's a *no* then."

"Magnus, I know you mean well. There's a lot on my plate, but I can handle it. I'll see you tonight at the feast for the . . ." Her expression soured. "You know, the newcomer."

She meant the soul she had gone to reap. As the responsible Valkyrie, Sam would have to be there at the nightly feast to introduce the newest einherji.

I studied the bruise under her eye, and something dawned on me.

"This soul you picked up," I said, "this new einherji punched you?"

Sam scowled. "It's complicated."

I'd met some violent einherjar, but never one who would dare punch a Valkyrie. That was suicidal behavior, even for someone who was already dead. "What kind of idiot . . . Wait. Did this have anything to do with that wolf howl I heard from across the Common?"

Sam's dark brown eyes smoldered, right on the edge of combustion.

"You'll hear about it tonight." She rose and picked up the assassin's ax. "Now go back to Valhalla. Tonight you'll have the pleasure of meeting . . ." She paused, considering her words. "My brother."

FOUR

A Cheetah Runs Me Over

WHEN CHOOSING an afterlife, it's important to consider location.

Suburban afterlives, as in Folkvanger and Niflheim, may offer lower costs-of-not-living, but Valhalla's Midgard entrance is right in the heart of the city, on Beacon Street across from the Boston Common. You'll be within easy walking distance of the best shops and restaurants, and less than a minute from the Park Street T station!

Yes, Valhalla. For all your Viking paradise needs.

(Okay, sorry. I told the hotel management I'd put in a plug. But it *was* pretty easy getting back home.)

After buying a bag of chocolate-covered espresso beans at the coffee shop, I made my way through the Public Garden, passing my old camping spot under the footbridge. A couple of grizzled dudes sat in a nest of sleeping bags, sharing garbage-bin leftovers with a little rat terrier.

"Hey, guys." I handed them Otis's trench coat and hat, along with all the mortal money I had on me—about twenty-four bucks. "Have a good day."

The guys were too startled to respond. I kept walking, feeling like I had an ax sticking out of my sternum.

Just because I'd been killed by a fire giant two months ago, I got to live in luxury. Meanwhile, these guys and their terrier ate from garbage bins. It wasn't fair.

I wished I could round up every homeless person in Boston and say, *Hey, there's a big mansion right over here with thousands of comfy suites and free food forever. Follow me!*

But that wouldn't work.

You couldn't bring mortals into Valhalla. You couldn't even die on purpose to get in. Your death had to be an unplanned selfless act, and you had to hope there was a Valkyrie around to see it.

Of course, that still made Valhalla better than the high-rise condos sprouting up all around downtown. Most of them were full of empty luxury apartments, too—shiny fourth or fifth homes for billionaires. You didn't need a brave death to get in, just a lot of money. If the giants *did* invade Boston, maybe I could convince them to do some strategic condo-stomping.

Finally, I reached the Midgard facade of the Hotel Valhalla. From the outside, it looked like an eight-story mansion of white-and-gray stone—just another piece of super-expensive real estate in a row of Colonial town houses. The only difference: the hotel's front garden was completely enclosed by a fifteen-foot-tall limestone wall with no entryway—the first of many defenses to keep non-einherjar from trespassing.

I jumped straight over and into the Grove of Glasir.

A couple of Valkyries hovered in the branches of the white birch tree, collecting its twenty-four-karat-gold foliage. They waved to me, but I didn't stop to chat. I marched up the front steps and pushed open the heavy double doors.

In the cathedral-size lobby, the usual scene was going on. In front of the roaring fireplace, teenage einherjar hung out playing board games or just chillaxing (which is like chilling, except with battle-axes). Other einherjar in fuzzy green hotel bathrobes chased each other around the rough-hewn pillars that lined the hall, playing hide-and-seek-and-kill. Their laughter echoed off the ceiling high above, where the rafters gleamed with the points of thousands of bundled spears.

I glanced over at the reception desk, wondering if Sam's mysterious eye-punching brother might be checking in. The only person there was the manager, Helgi, glowering at his computer screen. One sleeve of his green suit had been ripped off. Chunks of his epic-size beard had been pulled out. His hair looked even more like a dead buzzard than usual.

"Don't go over there," warned a familiar voice.

Hunding the bellhop sidled up next to me, his warty red face covered with fresh scratches. His beard, like Helgi's, looked like it had recently been caught in a chicken-plucking machine. "Boss is in a *foul* mood," he said. "Like, beat-you-with-a-stick foul mood."

"You don't look so happy yourself," I noted. "What happened?"

Hunding's beard quivered with anger. "Our newest guest happened."

"Samirah's brother?"

"Hmph. If you want to call him that. I don't know what Samirah was thinking, bringing that monster to Valhalla."

"Monster?" I had a flashback to X, the half-troll Samirah had once admitted to Valhalla. She'd gotten flak for that, too, though X had later turned out to be Odin in disguise. (Long story.) "You mean this newcomer is an *actual* monster, like Fenris or—"

"Worse, if you ask me." Hunding brushed a tuft of whiskers off his uniform name tag. "Cursed *argr* nearly tore my face off when he saw his accommodations. Not to mention the *complete* lack of a proper tip—"

"Bellhop!" the manager shouted from the reception desk. "Stop fraternizing and get over here! You have dragon teeth to floss!"

I looked at Hunding. "He makes you floss the dragons' teeth?"

Hunding sighed. "Takes forever, too. I gotta go."

"Hey, man." I handed him the bag of chocolate-covered espresso beans I'd bought at the Thinking Cup. "Hang in there."

The old Viking's eyes turned misty. "Magnus Chase, you're a fine lad. I could hug you to death—"

"BELLHOP!" Helgi shouted again.

"ALL RIGHT! HOLD YOUR EIGHT-LEGGED HORSES!" Hunding scurried toward the front desk, which spared me from a hug to the death.

As low as I felt, at least I didn't have Hunding's job. The poor guy had reached Valhalla only to be forced into servitude by Helgi, his archenemy from mortal life. I figured he deserved some chocolate now and then. Also, his friendship had already proven invaluable to me several times. Hunding knew his way around the hotel better than anybody, and he had all the juicy gossip.

I headed for the elevators, wondering what an "argr" was and why Sam would bring one into Valhalla. Mostly I wondered if I had time for lunch and a nap before this afternoon's battle. It was important to be well fed and well rested when dying in combat.

In the corridors, a few einherjar gave me sidelong glances. Most ignored me. Sure, I'd retrieved the Sword of Summer and defeated Fenris Wolf, but the majority of my fellow warriors just saw me as the kid who'd gotten three Valkyries killed and almost started Ragnarok. The fact that I was a son of Frey, the Vanir summer god, didn't help. His offspring weren't usually found in Valhalla. I wasn't cool enough to hang with the popular crowd—the children of war gods like Thor, Tyr, and Odin.

Yes, Valhalla had cliques just like high school. And while high school *seemed* to last for eternity, Valhalla actually did. The only einherjar who truly accepted me were my hallmates on floor nineteen, and I was anxious to get back to them.

In the elevator, the Viking easy-listening music did not help my mood. Questions swam around in my brain: Who had killed Otis? What had the goat wanted to warn me about? Who was Sam's brother? What were Blitz and Hearth hiding from? And who in their right mind would want to record "Fly Me to the Moon" in Old Norse?

The elevator doors opened at floor nineteen. I stepped out and promptly got sideswiped by a large animal. It was moving so fast I only registered a blur of tan and black before it turned a corner and was gone. Then I noticed holes in my sneakers where the animal had run over them. Tiny geysers of pain erupted from the tops of my feet.

"Ow," I said, belatedly.

"Stop that cheetah!" Thomas Jefferson, Jr. came charging

down the corridor with his bayonet fixed, my other hallmates Mallory Keen and Halfborn Gunderson close behind him. They stumbled to a stop in front of me, all three panting and sweating.

"Did you see it?" T.J. demanded. "Where'd it go?"

"Um . . ." I pointed to the right. "Why do we have a cheetah?"

"It wasn't our idea, believe me." T.J. shouldered his rifle. As usual, he wore his blue Union Army uniform, his jacket unbuttoned over a green Hotel Valhalla T-shirt. "Our new hallmate isn't happy to be here."

"New hallmate," I said. "A cheetah. You mean . . . the soul Sam brought in. A child of Loki. He's a shape-shifter?"

"Among other things," said Halfborn Gunderson. Being a berserker, he had the physique of Sasquatch and wore only hide britches. Runic tattoos swirled across his massive chest. He banged his battle-ax on the floor. "I almost got my face smashed in by that *meinfretr*!"

Since moving to Valhalla, I'd learned an impressive number of Old Norse cusswords. *Meinfretr* translated as something like *stinkfart*, which was, naturally, the worst kind of fart.

Mallory sheathed her two knives. "Halfborn, your face could use an occasional smashing." Her brogue got thicker whenever she was angry. With her red hair and flushed cheeks, she could have passed for a small fire giant, except fire giants were not as intimidating. "I'm more concerned about that demon destroying the hotel! Did you see what he did to X's room?"

"He took over X's old room?" I asked.

"And proceeded to tear it up." Mallory made a V with her fingers and flicked them under her chin in the direction the cheetah had fled. Miss Keen was Irish, so her V did not mean *peace* or *victory*—it meant something much ruder. "We came by to welcome him, found the place in ruins. No respect!"

I remembered my own first day in Valhalla. I had thrown a sofa across the living room and put my fist through the bathroom wall. "Well . . . adjusting can be tough."

T.J. shook his head. "Not like this. The kid tried to kill us on sight. Some of the stuff he said—"

"First-rate insults," Halfborn conceded. "I'll give him credit for that. But I've never seen one person do so much damage. . . . Come have a look, Magnus. See for yourself."

They led me down to X's old room. I'd never been inside, but now the door was wide open. The interior looked like it had been redecorated by a Category 5 hurricane.

"Holy Frigg." I stepped over a pile of busted furniture into the foyer.

The layout was a lot like my own suite—four square sections jutting out from a central atrium like a giant plus sign. The foyer had once been a sitting area with a sofa, bookshelves, a TV, and a fireplace. Now it was a disaster zone. Only the fireplace was still intact, and gouge marks scarred the mantel as if our new neighbor had taken a broadsword to it.

From what I could see, the bedroom, kitchen, and bathroom wings had been similarly destroyed. In a daze, I moved toward the atrium.

Just like mine, it had a huge tree in the middle. The lowest branches spread across the apartment's ceiling, interweaving with the rafters. The upper branches stretched into a cloudless blue sky. My feet sank into green grass. The breeze from above smelled like mountain laurel—a sort of grape Kool-Aid scent. I'd been in several of my friends' rooms, but none of them had an open-air atrium.

"Was it like this for X?" I asked.

Mallory snorted. "Hardly. X's atrium was a big pool—a natural hot spring. His place was always as hot, humid, and sulfurous as a troll's armpit."

"I miss X." Halfborn sighed. "But, yes, all this is completely new. Each suite arranges itself to fit its owner's style."

I wondered what it meant that my atrium was exactly like the newcomer's. I didn't want to share styles with a murderous wildcat son of Loki who ran over people's feet.

At the edge of the atrium lay another pile of wreckage. Freestanding shelves had been overturned. The grass was littered with ceramic bowls and cups—some colorfully glazed, others unfired clay.

I knelt and picked up the base of a broken flowerpot. "You think Cheetah Boy made all these?"

"Yep." T.J. gestured with his bayonet. "There are a kiln and a potter's wheel in the kitchen, too."

"Good quality stuff," Halfborn said. "The vase he threw at my face was beautiful and deadly. Just like Miss Keen, here."

Mallory's face went from strawberry red to habanero orange. "You're an idiot." Which was her way of expressing affection for her boyfriend.

I turned over the shard. On the base, the initials A.F. were etched in the clay. I did not want to speculate what they might stand for. Under the initials was a decorative stamp: two snakes curled in an elaborate *S* pattern, their tails looped around each other's heads.

My fingertips felt numb. I dropped the shard and picked up another broken pot: same initials on the bottom, same serpentine stamp.

"It's a symbol of Loki," Halfborn offered. "Flexibility, change, slipperiness."

My ears buzzed. I'd seen this symbol before . . . recently, in my own room. "How—how do you know?"

Halfborn puffed out his already puffed-out chest. "As I've told you, I've spent my time well in Valhalla. I have a PhD in Germanic literature."

"Which he only mentions several times a day," Mallory added.

"Hey, guys," T.J. called from the bedroom. He speared his bayonet into a pile of clothing and held up a dark green sleeveless silk dress.

"Posh," Mallory said. "That's a Stella McCartney."

Halfborn frowned. "How can you be sure?"

"I've spent my time well in Valhalla." Mallory did a decent imitation of Halfborn's gruff voice. "I have a PhD in fashion."

"Oh, shut up, woman," Halfborn muttered.

"And look at this." T.J. held up a tuxedo jacket, also dark green, with pink lapels.

I'll admit my brain was fuzzy. All I could think about was

the symbol of Loki on the pottery, and where I'd seen the snake design before. The whirlwind of clothes in this room didn't make sense to me—jeans, skirts, jackets, ties, and party gowns, most in shades of pink and green.

"How many people live here?" I asked. "Does he have a sister?"

Halfborn snorted. "T.J., should you explain, or should I?"

FLOOOOOOOM. The sound of a ram's horn echoed down the corridor.

"Lunchtime," T.J. announced. "We can talk then."

My friends headed for the door. I remained crouched over the pile of pottery shards, staring at the initials A.F. and the entwined serpents.

"Magnus?" T.J. called. "You coming?"

My appetite was gone. So was any desire to take a nap. Adrenaline screamed through my system like a high note on an electric guitar.

"You guys go ahead." My fingers curled around the broken pot with the symbol of Loki. "There's something I need to check first."

FIVE

My Sword Has a Better Social Life Than I Do

IT'S A GOOD THING I didn't go to lunch.

The buffet was usually fought to the death, and as distracted as I felt, I would've gotten impaled by a fondue fork before I filled my plate.

Most activities in Valhalla were done to the death: Scrabble, whitewater rafting, pancake eating, croquet. (Tip: Don't *ever* play Viking croquet.)

I got to my room and took a few deep breaths. I half expected the place to be as trashed as A.F.'s room—like maybe the suites were so similar, mine would decide to mess itself up in solidarity. Instead, it was just the way I'd left it, only cleaner.

I'd never seen the housekeeping staff. Somehow, they always managed to tidy up when I was gone. They made the bed whether I'd slept in it or not. They scrubbed the bathroom even if I'd just done that myself. They pressed and folded my laundry, though I was careful never to leave my clothes lying around. Seriously, who irons and starches underwear?

I felt guilty enough having this huge suite to myself; the idea of housekeepers picking up after me only made it worse. My mom had raised me to take care of my own messes. Still, as much as I tried to do that here, the hotel staff swooped in daily and sanitized everything without mercy.

The other thing they did was leave me presents. That bothered me more than the starched underwear.

I made my way over to the fireplace. When I first checked in, there had been only one photo on the mantel—a shot of my mom and me when I was eight, standing at the summit of Mount Washington. Since then, more pictures had appeared—some that I remembered from childhood, some that I had never seen before. I didn't know where the hotel staff found them. Maybe as the suite became more attuned to me, the photos just emerged from the cosmos. Maybe Valhalla kept a backup copy of every einherji's life on the iCloud.

In one shot, my cousin Annabeth stood on a hill, the Golden Gate Bridge and San Francisco in the background. Her blond hair blew sideways. Her gray eyes gleamed as if somebody had just told her a joke.

Looking at her made me happy because she was family. It also made me anxious because it was a constant reminder of our last conversation.

According to Annabeth, our family, the Chases, had some sort of special appeal to the ancient gods. Maybe it was our winning personalities. Maybe it was our brand of shampoo. Annabeth's mom, the Greek goddess Athena, had fallen in love with her dad, Frederick. My dad, Frey, had fallen in love with my mother, Natalie. If somebody came up to me tomorrow and told me—surprise!—the Aztec gods were alive and well in Houston and my second cousin was the granddaughter of Quetzalcoatl, I would totally believe them. Then I would run screaming off a cliff into Ginnungagap.

The way Annabeth figured it, all the old myths were true. They fed off human memory and belief—dozens of musty pantheons still muscling up against one another like they did in the old days. As long as their stories survived, the gods survived. And stories were almost impossible to kill.

Annabeth had promised we would talk about it further. So far, we hadn't had the chance. Before she returned to Manhattan, she'd warned me that she rarely used a cell phone because they were dangerous for demigods (though I had never noticed any problems). I tried not to worry that she'd been totally silent since January. Still, I wondered what might be going on down there in Greek and Roman land.

My hand drifted across the mantel to the next photo.

This one was harder to look at. My mother and her two brothers, all in their twenties, sat together on the steps of the family brownstone. Mom looked just as I always remembered her—pixie haircut, infectious smile, freckles, tattered jeans, and flannel shirt. If you could've hooked up a generator to her joy of life, you could've powered the entire city of Boston.

Sitting next to her was my Uncle Frederick, Annabeth's father. He wore a too-big cardigan over an oxford shirt, and beige slacks riding halfway up his calves. He held a model World War I biplane in one hand and grinned like a huge dork.

On the top step behind them, with his hands planted on his siblings' shoulders, sat their big brother, Randolph. He looked about twenty-five, though he was one of those people who was born to be old. His close-cropped hair was so blond it passed for gray. His large round face and burly frame made him resemble a club bouncer more than an Ivy League grad student. Despite the smile, his eyes were piercing, his posture guarded. He looked as if any second he would charge the photographer, take the camera, and stomp on it.

My mom had told me over and over: *Don't go to Randolph. Don't trust him.* She'd shunned him for years, refused to take me to the family mansion in Back Bay.

When I'd turned sixteen, Randolph had found me anyway. He'd told me about my godly father. He'd guided me to the Sword of Summer and promptly gotten me killed.

That made me a little wary of seeing good old Uncle Randolph again, though Annabeth thought we should give him the benefit of a doubt.

He's family, Magnus, she told me before she left for New York. *We can't give up on family.*

Part of me supposed she was right. Part of me thought Randolph was a dangerous piece of work. I didn't trust him farther than I could throw him, and even with einherji strength, I couldn't throw him very far.

Gee, Magnus, you might be thinking, *that's really harsh of you. He's your uncle. Just because your mom hated him, he ignored you most of your life, and then he got you killed, you don't trust him?*

Yeah, I know. I was being unreasonable.

The thing is, what bothered me most about Uncle Randolph wasn't our past. It was the way the photo of the three siblings had changed since last week. At some point, I don't get how, a new mark had appeared on Randolph's cheek—a symbol as faint as a water stain. And now I knew what it meant.

I held up the pot I'd taken from A.F.'s room—the initials etched in clay, the stamp with the two entwined snakes. Definitely the same design.

Somebody had branded my uncle's face with the mark of Loki.

I stared at the snake mark for a long time, trying to make sense of it.

I wished I could talk to Hearthstone, my expert on runes and symbols. Or Blitzen, who knew about magic items. I wished Sam were here, because if I was going crazy and seeing things, she would be the first to slap some sense into me.

Since I didn't have any of them to talk to, I pulled out my pendant and summoned Jack.

"Hey, *señor!*" Jack somersaulted through the air, his runes glowing blue and red. Nothing like a little disco lighting when you want to have a serious conversation. "Glad you woke me up. I have a date this afternoon with a *hot* spear, and if I missed that . . . Oh, man, I would stab myself."

"Jack," I said, "I'd rather not hear about your dates with other magical weapons."

"C'mon. You need to get out more! If you want to be my wingman, I could totally set you up. This spear has a friend—"

"Jack."

"Fine." He sighed, which caused his blade to glow a lovely shade of indigo. No doubt the lady spears found that very attractive. "So what's up? No more ninjas to fight, I hope?"

I showed him the serpent mark on the piece of pottery. "You know anything about this symbol?"

Jack floated closer. "Yeah, sure. That's one of Loki's marks. I don't have a PhD in Germanic literature or anything, but I think it represents, you know, snakiness."

I started to wonder if summoning Jack had been a good

idea. "So our new neighbor across the hall makes pottery. And every pot has this on the bottom."

"Huh. I would guess he's a son of Loki."

"I *know* that. But why would he brag about it? Sam doesn't even like to mention her dad. This guy stamps Loki's symbol on all his work."

"No accounting for taste," Jack said. "Once I met a throwing dagger with a green acrylic grip. Can you imagine?"

I picked up the photo of the three Chase siblings. "But sometime during the last week, that same Loki symbol appeared on my uncle's face. Any thoughts?"

Jack planted the tip of his blade in the living room carpet. He bent forward until his hilt was an inch from the photo. Maybe he was getting nearsighted. (Near-hilted?)

"Hmm," he said. "You want my opinion?"

"Yeah."

"I think that's pretty strange."

I waited for more. Jack did not elaborate.

"Okay, then," I said. "You don't think maybe there's a connection between . . . I don't know, another child of Loki showing up in Valhalla, and this weird mark on Randolph's face, and the fact that suddenly, after a couple of months of quiet, we have to find Thor's hammer right away to avoid some invasion?"

"When you put it like that," Jack said, "you're right, it's *very* strange. But Loki is always showing up in weird places. And Thor's hammer . . ." Jack vibrated in place like he was either shuddering or suppressing a laugh. "Mjolnir is *always* getting misplaced. I swear, Thor needs to have that hammer duct-taped to his face."

I doubted I would be getting that image out of my head anytime soon. "How can Thor lose it so easily? How could anyone steal it? I thought Mjolnir was so heavy nobody else could pick it up."

"Common misconception," Jack said. "Forget all that only-the-worthy-can-lift-it stuff from the movies. The hammer is heavy, but you get enough giants together? Sure, they can lift it. Now *wielding* it—throwing it correctly, catching it again, summoning lightning with it—that takes some skill. But I've lost count of the number of times Thor has fallen asleep in some forest, prankster giants have rolled up in a backhoe loader, and the next thing you know, the thunder god is hammerless. Most of the time he gets it back quickly, kills the pranksters, and lives happily ever after."

"But not this time."

Jack wobbled back and forth, his version of a shrug. "I suppose getting Mjolnir back is important. The hammer *is* powerful. Inspires fear in the giants. Smashes entire armies. Keeps the forces of evil from destroying the universe and whatever. Personally, I've always found him kind of a bore. He just *sits* there most of the time. Doesn't say a word. And don't *ever* invite him to karaoke night at the Nuclear Rainbow. *Disaster.* I completely had to carry both parts on 'Love Never Felt So Good.'"

I wondered if Jack's blade was sharp enough to cut off the too-much information he was giving me. I guessed not.

"Last question," I said. "Halfborn mentioned that this new child of Loki was an 'argr.' You have any idea—"

"I LOVE argrs!" Jack somersaulted with glee, nearly slicing

off my nose. "Frey's Fripperies! We have an argr across the hall? That's great news."

"Um, so—"

"One time we were in Midgard—me and Frey and a couple of elves, right? It was like three in the morning, and this argr walked up to us . . ." Jack howled with laughter, his runes pulsing in full *Saturday Night Fever* mode. "Oh, wow. That was an *epic* night!"

"But what exactly—?"

Someone knocked on my door. T.J. poked his head in. "Magnus, sorry to bother— Oh, hey, Jack, what's up?"

"T.J.!" Jack said. "You recover from last night?"

T.J. chuckled, though he looked embarrassed. "Just about."

I frowned. "You guys went partying last night?"

"Oh, *señor, señor*," Jack chided, "you *really* need to come out with us. You haven't lived until you've gone clubbing with a Civil War bayonet."

T.J. cleared his throat. "So, anyway, I came to get you, Magnus. The battle's about to start."

I looked around for a clock, then remembered I didn't have one. "Isn't it early?"

"It's Thursday," T.J. reminded me.

I cursed. Thursdays were special. And complicated. I hated them. "Let me grab my gear."

"Also," T.J. said, "the hotel ravens have tracked down our new hallmate. I thought we should probably go be with him. They're bringing him to the battle . . . whether he wants to be there or not."

SIX

Love Me Some Weasel Soup

THURSDAY MEANT dragons. Which meant an even more painful death than usual.

I would've brought Jack, but 1) he thought practice battles were beneath him, and 2) he had a hot date with a polearm.

By the time T.J. and I arrived at the battlefield, the fighting had already started. Armies streamed into the hotel's interior courtyard—a topographical killing zone big enough to be its own sovereign country, with woods, meadows, rivers, hills, and mock villages. On all four sides, soaring into the hazy white fluorescent sky, tiers of gold-rimmed balconies overlooked the field. From the upper levels, catapults hurled fiery projectiles toward the warriors below like deadly ticker tape.

The blare of horns echoed through the forests. Plumes of smoke rose from burning huts. Einherjar charged into the river, fighting on horseback, laughing as they cut each other down.

And, because it was Thursday, a dozen large dragons had also joined the slaughter.

The older einherjar called them *lindworms*. If you ask me, that made them sound like a mildly annoying skin rash. Instead, lindworms were the size and length of eighteen-wheelers. They had just two front legs, with leathery brown bat-type wings too small for effective flight. Mostly they dragged themselves across the ground, occasionally flapping, leaping, and swooping down on their prey.

From a distance, with their brown, green, and ocher hides, they looked like an angry flock of giant carnivorous turkey snakes. But trust me: up close, they were bad news.

Our goal for Thursday's battle? Stay alive as long as possible while the dragons tried very hard not to let us. (Spoiler: The dragons always won.)

Mallory and Halfborn waited for us at the edge of the field. Halfborn was adjusting the straps on Mallory's armor.

"You're doing it wrong," she growled. "That's too tight across the shoulders."

"Woman, I've been putting on armor for centuries."

"When? You always go into battle bare-chested."

"Are you complaining about that?" Halfborn asked.

Mallory blushed. "Shut up."

"Ah, look, here's Magnus and T.J.!" Halfborn clapped me on the shoulder, dislocating several of my joints. "Floor nineteen is accounted for!"

Technically, that wasn't true. Floor nineteen had almost a hundred residents. But our particular corridor—our neighborhood within the neighborhood—consisted of us four. Plus, of course, the newest resident . . .

"Where's the cheetah?" T.J. asked.

As if on cue, a raven dive-bombed us. It dropped a burlap bag at my feet then landed nearby, flapping its wings and croaking angrily. The burlap bag moved. A long skinny animal squirmed out of it—a brown-and-white weasel.

The weasel hissed. The raven cawed. I didn't speak raven,

but I was pretty sure it was telling the weasel, *Behave yourself or I will peck your weaselly eyes out.*

T.J. pointed his rifle at the animal. "You know, when the Fifty-Fourth Massachusetts was marching toward Darien, Georgia, we used to shoot weasels and cook them in a soup. Tasty stuff. You guys think I should get out my old recipe?"

The weasel transformed. I'd heard so much about this new recruit being a monster that I half expected him to turn into a living corpse like the goddess Hel, or a miniature version of the sea serpent Jormungand. Instead, the animal grew into a regular human teen, long and lanky, with a swirl of dyed green hair, black at the roots, like a plug of weeds pulled out of a lawn.

The weasel's brown-and-white fur changed into green and pink clothes: battered rose high-tops, skinny lime green corduroy pants, a pink-and-green argyle sweater-vest over a white tee, and another pink cashmere sweater wrapped around the waist like a kilt. The outfit reminded me of a jester's motley, or the coloration of a venomous animal warning the whole world: *Try me and you die.*

The newcomer looked up, and I forgot how to breathe. It was Loki's face, except younger—the same wry smile and sharp features, the same unearthly beauty, but without the scarred lips or the acid burns across the nose. And those eyes—one dark brown, the other pale amber. I'd forgotten the term for that, having different-colored irises. My mom would've called it David Bowie eyes. I called it completely unnerving.

The weirdest thing of all? I was pretty sure I had seen this kid before.

Yeah, I know. You're thinking a kid like that would stand out. How could I not remember exactly where we'd crossed paths? But when you live on the streets, wild-looking people are normal. Only normal people stand out as strange.

The kid flashed a perfect white smile at T.J., though there was no warmth in those eyes. "Point that rifle somewhere else, or I will wrap it around your neck like a bow tie."

Something told me this was not an idle threat. The kid might actually know how to tie a bow tie, which was kinda scary arcane knowledge.

T.J. laughed. He also lowered his rifle. "We didn't get a chance to introduce ourselves earlier, when you were trying to kill us. I'm Thomas Jefferson, Jr. This is Mallory Keen, Halfborn Gunderson, and Magnus Chase."

The newcomer just stared at us. Finally the raven made an irritated squawk.

"Yeah, yeah," the kid told the bird. "Like I said, I'm calmer now. You didn't mess me up, so it's all cool."

Screeeak!

The kid sighed. "Fine, I'll introduce myself. I'm Alex Fierro. Pleased to meet you all, I guess. Mr. Raven, you can go now. I promise not to kill them unless I have to."

The raven ruffled his feathers. He gave me the stink eye, like, *It's your problem now, buddy.* Then he flew away.

Halfborn grinned. "Well, that's settled! Now that you've promised not to kill us, let's start killing other people!"

Mallory crossed her arms. "He doesn't even have a weapon."

"She," Alex corrected.

"What?" Mallory asked.

"Call me *she*—unless and until I tell you otherwise."

"But—"

"She it is!" T.J. interceded. "I mean, she *she* is." He rubbed his neck as if still worrying about a rifle bow tie. "Let's get to battle!"

Alex rose to her feet.

I'll admit that I was staring. Suddenly my whole perspective had flipped inside out, like when you look at an inkblot picture and see just the black part. Then your brain inverts the image and you realize the white part makes an entirely different picture, even though nothing has changed. That was Alex Fierro, except in pink and green. A second ago, he had been very obviously a boy to me. Now she was very obviously a girl.

"What?" she demanded.

"Nothing," I lied.

Above us, more ravens began to circle, cawing accusingly.

"We'd better get moving," Halfborn said. "The ravens don't like slackers on the battlefield."

Mallory drew her knives and turned toward Alex. "Come on, then, sweetheart. Let's see what you can do."

SEVEN

Have You or Someone You Love Ever Suffered from Lindworms?

WE WADED into combat like one happy family.

Well, except for the fact that T.J. grabbed my arm and whispered, "Keep an eye on her, will you? I don't want to get mauled from behind."

So I brought up the rear with Alex Fierro.

We moved inland, picking our way through a field of corpses, all of whom we would see later, alive, at dinnertime. I could've taken some pretty funny photos, but camera phones were heavily discouraged on the field of combat. You know how it is. Somebody snaps a picture of you dead in an embarrassing pose, it makes the popular page on Instagram, then you get teased about it for centuries.

Halfborn and Mallory chopped us a path through a pack of berserkers. T.J. shot Charlie Flannigan in the head. Charlie thinks it is hilarious to get shot in the head. Don't ask me why.

We dodged a volley of fiery tar balls from the balcony catapults. We had a brief sword battle with Big Lou from floor 401—great guy, but he always wants to die by decapitation. That's hard, since Lou is almost seven feet tall. He seeks out Halfborn Gunderson on the battlefield since Halfborn is one of the few einherjar tall enough to oblige.

Somehow, we made it to the edge of the woods without

getting stomped by a lindworm. T.J., Mallory, and Halfborn fanned out in front and led us into the shadows of the trees.

I moved warily through the underbrush, my shield up, my standard-issue combat sword heavy in my left hand. The sword wasn't nearly as well-balanced or as lethal as Jack, but it was a lot less talkative. Next to me, Alex strolled along, apparently unconcerned that she was empty-handed and the most brightly colored target in our group.

After a while, the silence got to me.

"I've seen you before," I told her. "Were you at the youth shelter on Winter Street?"

She sniffed. "I hated that place."

"Yeah. I lived on the streets for two years."

She arched her eyebrow, which made her amber left eye look paler and colder. "You think that makes us friends?"

Everything about her posture said, *Get away from me. Hate me or whatever. I don't care as long as you leave me alone.*

But I'm a contrary person. On the streets, plenty of homeless folks had acted belligerent toward me and pushed me away. They didn't trust anybody. Why should they? That just made me more determined to get to know them. The loners usually had the best stories. They were the most interesting and the savviest about staying alive.

Sam al-Abbas must've had some reason for bringing this kid to Valhalla. I wasn't going to let Fierro off the hook just because she had startling eyes, an impressive sweater-vest, and a tendency to hit people.

"What did you mean earlier?" I asked. "When you said—"

"Call me *she*? I'm gender fluid and transgender, idiot. Look it up if you need to, but it's not my job to educate—"

"That's not what I meant."

"Oh, please. I saw your mouth hanging open."

"Well, yeah. Maybe for a second. I was surprised. But . . ." I wasn't sure how to continue without sounding like even more of an idiot.

The gender thing wasn't what surprised me. A *huge* percentage of the homeless teens I'd met had been assigned one gender at birth but identified as another, or they felt like the whole boy/girl binary didn't apply to them. They ended up on the streets because—shocker—their families didn't accept them. Nothing says "tough love" like kicking your non-heteronormative kid to the curb so they can experience abuse, drugs, high suicide rates, and constant physical danger. Thanks, Mom and Dad!

What surprised me was the way I'd reacted to Alex—how fast my impression of her had slingshot, and the kind of emotions that had stirred up. I wasn't sure I could put that into words without turning as red as Mallory Keen's hair.

"Wh-what I was sighing—*saying*—is when you were talking to the raven, you mentioned you were worried you'd been messed up. What did you mean?"

Alex looked like I'd just offered her a huge wedge of Limburger cheese. "Maybe I overreacted. I wasn't expecting to die today or get scooped up by some Valkyrie."

"That was Sam. She's okay."

Alex shook her head. "I *don't* forgive her. I got here and found out . . . whatever. I'm dead. Immortal. I'll never age and never change. I thought that meant . . ." Her voice frayed. "It doesn't matter."

I was pretty sure it mattered. I wanted to ask her about

life back in Midgard, why she had an outdoor atrium just like mine in her suite, why all the pottery, why she would want to put the mark of Loki next to her initials on her work. I wondered if her arrival was just a coincidence . . . or whether it had something to do with the mark on Uncle Randolph's face in the photo and our sudden urgent need to find Thor's hammer.

On the other hand, I suspected that if I tried to ask her all that, she would turn into a mountain gorilla and rip my face off.

Happily, I was spared that fate when a lindworm crashlanded in front of us.

The monster hurtled out of the sky, flapping its ridiculous wings and roaring like a grizzly bear with a hundred-watt amp. Trees cracked and splintered under its weight as it landed in our midst.

"*AWRGGG!*" Halfborn yelled—which was Old Norse for *HOLY CRUD, THERE'S A DRAGON!*—just before the lindworm smacked him into the sky. Judging from the arc, Halfborn Gunderson was going to end up somewhere around floor twenty-nine, which would be a surprise to anyone relaxing on their balcony.

T.J. fired his rifle. Gun smoke blossomed harmlessly against the dragon's chest. Mallory yelled a curse in Gaelic and charged.

The lindworm ignored her and turned toward me.

I should mention . . . lindworms are ugly. Like if Freddy Krueger and a *Walking Dead* zombie had a child—*that* kind of ugly. Their faces have no flesh or hide, just a carapace of bone and exposed tendons, gleaming fangs, and dark, sunken eye sockets. When the monster opened its maw, I could see straight down its rotten-meat-colored throat.

Alex crouched, her hands fumbling for something at her belt. "This isn't good."

"No kidding." My hand was so sweaty I could barely hold my sword. "You go right, I'll go left. We'll flank it—"

"No, I mean that isn't just *any* dragon. That's Grimwolf, one of the ancient worms."

I stared up into the monster's dark eye sockets. He *did* seem bigger than most of the lindworms I'd fought, but I was usually too busy dying to ask a dragon its age or name.

"How do you know?" I asked. "And why would anybody call a dragon Grim*wolf*?"

The lindworm hissed, filling the air with a scent like burning tires. Apparently he was sensitive about his name.

Mallory stabbed at the dragon's legs, screaming more angrily the longer the lindworm ignored her. "Are you two going to help," she called back at us, "or just stand there and chat?"

T.J. stabbed at the monster with his bayonet. The point just bounced off the creature's ribs. Being a good soldier, T.J. backed up and tried again.

Alex tugged some sort of cord from her belt loops—a dull steel wire no thicker than a kite string, with simple wooden dowels on either end for handles. "Grimwolf is one of the dragons that live at the roots of Yggdrasil. He shouldn't be here. No one would be crazy enough to . . ." Her face blanched, her expression hardening as if turning into lindworm bone. "*He* sent it for me. He knows I'm here."

"Who?" I demanded. "What?"

"Distract him," she ordered. She leaped into the nearest tree and began to climb. Even without turning into a gorilla, she could definitely move like one.

I took a shaky breath. "Distract him. Sure."

The dragon snapped at Alex, biting off several tree branches. Alex moved fast, scampering higher up the trunk, but one or two more snaps and she'd be a lindworm Lunchable. Meanwhile, Mallory and T.J. were still hacking away at the creature's legs and belly, but they were having no luck convincing the dragon to eat them.

It's only a practice battle, I told myself. *Charge in there, Magnus! Get yourself killed like a pro!*

That was the whole point of daily combat: to learn to fight any foe, to overcome our fear of death—because on the day of Ragnarok, we'd need all the skill and courage we could muster.

So why did I hesitate?

First, I'm way better at healing than I am at fighting. Oh, and running away—I'm *really* good at that. Also, it's hard to charge straight to your own demise, even if you know it won't be permanent—especially if that demise involves large amounts of pain.

The dragon snapped at Alex again, missing her rose high-tops by an inch.

As much as I hated dying, I hated even more seeing my comrades get killed. I screamed "FREY!" and ran at the lindworm.

Just my luck, Grimwolf was happy to turn his attention to me. When it comes to drawing aggro from ancient monsters, I've got the golden touch.

Mallory stumbled back out of my way, chucking one of her knives at the dragon's head. T.J. also retreated, yelling, "All yours, buddy!"

As far as encouraging words you might hear before an excruciating death go, those sucked pretty bad.

I raised my shield and sword like the nice instructors had demonstrated in Viking 101. The dragon's mouth opened wide, revealing several extra rows of teeth—just in case the outer row of teeth didn't kill me dead enough.

Out of the corner of my eye, I saw Alex swaying at the top of the tree—a tense bundle of pink and green, ready to spring. I realized what she was planning: she wanted to jump onto the dragon's neck. That was such a stupid plan it made me feel better about my own stupid way of dying.

The dragon struck. I jabbed my sword upward, hoping to impale the monster's upper palate.

Instead, a sudden pain blinded me. My face felt like it had been doused with industrial cleaning fluid. My knees buckled, which probably saved my life. The dragon bit empty air where my head had been a millisecond before.

Somewhere to my left, Mallory screamed, "Get up, you fool!"

I tried to blink away the pain. It only got worse. My nostrils filled with the stench of burning flesh.

Grimwolf recovered his balance, snarling with irritation.

Inside my head, a familiar voice said, *Come, now, my friend. Don't struggle!*

My vision doubled. I could still see the forest, the dragon looming over me, a small pink-and-green figure leaping toward the monster from the top of a tree. But there was another layer to reality—a gauzy white scene trying to burn its way through my corneas. I knelt in Uncle Randolph's study, in the Chase family mansion in Back Bay. Standing over me was someone much worse than a lindworm—Loki, the god of evil.

He grinned down at me. *There we are. How nice!*

At the same time, the dragon Grimwolf struck again, opening his maw to devour me whole.

EIGHT

I Am Saved from Certain Death by Being Killed

I'D NEVER EXISTED in two places at once before. I decided I didn't like it.

Through the pain, I was dimly aware of the fight in the forest—Grimwolf was about to bite me in half, when suddenly his head bucked upward; now Alex was straddling his neck, pulling her cord so tight around the dragon's throat that he thrashed and stuck out his forked black tongue.

T.J. and Mallory rushed in front of me, acting as a shield. They yelled at Grimwolf, waving their weapons and trying to herd him back.

I wanted to help them. I wanted to get to my feet or at least roll out of the way. But I was paralyzed, on my knees, trapped between Valhalla and my Uncle Randolph's study.

I told you, Randolph! Loki's voice dragged me further into the vision. *See? Blood is thicker than water. We have a solid connection!*

The hazy white scene resolved into full color. I knelt on the oriental carpet in front of Randolph's desk, sweating in a square of sunlight that was tinted green from the stained glass transom. The room smelled of lemon wood polish and burning meat. I was pretty sure the second odor was coming from my face.

In front of me stood Loki—his tousled hair the color of fall foliage, his delicately sculpted face marred by acid burns across his nose and cheekbones and suture scars around his lips.

He grinned and spread his arms in delight. *What do you think of my outfit?*

He was wearing an emerald green tuxedo with a frilly maroon shirt, a paisley bow tie, and a matching cummerbund. (If anything about the ensemble could be said to be *matching*.) A price tag dangled from his left coat sleeve.

I couldn't speak. I couldn't throw up, as much as I wanted to. I couldn't even offer him a free consultation at Blitzen's Best.

No? Loki's expression soured. *I told you, Randolph. You should've bought me the canary yellow one, too!*

A strangled sound came from my throat. "Magnus," said Uncle Randolph's voice, "don't listen—"

Loki extended his hand, the ends of his fingers smoking. He didn't touch me, but the pain across my face tripled, as though someone were branding me with an iron. I wanted to collapse, to beg Loki to stop, but I couldn't move.

I realized I was seeing everything through my uncle's eyes. I was inhabiting his body, feeling what he was experiencing. Loki was using Randolph as some sort of agony-operated telephone to contact me.

The pain eased, but Randolph's extra weight enveloped me like a lead wet suit. My lungs rattled. My worn-out knees ached. I didn't like being an old man.

Now, now, Randolph, Loki chided, *behave yourself. Magnus, I apologize about your uncle. Where was I? Oh, yes! Your invitation!*

Meanwhile, in Valhalla, I remained paralyzed on the battlefield while the dragon Grimwolf staggered around, knocking down entire swaths of forest. One of the lindworm's feet caught Mallory Keen, stomping her flat. T.J. yelled and waved pieces of his now-broken rifle, trying to draw the monster's attention. Somehow, Alex Fierro managed to stay on the dragon's neck, tightening her cord as Grimwolf whipped back and forth.

A wedding! Loki announced cheerfully. He held up a green invitation, then folded it and tucked it into Randolph's shirt pocket. *Five days from today! I apologize for the short notice, but I hope you can come, especially since it's up to you to bring the bride and the bride-price. Otherwise, well—war, invasion, Ragnarok, et cetera. A wedding will be much more fun! Now, let's see. How much has Samirah told you?*

My skull constricted until it felt like my brain would come out of my sinus cavity. A ragged scream escaped my lips, but I wasn't sure if it was mine or Uncle Randolph's.

From the dragon's neck, Alex yelled, "What's wrong with Magnus?"

T.J. ran to my side. "I don't know! His head is smoking! That's bad, right?"

"Grab his sword!" Alex pulled her cord tighter, causing black blood to trickle down the dragon's neck. "Get ready!"

Oh, dear. Loki tapped me/Randolph on the nose. The pressure in my head subsided from blackout misery to moderate torture. *Samirah hasn't shared. The poor thing is embarrassed, I suppose. I understand! It's difficult for me, too, giving away my favorite daughter. They grow up so quickly!*

I tried to speak. I wanted to say, *Go away! You suck! Get out of my head and leave Samirah alone!*

It came out as *"Gaaaaah."*

No need to thank me, Loki said. *Neither of us wants Ragnarok to start just yet, eh? And I'm the only one who can help you! It wasn't an easy negotiation, but I can be* very *persuasive. The hammer in exchange for the bride. A one-time offer. I'll tell you more when you secure the bride-price.*

"Now!" Alex yelled. She pulled her wire so hard the dragon arched his back, separating the segments of armored hide that protected his belly. T.J. charged forward and thrust my practice sword into a soft spot below Grimwolf's heart. T.J. rolled aside as the monster came down with his full weight, impaling himself. Alex leaped from the lindworm's neck, her garrote dangling from one hand, slick with blood.

Was that Alex I heard? Loki curled his scarred lip. *She's not invited to the wedding. She'll ruin everything. In fact—*Loki's eyes gleamed with mischief—*give her a little present for me, will you?*

My lungs tightened, even worse than when I was an asthmatic kid. My body began to superheat; I was in so much pain my organs seemed to be dissolving into molecules, my skin glowing and steaming. Loki was turning my brain to fire, filling me with flashes of memories that weren't mine—centuries of anger and the need for revenge.

I tried to push him out of my head. I tried to breathe.

Alex Fierro stood over me, frowning. Her face and Loki's melded together.

"Your friend is going to explode," Alex said, as if this were a perfectly normal thing that happened to people.

T.J. wiped his brow. "What exactly do you mean . . . *explode?*"

"I mean Loki is channeling power through him," Alex said. "It's too much. Magnus will blow up, destroying most of this courtyard."

I gritted my teeth. I managed one word: *"Run."*

"It won't help," Alex told me. "Don't worry, I've got a solution."

She stepped forward and calmly wrapped her metal wire around my neck.

I managed another word: *"Wait."*

"It's the only way to get him out of your head." Alex's brown and amber eyes were impossible to read. She winked at me . . . or maybe that was Loki, his face glowing hazily just under Alex's skin.

See you soon, Magnus, said the god.

Alex yanked both ends of her garrote and snuffed out my life.

NINE

Never Take a Bubble Bath with a Decapitated God

SOMEONE PLEASE explain to me why I have to dream when I'm dead.

There I was, floating in the darkness of nonexistence, minding my own business, trying to get over the fact that I'd just been decapitated. Then I got dropped into these weird vivid nightmares. *Really* annoying.

I found myself on a thirty-foot yacht in the middle of a storm. The deck heaved. Waves crashed over the bow. Sheets of gray rain slammed into the wheelhouse windows.

In the captain's chair sat Uncle Randolph, one hand clenching the wheel, the other strangling his radio handset. His yellow raincoat dripped puddles around his feet. His close-shaved head glistened with salt water. In front of him, the control board's monitors showed nothing but static.

"Mayday!" He yelled into the handset like it was a stubborn dog refusing to do a trick. "Mayday, curse you. Mayday!"

On the bench behind him, a woman and two young girls huddled together. I'd never known them in life, but I recognized them from photographs in Uncle Randolph's office. Perhaps because I had just been inside Randolph's head, I was able to pull their names from his memories: his wife, Caroline; and his daughters, Aubrey and Emma.

Caroline sat in the middle, her dark brown hair plastered against her face, her arms around her daughters' shoulders. "It'll be all right," she told the girls. She glanced at Randolph with a silent accusation: *Why have you done this to us?*

Aubrey, the youngest, had the Chase family's wavy blond hair. Her head was bowed, her face set in deep concentration. She held a model of the yacht in her lap, trying to keep the toy level despite the fifteen-foot swells that rocked the wheelhouse, as if by doing so she could help her father.

Emma was not as calm. She looked about ten, with dark hair like her mother's and sad, weary eyes like her father's. Somehow I knew that she'd been the most excited about this trip. She had insisted on coming along for Dad's big adventure—his search for a missing Viking sword that would finally prove his theories. Dad would be a hero! Randolph had not been able to refuse her.

Now, though, Emma trembled with fear. The faint scent of urine told me that her bladder was not holding up under the stress. With each pitch of the boat, Emma shrieked and clutched a pendant to her chest—a runestone Randolph had given her for her last birthday. I couldn't see the symbol, but somehow I knew what it was:

Othala: inheritance. Randolph saw Emma as his successor, the next great historian-archaeologist of the family.

"I'll bring us home." Randolph's voice cracked with despair.

He had been so sure of his plans, and confident about the weather. They would make an easy trip from the harbor. He had done extremely thorough research. He *knew* the Sword of Summer must lie at the bottom of Massachusetts Bay. He imagined himself making one quick dive. The old gods of Asgard would bless his efforts. He would bring the sword to the surface and lift its blade into the sunlight for the first time in a thousand years. His family would be there to witness his triumph.

Yet here they were, caught in a freak tempest, their yacht being thrown about like the toy in Aubrey's lap.

The boat rolled to starboard. Emma screamed.

A wall of water engulfed me.

I surfaced in a different dream. My disembodied head bobbed up and down in a full bathtub that smelled of strawberry soap and mildewed washcloths. To my right floated a cheerful rubber ducky with worn-away eyes. To my left floated the not-so-cheerful head of the god Mimir. Seaweed and dead minnows swirled in his beard. Bubble bath foam dribbled from his eyes, ears, and nose.

"I'm telling ya"—his voice echoed in the tiled bathroom— "you guys gotta go. And not just because I'm your boss. Destiny *demands* it."

He wasn't talking to me. Next to the tub, sitting on a lovely avocado porcelain commode, was my friend Hearthstone, his shoulders slumped, his expression despondent. He wore his usual black leather coat and pants, a starched white shirt, and a polka-dotted scarf that looked like it had been cut from a Twister game mat. His spiky blond hair was almost as pale as his face.

Hearth gesticulated in sign language, so quickly and with

such annoyance that I could only catch some of his words: *Too dangerous. . . . death . . . protect this idiot.*

He pointed to Blitzen, who leaned against the sink with his arms crossed. The dwarf was as dapper as always in a walnut colored three-piece suit that matched his skin tone, a bow tie as black as his beard, and a Frank Sinatra–style hat that somehow pulled the whole look together.

"We have to go," Blitz insisted. "The kid *needs* us."

I wanted to tell them how much I missed them, how much I wanted to see them, but also that they shouldn't risk their lives for me. Unfortunately, when I opened my mouth, the only thing that came out was a goldfish frantically wriggling its way to freedom.

My face pitched forward into the bubbles. When I surfaced again, the dream had changed.

I was still a disembodied head, but now I was floating in a massive open jar filled with pickles and vinegar. It was difficult to see through the greenish liquid and the curved glass, but I seemed to be on a bar. Neon drink ads glowed on the walls. Huge, hazy shapes sat hunched on the stools. Laughter and conversation sent ripples through the pickle juice.

I didn't spend a lot of time in bars. I certainly didn't spend a lot of time staring at one through a filthy pickle jar. But something about this place seemed familiar—the arrangement of the tables, the diamond-patterned beveled glass window on the opposite wall, even the rack of wineglasses suspended above me like pendant lamps.

A new shape moved into my vision—someone even larger than the patrons and dressed all in white. "GET OUT!" Her voice was harsh and ragged, as if she spent her spare time gargling gasoline. "ALL OF YOU, OUT! I WOULD TALK TO MY BROTHER!"

With a lot of grumbling, the crowd dispersed. The bar fell silent except for the sound of a TV somewhere across the room—a sports broadcast, a commentator saying, "Oh, would you look at that, Bill? His head came right off!"

I took that comment personally.

At the far end of the bar, someone else moved—a figure so dark and large I had thought it was just a shadow.

"It's my bar." His voice was a deep baritone, huffy and wet. If a bull walrus could speak English, he would sound like that. "Why do you always kick out my friends?"

"*Friends?*" the woman yelled. "They are your *subjects*, Thrym, not your friends! Start acting like a king!"

"I am!" the man said. "I'm going to destroy Midgard!"

"Huh. I'll believe *that* when I see it. If you were a real king, you would've used that hammer immediately rather than hide it away and dither for months about what to do. You certainly wouldn't trade it to that no-good—"

"It's an alliance, Thrynga!" the man bellowed. I doubted this guy Thrym was really a walrus, but I imagined him hopping from flipper to flipper, his whiskers bristling. "You don't understand how important that is. I *need* allies in order to take on the human world. Once I have married Samirah al-Abbas—"

BLOOP.

I didn't mean to, but as soon as I'd heard Samirah's name, I screamed inside my pickle jar, causing a huge bubble to break the surface of the greasy green liquid.

"What was that?" Thrym demanded.

The white shape of Thrynga loomed over me. "It came

from the pickle jar." She said this like it was the title of a horror film.

"Well, kill it!" Thrym yelled.

Thrynga picked up a barstool and whacked my jar with it, hurling me against the wall and leaving me on the floor in a puddle of pickles, juice, and broken glass.

I woke up in my own bed, gasping for air. My hands flew to my neck.

Thank Frey, my head was once again attached to my body. My nostrils still burned from the scent of pickles and strawberry bubble bath.

I tried to parse what had just happened—which parts were real, and which were dreams. The dragon Grimwolf. Alex Fierro and her garrote. Loki burning his way inside my head, somehow using Uncle Randolph to get to me. His warning about a wedding in five days.

All that had actually happened.

Unfortunately, my dreams seemed just as concrete. I'd been with Randolph on his boat the day his family had perished. His memories were now tangled with mine. His anguish sat on my chest like a block of steel—his loss of Caroline, Aubrey, and Emma felt as painful to me as the death of my own mother. Worse, in a way, because Randolph had never gotten any kind of closure. He still suffered every hour of every day.

The rest of the visions: Hearthstone and Blitzen coming to help me. I should have been elated, but I remembered Hearthstone's frantic signs: *Too dangerous. Death.*

And the scene from the pickle jar. What the Helheim was that? Those mystery siblings, Thrym and Thrynga—I was willing to bet fifty pieces of red gold and a falafel dinner that they were giants. The one named Thrym had Thor's hammer and planned on trading it for—I swallowed back pickle-flavored bile—for Sam.

It's up to you to bring the bride and the bride-price, Loki had said. *An alliance. A one-time offer.*

Loki must have been out of his mind. He wanted to "help us" get Thor's hammer back by marrying off Samirah?

Why hadn't Sam said anything about this?

The poor thing is embarrassed, Loki had said.

I remembered the urgency in Sam's voice when we'd talked at the café, the way her fingers had trembled on her coffee cup. No wonder she needed to find the hammer so badly. It wasn't just to save the world from invasion, blah, blah, blah. We were always saving the world. Sam wanted to prevent this marriage deal.

But why would she even think she'd have to honor such a stupid trade? Loki had no right to tell her what to do. She was betrothed to Amir. She loved the guy. I would raise an army of einherjar, magic elves, and well-dressed dwarves and burn down Jotunheim before I let them coerce my friend.

Whatever the case, I needed to talk to her again, and *soon.*

I struggled out of bed. My knees still felt worn and achy like Randolph's, though I knew it was only in my head. I limped to my closet, wishing I had my uncle's cane.

I got dressed and retrieved my phone from the kitchenette. The screen read 7:02 P.M. I was late for Valhalla's nightly feast.

I'd never taken so long to resurrect after dying in battle. Usually I was one of the first ones reborn. I remembered Alex

Fierro standing over me, calmly slicing off my head with her garrote.

I checked my texts. Still nothing from Annabeth. I shouldn't have been surprised, but I kept hoping. I needed my cousin's outside perspective right now, her smarts, her assurance that I could handle all the weirdness.

My door blew open. Three ravens flew in, spiraled around my head, then landed in the lowest branch of the atrium tree. They glared at me the way only ravens can do, like I was not worthy of being their roadkill dinner.

"I know I'm late," I told them. "I just woke up."

CAW!

CAW!

CAW!

Most likely translation:

"GET!"

"MOVING!"

"STUPID!"

Samirah would be at the feast. Maybe I could talk to her.

I grabbed my neck chain and slipped it over my head. The runestone pendant felt comfortingly warm against my collarbone, as though Jack were trying to reassure me. Or maybe he was just in a good mood after an enjoyable date with a fine spear. Either way, I was glad to have him back.

I got the feeling I wouldn't be using a practice sword for the next five days. Things were about to get Jack-worthy.

TEN

The Most Awkward
Viking Luau Ever

AS IF DRAGON Thursday wasn't bad enough, it was also
theme night in the feast hall: Hawaiian luau.

Ugh.

I understood that the management needed to keep things
interesting, especially for warriors who had been waiting here
for Doomsday since the Middle Ages. Still, the luau seemed a
little cultural appropriation-y to me. (Vikings were notorious
for appropriating from other cultures. Also for pillaging and
burning said cultures.) Besides, seeing thousands of einherjar
in Hawaiian shirts and flower leis was like getting a neon-paint
grenade between the eyes.

The feast hall was packed right up to the nosebleed
section—hundreds of tables arranged like stadium seating, all
facing the central court, where a tree as big as the Prudential
Center spread its branches across the vast domed roof. Near
its roots, turning on a spit above the fire pit, was our usual
dinner: the carcass of Saehrimnir the feast beast, who tonight
wore a lovely necklace of orchids. Stuffed in his mouth was a
pineapple the size of Wisconsin.

Valkyries flew back and forth across the hall, filling pitchers, serving food, and somehow managing to avoid setting

their grass skirts on fire in the tiki torches that flickered along the aisles.

"Magnus!" T.J. called, waving me over. His rifle was propped next to him, the broken stock patched up with duct tape.

We didn't have assigned tables. That would've cut down on the fun of fighting each other for the best seats. Tonight, my hallmates had scored a great location on the third tier, a few rows from the thanes' table.

"There's our sleepy boy!" Halfborn grinned, his teeth flecked with roasted Saehrimnir. "*Alicarl*, my friend!"

Mallory elbowed him. "It's *aloha*, moron." She rolled her eyes at me. "*Alicarl* is Norse for fatso, as Halfborn knows perfectly well."

"Close enough!" Halfborn pounded his goblet to get the Valkyries' attention. "Some mead and meat for my friend!"

I took a seat between Mallory and T.J. Soon I had a cold mug of mead and a hot plate of Saehrimnir with biscuits and gravy. Despite all the craziness I'd gone through today, I had a huge appetite—getting resurrected always did that to me. I dug in.

Sitting at the thanes' table was the usual assortment of famous dead people. I recognized Jim Bowie, Crispus Attucks, and Ernie Pyle, all of whom had died bravely in combat, along with Helgi, the hotel manager, and some other ancient Viking dudes. The central throne for Odin was empty, as usual. Sam supposedly received orders from the All-Father once in a while, but Odin hadn't appeared in person since the end of our quest back in January. Probably he was working on his next book—*Five Days to Your Best Ragnarok Ever!*—and the accompanying PowerPoint presentation.

To the left of the thanes was the table of honor. Tonight, it was occupied by only two people: Alex Fierro and her Valkyrie sponsor, Samirah al-Abbas. This meant that, in all the Nine Worlds, in the last twenty-four hours, only Alex had died a death worthy of Valhalla.

That wasn't necessarily unusual. The nightly numbers ranged from zero to twelve. Still, I couldn't shake the feeling that nobody else had died bravely today merely because they didn't want to share a table with Alex. Two Valkyrie guards stood behind her as if ready to prevent an escape attempt.

Sam's body language looked pretty stiff. I was too far away to hear, but I imagined her conversation with Alex was something like:

Sam: *Awkward.*

Alex: *Awkward, awkward.*

Sam (nodding): *Awkward, awkward, awkward.*

Next to me, T.J. pushed away his empty plate. "Some combat today. I've never seen anyone do that"—he drew a line across his neck—"so quick and cold."

I resisted the urge to touch my throat. "First time I've been decapitated."

"Not fun, is it?" Mallory said. "What was going on with you, steaming and threatening to explode like that?"

I'd known my hallmates a while now. I trusted them like family—and I mean like *Annabeth* family, not *Uncle Randolph* family. I told them everything: Loki in his ghastly green tuxedo inviting me to a wedding; the dreams about my uncle, Hearth and Blitz, and the giant siblings in the bar.

"Thrym?" Halfborn Gunderson picked some biscuit out of his beard. "I know that name from the old legends. He was one of the earth giant kings, but it couldn't be the same guy. That Thrym was killed good and proper centuries ago."

I thought about Otis the goat, who could supposedly reform from the mist of Ginnungagap. "Giants don't, like, resurrect?"

Halfborn scoffed. "Not that *I've* ever heard of. Probably this is another Thrym. It's a common name. Still, if he has Thor's hammer—"

"We should probably not spread the news that it's missing," I said.

"Too right," Mallory grumbled. "You say this giant plans on marrying . . ." Her finger drifted in the direction of Samirah. "Does Sam *know* about this scheme?"

"I need to ask her," I said. "Either way, we've got five days. Then, if this giant Thrym doesn't get his bride—"

"He jumps on the telegraph," T.J. said, "and he tells all the other giants that he's got Thor's hammer. Then they invade Midgard."

I decided not to remind T.J. that no one used telegraphs anymore.

Halfborn picked up his steak knife and started cleaning his teeth. "Don't understand why this Thrym fellow waited so long. If he's had the hammer for months, why aren't we already under attack?"

I didn't have an answer, but I imagined it had something to do with Loki. As always, he would be whispering in people's ears, manipulating events from behind the scenes. Whatever Loki wanted from this weird marriage transaction, I was sure of one thing: he wasn't trying to get Thor's hammer back just because he was a swell guy.

I stared across the hall at Alex Fierro. I remembered what she had said on the battlefield when we faced Grimwolf: *He sent it for me. He knows I'm here.*

Mallory nudged me. "You're thinking the same thing, eh? Can't be a coincidence that Alex Fierro arrived in the midst of all this. You think Loki sent her?"

I felt like the bathtub goldfish was wriggling its way back down my throat. "How could Loki arrange for someone to become an einherji?"

"Oh, my friend . . ." T.J. shook his head. The combination of his floral-patterned Hawaiian shirt with his Union Army jacket made him look like a detective from *Hawaii Five-0: 1862.* "How could Loki release an elder lindworm into Valhalla? How could he help Johnny Reb win the First Battle of Bull Run?"

"Loki did what?"

"My point is, Loki can do many things," T.J. said. "Don't *ever* underestimate him."

It was good advice. Still . . . staring at Alex Fierro, I had trouble believing she was a spy. Terrifying and dangerous, yes. A pain in the loincloth, sure. But working for her father?

"Wouldn't Loki pick somebody who . . . blended in a little more?" I asked. "Besides, when Loki was in my head, he told me not to bring Alex to this wedding. He said she would ruin everything."

"Reverse psychology," Halfborn suggested, still working the knife between his teeth.

Mallory snorted. "What do you know about psychology, you oaf?"

"Or reverse reverse reverse psychology!" Halfborn wriggled his bushy eyebrows. "That Loki is a tricky one."

Mallory threw a baked potato at him. "All I'm saying is that Alex Fierro bears watching. After she killed the lindworm—"

"With a little help from me," T.J. added.

"—she disappeared into the woods. She left T.J. and me to fend for ourselves. Then the rest of the dragons descended on us out of nowhere—"

"And killed us," T.J. said. "Yes, that *was* a little odd. . . ."

Halfborn grunted. "Fierro *is* a child of Loki, and an argr. You can't trust an argr in combat."

Mallory swatted his arm. "Your attitude is more offensive than your smell."

"I find your offense offensive!" Halfborn protested. "Argrs aren't warriors. That's all I meant!"

"Okay, what is an argr?" I asked. "When you first said it, I thought it was a monster. Then I thought maybe it was another word for pirate, like *one who arghs.* Does it mean a transgender person or what?"

"Literally, it means *unmanly*," Mallory said. "It's a deadly insult among big loutish Vikings like this guy." She poked Halfborn in the chest.

"Bah," said Halfborn. "It's only an offense if you call someone argr who isn't argr. Gender-fluid people are hardly a new thing, Magnus. There were plenty of argr among the Norse. They serve their purposes. Some of the greatest priests and sorcerers were . . ." He made circles in the air with his steak knife. "You know."

Mallory frowned at me. "My boyfriend is a Neanderthal."

"Not at all!" Halfborn said. "I'm an enlightened modern

man from the year 865 C.E. Now, if you talk to those einherjar from 700 C.E., well . . . they're not as open-minded about such things."

T.J. sipped his mead, his eyes fixed in the distance. "During the war, we had a scout from the Lenape tribe. Called himself—or herself—Mother William."

"That's an awful war name!" Halfborn complained. "Who would tremble in terror before someone called Mother William?"

T.J. shrugged. "I'll admit most of us didn't know what to make of him. His identity seemed to change day to day. He said he had two spirits in his body, one male and one female. But I'm telling you—great scout. Saved us from an ambush during the march through Georgia."

I watched Alex eat her dinner, gingerly picking pieces of carrot and potato from her plate. It was hard to believe that a few hours ago those same delicate fingers had taken down a dragon—and cut off my head—with a wire.

Halfborn leaned toward me. "There's no shame in being attracted, Magnus."

I choked on a piece of feast beast. "What? No, I wasn't—"

"Staring?" Halfborn grinned. "You know, Frey's priests were very fluid. During the harvest festival, they used to wear dresses and do some *amazing* dances—"

"You're messing with me," I said.

"Nope." Halfborn chuckled. "One time in Uppsala, I met this lovely—"

His story was cut short by the sound of horns echoing through the hall.

At the thanes' table, Helgi rose. Since this morning, he'd repaired his suit jacket and clipped his beard, but he was now wearing an oversize war helmet—probably to hide the damage Alex Fierro had done to his dead-buzzard hairdo.

"Einherjar!" his voice boomed. "Tonight, only one fallen warrior has joined us, but I'm told the story of his death is quite impressive." He scowled at Samirah al-Abbas as if to say, *It had* better *be.* "Rise, Alex Fierro, and dazzle us with your glorious deeds!"

ELEVEN

What's a Guy Gotta Do
to Get a Standing Ovation?

ALEX DIDN'T LOOK excited about having to dazzle us.

She rose, tugging at her sweater-vest, then scanned the crowd as if challenging each and every warrior to a duel.

"Alex, son of Loki!" Helgi began.

"Daughter," Alex corrected him. "Unless I tell you otherwise, it's daughter."

At the end of the thanes' table, Jim Bowie coughed into his mead cup. "What, now?"

Ernie Pyle muttered something in Bowie's ear. They put their heads together. Pyle brought out his journalist's notepad and a pen. He seemed to be drawing Bowie a diagram.

Helgi's face twitched. "As you wish, daughter of Loki—"

"And don't feel obliged to mention my dad," Alex added. "I don't like him very much."

A ripple of nervous laughter went around the room. Next to Alex, Samirah clenched her fists as if warming up her strangling muscles. I doubted she was mad at Alex—Sam didn't like Loki either. But if for any reason the thanes decided Alex wasn't a worthy choice for Valhalla, Sam could get kicked out of the Valkyries and exiled to Midgard. I knew this because that's what had happened when she'd introduced me.

"Very well, person who is the child of some parent." Helgi's voice was as dry as Odin's empty eye socket. "Let us watch your exploits, courtesy of Valkyrie Vision!"

These Vikings today and their new-fangled technology . . . Around the trunk of the Tree of Laeradr, huge holographic screens winked into existence. Footage from Samirah's Valkyrie body-cam began to play.

Sam was an expert at trigonometry, calculus, and aviation, so you'd think she could figure out how to use a camera. Nope. She always forgot when to turn it on and off. Half the time her videos came out sideways because she'd clipped the camera on wrong. Sometimes she recorded entire missions where the camera showed nothing but her own nostrils.

Tonight the video quality was good, but Sam had started recording way too early. Time stamp 7:03 that morning: we were treated to a view of her grandparents' living room—a small but tidy space with a low coffee table and two suede sofas. Over the fireplace hung a framed piece of Arabic calligraphy—a swirling gold ink design on white parchment. Proudly displayed on the mantel underneath were pictures of Sam as a toddler with a toy plane, as a middle schooler on the soccer field, and as a high schooler holding a large trophy.

As soon as Sam realized where the video had started, she stifled a yelp. But there was nothing she could do to stop it.

The video panned left to a dining area where three older people sat drinking tea from fancy gold-rimmed teacups. One guy I knew: Abdel Fadlan, the owner of Fadlan's Falafel. There was no mistaking his mane of silver hair and that tailored blue business suit. The other two must have been Sam's grandparents, Jid and Bibi. Jid looked like Santa Claus or Ernest Hemingway—barrel-chested and moonfaced with a snowy beard and lots of smile wrinkles, though today he was frowning. He wore a gray suit that had probably fit him twenty years and twenty pounds ago. Bibi wore an elegantly embroidered red-and-gold dress with a matching hijab. She sat with perfect poise, like royalty, as she poured tea for her guest, Mr. Fadlan.

From the angle of the camera, I guessed Samirah was sitting on a chair between the two sofas. About ten feet away, in front of the fireplace, Amir Fadlan paced in agitation, running his hands through his slick dark hair. He looked as dashing as always in his skinny jeans, white T-shirt, and stylish vest, but his usual easy smile was gone. His expression was anguished, like someone had stomped on his heart.

"Sam, I don't understand," he said. "I love you!"

The entire crowd in the feast hall went "Ooh!"

"Shut up!" Samirah snapped at them, which only made them laugh. I could see that it was taking all her willpower not to cry.

The video fast-forwarded. I watched as Sam flew to meet me at the Thinking Cup, then got a message on her phone for a possible code 381.

She flew from the coffee shop and sped across the park toward Downtown Crossing.

She spiraled down and floated over a dark dead-end alley between two dilapidated theaters. I knew exactly where it was, right around the corner from a homeless shelter. Heroin junkies liked to shoot up in that alley, which made it a great place to get beaten, robbed, or killed.

At the moment Sam arrived, it was also a great place to get attacked by vicious glowing wolves.

Against the back wall, three large beasts had cornered a

grizzled homeless guy. The only thing between him and certain death was a Roche Bros. shopping cart filled with cans for recycling.

My dinner congealed in my gut. The wolves brought back too many memories of my mother's murder. Even if they hadn't been the size of full-grown horses, I would've known they weren't regular Midgard wolves. Blue phosphorescent mist clung to their fur, throwing aquarium-like ripples of light across the brick walls. Their faces were too expressive, with human-like eyes and sneering lips. These were the children of Fenris. They padded back and forth, snarling and sniffing the air, enjoying the scent of fear coming from their prey.

"Back!" the old man croaked, jabbing his grocery cart toward the animals. "I told you, I don't want it! I don't believe in it!"

In the feast hall, the assembled einherjar muttered with disapproval.

I'd heard stories about some modern demigods—sons and daughters of Norse gods or goddesses—who refused to accept their destiny. They turned their backs on the weirdness of the Nine Worlds. Instead of fighting when monsters appeared, they ran and hid. Some decided they were legitimately crazy. They took meds. They checked themselves into hospitals. Others became alcoholics or junkies and ended up on the streets. This guy must have been one of them.

I could feel the pity and disgust in the feast hall. This old man might have spent his whole life running, but now he was trapped. Rather than come to Valhalla as a hero, he would die a coward's death and go to the cold land of Hel—the worst fate any einherji could imagine.

Then, at the mouth of the alley, a voice yelled, "Hey!"

Alex Fierro had arrived. She stood with her feet planted apart, her fists on her waist like Supergirl—if Supergirl had green hair and sported a pink-and-green sweater-vest.

Alex must have been passing by. Maybe she heard the old man shouting or the wolves growling. There was no reason she had to get involved. The wolves were so focused on their prey they never would have noticed her.

Yet she charged the beasts, morphing as she moved and launching herself into battle as a German shepherd.

Despite the size difference, Alex managed to knock the largest wolf off its feet. She sank her fangs into its neck. The beast writhed and snarled, but Alex jumped away before it could bite back. As the wounded wolf staggered, the other two attacked her.

As quick as flowing water, Alex changed back to human form. She lashed out with her wire, using it like a whip. With a single flick, one of the wolves lost its head.

"Ooh!" the audience said with appreciation.

Before she could strike again, the other wolf tackled her. The two of them rolled across the alley. Alex changed to a German shepherd again, clawing and biting, but she was out of her weight class.

"Turn into something bigger," I found myself murmuring. But for whatever reason, Alex didn't.

I'd always liked dogs—more than I liked most people, and *definitely* more than wolves. It was hard to watch as the wolf tore into the German shepherd, ripping at Alex's snout and throat, matting her fur with blood. Finally, Alex managed to change form—shrinking into a lizard and skittering out from under her attacker. She turned human again a few feet away, her clothes in tatters, her face a horror show of slashes and bite marks.

Unfortunately, the first wolf had recovered its wits. It howled in rage—a sound that echoed through the alley and ricocheted off the surrounding buildings. I realized it was the same howl I'd heard from across town while I fought the goat-assassin.

Together, the two remaining wolves advanced toward Alex, their blue eyes flickering with hatred.

Alex fumbled with the sweater tied around her waist. One reason she wore it became evident: it concealed a hunting knife at her belt. She drew the weapon and tossed it toward the homeless guy.

"Help me!" she yelled. "Fight!"

The blade skittered across the asphalt. The old man backed away, keeping his shopping cart between himself and the battle.

The wolves lunged at Alex.

Finally, she tried to change into something larger—maybe a buffalo or a bear, it was hard to tell—but I guess she didn't have enough strength. She collapsed back into human form as the wolves tackled her and brought her down.

She fought ferociously, wrapping her garrote around the neck of one wolf, kicking the other, but she was outmatched and had lost too much blood. She managed to choke the larger wolf. It slumped over, crushing her. The last beast took her by the throat. She wrapped her fingers around its neck, but her eyes were losing focus.

Much too late, the old man picked up the knife. He edged

toward the last wolf. With a horrified shriek, he drove the blade into its back.

The monster fell dead.

The old man stepped away from the scene—three dead wolves, their fur still glowing in faint clouds of neon blue; Alex Fierro, her final breath rattling in her chest, a pool of blood spreading around her like a halo.

The old man dropped the knife and ran away sobbing.

The camera zoomed in as Samirah al-Abbas descended toward the fallen warrior. Sam reached out. From the broken body of Alex Fierro, a shimmering golden spirit floated up, already scowling at the unexpected summons.

The video went dark. It did not show Alex arguing with Sam, punching her in the eye, or causing chaos when she finally reached Valhalla. Maybe Sam's camera ran out of batteries. Or maybe Sam intentionally ended the video there to make Alex look like more of a hero.

The feast hall was quiet except for the crackle of tiki torches. Then the einherjar burst into applause.

The thanes rose to their feet. Jim Bowie wiped a tear from his eye. Ernie Pyle blew his nose. Even Helgi, who had looked so angry a few minutes ago, openly wept as he clapped for Alex Fierro.

Samirah looked around, clearly stunned by the reaction.

Alex might as well have been a statue. Her eyes stayed fixed on the dark place where the video screen had been, as if she could make her death rewind by sheer force of will.

Once the ovation quieted, Helgi raised his goblet. "Alex Fierro, you fought against great odds, with no thought for your own safety, to save a weaker man. You offered this man a weapon, a chance to redeem himself in battle and achieve Valhalla! Such bravery and honor in a child of Loki is . . . is truly exceptional."

Sam looked like she had some choice words to share with Helgi, but she was interrupted by another round of applause.

"It's true," Helgi continued, "that we have learned not to judge Loki's children too harshly. Recently, Samirah al-Abbas was accused of un-Valkyrie-like behavior, and we forgave her. Here again is proof of our wisdom!"

More applause. The thanes nodded and patted each other on the back as if to say, *Yes, wow! We really are wise and open-minded! We deserve cookies!*

"Not only that," Helgi added, "but such heroism from an *argr*!" He grinned at the other thanes to share his amazement. "I don't even know what to say. Truly, Alex Fierro, you have risen above what we would expect from one of your kind. To Alex Fierro!" he toasted. "To bloody death!"

"BLOODY DEATH!" the crowd roared.

No one else seemed to notice how tightly Alex was clenching her fists, or the way she glared at the thanes' table. My guess was that she hadn't appreciated some of his word choices.

Helgi didn't bother calling a *vala*, or seer, to read Alex's destiny in the runes like he did when I first arrived in Valhalla. He must have figured the thanes already knew that Fierro would do great things when we all charged to our deaths at Ragnarok.

The einherjar kicked into full party mode. They laughed and wrestled and called for more mead. Valkyries buzzed around in their grass skirts and leis, filling pitchers as fast as they could. Musicians struck up some Norse dance tunes that sounded like acoustic death metal performed by feral cats.

For me, two things dampened the party mood.

First, Mallory Keen turned toward me. "You still think Alex is a legitimate einherji? If Loki wanted to place an agent in Valhalla, he couldn't have arranged a better introduction. . . ."

The thought made me feel like I was back on Randolph's boat, being tossed around in fifteen-foot swells. I wanted to give Alex the benefit of the doubt. Sam had told me it was impossible to cheat your way into Valhalla. Then again, since becoming an einherji, I ate impossible for breakfast, lunch, and dinner.

The second thing that happened: I caught a flash of movement somewhere above me. I glanced at the ceiling, expecting to see a high-flying Valkyrie or maybe one of the animals that lived in the Tree of Laeradr. Instead, a hundred feet up, almost lost in the gloom, a figure in black reclined in the crook of a branch, slow clapping as he watched our celebration. On his head was a steel helmet with the face mask of a wolf.

Before I could even say, *Hey, look, there's a goat-killer in the tree,* I blinked and he was gone. From the spot where he'd been sitting, a single leaf fluttered down and landed in my mead cup.

TWELVE

Samirah and Magnus Sitting in a Tree, T-A-L-K-I-N-G

AS THE CROWDS streamed out of the hall, I spotted Samirah flying away.

"Hey!" I shouted, but there was no way she could've heard me over the rowdy einherjar.

I pulled off my pendant and summoned Jack. "Fly after Sam, will you? Tell her I need to talk to her."

"I can do better than that," Jack said. "Hang on."

"Whoa. You can *carry* me?"

"For a short hop, yeah."

"Why didn't you tell me that sooner?"

"I totally mentioned it! Plus, it's in the owner's manual."

"Jack, you don't have an owner's manual."

"Just hang on. Of course, once you put me back in pendant form, you'll feel—"

"Like I've been carrying myself through the air," I guessed. "And I'll pass out or whatever. Fine. Let's go."

There was nothing graceful about flying Jack Air. I did not look like a superhero or a Valkyrie. I looked like a guy dangling from the hilt of a sword as it shot skyward—my butt clenched, my legs swinging wildly. I lost a shoe somewhere over the twentieth tier. I nearly fell to my death a couple of times. Otherwise, yeah, great experience.

When we got within a few feet of Sam, I yelled, "On your left!"

She turned, hovering in midair. "Magnus, what are you—? Oh, hey, Jack."

"'Sup, Lion Lady? Can we put down somewhere? This guy is heavy."

We landed on the nearest branch. I told Sam about the goat-assassin lurking in Laeradr, and she zipped off to alert the Valkyries. About five minutes later she came back, just in time to cut short Jack's rendition of "Hands to Myself."

"That is disturbing," Sam said.

"I know," I said. "Jack *cannot* sing Selena Gomez."

"No, I mean the assassin," Sam said. "He's disappeared. We've got the entire hotel staff on alert, but"—she shrugged— "he's nowhere."

"Can I finish my song now?" Jack asked.

"No!" Sam and I said.

I almost told Jack to go back to pendant form. Then I remembered that if he did, I would probably pass out for twelve hours.

Sam settled on the branch next to me.

Far below, the last of the dinner crowd was exiting the hall. My friends from floor nineteen, T.J., Mallory, and Halfborn, surrounded Alex Fierro and guided her along. From here it was hard to tell if this was a congratulatory "buddy" kind of escort or a forced march to make sure she didn't kill anyone.

Sam followed my gaze. "You've got doubts about her, I know. But she deserves to be here, Magnus. The way she died . . . I'm as sure about her heroism as I was about yours."

Since I'd never been confident about my own heroism, Sam's comment didn't ease my mind.

"How's your eye?"

She touched the bruise. "It's nothing. Alex just freaked out. It took me a while to understand, but when you take someone's hand and lead them to Valhalla, you get a glimpse into their soul."

"Did that happen when you took me?"

"With you, there wasn't much to see. It's very dark in there."

"Good one!" Jack said.

"Is there a rune that would make both of you shut up?" I asked.

"Anyway," Sam continued, "Alex was angry and scared. After I dropped her off, I started to realize why. She's gender fluid. She thought that if she became an einherji, she'd be stuck in one gender forever. She *really* hated that idea."

"Ah," I said, which was short for *I get it, but I don't really get it.*

I'd been stuck in one gender my whole life. It never bothered me. Now I wondered how that would feel for Alex. The only analogy I could come up with wasn't a very good one. My second grade teacher, Miss Mengler (aka Miss Mangler), had forced me to write with my right hand even though I was left-handed. She'd actually taped my left hand to the desk. My mom had exploded when she found out, but I still remembered the panicky feeling of being restrained, forced to write in such an unnatural way because Miss Mengler had insisted, *This is the normal way, Magnus. Stop complaining. You'll get used to it.*

Sam let out a sigh. "I admit I don't have much experience with—"

Jack leaped to attention in my hand. "Argrs? Oh, they're great! One time me and Frey—"

"Jack . . ." I said.

His runes changed to a subdued magenta. "Fine, I'll just sit here like an *inanimate object.*"

That actually got a laugh out of Sam. She had uncovered her hair, as she often did in Valhalla. She'd told me that she considered the hotel her second home, and the einherjar and Valkyries part of her family, so she didn't feel the need to wear the hijab here. Her dark locks spilled around her shoulders, and her green silk scarf hung around her neck, shimmering as it tried to activate its magical camouflage. This was a little unsettling, since every once in a while Sam's shoulders and neck seemed to disappear.

"Does Alex Fierro bother you?" I asked. "I mean . . . her being transgender? Like, with you being religious and all?"

Sam arched an eyebrow. "Being 'religious and all,' a lot of things bother me about this place." She gestured around us. "I had to do some soul-searching when I first realized my dad was . . . you know, *Loki.* I still don't accept the idea that the Norse gods are *gods.* They're just powerful beings. Some of them are my annoying relatives. But they are no more than creations of Allah, the *only* god, just like you and I are."

"You remember I'm an atheist, right?"

She snorted. "Sounds like the beginning of a joke, doesn't it? *An atheist and a Muslim walk into a pagan afterlife.* Anyway, Alex being transgender is the least of my problems. I'm more worried about her . . . connection to our father."

Sam traced the life line on her palm. "Alex changes shape so often. She doesn't realize how dangerous it is to rely on

Loki's power. You can't give him any more of a hold than he already has."

I frowned. Samirah had told me something like this before—how she didn't like to shape-shift because she didn't want to become like her dad—but I didn't understand it. Personally, if I could shape-shift, I'd be turning into a polar bear, like, every two minutes and scaring the Saehrimnir out of people.

"What kind of *hold* are we talking about?"

She wouldn't meet my eyes. "Forget it. You didn't fly after me to talk about Alex Fierro, did you?"

"True." I described what had happened on the battlefield—the dragon, and the way Loki had invaded my head wearing an offensive tuxedo and invited me to a wedding. Then I told her about my dreams and how apparently this marriage just happened to be Sam's, to some bar-owning, walrus-voiced giant named Thrym who served the worst-smelling pickles in Jotunheim.

Some of this Jack hadn't heard yet, either. Despite his promise to remain inanimate, he gasped and cried "You're kidding me!" at all the appropriate spots and some of the inappropriate ones.

When I was done, Sam stayed quiet. A waft of cold passed between us like a Freon leak from an AC.

Down below, the cleaning crew had moved in. Ravens picked up the plates and cups. Bands of wolves ate the leftover food and licked the floor clean. We were all about hygiene here in Valhalla.

"I wanted to tell you," Sam said at last. "It all happened so quickly. It just . . . came crashing down on me."

She wiped a tear from her cheek. I'd never seen Sam cry. I wanted to console her—give her a hug, pat her hand or something, but Sam didn't do physical contact, even if I *was* part of her extended Valhalla family.

"That's how Loki is messing with your personal life," I guessed. "He came to see your grandparents? Amir?"

"He gave them *invitations*." Sam dug one from her pocket and handed it across: gold cursive on green card stock, just like the one Loki had tucked into Uncle Randolph's pocket.

The incomparable Loki
and some other people
invite you to celebrate with them
the marriage of
Samirah Al-Abbas Bint Loki
and
Thrym, Son of Thrym, Son of Thrym
WHEN:
Five Days Hence
WHERE:
We'll Get Back to You
WHY:
Because It's Better than Doomsday
Gifts Are Welcome
Dancing and Wild Pagan Sacrifices to Follow

I looked up. "Wild pagan sacrifices?"

"You can imagine how that went over with my grandparents."

I studied the invitation again. The *when* section shimmered, the *five* slowly fading, turning into a *four*. The *where* section also had a holographic sheen, as if it might eventually change to a specific address. "Couldn't you tell your grandparents this was a prank?"

"Not when my father delivered it personally."

"Oh."

I pictured Loki sitting at the al-Abbases' dining table, sipping tea from one of their lovely gold cups. I imagined Jid's Santa Claus face getting redder and redder, Bibi doing her best to keep her regal poise while angry steam spewed from the edges of her hijab.

"Loki told them everything," Sam said. "How he met my mom, how I became a Valkyrie, *everything*. He told them they had no right to arrange a marriage for me because he was my dad and he had already arranged one."

Jack quivered in my hand. "On the bright side," he said, "that's a very nice invitation."

"Jack . . ." I said.

"Right. Inanimate."

"Please tell me your grandparents were not okay with that," I said. "They don't expect you to marry a giant."

"They don't know *what* to think." Sam took back the invitation. She stared at it as if hoping it would burst into flames. "They'd had their suspicions about my mother's relationship. Like I told you, my family has been interacting with the Norse gods for generations. The gods have this . . . this *attraction* to my clan."

"Welcome to the club," I muttered.

"But Jid and Bibi had no idea of the extent of it until Loki showed up and sent them reeling. What hurt them most was that I'd kept my life as a Valkyrie from them." Another tear traced the base of her nose. "And Amir . . ."

"The video we saw on Valkyrie Vision," I guessed. "He and his father came over this morning, and you tried to explain."

She nodded, picking at the corner of the invitation. "Mr. Fadlan doesn't understand what's going on, just that there's a disagreement of some kind. But Amir . . . we talked again this afternoon, and I—I told him the truth. All of it. And I promised that I would *never* agree to this crazy marriage with Thrym. But I don't know if Amir can even *hear* me at this point. He must think I'm out of my mind. . . ."

"We'll figure it out," I promised. "There's no way you are going to be forced to marry a giant."

"You don't know Loki like I do, Magnus. He can burn down my whole life. He's already started. He has ways of . . ." She faltered. "The point is, he's decided that *he* is the only one who can negotiate for Thor's hammer. I can't imagine what he wants out of the deal, but it can't be good. The only way to stop him is to find the hammer first."

"Then we'll do that," I said. "We know this guy Thrym has it. Let's go get it. Or even better, just tell Thor and make him do it."

Across my knees, Jack hummed and glowed. "It won't be that easy, *señor*. Even if you could find Thrym's fortress, he wouldn't be stupid enough to keep Thor's hammer there. He's an earth giant. He could have buried it literally anywhere under the earth."

"The wight's barrow," Sam said.

"In Provincetown," I said. "You still think that's our best bet? Even with this goat-killer stalking us, telling us it's a trap?"

Sam stared right through me. She seemed to be watching the horizon, imagining a mushroom cloud rising from the nuke Loki had dropped on her future. "I have to try, Magnus. The wight's tomb. First thing in the morning."

I hated this idea. Unfortunately, I didn't have a better one.

"Fine. You contacted Hearth and Blitz?"

"They're meeting us on Cape Cod." She rose and crumpled up the wedding invitation. Before I could object that we might need it, she tossed it to the ravens and wolves. "Meet you after breakfast. And bring a coat. It'll be a chilly morning to fly."

THIRTEEN

Relax, It's Just a Little Death Prophecy

SURE ENOUGH, once Jack became a pendant again, I passed out for twelve hours.

In the morning, I woke with sore arms and legs, feeling like I'd spent the whole night flapping through the air with an einherji hanging from my ankle.

Alex Fierro was conspicuously absent from breakfast, though T.J. assured me he'd slipped a note under her door explaining where the lounge was for floor nineteen.

"She's probably still asleep," T.J. said. "She had a big first day."

"Unless she's that mosquito right there." Halfborn pointed to an insect crawling across the saltshaker. "That you, Fierro?"

The mosquito said nothing.

My friends promised to stay on high alert, ready to do whatever was needed to help stop Loki from holding his shotgun wedding in five (now four) days.

"We'll also keep an eye on Fierro," Mallory promised, scowling at the mosquito.

I just had time to scarf down a bagel before Sam arrived and led me to the stables above the floor 422 exercise room.

Whenever Sam said, "We're going to fly," I couldn't be sure what she meant.

Valkyries were perfectly capable of flying on their own. They were strong enough to carry at least one other person, so maybe she intended to put me in a large tote bag and schlep me to Cape Cod.

Or she might have meant *fly* as in *we're going to tumble off a cliff and plummet to our deaths.* We seemed to spend a lot of time doing that.

Today, she meant riding a flying horse. I wasn't clear on why Valkyries *had* flying horses. Probably just because they looked cool. Besides, nobody wanted to ride into battle on a lindworm, flapping and bouncing around like a turkey-snake cowboy.

Sam saddled a white stallion. She climbed on his back and pulled me up behind her, then we galloped out the gates of the stable, straight into the skies above Boston.

She was right about the cold. That didn't bother me, but the winds were strong, and Sam's hijab kept fluttering into my mouth. Since hijabs represented modesty and piety, I doubted Sam wanted hers to look like I'd been chewing on it.

"How much farther?" I asked.

She glanced back. The bruise under her eye had faded, but she still seemed distracted and exhausted. I wondered if she'd slept at all.

"Not long now," she said. "Hang on."

I'd flown with Sam enough times to take that warning seriously. I clenched my knees against the horse's rib cage and wrapped my hands around Sam's waist. As we plunged straight through the clouds, I may have screamed "Meinfretr!"

My butt went weightless in the saddle. FYI, I do not like having a weightless butt. I wondered if Sam flew her airplane like this, and if so, how many flight instructors she had sent into cardiac arrest.

We broke through the clouds. In front of us, Cape Cod stretched to the horizon—a parenthesis of green and gold in a blue sea. Directly below, the northern tip of the peninsula made a gentle curlicue around Provincetown harbor. A few sailboats dotted the bay, but it was too early in the spring for many visitors.

Sam leveled us off at about five hundred feet and flew us along the coast, racing over dunes and marshes, then following the arc of Commercial Street with its gray shingled cottages and neon-painted gingerbread houses. The shops were mostly shut down, the streets empty.

"Just scouting," Sam told me.

"Making sure an army of giants isn't hiding behind the Mooncusser Tattoo Shop?"

"Or sea trolls, or wights, or my father, or—"

"Yeah, I get the idea."

Finally, she banked us left, heading for a gray stone tower that loomed on a hill at the edge of town. The granite structure rose about two hundred and fifty feet and had a turreted top that resembled a fairy-tale castle. I had a vague memory of seeing the tower during my visit here as a kid, but my mom had been more interested in hiking the dunes and walking the beaches.

"What is that place?" I asked Sam.

"Our destination." A faint smile tugged at her mouth. "The first time I saw it, I thought it was the minaret for a mosque. It looks sort of like one."

"But it's not?"

She laughed. "No. It's a memorial for the Pilgrims. They landed here before they moved to Plymouth. Of course, Muslims have been in America for a long time, too. One of my friends at mosque? She has an ancestor, Yusuf ben Ali, who served with George Washington during the American Revolution." She stopped herself. "Sorry, you didn't want a history lesson. Anyway, we're not here for the tower. We're here for what's underneath."

I was afraid she wasn't talking about the gift shop.

We flew around the monument, scanning the clearing at its base. Just outside the tower's entrance, sitting on the stone retaining wall and swinging their feet like they were bored, were my two favorite people from alien worlds.

"Blitz!" I yelled. "Hearth!"

Hearth was deaf, so yelling his name didn't do much good, but Blitzen nudged him and pointed us out. They both jumped off the ledge and waved enthusiastically as our horse came in for a landing.

"Kid!" Blitzen jogged toward me.

He could have been mistaken for the ghost of a tropical explorer. From the rim of his pith helmet, a screen of white gauze covered him down to his shoulders. The gauze, I knew, was custom-designed to block sunlight, which turns dwarves to stone. He'd also put on leather gloves to protect his hands. Otherwise he was wearing the same outfit I'd seen in my dream: a walnut three-piece suit with a black bow tie, snappy pointed leather shoes, and a bright orange handkerchief for flair. Just the thing for a day excursion into a tomb of the undead.

He tackled me with a hug, almost losing his pith helmet. His cologne smelled like rose petals. "Hammers and anvils, I'm glad to see you!"

Hearthstone ran up next, smiling faintly and waving both palms in the ASL gesture for *Yay!* For Hearth, this was the equivalent of ecstatic fanboy screaming.

He wore his usual black leather jacket and jeans, with his Twister-dot scarf wrapped around his neck. His face was as pale as ever, with the perpetually sad eyes and the spiky platinum hair, but he had fleshed out a bit in the past few weeks. He looked healthier, at least by human standards. Maybe they'd been ordering a lot of pizza while they hid out in Mimir's safe house.

"You guys." I pulled Hearth into a hug. "You look exactly like when I saw you in the bathroom!"

In retrospect, that was probably not the line to lead with.

I backed up and explained what had been going on—the weird dreams, the weirder reality, Loki in my head, my head in a pickle jar, Mimir's head in the bathtub, et cetera.

"Yeah," Blitzen said. "The Capo *loves* to show up in the bathtub. Almost scared me out of my chain mail pajamas one night."

"That's an image I did not need," I said. "Also, we have to have a talk about communication. You guys just disappeared on me without a *word*."

"Hey, kid, it was *his* idea." He signed this for Hearth's benefit—pinky touching the forehead, then pointing at Hearth with two fingers. *Idea. His. H* for Hearthstone's name sign.

Hearthstone grunted in irritation. He signed back: *To save you, dummy. Tell Magnus.* He made an *M* for my name sign—a fist with three fingers wrapped over his thumb.

Blitzen sighed. "The elf is overreacting, as usual. He got me all terrified and hustled me out of town. But I've calmed down now. It was just a little death prophecy!"

Sam untangled her backpack from the horse's saddlebags. She patted the horse's muzzle and pointed toward the sky, and our white stallion buddy took off for the clouds.

"Blitzen . . ." She turned. "You understand there's no such thing as a *little* death prophecy, right?"

"I'm fine!" Blitzen gave us a confident smile. Through the gauze netting, he looked like a slightly happier ghost. "A few weeks ago, Hearthstone got back from his one-on-one rune magic class with Odin. He was all excited to read my future. So he cast the runes and . . . well, they didn't come out so good."

Not so good? Hearthstone stomped his foot. *Blitzen. Bloodshed. Cannot be stopped. Before O-S-T-A-R-A.*

"Right," Blitzen said. "That's what he read in the runes. But—"

"What's Ostara?" I asked.

"The first day of spring," Sam said. "Which is in, ah, four days."

"The same day as your supposed wedding."

"Believe me," she said sourly, "it wasn't my idea."

"So Blitzen is supposed to die before that?" My stomach started climbing up my throat. "Bloodshed that cannot be stopped?"

Hearthstone nodded emphatically. *He shouldn't be here.*

"I agree," I said. "It's too dangerous."

"Guys!" Blitzen tried for a hearty chuckle. "Look, Hearthstone is new at reading the future. Maybe he misinterpreted! *Bloodshed* might actually be . . . *toolshed.* A toolshed that cannot be stopped. That would be a *good* omen!"

Hearthstone held out his hands as if to strangle the dwarf, which needed no translation.

"Besides," Blitz said, "if there's a tomb here, it'll be underground. You need a dwarf!"

Hearth launched into a flurry of angry signs, but Samirah stepped in.

"Blitz is right," she said, signing the message with a hot-potato fist bump, both index fingers extended. She'd gotten good at ASL since meeting Hearthstone—just, you know, in her spare time between gathering souls, making honor roll, and flying jet planes.

"This is too important," she said. "I wouldn't ask you otherwise. We have to find Thor's hammer before the first of spring, or entire worlds will be destroyed. Or . . . I'll have to marry a giant."

Another way, Hearth signed. *Must be one. Don't even know hammer is here.*

"Buddy." Blitz took the elf's hands, which was kind of sweet but also kind of rude, because it was the ASL equivalent of putting a gag on someone's mouth. "I know you're worried, but it'll be fine."

Blitz turned toward me. "Besides, as much as I love this elf, I'm going *crazy* in that safe house. I'd rather die out here, being useful to my friends, than keep on watching TV and eating delivery pizza and waiting for Mimir's head to pop up in the bathtub. Also, Hearthstone snores like you wouldn't believe."

Hearth yanked his hands back. *You're not signing, but I can read lips, remember?*

"Hearth," Sam said. "Please."

Sam and Hearth had a staring contest so intense I could feel ice crystals forming in the air. I'd never seen those two so much at odds before, and I did *not* want to be in the middle. I was tempted to summon Jack and have him sing a Beyoncé song just to give them a common enemy.

At last Hearthstone signed: *If anything happens to him . . .*

I take responsibility, Sam mouthed.

"I can read lips, too," Blitzen said. "And I can take responsibility for myself." He rubbed his hands together eagerly. "Now, let's find the entrance to this barrow, eh? It's been months since I unearthed a malicious undead power!"

FOURTEEN

Cry Me a Blood River.
Wait. Actually, Don't

JUST LIKE the good old days: marching together into the unknown, searching for missing magical weapons, and risking painful death. I'd missed my buddies!

We walked halfway around the base of the tower before Blitzen said "Aha."

He knelt and ran his gloved fingertips along a crack in the paving stones. To me, it didn't look any different from the thousands of other cracks in the stone, but Blitzen seemed to like this one.

He grinned up at me. "Now you see, kid? You *never* would've found this without a dwarf. You would've walked around forever, looking for the entrance to the tomb, and—"

"That crack is the entrance?"

"It's the *trigger* for the entrance, yeah. But we'll still need some magic to get in. Hearth, double-check this for me, will you?"

Hearth crouched next to him. He nodded like, *Yep*, then traced a rune on the floor with his finger. Immediately, a ten-foot-square section of pavement vaporized, revealing a shaft that plunged straight down. Unfortunately, the four of us happened to be *on* that ten-foot square when it vaporized.

We dropped into the darkness with a fair amount of screaming, most of which was mine.

Good news: When I landed, I didn't break any bones. Bad news: Hearthstone did.

I heard a wet *snap*, followed by Hearth's grunt, and I knew immediately what had happened.

I'm not saying elves are fragile. In some ways, Hearth was the toughest guy I knew. But on occasion, I wanted to wrap him in blankets and slap a "handle with care" sticker on his forehead.

"Hold on, man," I told him, which was useless, since he couldn't see me in the dark. I found his leg and quickly located the break. Hearth gasped and tried to claw the skin off my hands.

"What's going on?" Blitz demanded. "Whose elbow is this?"

"That's me," Sam said. "Everyone okay?"

"Hearth has a broken ankle," I said. "I need to fix it. You two keep watch."

"It's totally dark!" Blitz complained.

"You're a dwarf." Sam slipped her ax from her belt, a sound I knew well. "I thought you thrived underground."

"I do!" said Blitz. "Preferably in a well-lit and tastefully decorated underground."

Judging from the echo of our voices, we were in a large stone chamber. There was no light, so I assumed the shaft we'd fallen through had closed above us.

In the plus column, nothing had attacked us . . . yet.

I found Hearth's hand and made sign letters against his palm so he wouldn't panic: *HEAL YOU. BE STILL.*

Then I put both my hands on his broken ankle.

I called on the power of Frey. Warmth blossomed in my chest and spread down my arms. My fingers glowed with a soft golden light, pushing back the darkness. I could feel the bones in Hearthstone's ankle knitting together, the swelling subsiding, his circulation returning to normal.

He let out a long sigh and signed, *Thanks.*

I squeezed his knee. "No problem, man."

"So, Magnus," Blitz said, his voice hoarse, "you might want to look around."

One side effect of my healing power was that I temporarily glowed. I don't mean I looked healthy. I mean I actually *glowed.* In the daytime it was hardly noticeable, but here, in a dark subterranean chamber, I looked like a human night-light. Sadly, that meant I could now see our surroundings.

We were in the middle of a domed chamber, like a giant beehive carved from rock. The apex of the ceiling, about twenty feet up, showed no sign of the hatch through which we'd fallen. All around the circumference of the walls, in closet-size niches, stood mummified men in rotted clothing, their leathery fingers clasped around the hilts of corroded swords. I saw no exit from the room.

"Well, this is perfect," I said. "They're going to wake up, aren't they? Those ten guys—"

"Twelve," Sam corrected.

"Twelve guys with big swords," I said.

My hand closed around my runestone pendant. Either Jack was trembling, or I was. I decided it must be Jack.

"They could just be terrifying inanimate corpses," Blitz said. "Think positive."

Hearthstone snapped his fingers for attention. He pointed to the sarcophagus that stood upright in the center of the room.

It's not that I hadn't noticed it. The big iron box was hard to miss. But I'd been trying to ignore it, hoping it would go away. The front was carved with ornate Viking images—wolves, serpents, and runic inscriptions swirling around a central picture of a bearded man with a big sword.

I had no idea what a coffin like this was doing on Cape Cod. I was pretty sure the Pilgrims hadn't brought it over on the *Mayflower*.

Sam motioned for us to stay put. She levitated off the floor and floated around the sarcophagus, her ax ready.

"Inscriptions on the back, too," she reported. "This sarcophagus is *old*. I don't see any sign that it's been opened recently, but perhaps Thrym hid the hammer inside."

"Here's an idea," Blitzen said. "Let's not check."

I glanced at him. "That's your expert opinion?"

"Look, kid, this tomb *reeks* of ancient power. It was built well over a thousand years ago, long before Viking explorers got to North America."

"How can you tell?"

"The marks on the rock," Blitzen said. "I can tell when a chamber was hewn as easily as I can gauge the age of a shirt by the wear of the threads."

That didn't sound very easy to me. Then again, I didn't have a degree in dwarven fashion design.

"So it's a Viking tomb built before the Vikings got here," I said. "Uh . . . how is that possible?"

It moved, Hearth signed.

"How can a tomb move?"

Blitzen took off his pith helmet. The gauze netting left a cowlick across his otherwise perfect hair. "Kid, stuff moves in the Nine Worlds all the time. We're connected by the World Tree, right? The branches sway. New branches grow. Roots deepen. This place has shifted from wherever it was originally built. Probably because . . . you know, it's imbued with evil magic."

Sam touched down next to us. "Not a fan of evil magic."

Hearth pointed to the floor in front of the sarcophagus. I hadn't noticed before, but all around the base of the coffin, a faint circle of runes was etched in the stone.

Hearth finger-spelled: *K-E-N-N-I-N-G.*

"What's that?" I asked.

Samirah edged a little closer to the inscription. "A kenning is a Viking nickname."

"You, mean like . . . 'Hey, Kenning. How's it going?'"

"No," Sam said, in that I-am-going-to-hit-you-with-the-stupid-stick tone. "It's a way of referring to somebody with a description instead of their name. Like instead of Blitzen, I might say *Clever-of-clothes,* or for Hearthstone, *Rune-lord.*"

Hearth nodded. *You may call me Rune-lord.*

Sam squinted at the inscription on the floor. "Magnus, could you glow a little closer please?"

"I'm not your flashlight." But I stepped toward the coffin.

"It says *Blood River,*" Sam announced. "Over and over, all the way around."

"You can read Old Norse?" I asked.

"Old Norse is easy. You want difficult? Try learning Arabic."

"Blood River." My bagel breakfast sat heavy in my gut. "Does this remind anybody of *bloodshed that cannot be stopped*? I don't like it."

Even without his gauze netting, Blitz looked a little gray. "It's . . . probably a coincidence. However, I would like to point out there are no exits from this room. My dwarven senses tell me these walls are solid all the way around. We've walked into a loaded trap. The only way out is to spring it."

"I'm starting to dislike your dwarven senses," I said.

"You and me both, kid."

Hearthstone glared at Blitzen. *You wanted to come here. What now? Break kenning circle. Open coffin?*

Sam readjusted her hijab. "If there's a wight in this tomb, it'll be in that sarcophagus. It's also the most secure place to hide a magical weapon, like a god's hammer."

"I need a second opinion." I pulled off my pendant.

Jack sprang to full length in my hand. "Hey, guys! Ooh, a tomb imbued with evil magic? Cool!"

"Buddy, can you sense Thor's hammer anywhere around here?"

Jack vibrated with concentration. "Hard to be sure. There's *something* powerful in that box. A weapon? A magical weapon? Can we open it? Please, please? This is exciting!"

I resisted the urge to smack him upside the hilt, which would have only hurt me. "You ever heard of an earth giant working with a wight? Like . . . using its tomb as a safe-deposit box?"

"That would be strange," Jack admitted. "Usually an earth giant just buries his stuff in . . . you know, the earth. Like, *deep* in the earth."

I turned to Sam. "So why would Otis send us here? And how is this a good idea?"

Sam glanced around the chamber like she was trying to decide which of the twelve mummies to hide behind. "Look, maybe Otis was wrong. Maybe—maybe this was a wild-goose chase, but—"

"But we're here now!" Jack said. "Aw, c'mon, guys. I'll protect you! Besides, I can't stand an unopened present. At least let me shake the coffin to guess what's inside!"

Hearthstone made a chopping motion against his palm. *Enough already.*

From the inside pocket of his jacket, he produced a small leather pouch—his collection of runestones. He pulled out one I'd seen before:

"That's *dagaz*," I said. "We use that for opening doors in Valhalla. Are you sure—?"

Hearth's expression stopped me. He didn't need sign language to convey how he felt. He regretted this whole situation. He hated putting Blitzen in danger. But we were here now. We'd brought him along because he knew magic. He wanted to get this over with.

"Magnus," Sam said, "you might want to step back."

I did, positioning myself in front of Blitzen, just in case Blood River sprang out of the coffin samurai-style and went directly for the nearest dwarf.

Hearth knelt. He touched dagaz to the inscription. Instantly, the Blood River kenning ignited like a ring of gunpowder. Hearth backed away as the sarcophagus's iron lid blew right off, hurtling past me and slamming into the wall. Before us stood a mummified king in a silver crown and silver armor, with a sheathed sword clasped in his hands.

"Wait for it," I muttered.

Naturally, the corpse opened his eyes.

FIFTEEN

All in Favor of Slaughtering Magnus, Please Say *Aye*

WITH MOST zombies, you don't expect conversation.

I figured King Mummy would say *RARRRR!* Or, at most, *BRAINS!* And then get down to the business of killing us.

I was not ready for "Thank you, mortals! I am in your debt!"

He stepped out of his coffin—a little unsteadily, since he was an emaciated corpse whose armor probably weighed more than he did—and did a tap dance of glee.

"A thousand years in that stupid box, and now I'm free! HAHAHAHAHA!"

Behind him, the inner walls of his coffin were scored with hundreds of marks where he'd been keeping track of years. There was no sign of Thor's hammer, though, which meant the zombie had been locked in there without a decent way to stream Netflix.

Jack quivered with excitement. "Will you *look* at that sword? She's *so* hot!"

I did not know 1) how he could tell the sword was female, or 2) how he could tell she was hot. I was not sure I wanted answers to those questions.

Sam, Blitz, and Hearth edged away from the zombie. Jack's point floated toward the lady sword, but I forced him to the floor and leaned on him. I didn't want him to offend Mr. Zombie or his blade by being too forward.

"Uh, hi," I told the zombie. "I'm Magnus."

"You have a lovely golden glow!"

"Thanks. So how is it that you're speaking English?"

"Am I?" The king tilted his ghoulish head. Wisps of white clung to his chin—maybe cobwebs or the remnants of a beard. His eyes were green and bright and entirely human. "Perhaps it's magic. Perhaps we are communicating on a spiritual level. Whatever the case, thank you for releasing me. I am Gellir, prince of the Danes!"

Blitzen peeked out from behind me. "Gellir? Is Blood River your nickname?"

Gellir's laugh sounded like a maraca filled with wet sand. "No, my dwarven friend. Blood River is a kenning I earned from my *blade*, the Skofnung Sword."

Clunk, clunk.

Hearth had backed into the coffin lid and fallen over it. He stayed in crab-walk position, his eyes wide with shock.

"Ah!" Gellir said. "I see your elf has heard of my sword."

Jack lurched under my elbow. "Uh, *señor*? I've heard of her, too. She's like . . . *wow*. She's *famous*."

"Wait," Sam said. "Prince Gellir, is there possibly a—a hammer around here somewhere? We heard you might have a hammer."

The zombie frowned, which caused fault lines to open on his leathery face. "A hammer? No. Why would I want a hammer when I am the Lord of the Sword?"

Sam's eyes dimmed, or maybe that was just my glow starting to fade.

"You're sure?" I asked. "I mean, the Lord of the Sword is great. But you could also be, I don't know, the Slammer of the Hammer."

Gellir kept his gaze on Sam. His frowned deepened. "One moment. Are you a woman?"

"Uh . . . yes, Prince Gellir. My name is Samirah al-Abbas."

"We call her the Max with the Ax," I offered.

"I will hurt you," Sam hissed at me.

"A woman." Gellir tugged at his chin, pulling off some of his cobweb whiskers. "That's a shame. I can't unsheathe my sword in the presence of a woman."

"Oh, what a bummer," Jack said. "I want to meet Skoffy!"

Hearthstone struggled to his feet. He signed: *We should leave. Now. Not let zombie draw sword.*

"What is your elf doing?" Gellir asked. "Why does he make those strange gestures?"

"It's sign language," I said. "He, uh, doesn't want you to draw your sword. He says we should leave."

"But I can't allow that! I must show my gratitude! Also, I need to kill you!"

My glow was definitely fading now. When Jack spoke, his runes lit the tomb in ominous red flashes. "Hey, zombie guy? Gratitude is usually more like sending a nice card, and less like *I need to kill you.*"

"Oh, I'm very grateful!" Gellir protested. "But I'm also a *draugr*, the chief wight of this barrow. You are trespassing. So, after I finish thanking you properly, I'll have to consume your flesh and devour your souls. But, alas, the Skofnung Sword has very clear restrictions. It cannot be drawn in daylight or in the presence of a woman."

"Those are stupid rules," Sam said. "I mean, those are very *sensible* rules. So, you can't kill us?"

"No," Gellir allowed. "But don't worry. I can still *have* you killed!"

He rapped the sheath of his sword three times against the floor. To absolutely no one's surprise, the twelve mummified warriors stepped out from their niches along the walls.

The draugr had zero respect for zombie clichés. They did not shamble. They didn't moan incoherently or act dazed like proper zombies should. They drew their weapons in perfect unison and stood ready for Gellir's order to kill.

"This is bad," said Jack, master of the obvious. "I'm not sure I can take out this many before they kill you guys. And I don't want to look incompetent in front of that hot lady sword!"

"Priorities, Jack," I said.

"Exactly! I hope you've got a plan that makes me look good!"

Sam gave us a new light source. In her free hand, a glowing spear appeared—the field weapon of a Valkyrie. Its harsh white light made the zombies' faces start to steam.

Hearthstone hefted his pouch of runestones. Blitzen whipped off his bow tie—which, like his entire line of spring fashion, was lined with ultra-flexible chain mail. He wrapped the tie around his fist, ready to smash some zombie faces.

I didn't like our odds: four against thirteen. Or five, if you included Jack as a separate person. I didn't, because that meant I would have to pull my own weight.

I wondered if I could invoke the Peace of Frey. Thanks to my dad, a pacifist-type god who didn't allow fighting in his sacred places, I could sometimes disarm everyone in a wide circle around me, blasting their weapons right out of their hands. That was kind of my finishing trick, though. I would look really dumb if I tried it now in this enclosed space and the zombies just picked up their swords again and killed us.

Before I could decide what would be most impressive to a hot lady sword, one of the zombies raised his hand. "Do we have a quorum?"

Prince Gellir slumped as though one of his vertebrae had disintegrated.

"Arvid," he said, "we've been locked in this chamber for centuries. Of *course* we have a quorum! We're all present because we can't leave!"

"Then I move that we call this meeting to order," said another dead man.

"Oh, for the love of Thor!" Gellir complained. "We're here to massacre these mortals, feed on their flesh, and take their souls. That's *obvious*. Then we'll have enough strength to break free of our tomb and wreak havoc upon Cape Cod. Do we really need—?"

"I second," called another zombie.

Gellir smacked his own skeletal forehead. "Fine! All in favor?"

The twelve other dead guys raised their hands.

"Then this massacre, er, meeting is called to order." Gellir turned to me, his eyes gleaming with irritation. "My apologies, but we vote on everything in this group. It's the tradition of the Thing."

"What thing?"

"You know, the Thing," Gellir said. "From the word

thingvellir, meaning *field of the assembly.* The Norse voting council."

"Ah." Sam wavered between her ax hand and her spear hand, as if unsure which to use . . . or whether that decision would require a new motion. "I've heard of the Thing. It was a site where ancient Norse met to settle legal disputes and make political decisions. The meetings inspired the idea of Parliament."

"Yes, yes," Gellir said. "Now, the *English* Parliament—that wasn't my fault personally. But when the Pilgrims came along—" He pointed his chin toward the ceiling. "Well, by that time, our tomb had been here for centuries. The Pilgrims landed, camped out over us for a few weeks. They must have subconsciously felt our presence. I'm afraid we inspired the Mayflower Compact, started all that business about rights and democracy in America, blah, blah, blah."

"May I take the minutes?" asked a zombie.

Gellir sighed. "Dagfinn, honestly . . . Fine, you're secretary."

"I love being secretary." Dagfinn stuck his sword back in its sheath. He pulled a notepad and a pen from his belt, though what a Viking corpse was doing with school supplies I couldn't tell you.

"So . . . wait," Sam said. "If you've been stuck in that box, how do you know what was going on outside the tomb?"

Gellir rolled his lovely green eyes. "Telepathic powers. *Duh.* Anyway, ever since we inspired the Pilgrims, my twelve body-guards have been insufferably proud of themselves. We have to do *everything* by parliamentary rules . . . or Thing-a-mentary rules. Not to worry, though. We'll kill you soon enough. Now, I make a motion—"

"First," another zombie interrupted, "is there any old business?"

Gellir made a fist so tight I thought his hand would crumble. "Knut, we are draugr from the sixth century. For us, *everything* is old business!"

"I move that we read the minutes from the last meeting," said Arvid. "Do I hear a second?"

Hearthstone raised two fingers. I didn't blame him. The more time they spent reading the minutes of past massacres, the less time they'd have for killing us in a future one.

Dagfinn flipped back in his notebook. The pages turned to dust in his fingers. "Ah, actually, I don't have those minutes."

"Well, then!" Gellir said. "Moving right along—"

"Wait!" Blitzen cried. "We need an oral accounting! I want to hear about your pasts—who you are, why you were all buried together, and the names and histories of all your weapons. I'm a dwarf. The heritage of things is important to me, especially if those things are going to kill me. I motion that you tell us everything."

"I second the motion," Samirah said. "All in favor?"

Every zombie raised his hand, including Gellir—I guess out of habit—who then looked quite annoyed with himself. Jack shot into the air to make the vote unanimous.

Gellir shrugged, causing his armor and bones to creak. "You're making this massacre very difficult, but all right, I will recount our story. Gentlemen, at ease."

The other zombies sheathed their swords. Some sat on the floor. Others leaned against the wall and crossed their arms. Arvid and Knut retrieved bags of yarn and knitting needles from their niches and began to work on mittens.

"So I am Gellir," began the prince, "son of Thorkel, a prince among the Danes. And this"—he patted his sword—"is Skofnung, the most famous blade ever wielded by a Viking!"

"Present company excepted," Jack murmured. "But, oh, *man*, Skofnung is a *hot* name."

I didn't agree with him. I also didn't like the look of terror on Hearthstone's face. "Hearth, you know this sword?"

The elf signed cautiously, as if the air might burn his fingers. *First belonged to King H-R-O-L-F. Was forged with souls of his twelve followers, all berserkers.*

"What is he saying?" Gellir demanded. "Those hand gestures are very annoying."

I started to translate, but Blitzen interrupted, shrieking so loudly that Arvid and Knut dropped their knitting needles.

"*That* sword?" Blitz stared at Hearthstone. "The one with . . . the stone . . . your house?"

This made no sense to me, but Hearth nodded.

Now you see? he signed. *We should not have come.*

Sam turned, her spear's light making dust sizzle on the floor. "What do mean? What stone? And what does it have to do with Thor's hammer?

"Excuse me," Gellir said. "I believe I was speaking. If you came here looking for Thor's hammer, I'm afraid someone gave you very bad information."

"We have to live through this," I told my friends. "There's a goat I need to kill."

"Ahem," Gellir continued. "As I was saying, the Skofnung Sword was created by a king named Hrolf. His twelve berserkers sacrificed their lives so their souls could instill the blade with power." Gellir scowled at his own men, two of whom were now playing cards in the corner. "Those were the days when a prince could find *good* bodyguards. At any rate, a man named Eid stole the sword from Hrolf's grave. Eid lent it to my father, Thorkel, who sort of . . . forgot to return it. My dad died in a shipwreck, but the sword washed ashore in Iceland. I found it and used it in many glorious massacres. And now . . . here we are! When I died in battle, the sword was buried with me, along with my twelve berserkers, for protection."

Dagfinn flipped a page in his notebook and jotted. "*For . . . protection.* Can I add that we expected to go to Valhalla? That we were cursed to stay in this tomb forever because your sword was stolen property? And that we hate our afterlives?"

"NO!" Gellir snapped. "How many times do you want me to apologize?"

Arvid looked up from his half-finished mittens. "I move that Gellir apologize a million more times. Do I hear a second?"

"Stop that!" Gellir said. "Look, we have guests. Let's not air our dirty under-tunics, eh? Besides, once we kill these mortals and devour their souls, we'll have enough power to break out of this tomb! I can't *wait* to check out Provincetown."

I imagined thirteen zombie Vikings marching down Commercial Street, barging into the Wired Puppy Coffee Shop and demanding espresso drinks at sword point.

"But enough old business!" Gellir said. "Can I *please* introduce a motion to kill these intruders?"

"I second." Dagfinn shook his ballpoint pen. "I'm out of ink anyway."

"No!" Blitzen said. "We need more discussion. I don't know the names of these other weapons. And those knitting needles! Tell me about them!"

"You're out of order," Gellir said.

"I move that we be shown the nearest exit," I said.

Gellir stomped his foot. "You're also out of order! I call for a vote!"

Dagfinn looked at me apologetically. "It's a Thing thing. You wouldn't understand."

I should have attacked immediately, while they were off guard, but that seemed undemocratic.

"All in favor?" Gellir called.

"Aye!" the dead Vikings cried in unison. They got to their feet, put away their cards and various knitting projects, and drew their swords once again.

SIXTEEN

Hearthstone Unleashes His Inner Bovine

JACK DECIDED this was an excellent time to give me a training session.

Despite being fully capable of fighting on his own, he had this strong belief that I should learn to wield him with my own power. Something about me being worthy and competent or whatever. The thing is, I sucked at swordplay. Also, Jack always decided to train me in the *worst* possible situations.

"No time like the present!" he yelled, turning heavy and unhelpful in my grip.

"Come on, man!" I ducked the first blade that swung toward my head. "Let's practice later, on mannequins or something!"

"Dodge left!" Jack yelled. "Your other left! Make me proud, *señor*. The Skofnung blade is watching!"

I was almost tempted to die just to embarrass Jack in front of the lady sword. But since I was outside Valhalla and my death would be permanent, I decided that particular plan might be shortsighted.

The zombies crowded in.

The cramped quarters were our only advantage. Each draugr was armed with a broadsword, which requires about five feet of free space for effective swinging. Twelve dead berserkers with broadswords, surrounding a tight-knit group of defenders in a small chamber? I don't care how good you are at forming a quorum, you're just not going to be able to massacre those defenders very easily without hacking apart your comrades as well.

Our melee turned into an awkward shuffle with a lot of shoving, cursing, and bad zombie breath. Samirah thrust her spear under Arvid's jaw. The weapon's light burned away his head like a flame going through toilet paper.

Another zombie jabbed at Blitzen's chest, but Blitz's chain-mail-lined vest bent the blade. Blitz slammed his bow tie–wrapped fist into the zombie's gut and—much to everyone's disgust—got his hand stuck in the zombie's abdominal cavity.

"Gross!" Blitzen proceeded to lurch backward, yanking the zombie along, swinging him like a clumsy dance partner and knocking other draugr out of the way.

Hearthstone took the award for Most Improved in Melee Combat. He slammed down a runestone:

$$\mathsf{\Pi}$$

He was immediately encased in golden light. He grew taller. His muscles swelled as though someone were inflating his clothes. His eyes turned bloodshot. His hair splayed with static. He grabbed the nearest zombie and tossed him across the room. Then he picked up another one and literally broke him in half over his knee.

As you can guess, the other zombies backed away from the crazy overinflated elf.

"What rune is *that*?" I accidentally swung Jack through the top of Gellir's sarcophagus, giving it a sunroof.

Blitz yanked his hand free from his dance partner, who collapsed into pieces. *"Uruz,"* Blitz said. "The rune of the ox."

I silently added an uruz rune to my Christmas wish list.

Meanwhile, Samirah cut through her enemies, twirling her spear in one hand like a shiny baton of death. Any zombie who managed to avoid going up in flames, she chopped down with her ax.

Jack continued shouting unhelpful advice. "Parry, Magnus! Duck! Defense Pattern Omega!"

I was pretty sure that wasn't even a thing. The few times I managed to hit a zombie, Jack cut him to pieces, but I doubted the moves were impressive enough to win Jack a date with the lady sword.

When it became clear that Gellir was running out of bodyguards, he leaped into battle himself, whacking me with his sheathed sword and yelling, "Bad mortal! Bad mortal!"

I tried to fight back, but Jack resisted. Probably he thought it would be unchivalrous to fight a lady, especially one who was stuck in her sheath. Jack was old-fashioned that way.

Finally, Gellir was the only draugr left. His bodyguards lay strewn across the floor in a ghastly collection of arms, legs, weapons, and knitting supplies.

Gellir backed toward his sarcophagus, cradling the Skofnung Sword against his chest.

"Hold on. Point of order. I move that we table all further combat until—"

Hearthstone objected to Gellir's motion by rushing the prince and ripping his head off. Gellir's body toppled forward, and our 'roid-raging elf stomped him flat, kicking and scattering the desiccated remains until there was nothing left but the Skofnung Sword.

Hearthstone started to kick that, too.

"Stop him!" Jack yelled.

I grabbed Hearth's arm, which was definitely the bravest thing I'd done that day. He rounded on me, his eyes blazing with fury.

He's dead, I signed. *You can stop now.*

Chances were high that I was going to get decapitated again.

Then Hearthstone blinked. His bloodshot eyes cleared. His muscles deflated. His hair settled against his scalp. He crumpled, but Blitzen and I were both there to catch him. We'd gotten used to Hearthstone's post-magic pass-outs.

Sam stuck her spear into Dagfinn's corpse and left it standing up like a giant glow stick. She paced the tomb, cursing under her breath. "I'm sorry, guys. All that risk, all that effort, and no Mjolnir."

"Hey, it's cool," Jack said. "We rescued the Skofnung Sword from her evil master! She's going to be *so* grateful. We have to take her with us!"

Blitzen waved his orange handkerchief in Hearth's face, trying to revive him. "Taking that sword would be a *very* bad idea."

"Why?" I asked. "And why did Hearth look so freaked-out when he heard its name? You said something about a stone?"

Blitz cradled Hearth's head in his lap like he was trying to protect the elf from our conversation. "Kid, whoever sent us here . . . it was a trap, all right. But the draugr were the least dangerous things in this chamber. Somebody wanted us to free that sword."

A familiar voice said, "You're absolutely right."

My heart jackknifed. Standing in front of Gellir's sarcophagus were the two men I least wanted to see in the Nine Worlds: Uncle Randolph and Loki. Behind them, the back panel of the sawed-off coffin had become a shimmering doorway. On the other side lay Randolph's study.

Loki's scarred lips twisted into a grin. "Good job finding the bride-price, Magnus. The sword is *perfect!*"

SEVENTEEN

Uncle Randolph Gets on My Naughty List BIG-TIME

SAM REACTED fastest. She grabbed her spear and lunged toward her father.

"No, dear." Loki snapped his fingers.

Instantly, Sam's legs buckled. She collapsed sideways on the floor and lay immobile, her eyes half-closed. Her glowing spear rolled across the stones.

"Sam!" I lurched toward her, but Uncle Randolph intercepted me.

His bulk eclipsed everything. He gripped my shoulders, his breath an overwhelming combination of cloves and rotten fish.

"Don't, Magnus." His voice fractured with panic. "Don't make it worse."

"*Worse?*" I pushed him away.

Anger hummed through my system. Jack felt light in my hand, ready to lash out. Seeing Samirah unconscious at her father's feet (oh, gods, I hoped she was only unconscious), I wanted to blade-smack my uncle. I wanted to go full uruz on Loki's face.

Give Randolph a chance, Annabeth's voice whispered in the back of my mind. *He's family.*

I hesitated . . . just enough to notice Uncle Randolph's condition.

His gray suit was threadbare and smeared with ashes, as though he'd been crawling through a chimney. And his face . . . across his nose, left cheek, and eyebrow spread a horrible crater of red-and-brown scar tissue—a barely healed burn mark in the shape of a hand.

I felt like a dwarf had punched through my abdominal cavity. I remembered the mark of Loki that had appeared on Randolph's cheek in the family photograph. I thought about my dream on the battlefield in Valhalla and recalled the searing agony on my own face when Loki had communicated with me, using Randolph as a conduit. Loki had *branded* my uncle.

I fixed my gaze on the god of trickery. He still wore the offensive green tuxedo he'd been modeling in my battlefield vision, with his paisley bow tie at a rakish angle. His eyes gleamed as if he was thinking, *Go on. Kill your uncle. This could be amusing.*

I decided not to give Loki the pleasure. "You tricked us into coming here," I growled. "Why, if you could just step through a magic doorway in a coffin?"

"Oh, but we couldn't!" Loki said. "Not until you opened the way. Once you did, well . . . you and Randolph are connected. Or didn't you notice?" He tapped the side of his own face. "Blood is a powerful thing. I can always find you through him."

"Unless I kill you," I said. "Randolph, get out of the way."

Loki chuckled. "You heard the boy, Randolph. Step aside."

My uncle looked like he was trying to swallow a horse pill. "Please, Loki. Don't—"

"Wow!" Loki raised his eyebrows. "It sounds like you're

trying to give me an order! But that can't be right, can it? That would violate our agreement!"

The words *our agreement* made Randolph wince. He shuffled aside, his facial muscles twitching around the edges of his new scar.

Out of the corner of my eye, I saw Blitzen helping Hearthstone to his feet. I silently willed them to back away and stay safe. I didn't want anyone else in Loki's path.

Sam still wasn't moving.

My heart hammered against my ribs. I took a step forward. "Loki, what did you do to her?"

The god glanced down at his daughter. "Who, Samirah? She's fine. I just willed her to stop breathing."

"You *what?*"

Loki waved away my concern. "Not permanently, Magnus. I just like to keep a firm hand with my children. So many parents are *lackadaisical* these days, don't you think?"

"He controls them," Randolph croaked.

Loki shot him an irritated look. "Remind me how well *you* did as a father, Randolph? Oh, that's right. Your family is *dead*, and your only hope of seeing them again is *me*."

Randolph curled inward, withering.

Loki turned back to me. His grin sent paisley patterns of *ick* crawling up my spine. "You see, Magnus, my children owe their powers to me. In exchange, they must bend to my will when I require it. It's only fair. As I said, family blood is a strong connection. It's a good thing you listened to me and left Alex in Valhalla. Otherwise we'd have two of my children unconscious!"

He rubbed his hands together. "Now, would you like to see

more? Samirah's always so reluctant to shape-shift. Maybe I should force her into the shape of a cat for you. Or a wallaby? She'd make a very cute wallaby."

The paisley *ick* swirled into my stomach, threatening to erupt.

Finally I understood Samirah's reluctance to shape-shift.

Every time I do it, she'd once told me, *I feel more of my father's nature trying to take hold of me.*

No wonder Sam was afraid Loki could make her go through with the marriage to the giant. No wonder she worried about Alex Fierro, who shape-shifted without a second thought.

Did other gods have that kind of control over their children? Could Frey . . . ? No, I wouldn't allow myself to think about that.

"Leave her alone."

Loki shrugged. "As you wish. I merely needed her out of commission. No doubt Gellir told you—the Skofnung Sword cannot be unsheathed in the presence of a woman. Fortunately, comatose women don't count! Randolph, hurry up now. This is the part where you draw the sword."

Uncle Randolph licked his lips. "Perhaps it would be better if—" His voice deteriorated into a guttural scream. He doubled over, smoke curling from the scar tissue on his cheek. My face burned in sympathy.

"Stop it!" I yelled.

My uncle gasped. He stood up, steam still rising from the side of his nose.

Loki laughed. "Randy, Randy, Randy. You look *ridiculous.* Now, we've been through this before. You want your family back from Helheim? I require full payment in *advance.* You bear my mark, you do what I say. It's really not that hard." He pointed to the Skofnung blade. "Fetch, boy. And Magnus, if you try to interfere, I can always make Sam's coma permanent. I hope you won't, though. It would be terribly inconvenient with the wedding coming up."

I wanted to slice him down the middle like Hel. (I mean his daughter Hel, who had two different sides.) Then I wanted to glue him back together and slice him in half again. I couldn't believe I'd ever thought Loki was charismatic and silver-tongued. He'd called my uncle "Randy." That by itself required the death penalty.

But I didn't know the extent of Loki's control over Sam. Could he really make her permanently cataleptic with just a thought? I was also worried—sort of—about what might happen to Randolph. The idiot may have gotten himself into an evil bargain with Loki, but I understood why he'd done it. I remembered his wife, Catherine, on that sinking ship; Aubrey with her toy boat; Emma shrieking as she clutched her rune-stone *inheritance*—the symbol of all the dreams she would never grow up to realize.

To my left, Hearthstone and Blitzen edged forward. Hearthstone had recovered enough to walk on his own. Blitz held a broadsword he must have retrieved from a zombie. I put out my hand, urging them to stay back.

Randolph picked up the Skofnung Sword. He drew it slowly from its sheath—a double-edged blade of cold gray iron. Along its central ridge, runes glowed faintly in every shade of blue from permafrost to vein blood.

Jack quivered. "Oh . . . oh, *wow*."

"Yes, indeed," Loki said. "Now, if *I* could wield a blade, and

I couldn't have the fabled Sword of Summer, I would choose the Skofnung Sword."

"Dude may be evil," Jack whispered to me, "but he has good taste."

"Unfortunately," Loki continued, "in my present state, I'm not really all here."

Blitzen grunted. "First thing he's said I agree with. That sword should never be drawn."

Loki rolled his eyes. "Blitzen, son of Freya, you're *such* a drama dwarf when it comes to magic weapons! I can't wield Skofnung, no, but the Chases are descended from the Norse kings of old! They're perfect."

I remembered Randolph telling me something about that—how the Chase family was descended from ancient Swedish royalty, blah, blah, blah. But I'm sorry. If it qualified us to wield evil swords, I was *not* going put that on my resumé.

Too dangerous. Hearthstone's signing was listless and weak. His eyes brimmed with fear. *Death. The prophecy.*

"So the blade has a few quirks," said Loki. "I like quirks! It can't be used in the presence of women. It can't be drawn in daylight. It can only be used by one of noble lineage." Loki nudged Randolph's arm. "Even *this* guy qualifies. Also, once the blade is drawn, it cannot be sheathed again until it has tasted blood."

Jack buzzed with a metallic whimper. "That's not fair. That is *too* attractive."

"I know, right?" Loki said. "And the last little quirk of the sword . . . Hearthstone, my friend, would you like to tell them, or should I?"

Hearthstone swayed. He grabbed Blitzen's shoulder. I

wasn't sure if it was for support or just to make sure the dwarf was still there.

Blitzen hefted his broadsword, which was almost as tall as he was. "Loki, you won't do this to Hearth. I won't let you."

"My dear dwarf, I appreciate you finding the tomb's entrance! And of course I needed Hearthstone to break the magic seal around that sarcophagus. You each played your part well, but I'm afraid I require just a *bit* more from you both. You want to see Samirah happily married, don't you?"

"To a giant?" Blitzen snorted. "No."

"But it's for a good cause! The return of what's-his-name's hammer! That means I need a proper bride-price, and Thrym has asked for the Skofnung Sword. It's a very reasonable exchange. The thing is, the sword isn't complete without the stone. The two are a set."

"What do you mean?" I asked. "What stone?"

"The Skofnung Stone—the whetstone that was made to sharpen the blade!" With his thumbs and fingers, Loki made a circle about the size of a dessert plate. "About yea big, blue with gray flecks." He winked at Hearthstone. "Sound familiar?"

Hearthstone looked as if his scarf was choking him.

"Hearth," I said, "what's he talking about?"

My elf friend didn't answer.

Uncle Randolph stumbled, now using both hands to hold up the cursed sword. The iron blade turned darker, and wisps of ice vapor twisted from its edges.

"It's getting heavier," Randolph gasped. "Colder."

"Then we should hurry." Loki looked down at the unconscious form of Samirah. "Randolph, let's feed this hungry sword, shall we?"

"No way." I raised my own blade. "Randolph, I don't want to hurt you, but I will."

My uncle let out a broken sob. "Magnus, you don't understand. You don't know what he's planning—"

"*Randolph,*" Loki hissed, "if you want to see your family again, strike!"

Randolph lunged, thrusting the cursed blade—and I completely misjudged his target.

Stupid, Magnus. Unforgivably stupid.

I was only thinking about Sam lying helpless at Loki's feet. I needed to defend her. I wasn't thinking about prophecies, or how everything Loki did, even a casual glance at his daughter, was a trick.

I stepped to intercept my uncle's strike, but he charged right past me. With a cry of horror, he buried the Skofnung Sword in Blitzen's gut.

EIGHTEEN

I Need to Learn Many, Many More Cusswords in Sign Language

I HOWLED with rage.

I slashed upward, and the Skofnung Sword flew out of Randolph's grip, along with—ew, you might want to skip this part—a couple of pink things that looked like fingers.

Randolph stumbled back, cradling his fist against his chest. The Skofnung Sword clanged to the floor.

"Oh." Blitzen's eyes widened. The sword had gone straight through his chain mail vest. Blood seeped between his fingers.

He stumbled. Hearthstone caught him and dragged him away from Randolph and Loki.

I wheeled around on Loki. I raised Jack's blade again and sliced through the god's smug face, but his form just shimmered like a projection.

"He swings! He misses!" Loki shook his head. "Really, Magnus, we both know you can't hurt me. I'm not fully *here*! Besides, fighting isn't your strong suit. If you need to take out your anger on someone, go ahead and kill Randolph, but do it quickly. We have a lot to talk about, and your dwarf is bleeding out."

I couldn't breathe. I felt like someone was pouring pure hate right down my throat. I wanted to cut down my own uncle. I wanted to pull this tomb apart stone by stone. Suddenly I understood Ratatosk, the squirrel who only spoke malice and wanted to destroy the very tree he lived in.

It wasn't easy, but I pushed down the anger. Saving Blitz was more important than getting revenge.

"Jack," I said, "watch these meinfretrs. If they try to hurt Sam or take the Skofnung Sword, go into Cuisinart mode."

"You got it." Jack spoke in a deeper voice than usual, probably to impress the Skofnung Sword. "I'll protect the hot lady blade with my life! Oh, and also Sam."

I ran to Blitzen's side.

"That's it!" Loki cheered. "There's the Magnus Chase I know and love! Always thinking of others. Always the healer!"

I put my hands on Blitzen's gut, then glanced up at Hearthstone. "You got any runes that might help?"

Hearth shook his head. His own Ratatosk-level hatred smoldered in his eyes. I could see how desperately he wanted to do something, *anything*, but he'd already used two runes this morning. Any more would probably kill him.

Blitzen coughed. His face turned the color of putty. "I—I'm good, guys. Just need . . . a minute."

"Hold on, Blitz." Again, I summoned the power of Frey. My hands heated like the coils of an electric blanket, sending warmth into every cell of Blitzen's body. I slowed his circulation. I eased his pain. But the wound itself refused to heal. I felt it fighting me, tearing open tissue and capillaries faster than I could mend them, gnawing at Blitzen with malicious hunger.

I remembered Hearthstone's prophecy: *Blitzen. Bloodshed. Cannot be stopped.*

This was my fault. I should have seen it coming. I

should've insisted that Blitz stay in Mimir's safe house eating delivery pizza. I should have listened to that stupid Back Bay goat-assassin.

"You're going to be fine," I said. "Stay with me."

Blitz's eyes were starting to lose focus. "Got . . . sewing kit in my vest pocket . . . if that helps."

I wanted to scream. It's a good thing Jack was no longer in my hands, because I would've pulled a full-on Kylo Ren temper tantrum.

I rose and faced Loki and Randolph. My expression must have been pretty frightening. Randolph backed all the way into a zombie niche, leaving a trail of blood from his wounded hand. I probably could've healed that for him, but I wasn't even tempted.

"Loki, what do you want?" I demanded. "How do I help Blitzen?"

The god spread his arms. "I am *so* glad you asked. Happily, those two questions have the same answer!"

"The stone," Blitz gasped. "He wants . . . the stone."

"Exactly!" Loki agreed. "You see, Magnus, wounds from the Skofnung Sword *never* heal. They just keep bleeding forever . . . or until death, whichever comes first. The only way to close that wound is with the Skofnung Stone. That's why the two are such an important set."

Hearthstone launched into a bout of sign language cursing so impressive it would've made a beautiful piece of performance art. Even if you didn't know ASL, his gestures conveyed his anger better than any amount of yelling.

"Dear me," Loki said. "I haven't been called some of those names since my last flyting with the Aesir! I'm sorry you feel that way, my elfish friend, but you're the only one who can get that stone. You *know* it's the only solution. You'd better run along home!"

"Home?" My mind moved at the speed of cold syrup. "You mean . . . Alfheim?"

Blitzen groaned. "Don't make Hearth go. Not worth it, kid."

I glared at Uncle Randolph, who was making himself at home in his zombie niche. With his ratty suit and scarred face, his eyes glazed from pain and blood loss, Randolph was already halfway to being undead.

"What is Loki after?" I asked him. "What does any of this have to do with Thor's hammer?"

He gave me the same desolate expression he'd worn in my dream, when he'd turned to his family on the storm-tossed yacht and said *I'll bring us home.* "Magnus, I—I'm so—"

"Sorry?" Loki supplied. "Yes, you're very sorry, Randolph. We know. But really, Magnus, do you not see the connection? Maybe I need to be clearer. Sometimes I forget how slow you mortals can be. A—giant—has—the—hammer."

He illustrated each word with exaggerated sign language. "Giant—gives—hammer—back—for—Samirah. We—exchange—gifts—at—wedding. Hammer—for—S-K-O-F-N-U-N-G."

"Stop that!" I snarled.

"You understand, then?" Loki shook his hands out. "Good, because my fingers were getting tired. Now, I can't give *half* a bride-price, can I? Thrym will never accept that. I need the blade *and* the stone. Fortunately, your friend Hearthstone knows exactly where the stone can be found!"

"*That's* why you arranged all this? Why you . . . ?" I gestured at Blitz, who lay in an expanding pool of red.

"Call it incentive," Loki said. "I wasn't sure you'd get me the stone merely for the purpose of Samirah's wedding, but you'll do it to save your friend. And, I'll remind you, this is all so *I* can help *you* get back what's-his-name's stupid hammer. It's a win-win. Unless, you know, your dwarf dies. They are such small, pitiful creatures. Randolph, come along now!"

My uncle shuffled toward Loki like a dog expecting a beating. I didn't feel much love for my uncle at the moment, but I also hated the way Loki treated him. I remembered the connection I'd had to Randolph during my dreams . . . feeling the overwhelming grief that motivated him.

"Randolph," I said, "you don't have to go with him."

He glanced at me, and I saw how wrong I was. When he stabbed Blitzen, something inside him had broken. He'd been drawn so far into this evil bargain now, given up so much to get back his dead wife and children, he couldn't imagine any other way.

Loki pointed to the Skofnung blade. "The sword, Randolph. Get the sword."

Jack's runes pulsed an angry purple. "Try it, compadre, and you'll lose more than a couple of fingers."

Randolph hesitated, as people tend to do when they are threatened by talking glowing swords.

Loki's smug confidence wavered. His eyes darkened. His scarred lips curled. I saw how badly he wanted that sword. He needed it for something much more important than a wedding gift.

I put my foot over the Skofnung blade. "Jack's right. This isn't going anywhere."

The veins in Loki's neck looked like they might explode.

I was afraid he would kill Samirah and paint the walls with abstract swaths of dwarf, elf, and einherji.

I stared him down anyway. I didn't understand his plan, but I was starting to realize that he needed us alive . . . at least for now.

In the space of a nanosecond, the god regained his composure.

"Fine, Magnus," he said breezily. "Bring the sword and the stone with you when you bring the bride. Four days. I'll let you know where. And *do* get a proper tuxedo. Randolph, come along. Chop-chop!"

My uncle winced.

Loki laughed. "Oh, sorry." He wriggled his pinky and ring finger. "Too soon?"

He grabbed Randolph's sleeve. The two men shot backward into the coffin portal like they were being sucked out of a moving jet plane. The sarcophagus imploded behind them.

Sam stirred. She sat up abruptly, as though her alarm had gone off. Her hijab slipped over her right eye like a pirate's patch. "What—what's going on?"

I felt too numb to explain. I was kneeling next to Blitzen, doing what I could to keep him stable. My hands glowed with enough Frey-power to cause a nuclear meltdown, but it wasn't helping. My friend was slipping away.

Hearth's eyes brimmed with tears. He sat next to Blitz, his polka-dot scarf trailing in blood. Every once in a while he smacked a *V* sign against his own forehead: *Stupid. Stupid.*

Sam's shadow fell across us. "No! No, no, no. What *happened*?"

Hearthstone flew into another sign language tirade: *Told you! Too dangerous! Your fault we–*

"Buddy . . ." Blitzen pulled weakly at Hearthstone's hands. "Not Sam's . . . fault. Not yours. Was . . . my idea."

Hearthstone shook his head. *Stupid Valkyrie. Stupid me, also. Must be a way to heal you.*

He looked to me, desperate for a miracle.

I *hated* being a healer. Frey's Fripperies, I wished I were a warrior. Or a shape-shifter like Alex Fierro, or a rune caster like Hearthstone, or even a berserker like Halfborn, charging into battle in my underwear. Having my friends' lives depend on my abilities, watching the light go out of Blitzen's eyes and knowing there was nothing I could do about it . . . that was unbearable.

"Loki wouldn't leave us another choice," I said. "We have to find the Skofnung Stone."

Hearthstone grunted in frustration. *I would do it. For Blitz. But no time. Would take a day at least. He will die.*

Blitzen tried to say something. No words came out. His head lolled sideways.

"No!" Sam sobbed. "No, he can't die. Where's this stone? I'll go get it myself!"

I scanned the tomb, frantic for ideas. My eyes fixed on the only source of light—Samirah's spear, lying in dust.

Light. *Sunlight.*

There was one last miracle I could try—a lame, bottom-shelf miracle, but it was all I had.

"We need more time," I said, "so we'll *make* more time." I wasn't sure Blitzen was still lucid, but I squeezed his shoulder. "We'll bring you back, buddy. I promise."

I stood. I raised my face toward the domed ceiling and imagined the sun overhead. I called on my father—the god of warmth and fertility, the god of living things that broke through the earth to reach the light.

The tomb rumbled. Dust rained down. Directly above me, the domed ceiling cracked like an eggshell and a jagged canyon of sunlight spilled through the darkness, illuminating Blitzen's face.

As I watched, one of my best friends in the Nine Worlds turned to solid rock.

NINETEEN

Should I Be Nervous that the Pilot Is Praying?

THE PROVINCETOWN airport was the most depressing place I'd ever been. To be fair, that might have been because I was in the company of a petrified dwarf, a heartbroken elf, a furious Valkyrie, and a sword that would not shut up.

Sam had called an Uber car to get us from the Pilgrim Monument. I wondered if she used Uber as a backup for transporting souls to Valhalla. All the way to the airport, crammed in the backseat of a Ford Focus station wagon, I couldn't stop humming "Flight of the Valkyries."

Next to me, Jack hogged the seat belt and pestered me with questions. "Can we unsheathe Skofnung again just for a minute? I want to say hi."

"Jack, no. She can't be drawn in sunlight or in the presence of women. And if we *did* unsheathe her, she'd have to kill somebody."

"Yeah, but except for that, wouldn't it be awesome?" He sighed, his runes lighting up his blade. "She's *so* fine."

"Please go into pendant mode."

"Do you think she liked me? I didn't say anything stupid, did I? Be honest."

I bit back a few scathing remarks. It wasn't Jack's fault we were in this predicament. Still, I was relieved when I finally convinced him to turn into a pendant. I told him he needed his beauty rest in case we unsheathed Skofnung later.

When we got to the airport, I helped Hearthstone wrestle our granite dwarf out of the station wagon while Sam went into the terminal. The airport itself wasn't much to look at—just a one-room shack for arrivals and departures, a couple of benches out front, and beyond the security fence, two runways for small planes.

Sam hadn't explained why we were here. I guessed she was using her pilot-y connections to get us a charter flight back to Boston. Obviously she couldn't fly all four of us under her own power, and Hearthstone was in no shape to cast any more runes.

Hearth had spent his last bit of magical energy to summon Bubble Wrap and strapping tape, using a rune that looked like a regular *X*. Maybe it was the ancient Viking symbol for shipping materials. Maybe it was the rune for Alfheim Express. Hearthstone was so angry and miserable I didn't dare ask him. I just stood outside the terminal, waiting for Sam to come back, while Hearth carefully wrapped up his best friend.

We'd come to a sort of truce while waiting for the Uber car. Hearth, Sam, and I all felt like stripped high-voltage wires, supercharged with guilt and resentment, ready to kill anyone who touched us. But we knew that wasn't going to help Blitzen. We hadn't discussed it, but we'd formed a silent agreement not to yell and scream and hit each other until later. Right now, we had a dwarf to heal.

Finally, Sam emerged from the terminal. She must have

stopped by the restroom, because her hands and face were still damp.

"The Cessna is on its way," she said.

"Your instructor's plane?"

She nodded. "I had to beg and plead. But Barry's really nice. He understands it's an emergency."

"Does he know about . . . ?" I gestured around, weakly implying the Nine Worlds, petrified dwarves, undead warriors, evil gods, and all the other messed-up things about our lives.

"No," Sam said. "And I'd like to keep it that way. I can't fly airplanes if my instructor thinks I'm delusional."

She glanced over at Hearthstone's Bubble-Wrapping project. "No change in Blitzen? He hasn't started . . . crumbling yet?"

A slug wriggled down my throat. "Crumbling? Please tell me that's not going to happen."

"I hope not. But sometimes . . ." Sam closed her eyes and took a second to compose herself. "Sometimes after a few days . . ."

As if I needed a reason to feel guiltier. "When we find the Skofnung Stone . . . there *is* a way to un-petrify Blitz, right?"

That seemed like I question I should have asked *before* turning my friend into a chunk of granite, but, hey, I'd been under a lot of pressure.

"I—I hope so," Sam said.

That made me feel a whole lot better.

Hearthstone looked over at us. He signed to Sam in small angry gestures: *Plane? You will drop Magnus, me. You don't come.*

Sam looked stung, but she held her hand up next to her face, index finger pointing skyward. *Understand.*

Hearthstone went back to packaging our dwarf.

"Give him time," I told Sam. "It isn't your fault."

Sam studied the pavement. "I wish I believed that."

I wanted to ask about Loki's control over her, to tell her how bad I felt for her, to promise we would find a way to fight her father. But I guessed it was too soon to bring up all that. Her shame was still too raw.

"What did Hearthstone mean about dropping us?" I asked.

"I'll explain when we're in the air." Sam pulled out her phone and checked the time. "It's *zuhr.* We've got about twenty minutes before the plane lands. Magnus, can I borrow you?"

I didn't know what *zuhr* meant, but I followed her to a little grassy area in the middle of the circular driveway.

Samirah rummaged through her backpack. She pulled out a folded blue piece of cloth like an oversize scarf and spread it on the grass. My first thought: *We're having a picnic?*

Then I realized she was aligning the cloth so it pointed southeast. "That's a prayer rug?"

"Yeah," she said. "It's time for noon prayers. Would you stand watch for me?"

"I . . . wait. What?" I felt like she was handing me a newborn baby and asking me to take care of it. In all the weeks I'd known Sam, I'd never seen her pray. I figured she just didn't do it very often. That's what I would've done in her place—as little religious stuff as possible. "How can you pray at a time like this?"

She laughed without humor. "The real question is, how

can I *not* pray at a time like this? It won't take long. Just stand
guard in case . . . I don't know, trolls attack or something."

"Why haven't I ever seen you do this before?"

Sam shrugged. "I pray every day. Five times, as required.
Usually I just slip away to somewhere quiet, though if I'm
traveling or in a dangerous situation, sometimes I postpone
prayers until I'm sure it's safe. That's permissible."

"Like when we were in Jotunheim?"

She nodded. "That's a good for instance. Since we're not
in danger at the moment, and since you're here, and since it's
time . . . do you mind?"

"Uh . . . no. I mean, yeah, sure. Go for it."

I'd been in some pretty surreal situations. I'd bellied up to
a dwarven bar. I'd run from a giant squirrel through the tree
of the universe. I'd rappelled down a curtain into a giant's dining room. But guarding Samirah al-Abbas while she prayed in
an airport parking lot . . . that was a new one.

Sam took off her shoes. She stood very still at the foot of
her rug, her hands clasped at her stomach, her eyes half-closed.
She whispered something under her breath. She momentarily
brought her hands to her ears—the same gesture we'd use in
ASL for *listen carefully*. Then she began her prayers, a soft,
singsong chanting of Arabic that sounded like she was reciting
a familiar poem or a love song. Sam bowed, straightened, and
knelt with her feet tucked under her and pressed her forehead
against the cloth.

I'm not saying I stared at her. It felt wrong to gawk. But I
kept watch from what I hoped was a respectful distance.

I have to admit I was kind of fascinated. Also maybe a little envious. Even after all that had just happened to her, after being controlled and knocked unconscious by her evil father, Sam seemed momentarily at peace. She was generating her own little bubble of tranquility.

I never prayed, because I didn't believe in one all-powerful God. But I wished I had Sam's level of faith in something.

The prayer didn't take long. Sam folded her rug and stood. "Thanks, Magnus."

I shrugged, still feeling like an intruder. "Any better now?"

She smirked. "It's not magic."

"Yeah, but . . . we see magic all the time. Isn't it hard, like, believing there's something more powerful out there than all these Norse beings we deal with? Especially if—no offense—the Big Dude doesn't step in to help out?"

Sam tucked her prayer mat into her bag. "Not stepping in, not interfering, not forcing . . . to me, that seems more merciful and more divine, don't you think?"

I nodded. "Good point."

I hadn't seen Sam crying, but the corners of her eyes were tinged with pink. I wondered if she cried the same way she prayed—privately, stepping away to some quiet place so we didn't notice.

She glanced at the sky. "Besides, who says Allah doesn't help?" She pointed to the gleaming white shape of an airplane making its approach. "Let's go meet Barry."

Surprise! Not only did we get an airplane and a pilot, we also got Sam's boyfriend.

Sam was jogging across the tarmac when the plane's door opened. The first person down the steps was Amir Fadlan, a brown leather jacket over his white Fadlan's Falafel T-shirt, his hair slicked back, and gold-rimmed sunglasses over his eyes so he looked like one of those aviator dudes in a Breitling watch ad.

Sam slowed when she saw him, but it was too late for her to hide. She glanced back at me with a panicked expression, then went to meet her betrothed.

I missed the first part of their conversation. I was too busy helping Hearthstone lug a stone dwarf to the plane. Sam and Amir stood at the bottom step, trading exasperated hand gestures and pained expressions.

When I finally reached them, Amir was pacing back and forth like he was practicing a speech. "I shouldn't even be here. I thought you were in danger. I thought it was life and death. I—" He froze in his tracks. "Magnus?"

He stared at me as if I'd just fallen out of the sky, which wasn't fair, since I hadn't fallen out of the sky in hours.

"Hey, man," I said. "There is totally a good reason for all this. Like, a really good reason. Like, Samirah didn't do . . . *anything* that you might be thinking that she did that was wrong. Because she didn't do that."

Sam glared at me: *Not helping.*

Amir's gaze drifted to Hearthstone. "I recognize you, too. From a couple of months ago, at the food court. Sam's so-called math study group . . ." He shook his head in disbelief. "So you're the elf Sam was talking about? And Magnus . . . you're . . . you're dead. Sam said she took your soul to Valhalla. And the dwarf"—he stared at our Bubble-Wrapped carry-on Blitzen—"is a *statue*?"

"Temporarily," I said. "That wasn't Sam's fault, either."

Amir let out one of those crazy laughs you never want to hear—the kind that indicates the brain has developed a few cracks that will not come out with buffing. "I don't even know where to start. Sam, are you okay? Are . . . are you in trouble?"

Samirah's cheeks turned the color of cranberry sauce. "It's . . . complicated. I'm so sorry, Amir. I didn't expect—"

"That he would be here?" said a new voice. "Darling, he wouldn't take *no* for an answer."

Standing in the plane's doorway was a thin, dark-skinned man so well dressed that Blitzen would have wept with joy: maroon skinny jeans, pastel green shirt, double-breasted vest, and pointy leather boots. The laminated pilot's ID hanging around his neck read BARRY AL-JABBAR.

"My dears," said Barry, "if we're going to keep to our flight plan, you should come aboard. We just need to refuel and we'll be on our way. And as for you, Samirah . . ." He raised an eyebrow. He had the warmest gold eyes I'd ever seen. "Forgive me for telling Amir, but when you called, I was worried sick. Amir *is* a dear friend. And whatever drama is going on between you two, I expect you to fix it! As soon as he heard you were in trouble, he insisted on coming along. So . . ." Barry cupped his hand to his mouth and stage-whispered, "We'll just say I'm your chaperone, shall we? Now, all aboard!"

Barry whirled and disappeared back inside the plane. Hearthstone followed, lugging Blitzen up the steps behind him.

Amir wrung his hands. "Sam, I'm trying to understand. Really."

She looked down at her belt, maybe just realizing she was still wearing her battle-ax. "I—I know."

"I'll do anything for you," Amir said. "Just . . . don't stop talking to me, okay? *Tell* me. No matter how crazy it is, *tell* me."

She nodded. "You'd better get on board. I need to do my walk-around inspection."

Amir glanced at me once more—as if he was trying to figure out where my death wounds were—then he climbed the steps.

I turned to Sam. "He flew out here for you. Your safety is all he cares about."

"I know."

"That's *good*, Sam."

"I don't deserve it. I wasn't honest with him. I just . . . I didn't want to infect the one *normal* part of my life."

"The abnormal part of your life is standing right here."

Her shoulders slumped. "I'm sorry. I know you're trying to help. I wouldn't change having you in my life, Magnus."

"Well, that's good," I said. "Because there's a whole lot more crazy coming up."

Sam nodded. "Speaking of which, you'd better find a seat and buckle in."

"Why? Is Barry a bad pilot?"

"Oh, Barry's an excellent pilot, but he's not flying you. *I* am—straight to Alfheim."

TWENTY

In Case of Demonic Possession, Please Follow Illuminated Signs to the Nearest Exit

BARRY STOOD in the aisle to address us, his elbows on the seatbacks on either side. His cologne made the plane smell like the Boston Flower Exchange. "So, my dears, have you ever flown in a Citation XLS before?"

"Uh, no," I said. "I think I would remember."

The cabin wasn't big, but it was all white leather with gold trim, like a BMW with wings. Four passenger seats faced each other to form a sort of conference area. Hearthstone and I sat looking forward. Amir sat across from me, and petrified Blitzen was strapped in opposite Hearth.

Sam was up in the pilot's seat, checking dials and flipping switches. I'd thought all planes had doors separating the cockpit from the passenger area, but not the Citation. From where I sat, I could see straight out the front windshield. I was tempted to ask Amir to trade places with me. A view of the restroom would have been less nerve-racking.

"Well," said Barry, "as your copilot on this flight, it's my job to give you a quick safety briefing. The main exit is here." He rapped his knuckles on the cabin door through which we'd entered. "In case of emergency, if Sam and I aren't able to open it for you, you—*SHOULD HAVE LISTENED TO ME, MAGNUS CHASE.*"

Barry's voice deepened and tripled in volume. Amir, who was sitting right under his elbow, nearly leaped into my lap.

In the cockpit, Sam turned around slowly. "Barry?"

"*I WARNED YOU.*" Barry's new voice crackled with distortion, and fluctuated up and down in pitch. "*YET YOU FELL INTO LOKI'S TRAP.*"

"Wh-what's wrong with him?" Amir asked. "That's not Barry."

"No," I agreed, my throat as dry as a zombie berserker's. "That's my favorite assassin."

Hearthstone looked even more confused than Amir. He couldn't hear the change in Barry's voice, obviously, but he could tell that the safety briefing had gone off the rails.

"*NOW THERE IS NO CHOICE,*" said Barry-not-Barry. "*ONCE YOU HEAL YOUR FRIEND, FIND ME IN JOTUNHEIM. I WILL GIVE YOU THE INFORMATION YOU NEED TO DEFEAT LOKI'S PLAN.*"

I studied the copilot's face. His gold eyes looked unfocused, but otherwise I couldn't see anything different about him.

"You're the goat-killer," I said. "The guy who was watching me from the tree branch at the feast."

Amir couldn't stop blinking. "Goat-killer? Tree branch?"

"*SEEK OUT HEIMDALL,*" said the distorted voice. "*HE WILL POINT YOU IN MY DIRECTION. BRING THE OTHER, ALEX FIERRO. SHE IS NOW YOUR ONLY HOPE FOR SUCCESS.* —And that covers everything. Any questions?"

Barry's voice had returned to normal. He smiled contentedly, like he could think of no better way to spend his day than flying back and forth from Cape Cod, helping his friends, and channeling the voices of otherworldly ninjas.

Amir, Hearth, and I shook our heads vehemently.

"No questions," I said. "Not a single one."

I locked eyes with Sam. She gave me a shrug and a head shake, like, *Yes, I heard. My copilot was briefly possessed. What do you want me to do about it?*

"Okay, then." Barry patted Blitzen's granite noggin. "Headsets are in the compartments next to you if you want to talk to us in the cockpit. It's a very short flight to Norwood Memorial. Sit back and enjoy!"

Enjoy was not the word I would've used.

Small confession: not only had I never flown in a Citation XLS, I had never flown in an airplane. My first time probably should not have been in an eight-seat Cessna flown by a girl my age who'd only been taking lessons for a few months.

That wasn't Sam's fault. I had nothing to compare it to, but the takeoff seemed smooth. At least we got airborne without any fatalities. Still, my fingernails left permanent gouges in the armrests. Every bump of turbulence jolted me so badly I felt nostalgic for our old friend Stanley, the canyon-diving eight-legged flying horse. (Well, almost.)

Amir declined to use a headset, maybe because his brain was already overloaded with crazy Norse information. He sat with his arms crossed, staring morosely out the window as if wondering whether we would ever land in the real world again.

Sam's voice crackled in my headphones. "We've reached cruising altitude. Thirty-two minutes left in flight."

"Everything good up there?" I asked.

"Yeah . . ." The connection beeped. "There. No one else is

on this channel. Our *friend* seems okay now. Anyway, there's no need to worry. I've got the controls."

"Who, me? Worry?"

From what I could see, Barry seemed pretty chill at the moment. He was kicking back in the copilot's seat staring at his iPad. I wanted to believe he was keeping an eye on important aviation readings, but I was pretty sure he was playing *Candy Crush.*

"Any thoughts?" I asked Sam. "I mean about Goat-Killer's advice?"

Static. Then: "He said we should seek him out in Jotunheim. So he's a giant. That doesn't necessarily mean he's bad. My father"—she hesitated, probably trying to get the word's sour taste out of her mouth—"he has lots of enemies. Whoever Goat-Killer is, he's got some powerful magic. He was right about Provincetown. We should listen to him. *I* should've listened sooner."

"Don't do that," I said. "Don't beat yourself up."

Amir tried to focus on me. "Sorry, what?"

"Not you, man." I tapped the headset mic. "Talking to Sam."

Amir mouthed a silent *Ah*. He returned to practicing his forlorn stare out the window.

"Amir isn't on this channel?" Sam asked.

"No."

"After I drop you guys, I'm going to take the Skofnung Sword to Valhalla for safekeeping. I can't take Amir into the hotel, but . . . I'm going to try to show him what I can. Show him my life."

"Good call. He's strong, Sam. He can handle it."

A three-second count of white noise. "I hope you're right. I'll also update the gang on floor nineteen."

"What about Alex Fierro?"

Sam glanced back at me. It was weird seeing her a few feet away but hearing her voice right in my ears. "Bringing her along is a bad idea, Magnus. You saw what Loki could do to me. Imagine what he . . ."

I could imagine. But I also sensed that Goat-Killer had a point. We would need Alex Fierro. Her arrival in Valhalla wasn't a coincidence. The Norns, or some other weird prophecy gods, had interwoven her fate with ours.

"I don't think we should underestimate her," I said, remembering her fighting those wolves, and riding a bucking lindworm. "Also, I trust her. I mean, as much as you can trust somebody who has cut your head off. Do you have any idea how to find the god Heimdall?"

The static sounded heavier, angrier. "Unfortunately, yes," Sam said. "Get ready. We're almost in position."

"For landing in Norwood? I thought you said we were going to Alfheim."

"*You* are. I'm not. The flight path to Norwood puts us just over the optimal drop zone."

"*Drop* zone?" I really hoped I had misheard her.

"Look, I have to concentrate on flying this plane. Ask Hearthstone." My headphones went silent.

Hearthstone was having a staring contest with Blitzen. The dwarf's granite face poked out from his Bubble-Wrap cocoon, his expression frozen in dying agony. Hearthstone didn't look much happier. The misery swirling around him was almost as easy to see as his bloodstained polka-dotted scarf.

Alfheim, I signed. *How do we get there?*

Jump, Hearth told me.

My stomach dropped out from under me. "Jump? Jump out of the *plane?*"

Hearth stared past me, the way he does when he's considering how to explain something complicated in sign language . . . usually something I won't like.

Alfheim kingdom of air, light, he signed. *Can only be entered . . .* He pantomimed free-falling.

"This is a jet plane," I said. "We can't jump—we'll die!"

Not die, Hearth promised. *Also, not jump exactly. Just . . .* He made a *poof* gesture, which did not reassure me. *We cannot die until we save Blitzen.*

For a guy who rarely made a sound, Hearthstone could speak in defiant shouts when he wanted to. He'd just given me my marching orders: poof out of this plane; fall to Alfheim; save Blitzen. Only after that would it be okay for me to die.

Amir shifted in his seat. "Magnus? You look nervous."

"Yeah." I was tempted to make up some simple explanation, something that wouldn't add any more cracks to Amir's generous mortal brain. But we were beyond that now. Amir was fully in Sam's life, for better or worse, normal or abnormal. He'd always been kind to me. He'd fed me when I was homeless, treated me like a person when most people pretended I was invisible. He'd come to our rescue today without knowing any details, just because Sam was in trouble. I couldn't lie to him.

"Apparently, Hearth and I are going to go *poof.*" I told him my marching orders.

Amir looked so lost I wanted to give the guy a hug.

"Until last week," he said, "my biggest worry was where to expand our falafel franchise, Jamaica Plain or Chestnut Hill. Now I'm not even sure what *world* we're flying through."

I checked to make sure my headset mic was switched off. "Amir, Sam is the same as she's always been. She's brave. She's strong."

"I know that."

"She's also head-over-heels crazy about you," I said. "She didn't ask for any of this weirdness in her life. Her biggest concern is that it doesn't mess up her future with you. Believe that."

He hung his head like a puppy in a kennel. "I . . . I'm trying, Magnus. It's just so strange."

"Yeah," I said. "Here's a heads-up: It's going to get stranger." I switched on my microphone. "Sam?"

"I could hear that entire conversation," she announced.

"Ah." Apparently I hadn't figured out the headset controls after all. "Um—"

"I'll kill you later," she said. "Right now, your exit is coming up."

"Wait. Won't Barry notice if we just disappear?"

"He's mortal. His brain will recalibrate. After all, people don't just vanish off jet planes in mid-flight. By the time we land in Norwood, he probably won't even remember you were here."

I wanted to think I was a little more memorable than that, but I was too nervous to worry about it.

Next to me, Hearthstone unlatched his seat belt. He pulled off his scarf and tied it around Blitzen, fashioning a sort of makeshift harness.

"Good luck," Sam told me. "I'll see you back in Midgard, assuming . . . you know."

Assuming we live, I thought. *Assuming we can heal Blitzen. Assuming our luck is better than it has been the past two days . . . or ever.*

Between one heartbeat and the next, the Cessna disappeared. I found myself floating in the sky, my headphones plugged into nothing at all.

Then I fell.

TWENTY-ONE

Loiterers Will Be Shot,
Then Arrested and Shot Again

BLITZEN ONCE told me that dwarves never left home without a parachute.

Now I understood the wisdom in that. Hearthstone and I plummeted through the frigid air, me waving my arms and screaming, Hearth in a perfect swan dive with granite Blitzen tied to his back. Hearth glanced over at me reassuringly, as if to say, *Don't worry. The dwarf is Bubble-Wrapped.*

My only response was more incoherent screaming, because I didn't know the ASL for *HOLY FREAKING AGGGHHH!*

We punched through a cloud and everything changed. Our fall slowed. The air turned warm and sweet. The sunlight intensified, blinding me.

We hit the ground. Well, sort of. My feet touched down on freshly mown grass and I bounced right off, feeling like I weighed about twenty pounds. I astronaut-skipped across the lawn until I found my balance.

I squinted through the searing sunlight, trying to get my bearings—acres of landscaping, tall trees, a big house in the distance. Everything seemed haloed in fire. No matter which direction I turned, I felt as though a spotlight was shining straight in my face.

Hearthstone grabbed my arm. He pressed something into

my hands: a pair of dark sunglasses. I put them on and the stabbing pain in my eyes subsided.

"Thanks," I muttered. "Is it this bright all the time?"

Hearthstone frowned. I must have been slurring my words. He was having trouble reading my lips. I repeated the question in sign language.

Always bright, Hearth agreed. *You get used to it.*

He scanned our surroundings as if looking for threats.

We'd landed on the front lawn of a big estate. Low stone walls hedged the property—a golf course–size expanse of well-kept flower beds and thin willowy trees that looked as if they'd been pulled upward by gravity as they grew. The house was a Tudor-style mansion with leaded glass windows and conical turrets.

Who lives here? I signed to Hearth. *President of Alfheim?*

Just a family. The Makepieces. He spelled out their name.

They must be important, I signed.

Hearth shrugged. *Regular. Middle-class.*

I laughed, then realized he wasn't joking. If this was a middle-class family in Alfheim, I didn't want to split a lunch tab with the one-percenters.

We should go, Hearth signed. *Makepieces don't like me.* He readjusted his scarf harness for Blitzen, who probably weighed no more than a regular backpack in Alfheim.

Together we headed for the road.

I have to admit, the lighter gravity made me feel . . . well, lighter. I bounded along, covering five feet with every step. I had to restrain myself from leaping farther. With my einherji strength, if I wasn't careful, I might have found myself jumping over the rooftops of middle-class mansions.

As far as I could tell, Alfheim was just row after row of estates like the Makepieces', each property at least several acres, each lawn dotted with flower beds and topiaries. In the cobblestone driveways, black luxury SUVs gleamed. The air smelled like baked hibiscus and crisp dollar bills.

Sam had said our flight path to Norwood would put us over the best drop zone. Now that made sense. In the same way Nidavellir resembled Southie, Alfheim reminded me of the posh suburbs west of Boston—Wellesley, maybe, with its huge houses and pastoral landscapes, its winding roads, picturesque creeks, and sleepy aura of absolute safety . . . assuming you belonged there.

On the downside, the sunlight was so harsh it accentuated every imperfection. Even one stray leaf or wilted flower in a garden stood out as a glaring problem. My own clothes looked dirtier. I could see every pore on the back of my hands and the veins under my skin.

I also understood what Hearthstone meant about Alfheim being made of air and light. The whole place seemed unreal, like it was whisked together from cotton candy fibers and might dissolve with a splash of water. Walking across the spongy ground, I felt uneasy and impatient. The super-dark sunglasses only did so much to alleviate my headache.

After a few blocks, I signed to Hearthstone: *Where are we going?*

He pursed his lips. *Home.*

I caught his arm and made him stop.

Your home? I signed. *Where you grew up?*

Hearth stared at the nearest quaint garden wall. Unlike

me, he wore no sunglasses. In the brilliant daylight, his eyes glittered like crystal formations.

Skofnung Stone is at home, he signed. *With . . . Father.*

The sign for *father* was an open hand, palm facing out, thumb across the forehead. It reminded me of *L* for *loser*. Given what I knew about Hearth's childhood, that seemed appropriate.

Once, in Jotunheim, I'd done some healing magic on Hearth. I'd gotten a glimpse of the pain he carried around inside. He'd been mistreated and shamed while growing up, mostly because of his deafness. Then his brother had died—I didn't know the details—and his parents had blamed Hearth. He couldn't possibly want to go back to a home like that.

I remembered how strongly Blitzen had protested the idea, even when he knew he was going to die. *Don't make Hearth go. Not worth it, kid.*

Yet here we were.

Why? I signed. *Why would your father (loser) have the Skofnung Stone?*

Instead of answering, Hearthstone nodded in the direction we'd come. Everything was so bright in Elf World, I hadn't noticed the flashing lights until the sleek black town car pulled up directly behind us. Along the sedan's front grill, red and blue sequencers pulsed. Behind the windshield, two elves in business suits scowled at us.

The Alfheim Police Department had come to say hello.

"Can we help you?" asked the first cop.

Right then, I knew we were in trouble. In my experience,

no cop ever said *can we help you* if he had any actual desire to help. Another giveaway: cop number one's hand was resting on the butt of his sidearm.

Cop number two edged around the passenger side, also looking ready to break out some helpful deadly force.

Both elves were dressed like plainclothes detectives—in dark suits and silk ties, with ID badges clipped to their belts. Their short-cropped hair was as blond as Hearthstone's. They had the same sort of pale eyes and eerily calm expressions.

Otherwise they looked nothing like my friend. The cops seemed taller, spindlier, more alien. They exuded a cold air of disdain as though they had personal AC units installed under their shirt collars.

The other thing I found strange: *they spoke.* I'd spent so much time around Hearthstone, who communicated in eloquent silence, that hearing an elf speak was really jarring. It just seemed wrong.

Both cops focused on Hearthstone. They looked right through me as if I didn't exist.

"I asked you a question, pal," the first cop said. "Is there a problem here?"

Hearthstone shook his head. He edged back, but I caught his arm. Retreating would only make things worse.

"We're good," I said. "Thanks, officers."

The detectives stared at me like I was from another world, which, to be fair, I was.

The ID tag on cop number one's belt read SUNSPOT. He didn't look much like a sunspot. Then again, I guessed I didn't look much like a chase.

Cop number two's ID read WILDFLOWER. With a handle

like that, I wanted him to be wearing a Hawaiian shirt or at least a floral-pattern tie, but his outfit was just as boring as his partner's.

Sunspot wrinkled his nose as if I smelled like a wight's barrow. "Where'd you learn Elfish, thick? That accent is horrible."

"*Thick?*" I asked.

Wildflower smirked at his partner. "What do you bet Elfish isn't his first language? Illegal *husvaettr* would be my guess."

I wanted to point out that I was a human speaking English, and it *was* my first language. Also my only language. Elfish and English just happened to be the same, like Hearth's Alf Sign Language was the same as American Sign Language.

I doubted the cops would listen or care. The way they spoke *was* a little strange to my ears: a sort of old-fashioned, aristocratic American accent I'd heard on newsreels and movies from the 1930s.

"Look, guys," I said, "we're just taking a walk."

"In a nice neighborhood," said Sunspot, "where I'm guessing you don't live. The Makepieces down the road—they called in a report. Somebody trespassing, loitering. We take that sort of thing seriously, thick."

I had to tamp down my anger. As a homeless person, I'd been a frequent target for rough treatment by law enforcement. My darker-skinned friends got it even worse. So, during the two years I lived on the street, I'd learned a whole new level of caution when dealing with "friendly" neighborhood police officers.

And yet . . . I didn't like being called a *thick*. Whatever that was.

"Officers," I said, "we've been walking for maybe five

minutes. We're heading to my friend's house. How is that loitering?"

Hearthstone signed to me: *Careful.*

Sunspot frowned. "What was that? Some kind of gang sign? Speak Elfish."

"He's deaf," I said.

"Deaf?" Wildflower's face scrunched up in disgust. "What kind of elf—?"

"Whoa, partner." Sunspot swallowed. He tugged at his collar like his personal AC had stopped working. "Is that . . . ? That's gotta be . . . you know, Mr. Alderman's kid."

Wildflower's expression shifted from contempt to fear. It would've been kind of satisfying to watch, except that a fearful cop was *way* more dangerous than a disgusted one.

"Mr. Hearthstone?" Wildflower asked. "Is that you?"

Hearthstone nodded glumly.

Sunspot cursed. "All right. Both of you, in the car."

"Whoa, why?" I demanded. "If you're arresting us, I want to know the charges—"

"We're not arresting you, thick," Sunspot growled. "We're taking you to see Mr. Alderman."

"After that," Wildflower added, "you won't be our problem anymore."

His tone made it sound like we'd be *no one's* problem, since we'd be buried under a lovely well-tended flower bed somewhere. The last thing I wanted to do was get in the car, but the cops tapped their fingers on their elfish firearms, showing us just how helpful they were prepared to be.

I climbed into the back of the cruiser.

TWENTY-TWO

Pretty Sure Hearthstone's Dad Is a Cow-Abducting Alien

IT WAS the nicest cop car I'd ever been in, and I'd been in quite a few. The black leather interior smelled of vanilla. The Plexiglas divider was squeaky clean. The bench seat had a massage feature so I could relax after a hard day of loitering. Obviously, they served only the finest criminals here in Alfheim.

After a mile of comfortable cruising, we pulled off the main road and stopped at a pair of iron gates monogrammed with a fancy *A*. On either side, ten-foot-tall stone walls were topped with decorative spikes to keep out the upper-middle-class riffraff who lived down the street. From the tops of the gateposts, security cameras swiveled to study us.

The gates opened. As we drove through into Hearthstone's family estate, my jaw nearly dropped off. I thought *my* family mansion was embarrassing.

The front yard was bigger than the Boston Common. Swans glided across a lake edged with willow trees. We drove over two different bridges crossing a winding creek, past four different gardens, then through a second set of gates before coming to the main house, which looked like a postmodern version of Sleeping Beauty Castle at Disneyland—white-and-gray slab walls jutting out at strange angles, slender towers like organ pipes, huge plate glass windows, and a burnished steel front door so large it probably had to be opened by chain-pulling trolls.

Hearthstone fidgeted with his bag of runes, occasionally glancing back toward the car's trunk, where the cops had stowed Blitzen.

The officers said nothing until we parked at the front door.

"Out," Wildflower said.

As soon as Hearthstone was free, he walked to the back of the cruiser and rapped on the trunk.

"Yeah, fine." Sunspot popped the lid. "Though I don't see why you care. That has to be the *ugliest* dwarf lawn ornament I've ever seen."

Hearthstone gently lifted out Blitzen and slung the granite dwarf over his shoulder.

Wildflower shoved me toward the entrance. "Move, thick."

"Hey!" I almost reached for my pendant but caught myself. At least the cops now treated Hearthstone as off-limits, but they still seemed perfectly fine pushing me around. "Whatever *thick* means," I said, "I'm not it."

Wildflower snorted. "Have you looked in the mirror recently?"

It dawned on me that, compared to elves, all willowy and delicate and handsome, I must have looked squat and clumsy—*thick*. I got the feeling the term also implied mentally slow, because why insult someone on one level when you can insult them on two?

I was tempted to wreak my revenge on the police officers by bringing out Jack to sing some top-forty hits. Before I could, Hearthstone took my arm and led me up the front steps. The cops trailed behind us, putting distance between themselves and Hearthstone as if they feared his deafness might be contagious.

When we reached the top step, the big steel door swung open silently. A young woman hurried out to meet us. She was almost as short as Blitzen, though she had blond hair and delicate features like an elf. Judging from her plain linen dress and white hair bonnet, I assumed she was a house servant.

"Hearth!" Her eyes lit up in excitement, but she quickly stifled her enthusiasm when she saw our police escorts. "Mr. Hearthstone, I mean."

Hearth blinked like he might start crying. He signed: *Hello/Sorry*, blending them together in a single word.

Officer Wildflower cleared his throat. "Is your master home, Inge?"

"Oh—" Inge gulped. She looked at Hearthstone, then back at the cops. "Yes, sir, but—"

"Go get him," snapped Sunspot.

Inge turned and fled inside. As she hurried away, I noticed something hanging from the back of her skirt—a cord of brown-and-white fur, frayed at the end like the tassel of a belt. Then the tassel flicked, and I realized it was a living appendage.

"She's got a cow tail," I blurted.

Sunspot laughed. "Well, she's a *hulder*. It would be illegal for her to hide that tail. We'd have to bring her in on charges of impersonating a proper elf."

The cop gave Hearthstone a quick look of distaste, making it clear that his definition of *proper elf* also did not include my friend.

Wildflower grinned. "I don't think the boy has ever seen a

hulder before, Sunspot. What's the matter, thick? They don't have domesticated forest sprites in whatever world you crawled out of?"

I didn't answer, though in my mind I was imagining Jack belting out Selena Gomez right in the policeman's ears. The thought comforted me.

I stared into the foyer—a sunlit colonnade of white stone and glass skylights that still managed to make me feel claustrophobic. I wondered how Inge felt about being required to display her tail at all times. Was it a source of pride to show her identity, or did it feel like a punishment—a constant reminder of her lesser status? I decided the really horrible thing was entwining the two together: *Show us who you are; now feel bad about it.* Not much different from Hearth signing *hello* and *sorry* as a single word.

I felt Mr. Alderman's presence before I saw him. The air turned cooler and carried a scent of spearmint. Hearthstone's shoulders slumped as if Midgard gravity were taking over. He shifted Blitzen to the middle of his back as if to hide him. The spots on Hearth's scarf seemed to swarm. Then I realized Hearth was shivering.

Footsteps echoed on the marble floor.

Mr. Alderman appeared, rounding one of the columns and marching toward us.

All four of us stepped back—Hearth, me, even the cops. Mr. Alderman was almost seven feet tall, and so thin that he looked like one of those UFO-flying, strange-medical-experiment-conducting aliens from Roswell. His eyes were too large. His fingers were too delicate. His jaw was so pointy I wondered if his face had been hung on a perfect isosceles triangle.

He dressed better than your average UFO traveler, though. His gray suit fit perfectly over a green turtleneck that made his neck look even longer. His platinum blond hair bristled like Hearth's. I could see some family resemblance in the nose and the mouth, but Mr. Alderman's face was much more expressive. He looked harsh, critical, dissatisfied—like someone who'd just had an outrageously expensive, terrible meal and was contemplating the one-star review he was going to write.

"Well." His eyes dug into his son's face. "You're back. At least you had enough sense to bring the son of Frey with you."

Sunspot choked on his own smug smile. "Sorry, sir. Who?"

"This lad." Mr. Alderman pointed to me. "Magnus Chase, son of Frey, isn't it?"

"That's me." I bit back the urge to add *sir*. So far, this dude hadn't earned it.

I wasn't used to people looking impressed when they found out my dad was Frey. Reactions normally ranged from *Gee, I'm sorry* to *Who is Frey?* to hysterical laughter.

So I'm not going to lie. I appreciated how quickly the cops' expressions changed from contempt to oh-poop-we-just-dissed-a-demigod. I didn't understand it, but I liked it.

"We—we didn't know." Wildflower brushed a speck off my shirt like that would make everything better. "We, um—"

"Thank you, officers," Mr. Alderman cut in. "I will take it from here."

Sunspot gaped at me like he wanted to apologize, or possibly offer me a coupon for fifty percent off my next imprisonment.

"You heard the man," I said. "Off you go, Officers Sunspot and Wildflower. And don't worry. I'll remember you."

They bowed to me . . . actually *bowed*, then made a hasty retreat to their vehicle.

Mr. Alderman scrutinized Hearthstone as if looking for visible defects. "You're the same," he pronounced sourly. "At least the dwarf has turned to stone. That's an improvement."

Hearthstone clenched his jaw. He signed in short angry bursts: *His name is B-L-I-T-Z-E-N.*

"Stop," Alderman demanded. "None of that ridiculous hand-waving. Come inside." He gave me the subzero once-over. "We must properly welcome our guest."

TWENTY-THREE

Yep, His Other Car
Is Definitely a UFO

WE WERE shown into the living room, where absolutely nothing was living. Light spilled in from huge picture windows. The thirty-foot ceiling glittered with a silver mosaic of swirling clouds. The polished marble floor was blindingly white. Lining the walls, illuminated niches displayed various minerals, stones, and fossils. All around the room, yet more artifacts sat under glass cases on white podiums.

As far as museums went—yeah, great space. As far as rooms where I wanted to hang out—no thanks. The only places to sit were two long wooden benches on either side of a steel coffee table. Above the mantel of the cold fireplace, a giant oil portrait of a young boy smiled down at me. He didn't look like Hearthstone. His dead brother, Andiron, I guessed. The boy's white suit and beaming face made him look like an angel. I wondered if Hearthstone had ever looked that happy as a child. I doubted it. The smiling elf boy was the only joyful thing in this room, and the smiling elf boy was dead—frozen in time like the other artifacts.

I was tempted to sit on the floor instead of the benches. I decided to try politeness. It hardly ever works for me, but once in a while I give it a shot.

Hearthstone put Blitzen down carefully on the floor. Then he sat next to me.

Mr. Alderman made himself uncomfortable on the bench across from us.

"Inge," he called, "refreshments."

The hulder materialized in a nearby doorway. "Right away, sir." She scurried off again, her cow tail swishing in the folds of her skirt.

Mr. Alderman fixed Hearthstone with a withering stare, or maybe it was his normal Wow-I-missed-you! expression. "Your room is as you left it. I assume you will be staying?"

Hearthstone shook his head. *We need your help. Then we will leave.*

"Use the slate, son." Mr. Alderman gestured at the end table next to Hearth, where a small whiteboard sat with a marker attached by a string. The old elf glanced at me. "The slate encourages him to think before he speaks . . . if you can call that hand-waving speech."

Hearthstone crossed his arms and glared at his father.

I decided to play translator before one of them killed the other. "Mr. Alderman, Hearth and I need your help. Our friend Blitzen—"

"Has turned to stone," said Mr. Alderman. "Yes, I can see that. Fresh running water will bring back a petrified dwarf. I don't see the issue."

That information alone would've made the unpleasant trip to Alfheim worth it. I felt like the weight of a granite dwarf had been lifted from my shoulders. Unfortunately, we needed more.

"But see," I said, "I turned Blitzen to stone on purpose. He was wounded by a sword. The Skofnung Sword."

Mr. Alderman's mouth twitched. "Skofnung."

"Yeah. Is that funny?"

Alderman showed his perfect white teeth. "You've come here for my help. To heal this dwarf. You want the Skofnung Stone."

"Yeah. You have it?"

"Oh, certainly." Mr. Alderman gestured to one of the nearby podiums. Under a glass case sat a stone disc about the size of a dessert plate—gray with blue flecks, just as Loki had described.

"I collect artifacts from all the Nine Worlds," said Mr. Alderman. "The Skofnung Stone was one of my first acquisitions. It was specially enchanted to withstand the magical edge of the sword—to sharpen it if necessary—and, of course, to provide an instant remedy in the event some foolish wielder cut himself."

"That's great," I said. "How do you heal with it?"

Alderman chuckled. "Quite simple. You touch the stone to the wound, and the wound closes."

"So . . . can we borrow it?"

"No."

Why was I not surprised? Hearthstone gave me a look like, *Yes, Nine Worlds' Best Dad.*

Inge returned with three silver goblets on a tray. After serving Mr. Alderman, she set a cup in front of me, then she smiled at Hearthstone and gave him his. When their fingers touched, Inge's ears turned bright red. She hurried off back to . . . wherever she was required to stay, out of sight but within shouting distance.

The liquid in my cup looked like melted gold. I hadn't eaten or drunk anything since breakfast, so I'd been kind of hoping for elfish sandwiches and sparkling water. I wondered if I was supposed to ask about the goblet's creation and its famous deeds before I drank, the way I would in Nidavellir, the world of the dwarves. Something told me no. The dwarves treated every object they made as unique, deserving of a name. From what I'd seen so far, elves surrounded themselves with priceless artifacts and didn't care about them any more than they cared about their servants. I doubted they named their goblets.

I took a sip. Without doubt, it was the best stuff I'd ever had—with the sweetness of honey, the richness of chocolate, and the coolness of glacier ice, yet it tasted unlike any of those. It filled my stomach more satisfyingly than a three-course meal. It completely quenched my thirst. The jolt it gave me made the mead of Valhalla seem like a knock-off brand of energy drink.

Suddenly, the living room was tinged with kaleidoscopic light. I gazed outside at the well-manicured lawn, the sculptured hedgerows, the garden topiaries. I wanted to pull off my sunglasses, break through the window, and go skipping merrily through Alfheim until the sun burned my eyes out.

I realized Mr. Alderman was watching me, waiting to see how I handled the elfish goofy juice. I blinked several times to get my thoughts back in order.

"Sir," I said, because politeness was working so well, "why won't you help us? I mean, the stone is right there."

"I will not help you," said Mr. Alderman, "because it would

serve me no purpose." He sipped his drink, raising his pinky finger to show off a glittering amethyst ring. "My . . . *son* . . . Hearthstone, deserves no help from me. He left years ago without a word." He paused, then barked a laugh. "Without a word. Well, of course he did. But you take my meaning."

I wanted to shove my goblet between his perfect teeth, but I restrained myself. "So Hearthstone left. Is that a crime?"

"It should be." Alderman scowled. "In doing so, he killed his mother."

Hearthstone choked and dropped his goblet. For a moment, the only sound was the cup rolling on the marble floor.

"You didn't know?" Mr. Alderman asked. "Of course you didn't. Why would you care? After you left, she was distracted and upset. You have no idea how you embarrassed us by disappearing. There were rumors about you studying rune magic, of all things, consorting with Mimir and his riffraff, befriending a *dwarf*. Well, one afternoon, your mother was crossing the street in the village, on her way back from the country club. She had endured awful comments from her friends at lunch. She feared her reputation was ruined. She wasn't looking where she was going. When a delivery truck ran the red light . . ."

Alderman gazed at the mosaic ceiling. For a second, I could almost imagine he had emotions other than anger. I thought I detected sadness in his eyes. Then his gaze froze over with disapproval again. "As if causing your brother's death hadn't been bad enough."

Hearthstone fumbled for his goblet. His fingers seemed to be made of clay. It took him three tries to stand the cup upright on the table. Spots of gold liquid made a trail across the back of his hand.

"Hearth." I touched his arm. I signed: *I'm here.*

I couldn't think of what else to say. I wanted him to know he wasn't alone—that someone in this room cared for him. I thought about the runestone he'd showed me months ago— *perthro,* the sign of the empty cup, Hearth's favorite symbol. Hearthstone had been drained by his childhood. He'd chosen to fill his life with rune magic and a new family—which included me. I wanted to yell at Mr. Alderman that Hearthstone was a better elf than his parents ever were.

But one thing I'd learned from being a son of Frey—I couldn't always fight my friends' battles. The best I could do was be there to heal their injuries.

Also, yelling at Mr. Alderman wouldn't get us what we needed. Sure, I could summon Jack, bust into the display case, and just take the stone. But I was betting Mr. Alderman had some first-rate security. It wouldn't do Blitzen any good to get healed only to be killed immediately by the Alfheim SWAT unit. I wasn't even sure the stone would *work* properly if it wasn't given freely by its owner. Magic items had weird rules, especially ones named Skofnung.

"Mr. Alderman." I tried to keep my voice even. "What do you want?"

He raised a platinum blond eyebrow. "Excuse me?"

"Aside from making your son feel miserable," I added. "You're really good at that. But you said helping us wouldn't serve a purpose for you. What *would* make it worth your while?"

He smiled faintly. "Ah, a young man who understands business. From you, Magnus Chase, I don't require much. You know the Vanir are our ancestral gods? Frey himself is our patron and lord. All of Alfheim was given to him as his teething gift when he was a child."

"So . . . he chewed on you and spit you out?"

Mr. Alderman's smile died. "My *point* is that a son of Frey would make a worthy friend for our family. All I would ask is that you stay with us for a while, perhaps attend a small reception . . . just a few hundred close associates. Show yourself, take a few photos with me for the press. That sort of thing."

The gold drink started to leave a bad aftertaste in my mouth. Photos with Alderman sounded almost as painful as getting decapitated by a wire. "You're worried about your reputation," I said. "You're ashamed of your son, so you want *me* to bolster your street cred."

Alderman's big alien eyes narrowed, making them almost normal size. "I do not know this term *street cred*. But I believe we understand each other."

"Oh, I understand you." I glanced at Hearthstone for guidance, but he still looked unfocused, miserable. "So, Mr. Alderman, I do your little photo op, and you give us the stone?"

"Well, now . . ." Alderman took a long sip from his goblet. "I would expect something from my wayward son, as well. He has unfinished business here. He must atone. He must pay his *wergild*."

"What's a *wergild*?" I silently prayed it wasn't like a werewolf.

"Hearthstone knows what I mean." Alderman stared at his son. "Not a hair must show. You do what must be done—what you should have done years ago. While you work on that, your friend will be a guest in our house."

"Wait," I said. "How long are we talking about? We've got somewhere important to be in, like, less than four days."

Mr. Alderman bared his white teeth again. "Well, then, Hearthstone had better hurry." He rose and shouted, "Inge!"

The hulder scurried over, a dishrag in her hands.

"Provide for my son and his guest as needed," said Mr. Alderman. "They will stay in Hearthstone's old room. And Magnus Chase, do not think you can defy me. My house, my rules. Try to take the stone and, son of Frey or not, it won't go well for you."

He tossed his goblet on the floor, as if he couldn't allow Hearthstone to have the most impressive spill.

"Clean that up," he snapped at Inge. Then he stormed out of the room.

TWENTY-FOUR

Oh, You Wanted to Breathe? That'll Be an Extra Three Gold

HEARTHSTONE'S ROOM? More like Hearthstone's isolation chamber.

After cleaning up the spill (we insisted on helping), Inge led us up a wide staircase to the second floor, down a hall bedecked with lush tapestries and more artifact niches, to a simple metal door. She opened it with a big old-fashioned key, though doing so made her wince as if the door was hot.

"Apologies," she told us. "The house's locks are all made of iron. They're uncomfortable for sprites like me."

Judging from the clammy look on her face, I think she meant *torturous*. I guessed Mr. Alderman didn't want Inge unlocking too many doors—or maybe he just didn't care if she suffered.

Inside, the room was almost as large as my suite in Valhalla, but whereas my suite was designed to be everything I could want, this place was designed to be nothing Hearthstone would want. Unlike every other part of the house I'd seen, there were no windows. Rows of fluorescent lights glowed harshly overhead, providing all the ambiance of a discount-furniture store. On the floor in one corner lay a twin mattress covered in white sheets. No blanket, no comforter, no pillows.

To the left, a doorway led to what I assumed was the bathroom. To the right, a closet stood open, revealing exactly one set of clothes: a white suit roughly Hearth's size but otherwise an exact match for the suit in the portrait of Andiron downstairs. Mounted on the walls, classroom-size whiteboards displayed to-do lists written in neat block letters.

Some lists were in black:
YOUR OWN LAUNDRY, TWICE WEEKLY = +2 GOLD
SWEEP THE FLOORS, BOTH LEVELS = +2 GOLD
WORTHY TASKS = +5 GOLD

Others were in red:
EACH MEAL = –3 GOLD
ONE HOUR OF FREE TIME = –3 GOLD
EMBARRASSING FAILURES = –10 GOLD

I counted maybe a dozen lists like this, along with hundreds of motivational statements like: NEVER FORGET YOUR RESPONSIBILITY. STRIVE TO BE WORTHY. NORMALCY IS THE KEY TO SUCCESS.

I felt as if I were surrounded by towering adults all wagging their fingers at me, heaping shame, making me smaller and smaller. And I'd only been here for a minute. I couldn't imagine *living* here.

Even the Ten Commandments whiteboards weren't the strangest thing. Stretched across the floor was the furry blue hide of a large animal. Its head had been removed, but its four paws still had the claws attached—curved ivory barbs that would've made perfect fishing hooks for catching great white sharks. Strewn across the rug were gold coins—maybe two or three hundred of them, glittering like islands in a sea of thick blue fur.

Hearthstone set Blitzen down gently at the foot of the mattress. He scanned the whiteboards, his face a mask of anxiety, as if looking for his name on a list of exam scores.

"Hearth?" I was so shocked by the room I couldn't form a coherent question like, *Why?* or, *May I please kick your father's teeth in?*

He made one of the first signs he'd ever taught me—back on the streets, when he was teaching me how to stay out of trouble with the police. He crossed two fingers and ran them down his opposite palm like he was writing a ticket: *Rules.*

It took a moment for my hands to remember how to sign. *Your parents made these for you?*

Rules, he repeated. His face gave away little. I started to wonder if, earlier in his life, Hearthstone had smiled more, cried more, shown *any* emotion more. Maybe he'd learned to be so careful with his expressions as a defense.

"But why the prices?" I asked. "It's like a menu. . . ."

I stared at the gold coins glittering on the fur rug. "Wait, the coins were your allowance? Or . . . your *payment*? Why throw them on the rug?"

Inge stood quietly in the doorway, her face lowered. "It's the hide of the beast," she said, also signing the words. "The one that killed his brother."

My mouth tasted like rust. "Andiron?"

Inge nodded. She glanced behind her, probably worried that the master would appear out of nowhere. "It happened when Andiron was seven and Hearthstone was eight." As she spoke, she signed almost as fluently as Hearth, like she'd been practicing for years. "They were playing in the woods behind the house. There's an old well . . ." She hesitated, looking at Hearthstone for permission to say more.

Hearthstone shuddered.

Andiron loved the well, he signed. *He thought it granted wishes. But there was a bad spirit. . . .*

He made a strange combination of signs: three fingers at the mouth—a W for water; then pointing down—the symbol for a well; then a V over one eye—the sign for taking a pee. (We used that one a lot on the streets, too.) Together, it looked like he was naming this bad spirit *Pees-in-the-Well.*

I frowned at Inge. "Did he just say—?"

"Yes," she confirmed. "That is the spirit's name. In the old language, it is called a *brunnmigi.* It came out of the well and attacked Andiron in the form of . . . *that.* A large bluish creature, a mixture of bear and wolf."

Always with the blue wolves. I hated them.

"It killed Andiron," I summed up.

In the fluorescent light, Hearthstone's face looked as petrified as Blitzen's. *I was playing with some stones,* he signed. *My back was turned. I didn't hear. I couldn't . . .*

He grasped at empty air.

"It wasn't your fault, Hearth," Inge said.

She looked so young with her clear blue eyes, her slightly pudgy rosy cheeks, her blond hair curling around the edges of her bonnet, but she spoke as if she'd seen the attack firsthand.

"Were you there?" I asked.

She blushed even more. "Not exactly. I was just a little girl, but my mother worked as Mr. Alderman's servant. I—I remember Hearthstone running into the house crying, signing for help. He and Mr. Alderman rushed out again. And then, later . . . Mr. Alderman came back, carrying Master Andiron's body."

Her cow tail flicked, brushing the doorjamb. "Mr. Alderman killed the brunnmigi, but he made Hearthstone . . . skin the creature, all by himself. Hearthstone wasn't allowed back inside until the job was done. Once the hide was cured and made into a rug, they put it in here."

"Gods." I paced the room. I tried to wipe some of the words off a whiteboard, but they were written in permanent marker. Of course they were.

"And the coins?" I asked. "The menu items?"

My voice came out harsher than I'd intended. Inge flinched.

"Hearthstone's wergild," she said. "The blood debt for his brother's death."

Cover the rug, Hearthstone signed mechanically, as if quoting something he'd heard a million times. *Earn gold coins until not a single hair can be seen. Then I have paid.*

I looked at the list of prices—the pluses and minuses of Hearthstone's guilt ledger. I stared at the sprinkling of coins lost in an expanse of blue fur. I imagined eight-year-old Hearthstone trying to earn enough money to cover even the smallest portion of this huge rug.

I shivered, but I couldn't shake off my anger. "Hearth, I thought your parents beat you or something. This is worse."

Inge wrung her hands. "Oh, no, sir, beatings are only for the house staff. But you are right. Mr. Hearthstone's punishment has been much more difficult."

Beatings. Inge mentioned them as if they were unfortunate facts of life, like burned cookies or stopped-up sinks.

"I'm going to tear this place down," I decided. "I'm going to throw your father—"

Hearthstone locked eyes with me. My anger backwashed in my throat. This wasn't my call. This wasn't my history. Still . . .

"Hearth, we can't play his sick little game," I said. "He wants you to complete this wergild before he helps us? That's impossible! Sam's supposed to marry a giant in four days. Can't we just take the stone? Travel to another world before Alderman realizes?"

Hearth shook his head. *Stone must be a gift. Only works if given freely.*

"And there are guards," Inge added. "Security spirits that . . . you don't want to meet."

I'd expected all of the above, but that didn't stop me from cursing until Inge's ears blushed.

"What about rune magic?" I asked. "Can you summon enough gold to cover the fur?"

Wergild cannot be cheated, Hearth signed. *Gold must be earned or won by some great effort.*

"That'll take years!"

"Perhaps not," Inge murmured, as if talking to the blue rug. "There is a way."

Hearth turned to her. *How?*

Inge clasped her hands in agitation. I wasn't sure if she

was aware that she was making the sign for *marriage*. "I—I
don't mean to speak out of turn. But there is the Careful One."

Hearth threw his hands up in the universal gesture for *Are
you kidding me?* He signed: *Careful One is a legend.*

"No," Inge said. "I know where he is."

Hearth stared at her in dismay. *Even if. No. Too dangerous.
Everyone who tries to rob him ends up dead.*

"Not everyone," Inge said. "It would be dangerous, but you
could do it, Hearth. I *know* you could."

"Hold up," I said. "Who's the Careful One? What are you
talking about?"

"There—there is a dwarf," Inge said. "The only dwarf in
Alfheim except for . . ." She nodded toward our petrified
friend. "The Careful One has a hoard of gold large enough
to cover this rug. I could tell you how to find him—if you don't
mind a fairly high chance that you'll die."

TWENTY-FIVE

Hearthstone? More Like *Hearthrob*. Am I Right?

YOU SHOULDN'T make a comment about imminent death and then say "Good night! We'll talk about it tomorrow!"

But Inge insisted we shouldn't go after the dwarf until the morning. She pointed out that we needed rest. She brought us extra clothes, food and drink, and a couple of pillows. Then she scurried off, maybe to clean up spills or dust artifact niches or pay Mr. Alderman five gold for the privilege of being his servant.

Hearth didn't want to talk about the killer dwarf Careful One or his gold. He didn't want to be consoled about his dead mother or his living father. After a quick gloomy meal, he signed, *Need sleep,* and promptly collapsed on his mattress.

Just out of spite, I decided to sleep on the rug. Sure, it was creepy, but how often do you get to recline on one hundred percent genuine Pees-in-the-Well fur?

Hearthstone had told me that the sun never set in Alfheim. It just sort of dipped to the horizon and came back up again, like in summer in the arctic. I'd wondered if I'd have trouble sleeping when there was no night. But I needn't have worried— here in Hearthstone's windowless room, one flick of the light switch left me in total darkness.

I'd had a long day, what with fighting democratic zombies

and then getting dropped out of an airplane into the wealthy suburbs of Elitist-heim. The evil creature's fur was surprisingly warm and comfortable. Before I knew it, I had drifted off into not-so-peaceful slumber.

Seriously, I don't know if there's a Norse god of dreams, but if there is, I'm going to find his house and hack apart his Sleep Number mattress with a battle-ax.

I got treated to a flurry of disturbing images, none of which made much sense. I saw my Uncle Randolph's ship listing in the storm, heard his daughters screaming from inside the wheelhouse. Sam and Amir—who had no business being there—clung to opposite sides of the deck, trying to reach each other's hands until a wave crashed over them and swept them out to sea.

The dream shifted. I saw Alex Fierro in her suite in Valhalla, throwing ceramic pots across the atrium. Loki stood in her bedroom, casually adjusting his paisley bow tie in the mirror as pots passed through him and smashed against the wall.

"It's such a simple request, Alex," he said. "The alternative will be unpleasant. Do you think because you're dead you have nothing left to lose? You are *very* wrong."

"Get out!" Alex screamed.

Loki turned, but he was no longer a *he*. The god had changed into a young woman with long red hair and dazzling eyes, an emerald green evening gown accentuating her figure. "Temper, temper, love," she purred. "Remember where you come from."

The words reverberated, shaking the scene apart.

I found myself in a cavern of bubbling sulfuric pools and

thick stalagmites. The god Loki, wearing only a loincloth, lay lashed to three rock columns—his arms spread wide, his legs bound together, his ankles and wrists tied with glistening dark cords of calcified guts. Coiled around a stalactite above his head was a massive green serpent, jaws open, fangs dripping venom into the god's eyes. But instead of screaming, Loki was laughing as his face burned. "Soon enough, Magnus!" he called. "Don't forget your wedding invitation!"

A different scene: a mountainside in Jotunheim in the middle of a blizzard. At the summit stood the god Thor, his red beard and shaggy hair flecked with ice, his eyes blazing. In his thick fur cloak, with his hide clothes dusted with snow, he looked like the Abominable Ginger Snowman. Coming up the slope to kill him were a thousand giants—an army of muscle-bound gargantuans in armor fashioned from slabs of stone, their spears the size of redwood trees.

With his gauntlets, Thor raised his hammer—the mighty Mjolnir. Its head was a slab of iron shaped roughly like a flattened circus tent, blunt on both ends and pointed in the middle. Runic designs swirled across the metal. In the god's double-fisted grip, Mjolnir's handle looked so stubby it was almost comical, like he was a child raising a weapon much too heavy for him. The army of giants laughed and jeered.

Then Thor brought down the hammer. At his feet, the side of the mountain exploded. Giants went flying in a million-ton maelstrom of rock and snow, lightning crackling through their ranks, hungry tendrils of energy burning them to ashes.

The chaos subsided. Thor glowered down at the thousand dead enemies now littering the slopes. Then he looked directly at me.

"You think I can do that with a *staff*, Magnus Chase?" he bellowed. "HURRY UP WITH THAT HAMMER!"

Then, being Thor, he lifted his right leg and farted a thunderclap.

The next morning, Hearthstone shook me awake.

I felt like I'd been bench-pressing Mjolnir all night, but I managed to stumble into the shower, then dress myself in elfish linen and denim. I had to roll up the sleeves and cuffs about sixteen times to make them fit.

I wasn't sure about leaving Blitzen behind, but Hearthstone decided that our friend would be safer here than where we were going. We set him on the mattress and tucked him in. Then the two of us crept out of the house, thankfully without encountering Mr. Alderman.

Inge had agreed to meet us at the back edge of the estate. We found her waiting where the well-kept lawn met a gnarled line of trees and undergrowth. The sun was on the rise again, turning the sky blood orange. Even with my sunglasses on, my eyeballs were screaming in pain. Stupid beautiful sunrise in stupid Elf World.

"I don't have long," Inge fretted. "I bought a ten-minute break from the master."

That made me angry all over again. I wanted to ask how much it would cost to buy ten minutes of stomping Mr. Alderman with cleats, but I figured I shouldn't waste Inge's valuable time.

She pointed to the woods. "Andvari's lair is in the river. Follow the current downstream to the waterfall. He dwells in the pool at its base."

"Andvari?" I asked.

She nodded uneasily. "That is his name—the Careful One, in the old language."

"And this dwarf lives underwater?"

"In the shape of a fish," said Inge.

"Oh. Naturally."

Hearthstone signed to Inge: *How do you know this?*

"I . . . well, Master Hearthstone, hulder still have some nature magic. We're not supposed to use it, but—I sensed the dwarf the last time I was in the woods. Mr. Alderman only tolerates this patch of wilderness on his property because . . . you know, hulder need a forest nearby to survive. And he can always . . . hire more help in there."

She said *hire*. I heard *catch*.

The ten-minute cleat-stomping session was sounding better and better.

"So this dwarf . . ." I said, "what's he doing in Alfheim? Doesn't the sunlight turn him to stone?"

Inge's cow tail flicked. "According to the rumors I've heard, Andvari is over a thousand years old. He has powerful magic. The sunlight barely affects him. Also, he stays in the darkest depths of the pool. I—I suppose he thought Alfheim was a safe place to hide. His gold has been stolen before, by dwarves, humans, even gods. But who would look for a dwarf and his treasure here?"

Thank you, Inge, Hearth signed.

The hulder blushed. "Just be careful, Master Hearth. Andvari is tricky. His treasure is sure to be hidden and protected by all sorts of enchantments. I'm sorry I can only tell you where to find him, not how to defeat him."

Hearthstone gave Inge a hug. I was afraid the poor girl's bonnet might pop off like a bottle cap.

"I—please—good luck!" She dashed off.

I turned to Hearthstone. "Has she been in love with you since you were kids?"

Hearth pointed at me, then circled his finger at the side of his head. *You're crazy.*

"Whatever, man," I said. "I'm just glad you didn't kiss her. She would've passed out."

Hearthstone gave me an irritated grunt. *Come on. Dwarf to rob.*

TWENTY-SIX

We Nuke All the Fish

I HAD trekked through the wilderness of Jotunheim. I had lived on the streets of Boston. Somehow the swath of uncultivated land behind the Alderman Manor seemed even more dangerous.

Glancing behind us, I could still see the house's towers peeking above the woods. I could hear traffic from the road. The sun shone down as glaringly cheerful as usual. But under the gnarled trees, the gloom was tenacious. The roots and rocks seemed determined to trip me. In the upper branches, birds and squirrels gave me the stink eye. It was as if this little patch of nature were trying doubly hard to stay wild in order to avoid getting turned into a tea garden.

If I even see you bringing a croquet set up in here, the trees seemed to say, *I will make you eat the mallets.*

I appreciated the attitude, but it made our stroll a little nerve-racking.

Hearthstone seemed to know where he was going. The thought of Andiron and him playing in these woods as boys gave me new respect for their courage. After picking our way through a few acres of thornbushes, we emerged in a small clearing with a cairn of stones in the center.

"What is that?" I asked.

Hearthstone's expression was tight and painful, as if he were still forging through the briar. He signed, *The well.*

The melancholy of the place seeped into my pores. This was the spot where his brother had died. Mr. Alderman must have filled in the well—or maybe he had forced Hearthstone to do it after he'd finished skinning the evil creature. The act had probably earned Hearth a couple of gold coins.

I circled my fist over my chest, the sign for *I'm sorry.*

Hearth stared at me as if the sentiment did not compute. He knelt next to the cairn and picked up a small flat stone from the top. Engraved on it in dark red was a rune:

Othala. *Inheritance.* The same symbol Randolph's little girl Emma had been clutching in my dream. Seeing it in real life, I felt seasick all over again. My face burned with the memory of Randolph's scar.

I recalled what Loki had said in the wight's tomb: *Blood is a powerful thing. I can always find you through him.* For a second, I wondered if Loki had somehow put the rune here as a message for me, but Hearthstone didn't seem surprised to find it.

I knelt next to him and signed, *Why is that here?*

Hearthstone pointed to himself. He set the stone carefully back on top of the pile.

Means home, he signed. *Or what is important.*

"Inheritance?"

He considered for a moment, then nodded. *I put it here when I left, years ago. This rune I will not use. It belongs with him.*

I stared at the pile of rocks. Were some of these the same

ones that eight-year-old Hearthstone had been playing with when the monster attacked his brother? This place was more than a memorial for Andiron. Part of Hearthstone had died here, too.

I was no magician, but it seemed wrong for a set of rune-stones to be missing one symbol. How could you master a language—especially the language of the universe—without all the letters?

I wanted to encourage Hearth to take back the rune. Surely Andiron would want that. Hearth had a new family now. He was a great sorcerer. His cup of life had been refilled.

But Hearthstone avoided my eyes. It's easy not to heed someone when you're deaf. You simply don't look at them. He rose and walked on, gesturing for me to follow.

A few minutes later, we found the river. It wasn't impressive—just a swampy creek like the one that meandered through the Fenway greenbelt. Clouds of mosquitos hovered over marsh grass. The ground was like warm bread pudding. We followed the current downstream through thick patches of bramble and bog up to our knees. The thousand-year-old dwarf Andvari had picked a lovely place to retire.

After last night's dreams, my nerves were raw.

I kept thinking about Loki bound in his cave. And his appearance in Alex Fierro's suite: *It's such a simple request.* If that had actually happened, what did Loki want?

I remembered the assassin, the goat-killer who liked to possess flight instructors. He'd told me to bring Alex to Jotunheim: *SHE IS NOW YOUR ONLY HOPE FOR SUCCESS.* That did not bode well.

Three days from now, the giant Thrym expected a wedding. He would want his bride, as well as a bride-price of the Skofnung Sword and Stone. In exchange, maybe, we would get back Thor's hammer and prevent hordes of Jotunheim from invading Boston.

I thought about the thousand giants I'd seen in my dream, marching into battle to challenge Thor. I wasn't anxious to face such a force—not without a big hammer that could explode mountains and fry invading armies into sizzly bits.

I guessed what Hearth and I were doing now made sense: trudging through Alfheim, trying to retrieve gold from some old dwarf so we could get the Skofnung Stone and heal Blitz. Still . . . I felt as if Loki was intentionally keeping us sidetracked, not giving us time to think. He was like a point guard waving his hands in our faces, distracting us from shooting for the net. There was more to this wedding deal than getting Thor's hammer back. Loki had a plan within a plan. He'd recruited my Uncle Randolph for some reason. If only I could find a moment to gather my thoughts without being pulled from one life-threatening problem to another. . . .

Yeah, right. You have just described your entire life and afterlife, Magnus.

I tried to tell myself everything would be fine. Unfortunately, my esophagus didn't believe me. It kept yo-yoing up and down from my chest to my teeth.

The first waterfall we found was a gentle trickle over a mossy ledge. Open meadows stretched out on either bank. The water wasn't deep enough for a fish to hide in. The meadows were too flat to conceal effective traps like poison spikes, land mines, or trip wires that launched dynamite or rabid rodents from catapults. No self-respecting dwarf would've hidden his treasure here. We kept walking.

The *second* waterfall had potential. The terrain was rockier, with lots of slippery moss and treacherous crevices between the boulders on either bank. The overhanging trees shaded the water and provided ample potential hiding places for crossbows or guillotine blades. The river itself cascaded down a natural stairwell of rock before tumbling ten feet into a pond the diameter of a trampoline. With all the churning froth and ripples, I couldn't see below the surface, but judging from the dark blue water, it must've been deep.

"There could be anything down there," I told Hearth. "How do we do this?"

Hearthstone gestured toward my pendant. *Be ready.*

"Uh, okay." I pulled off my runestone and summoned Jack.

"Hey, guys!" he said. "Whoa! We're in Alfheim! Did you bring sunglasses for me?"

"Jack, you don't have eyes," I reminded him.

"Yeah, but still, I look great in sunglasses! What are we doing?"

I told him the basics while Hearthstone rummaged through his bag of runestones, trying to decide which flavor of magic to use on a dwarf/fish.

"Andvari?" Jack said. "Oh, I've heard of that guy. You can steal his gold, but don't kill him. That would be really bad luck."

"Meaning what, exactly?"

Swords could not shrug, but Jack tilted from side to side, which was his closest equivalent. "I dunno what would happen. I just know it's right up there on the things-you-don't-do list, along with breaking mirrors, crossing paths with Freya's cats, and trying to kiss Frigg under the mistletoe. Boy, I made that mistake once!"

I had the horrible feeling Jack was about to tell me the story. Then Hearthstone raised a runestone over his head. I just had time to recognize the symbol:

Thurisaz: the rune of Thor.

Hearthstone slammed it into the pond.

KA-BLAM! Water vapor coated my sunglasses. The atmosphere turned to pure steam and ozone so fast, my sinuses inflated like car air bags.

I wiped off my lenses. Where the pond had been, a huge muddy pit went down thirty feet. At the bottom, dozens of surprised fish flailed around, their gills flapping.

"Whoa," I said. "Where did the waterfall . . . ?"

I looked up. The river arched over our heads like a liquid rainbow, bypassing the pond and crashing into the riverbed downstream.

"Hearth, how the heck—?"

He turned to me, and I took a nervous step back. His eyes blazed with anger. His expression was scarier and even less Hearth-like than when he'd *uruz*ed himself into Ox Elf.

"Uh, just saying, man . . ." I raised my hands. "You nuked about fifty innocent fish."

One of them is a dwarf, he signed.

He jumped into the pit, his boots sinking into the mud. He waded around, pulling out his feet with deep sucking noises, examining each fish. Above me, the river continued to arc through midair, roaring and glittering in the sunlight.

"Jack," I said, "what does the thurisaz rune do?"

"It's the rune of Thor, *señor.* Hey—*Thor, señor.* That rhymes!"

"Yeah, great. But, uh, why did the pond go boom? Why is Hearthstone acting so weird?"

"Oh! Because thurisaz is the rune of destructive force. Like Thor. Blowing stuff up. Also, when you invoke it, you can get a little . . . Thor-like."

Thor-like. Just what I needed. Now I really didn't want to jump into that hole. If Hearthstone started farting like the thunder god, the air down there was going to get toxic real fast.

On the other hand, I couldn't leave those fish at the mercy of an angry elf. Sure, they were just fish. But I didn't like the idea of so many dying just so we could weed out one disguised dwarf. Life was life. I guess it was a Frey thing. I also figured Hearthstone might feel bad about it once he shook off the influence of thurisaz.

"Jack, stay here," I said. "Keep watch."

"Which would be easier and cooler with sunglasses," Jack complained.

I ignored him and leaped in.

At least Hearth didn't try to kill me when I dropped down next to him. I looked around but saw no sign of treasure—no X's marking the spot, no trapdoors, just a bunch of gasping fish.

How do we find Andvari? I signed. *The other fish need water to breathe.*

We wait, Hearth signed. *Dwarf will suffocate too unless he changes form.*

I didn't like that answer. I crouched and rested my hands on the mud, sending out the power of Frey through the slime and the muck. I know that sounds weird, but I figured if I could heal with a touch, intuiting everything that was wrong inside someone's body, maybe I could extend my perception a little more—the same way you might squint to see farther—and sense all the different life-forms around me.

It worked, more or less. My mind touched the cold panicked consciousness of a trout flopping a few inches away. I located an eel that had burrowed into the mud and was seriously considering biting Hearthstone in the foot (I convinced him not to). I touched the tiny minds of guppies whose entire thought process was *Eek! Eek! Eek!* Then I sensed something different—a grouper whose thoughts were racing a little too fast, like he was calculating escape plans.

I snatched him up with my einherji reflexes. The grouper yelled, *"GAK!"*

"Andvari, I presume? Nice to meet you."

"LET ME GO!" wailed the fish. "My treasure is not in this pond! Actually, I don't have a treasure! Forget I said that!"

"Hearth, how 'bout we get out of here?" I suggested. "Let the pond fill up again."

The fire suddenly went out of Hearthstone's eyes. He staggered.

From above, Jack yelled, "Uh, Magnus? You might want to hurry."

The rune magic was fading. The arc of water started to dissolve, breaking into droplets. Keeping one hand tight on my captive grouper, I wrapped my other arm around Hearthstone's waist and leaped straight up with all my strength.

Kids, do not try this at home. I'm a trained einherji who died a painful death, went to Valhalla, and now spends most of his time arguing with a sword. I am a qualified professional who can jump out of thirty-foot-deep muddy holes. You, I hope, are not.

I landed on the riverbank just as the waterfall collapsed back into the pond, granting all the little fishies a very wet miracle and a story to tell their grandchildren.

The grouper tried to wriggle free. "Let me go, you scoundrel!"

"Counterproposal," I said. "Andvari, this is my friend Jack, the Sword of Summer. He can cut through almost anything. He sings pop songs like a demented angel. He can also fillet a fish faster than you would believe. I'm about to ask Jack to do all of those things at once—or you can turn into your normal form, slow and easy, and we can have a chat."

In two blinks, instead of holding a fish, my hand was wrapped around the throat of the oldest, slimiest dwarf I'd ever seen. He was so disgusting that the fact I didn't let go should've proven my bravery and gotten me into Valhalla all over again.

"Congratulations," the dwarf croaked. "You got me. And now you're gonna get a tragic demise!"

TWENTY-SEVEN

Let Me Go Immediately,
or I Will Make You a Billionaire

OOH, A DEMISE!

Normally I am not threatened with a *demise*. Most folks in the Nine Worlds don't use fancy words like that. They just say "IMMA KILL YOU!" Or they let their chain-mail-wrapped fists do the talking.

I was so impressed with Andvari's vocabulary, I squeezed his throat tighter.

"Ack!" The dwarf thrashed and wriggled. He was slippery, but not heavy. Even by dwarf standards, the dude was tiny. He wore a fish-skin tunic and underwear that was basically a moss diaper. Slime coated his limbs. His stubby arms hammered away at me, but it didn't feel any worse than getting hit with Nerf bats. And his face . . . well, you know how your thumb looks after it's been under a wet bandage too long—all wrinkly and discolored and gross? Imagine that as a face, with some scraggly white whiskers and mold-green eyes, and you've got Andvari.

"Where's the gold?" I demanded. "Don't make me unleash my sword's playlist."

Andvari writhed even more. "You fools don't want my gold! Don't you know what happens to people who take it?"

"They get rich?" I guessed.

"No! Well, yes. But after that, they die! Or . . . at least they *want* to die. They always suffer. And so does everyone around them!" He wiggled his slimy fingers like, *Woo, woo, threatening!*

Hearthstone was listing slightly to port, but he managed to stay on his feet. He signed: *One person stole gold, no consequences.* Then he made my least favorite name sign: index finger and thumb pinched together at the side of his head, a combination of the letter *L* and the sign for *devil*, which fit our friend Loki just fine.

"Loki took your gold once," I interpreted, "and *he* didn't die or suffer."

"Well, yeah, but that's Loki!" Andvari said. "Everybody else who got the gold after him—they went crazy! They had horrible lives, left a trail of dead bodies! Is that what you want? You want to be like Fafnir? Sigurd? The Powerball lottery winners?"

"The who?"

"Oh, come on! You've heard the stories. Every time I lose my ring, it bounces around the Nine Worlds for a while. Some schmuck gets ahold of it. They win the lottery and make millions. But they always end up broke, divorced, sick, unhappy, and/or dead. Is that what you want?"

Hearth signed: *Magic ring, yes. That's the secret of his wealth. We need that.*

"You mentioned a ring," I said.

Andvari went still. "Did I? Nope. Must have misspoken. No ring."

"Jack," I said, "how do his feet look to you?"

"Real bad, *señor*. They need a pedicure."

"Do it."

Jack flew into action. It's a rare sword that can remove caked-on pond scum, shave off calluses, trim gnarly toenails, and leave a pair of dwarf feet shiny clean without 1) killing said dwarf, 2) cutting off the flailing feet of said dwarf, or 3) cutting off the legs of the einherji who is holding said dwarf . . . and all the while singing "Can't Feel My Face." Jack is truly special.

"All right! All right!" Andvari shrieked. "No more torture! I'll show you where the treasure is! It's right under that rock!"

He pointed frantically to pretty much everything until his finger came to rest at a boulder near the edge of the waterfall.

Traps, Hearthstone signed.

"Andvari," I said, "if I move that boulder, what sort of traps will I spring?"

"None!"

"What if I move it using your head as a lever, then?"

"All right, it's booby-trapped! Exploding hexes! Trip wires to catapults!"

"I *knew* it," I said. "How do you disarm them? *All* of them."

The dwarf squinted with concentration. At least I *hoped* that's what he was doing. Otherwise he was making a deposit in his moss diaper.

"It's done." He sighed miserably. "I've disarmed all the traps."

I glanced at Hearthstone. The elf stretched out his hands, probably testing our surroundings for magic the way I could sense eels and guppies. (Hey, we all have different talents.)

Hearth nodded. *Safe.*

With Andvari still dangling from my hand, I walked to the boulder and flipped it over with my foot. (Einherji strength is also a good talent.)

Under the rock, a canvas-lined pit was filled with . . . Wow. I didn't usually care about money. I'm not about that. But my saliva glands went into overdrive when I saw the sheer volume of gold—bracelets, necklaces, coins, daggers, rings, cups, Monopoly tokens. I wasn't sure what the value of gold per ounce was these days, but I estimated I was looking at about a gajillion dollars' worth, give or take a bazillion.

Jack squealed. "Oh, look at those little daggers! They're *adorable.*"

Hearthstone's eyes regained their alertness. All that gold seemed to have the same effect on him as waving a cup of coffee under his nose.

Too easy, he signed. *Must be a catch.*

"Andvari," I said, "if your name means *Careful One,* why are you so easy to rob?"

"I know!" he sobbed. "I'm *not* careful! I get robbed all the time! I think the name is ironic. My mother was a cruel woman."

"So this hoard keeps getting stolen, but you keep getting it back? Because of that ring you mentioned?"

"What ring? Lots of rings in that pile. Take them!"

"No, the super-magic one. Where is it?"

"Um, probably in the pile somewhere. Go look!" Andvari quickly pulled a ring off his finger and slipped it into his diaper. His hands were so filthy I wouldn't have noticed the ring at all if he hadn't tried to hide it.

"You just dropped it down your pants," I said.

"No, I didn't!"

"Jack, I think this dwarf wants a full Brazilian waxing."

"No!" Andvari wailed. "All right, yes, my magic ring is in my pants. But *please* don't take it. Getting it back is always such a hassle. I *told* you, it's cursed. You don't want to end up like a lottery winner, do you?"

I turned to Hearth. "What do you think?"

"Tell him, Mr. Elf!" said Andvari. "You're obviously an elf of learning. You know your runes. I bet you know the story of Fafnir, eh? Tell your friend this ring will bring you nothing but trouble."

Hearth gazed into the distance as if reading a list on some heavenly whiteboard: –10 GOLD FOR BRINGING HOME A CURSED RING. +10 GAJILLION GOLD FOR STEALING A GAJILLION GOLD.

He signed, *Ring is cursed. But also key to treasure. Without ring, treasure will never be enough. Will always come up short.*

I looked at the Jacuzzi-size stash of gold. "I don't know, man. That seems like plenty to cover your wergild rug."

Hearth shook his head. *It will not be. Ring is dangerous. But we have to take it just in case. If we don't use it, we can return it.*

I twisted the dwarf to face me. "Sorry, Andvari."

Jack laughed. "Hey, that rhymes, too!"

"What did the elf *say*?" Andvari demanded. "I can't read those gestures!" He waved his grubby hands, accidentally signing *donkey waiter pancake* in ASL.

I was losing patience with the old slime-bucket, but I did my best to translate Hearth's message.

Andvari's moss green eyes darkened. He bared his teeth,

which looked like they hadn't been flossed since zombies inspired the Mayflower Compact.

"You're a fool, then, Mr. Elf," he growled. "The ring will come back to me eventually. It always does. In the meantime, it will cause death and misery to whoever wears it. And don't think it will solve your problems, either. This won't be the last time you have to come home. You've only delayed a much more dangerous reckoning."

The change in Andvari's tone unnerved me even more than his change from grouper to dwarf. No more wailing or crying. He spoke with cold certainty, like a hangman explaining the mechanics of a noose.

Hearthstone didn't look rattled. He wore the same expression he'd had at his brother's cairn—as if he was reliving a tragedy that had happened long ago and couldn't be changed.

The ring, he signed.

The gesture was so obvious even Andvari understood it.

"Fine." The dwarf glared at me. "You won't escape the curse either, human. Soon enough you'll see what comes of stolen gifts!"

The hairs on my arms stood up. "What do you mean?"

He grinned evilly. "Oh, nothing. Nothing at all."

Andvari did the shimmy-shimmy-shake. The ring dropped out the leg hole of his diaper. "One magic ring," he announced, "complete with curse."

"There is no way," I said, "that I am picking that up."

"Got it!" Jack dove in and made like a spatula, scooping the ring out of the mud with the flat of his blade.

Andvari watched wistfully as my sword played paddleball, flipping the ring from one side of his blade to the other.

"The usual deal?" the dwarf asked. "You spare my life and take everything I own?"

"The usual sounds great," I said. "What about all the gold in the pit? How do we carry it?"

Andvari scoffed. "Amateurs! The canvas lining of the pit is a big magical sack. Pull the drawstring and voila! I have to keep the stash ready for quick getaways for those *few* times I avoid getting robbed."

Hearthstone crouched next to the pit. Sure enough, poking from a hole in the hem of the canvas was a loop of string. Hearth pulled it and the bag snapped closed, shrinking to the size of a backpack. Hearth held it up for me to see—a gajillion dollars' worth of gold in a superconvenient carry-on size.

"Now honor your part of the deal!" Andvari demanded.

I dropped him.

"Humph." The old dwarf rubbed his neck. "Enjoy your demise, amateurs. I hope you have pain and suffering and win *two* lotteries!"

With that vile curse, he jumped back into his pond and disappeared.

"Hey, *señor!*" called Jack. "Heads up!"

"Don't you dare—"

He flipped the ring at me. I caught it out of reflex. "Aww, *gross.*"

Seeing as it was a magic ring, I half expected some big *Lord of the Rings* moment when it landed in my hand—cold heavy whispering, swirling gray mist, a line of Nazgûl doing the Watusi. None of that happened. The ring just sat there, looking very much like a gold ring, albeit one that had recently fallen from a thousand-year-old dwarf's moss diaper.

I slipped the ring into my pants pocket, then studied the circle of slime residue on my palm. "My hand will never feel clean again."

Hearthstone shouldered his expensive new backpack like Gajillionaire Santa Claus. He glanced at the sun, which was already past its zenith. I hadn't realized just how long we'd been trekking through the wilds of Mr. Alderman's backyard.

We should go, Hearth signed. *Father will be waiting.*

TWENTY-EIGHT

And If You Order Now, You Also Get This Cursed Ring!

FATHER WAS waiting, all right. He paced in the living room, sipping golden juice from a silver goblet while Inge stood nearby waiting for a spill to happen.

When we walked in, Mr. Alderman turned toward us, his face a mask of cold anger. "Where have you—?"

His isosceles jaw dropped.

I guess he didn't expect to see us soaked in sweat, covered in grass and twigs, our slime-caked shoes leaving slug trails across his white marble floor. Mr. Alderman's expression was one of the best rewards I'd ever gotten, right up there with dying and going to Valhalla.

Hearthstone plopped his canvas bag on the floor with a muffled clatter. He signed: *Payment*—palm up, brushing one finger toward his dad like he was flicking a coin at him. The way Hearth did it made it look like an insult. I liked that.

Mr. Alderman forgot that he wasn't supposed to acknowledge sign language. He asked, "Payment? But how—?"

"Come upstairs and we'll show you." I glanced behind Alderman, where Inge stood wide-eyed, a grin slowly spreading across her face. "We've got a demon-skin rug to cover."

Ah, the sound of golden Monopoly tokens cascading across a fur rug . . . There is nothing sweeter, I promise you. Hearthstone tipped over the canvas sack and walked around the rug, hosing it down with a torrent of wealth. Mr. Alderman's face got paler. In the doorway, Inge jumped up and down, clapping with excitement, heedless of the fact that she hadn't paid her master for the privilege.

When the last of the gold was out, Hearthstone stepped back and threw down the empty bag. He signed, *Wergild paid.*

Mr. Alderman looked stunned. He did not say *Good job, son!* Or *Oh, boy, I'm richer!* Or *Did you rob the Elfish Treasury Department?*

He crouched and inspected the pile, coin by coin, dagger by dagger. "There are miniature dogs and steam trains," he noted. "Why?"

I coughed. "I think the, uh, previous owner liked board games. Solid-*gold* board games."

"Hmm." Alderman continued his inspection, making sure that the entire rug was covered. His expression turned more and more sour. "Did you leave the property to acquire this? Because I did not give you permission—"

"Nope," I said. "You own the wilderness behind the backyard, right?"

"Yes, he does!" Inge said. The master glared at her, and she hastily added, "Because, ah, Mr. Alderman is a *very* important man."

"Look, sir," I said, "it's obvious Hearthstone succeeded. The rug is covered. Just admit it."

"I will be the judge!" he snarled. "This is all about *responsibility,* something you younger folks do not understand."

"You *want* Hearthstone to fail, don't you?"

Alderman scowled. "I *expect* him to fail. There is a difference. This boy earned his punishment. I am not convinced he has the potential to pay it off."

I almost screamed, *Hearthstone has been paying his entire life!* I wanted to pour Andvari's treasure straight down Alderman's throat and see if that convinced him of his son's potential.

Hearthstone brushed his fingers against my arm. He signed, *Calm. Ready with the ring.*

I tried to control my breathing. I didn't understand how Hearth could endure his father's insults. He'd had a lot of practice, sure, but the old elf was intolerable. I was glad Jack was back in pendant form, because I would've ordered him to give Mr. Alderman the full Brazilian treatment.

In the pocket of my jeans, Andvari's ring was so light I could barely feel it. I had to resist the urge to check on it every few seconds. I realized that was one reason I felt so irritated with Mr. Alderman. I wanted him to say that the debt was paid. I didn't want Hearthstone to be right about needing the ring, too.

I kind of wanted to keep it. No, wait. That's not right. I wanted to return it to Andvari so we didn't have to deal with the curse. My thoughts on the subject were starting to get muddled, as though my head was full of river sludge.

"Aha!" Mr. Alderman cried triumphantly. He pointed to the top of rug, at the nape of its neck, where the fur was thickest. A single blue hair sprouted from the treasure like a stubborn weed.

"Oh, come on," I said. "That'll just take a minor adjustment."

I shifted the treasure so the hair was covered. But as soon as I succeeded, another hair popped up from the spot where I'd taken the gold. It was like the same stupid blue hair was following me around, defying my efforts.

"This is no problem," I insisted. "Let me get out my sword. Or, if you have a pair of scissors—"

"The debt is *not* paid!" Mr. Alderman insisted. "Unless you can cover that last hair right now, with more gold, I am going to charge you for disappointing me and wasting my time. Say . . . half this treasure."

Hearthstone turned to me—no surprise in his face, just glum resignation. *The ring.*

A wave of murderous resentment washed over me. I didn't want to give up the ring. But then I looked at the whiteboards around the room: all the rules and menu items, all the expectations that Mr. Alderman expected Hearthstone *not* to meet. The curse of Andvari's ring was pretty strong. It whispered to me, telling me to keep it and get filthy rich. But the urge to see Hearthstone free of his father, reunited with Blitzen, and out of this toxic house . . . that was stronger.

I brought out our secret last bit of treasure.

A hungry light kindled in Mr. Alderman's space-alien eyes. "Very well. Place it on the pile."

Father, Hearthstone signed. *Warning: the ring is cursed.*

"I will not listen to your hand gestures!"

"You know what he's saying." I held up the ring. "This thing taints whoever owns it. It'll ruin you. Heck, I've only had it for a few minutes and it's already messing with my mind. Take the gold that's already on the rug. Call the debt paid. Show some forgiveness, and we'll return this ring to its previous owner."

Mr. Alderman laughed bitterly. *"Forgiveness? What can I buy with forgiveness? Will it bring Andiron back to me?"*

Personally, I would've punched the old dude in the face, but Hearthstone stepped toward his father. He looked genuinely worried. *Curse of F-A-F-N-I-R*, he signed. *Do not.*

Andvari had mentioned that name. It sounded vaguely familiar, but I couldn't place it. Maybe Fafnir was a Powerball lottery winner?

Hearthstone gestured *please*—hand flat against the chest, making a circle. It struck me that *please* was just a more relaxed, less angry version of *sorry*.

The two elves stared at each across the pile of gold. I could almost feel Alfheim swaying in the branches of the World Tree. Despite everything Alderman had done to him, Hearthstone still wanted to help his father . . . he was making one last effort to pull his dad out of a hole much deeper than Andvari's.

"No," Mr. Alderman decided. "Pay the wergild or stay in my debt—*both* of you."

Hearthstone bowed his head in defeat. He motioned at me to give up the ring.

"First the Skofnung Stone," I said. "Let me see that you're keeping your side of the bargain."

Alderman grunted. "Inge, bring the Skofnung Stone from its case. The security code is *Greta*."

Hearthstone flinched. I guessed Greta was his mother's name.

The hulder scurried off.

For a few tense moments, Hearthstone, Alderman, and I

stood around the rug and stared at each other. No one suggested a game of Monopoly. No one yelled "Yippee!" and jumped in the pile of gold (though I'll admit I was tempted).

Finally, Inge came back, the blue-gray whetstone cupped in her hands. She offered it to Alderman with a curtsey.

Alderman took it and handed it to his son. "I give this to you freely, Hearthstone, to do with as you please. Let its powers be yours." He glowered at me. "Now, the ring."

I was out of reasons to delay, but it was still difficult. With a deep breath, I knelt and added Andvari's ring to the treasure, covering the last bit of fur.

"The deal is done," I said.

"Eh?" Alderman's gaze was fixed on the treasure. "Yes, yes, except for one thing. You promised me media exposure, Magnus Chase. I have arranged a little party for tonight. Inge!"

The hulder jumped. "Yes, sir! Preparations are coming along. All four hundred guests have RSVP'd."

"Four hundred?" I asked. "How did you have time to set that up? How did you know we'd succeed?"

"Ha!" The crazy light in Mr. Alderman's eyes did not calm my nerves. "I didn't know you'd succeed, and I didn't care. I planned on arranging parties *every* night while you stayed here, Magnus, preferably forever. But since you have paid the wergild so quickly, we'll have to make tonight count. As for *how*, I am Alderman of House Alderman. No one would dare turn down my invitation!"

Behind his back, Inge gave me a frantic nod and drew a line across her neck.

"And now . . ." Mr. Alderman snatched the cursed ring out of the hoard. He placed it on his finger and held it out to admire it like someone newly engaged. "Yes, this will look *lovely* with my formal attire. Hearthstone, I will expect you and your guest— *Hearthstone,* where are you going?"

Apparently Hearth had had enough of his father. With the Skofnung Stone in one hand, he hauled Blitzen upright by the scarf harness and lugged him into the bathroom.

A moment later, I heard the shower running.

"I, uh, should go help them," I said.

"What?" Alderman snapped. "Yes, fine. Such a *lovely* ring. Inge, make sure our young scoundrels are dressed appropriately for the party, and send some of the staff to help me with this gold. I must have every piece of treasure weighed and counted. And polished! It will look wonderful polished. And while you're at it . . ."

I didn't want to leave Inge alone in the same room with Mr. Crazy Ring, but I was getting nauseated watching Alderman flirt with his fortune. I ran to join my friends in the bathroom.

The only thing more disturbing than a severed god's head in your bubble bath? A bleeding granite dwarf in your shower.

Hearth propped Blitzen under the showerhead. As soon as the running water cascaded over Blitz's head, his form began to soften. His cold gray face darkened into warm brown flesh. Blood flowed from his wounded gut and swirled around the drain. His knees buckled. I lurched into the stall to hold him up.

Hearthstone fumbled with the Skofnung Stone. He pressed it against the gushing wound and Blitz gasped. The flow of blood stopped instantly.

"I'm a goner!" Blitz croaked. "Don't worry about me, you crazy elf! Just—" He spit out water. "Why is it raining?"

Hearthstone hugged him fiercely, crushing Blitz's face against his chest.

"Hey!" Blitz complained. "Can't breathe here!"

Hearth, of course, couldn't hear him and didn't seem to care. He rocked back and forth with the dwarf in his arms.

"Okay, buddy." Blitz patted him weakly. "There, there." He looked up at me and silently asked several thousand questions with his eyes, including: *Why are the three of us taking a shower together? Why am I not dead? Why do you smell like pond scum? What is wrong with my elf?*

Once we were sure he'd fully un-petrified, Hearth shut off the water. Blitzen was too weak to move, so we slid him into a sitting position right there in the shower.

Inge rushed into the bathroom with a stack of towels and some fresh clothes. From Hearth's bedroom came the sound of spilling coins, like a dozen slot machines paying out, punctuated by the occasional crazy laugh.

"You might want to take your time in here," Inge warned us, glancing nervously behind her. "It's a bit . . . hectic out there." Then she left, closing the door behind her.

We did our best to get ourselves cleaned up. I used an extra belt to make a strap for the Skofnung Stone and tied it around my waist, tucking my shirt over it so it wouldn't be too obvious if Mr. Alderman got a case of takesy-backsies.

Blitzen's wound had closed nicely, leaving just a small white scar, but he bemoaned the damage to his suit—the sword slash in the vest, the heavy bloodstains. "No amount of lemon juice

will get these out," he said. "Once fabric turns to granite and
back again, well, the discoloration is permanent."

I didn't bother pointing out that at least he was alive. I
knew he was in shock and dealing with it by concentrating on
things he understood and could fix—such as his wardrobe.

We sat together on the bathroom floor. Blitzen used his
mending kit to stitch together bath towels for extra Alfheim
sun protection, while Hearthstone and I took turns filling him
in on what had been happening.

Blitzen shook his head in amazement. "You did all that for
me? You crazy, wonderful idiots, you could've gotten yourselves
killed! And Hearth, you subjected yourself to your father? I
never would have asked you to do that. You swore you'd never
come back here, and for good reason!"

I also swore to protect you, Hearth signed. *My fault you were
stabbed. And Samirah's.*

"Stop that right now," Blitz said. "It wasn't your fault or
hers. You can't cheat a prophecy. That mortal wound was
bound to happen, but now you've fixed it, so we can stop worrying about it! Besides, if you want to blame someone, blame that
fool Randolph." He glanced at me. "No offense, kid, but I have
a strong desire to murder your uncle with extreme prejudice."

"No offense taken," I said. "I'm tempted to help you."

And yet I remembered Randolph's horrified cry when he'd
stabbed Blitzen, and the way he'd followed Loki like an abused
dog. As much as I wanted to hate my uncle, I couldn't help
feeling sorry for him. Now that I'd met Mr. Alderman, I was
starting to realize that no matter how bad your family is, it
could always be worse.

Hearth finished bringing Blitzen up to speed in sign language, explaining how we'd robbed Andvari and been threatened with multiple Powerball jackpots.

"You were both out of your minds to face that dwarf," Blitzen said. "He's infamous in Nidavellir—even craftier and greedier than Eitri Junior!"

"Could we please not mention him?" I pleaded. I still had nightmares about the old dwarf who had challenged Blitz to a crafting contest last January. I never wanted to see another rocket-powered granny-walker as long as I lived.

Blitzen frowned at Hearth. "And you say your father has the ring now?"

Hearthstone nodded. *I tried to warn him.*

"Yes, but still . . . that thing can warp its owner's mind beyond recognition. After what happened to Hreidmar, Fafnir, Regin, and all those lottery winners . . . well, there's an endless list of people that ring has destroyed."

"Who are they?" I asked. "Those people you mentioned?"

Blitzen held up his bath-towel creation—a sort of terrycloth burka with sunglasses taped over the eyeholes. "Long, tragic story, kid. Lots of death. The important thing is, we must convince Mr. Alderman to give up that ring before it's too late. We have to stay at this party of his for a while, right? That'll give us a chance. Maybe he'll be in a good mood and we can make him see sense."

Hearthstone grunted. *My father? Doubtful.*

"Yeah," I said. "And if he won't see sense?"

"Then we run," Blitz said. "And we hope Alderman doesn't—"

From the next room, Inge called, "Mr. Hearthstone?"

Her tone verged on panic.

We stumbled out of the bath and found that Hearth's bedroom had been completely stripped. The mattress was gone. The whiteboards had been removed, leaving bright white shadows on only slightly less white walls. The pile of treasure and the blue fur rug had vanished as if the wergild had never happened.

Inge stood in the doorway, her bonnet askew on her head. Her face was flushed, and she was anxiously pulling tufts from the end of her tail. "Master Hearth, the—the guests have arrived. The party has started. Your father is asking for you, but . . ."

Hearthstone signed, *What's wrong?*

Inge tried to speak. No words came out. She shrugged helplessly, as if she could not describe the horrors she had witnessed at Mr. Alderman's mix-and-mingle. "It's—it's probably best you see for yourself."

TWENTY-NINE

Nøkk, Nøkk

ALDERMAN KNEW how to throw a party. He also knew how to throw things at a party.

From the top of the staircase, we gazed down at a living room jammed with well-groomed elves in elegant white, gold, and silver outfits. Their pale eyes, fair hair, and expensive jewelry gleamed in the evening sunlight streaming through the windows. Dozens of hulder servants moved through the crowd, offering drinks and hors d'oeuvres. And in all the cases and niches, where artifacts and minerals were once displayed, piles of Andvari's treasure glittered, making the whole room look like a jewelry warehouse after a tornado.

Above the fireplace mantel, across the foot of Andiron's portrait, hung a golden banner with red letters: WELCOME, MAGNUS CHASE, SON OF FREY, SPONSORED BY HOUSE ALDERMAN! And under that in smaller print: HEARTHSTONE HAS BEEN BROUGHT BACK.

Not "returned." *Been brought back.* As if the elfish marshal service had apprehended him and hauled him home in chains.

Alderman himself circulated through the crowd at double-speed, tossing gold coins to his guests, accosting them with jewelry, and muttering, "Can you believe all this treasure? Amazing, isn't it? Would you like a golden choo choo train? May I interest you in a dagger?"

In his white tuxedo, with his wild eyes and brilliant smile, he looked like a diabolical maître d' seating parties at Chez Mass Murder. His guests laughed nervously as he threw treasure at them. Once he passed, they muttered to one another, perhaps wondering how soon they could flee the party without seeming impolite. Alderman wove through the room, distributing golden trinkets, and the crowd moved away from him like cats avoiding an out-of-control Roomba.

Behind us, Inge murmured, "Oh, dear. He's getting worse."

Hearthstone signed: *The ring is affecting him.*

I nodded, though I wondered how strained Mr. Alderman's sanity had already been. For decades, he had been living off resentment, blaming Hearthstone for Andiron's death. Now, suddenly, Hearthstone had freed himself from that debt. Andvari's ring simply moved in to fill the void with a whole bunch of crazy.

Blitzen gripped the staircase with his gloved hands. "This isn't good."

He was wearing his bath-towel burka to protect himself from the Alfheim light. He'd explained to us that his usual pith helmet netting and sunscreen would not be sufficient, as he was still weak from petrification. Still, the outfit was a little disturbing. He looked like a miniature version of Cousin Itt from the Addams Family.

"Aha!" Mr. Alderman spotted us on the stairs and grinned even wider. "Behold, my son and his companions! The dwarf— at least I assume that's the dwarf under those towels. And Magnus Chase, son of Frey!"

The crowd turned and looked up at us, emitting a fair number of *ooh*s and *ahh*s. I've never liked being the center of attention. I hated it at school, and later in Valhalla. I hated even more these glamorous elves ogling me like I was a delectable chocolate fountain that had just opened for business.

"Yes, yes!" Mr. Alderman cackled like a maniac. "All this treasure you see, my friends? That is nothing compared to Magnus Chase! My son finally did something right. He brought me a child of Frey as part of his wergild payment. And now this boy Magnus Chase will be my permanent houseguest! We will start a line for photo ops at the bar—"

"Hold up," I said. "That was *not* the deal, Alderman. We're not staying past this party."

Hearthstone signed: *Father, the ring. Dangerous. Take it off.*

The crowd stirred restlessly, not sure what to make of this.

Alderman's smile eroded. His eyes narrowed. "My son is asking me to take off my new ring." He held up his hand and wiggled his finger, letting the gold band catch the light. "Now, why would he ask that? And why would Magnus Chase threaten to leave . . . unless these scoundrels are planning to steal my treasure?"

Blitzen scoffed. "They just *brought* you that treasure, you daft elf. Why would they steal it again?"

"So you admit it!" Alderman clapped his hands. All the doors to the living room slammed shut. Around the perimeter of the room, a dozen columns of water erupted from the floor and formed vaguely humanoid shapes, like balloon animals filled with water . . . minus the balloons.

Blitzen yelped. "Those are security *nøkks*."

"What?" I asked.

"Also called *nixies*," he said. "Water spirits. Bad news."

Hearthstone caught Inge's arm. He signed: *You still have family in woods?*

"Y-yes," she said.

Go now, he said. *I release you from my family's service. Don't come back. Also, call police.*

Inge looked stunned and hurt, but then she glanced at the water spirits surrounding the crowd below.

She pecked Hearthstone on the cheek. "I—I love you."

She vanished in a puff of fresh laundry-scented smoke.

Blitzen arched his eyebrow. "Did I miss something?"

Hearthstone shot him an irritated look, but he didn't have time to explain.

Down in the living room, an older elf shouted, "Alderman, what is the meaning of this?"

"The meaning, Lord Mayor?" Alderman grinned with an intensity that was not at all sane. "I now understand why you all came here. You meant to steal my treasure, but I've caught you gold-handed! Security nøkks, subdue these thieves! No one leaves here alive!"

Etiquette tip: If you're looking for the right time to leave a party, when the host yells, "No one leaves here alive," that's your cue.

Elves screamed and ran for the exits, but the glass doors were shut fast. Security nixies moved through the crowd, changing shape from animal-like to human-like to solid wave, enveloping the elves one by one and leaving them passed out on the floor in elegant wet lumps. Meanwhile, Alderman laughed and danced around the room, retrieving his gold trinkets from his fallen guests.

"We've got to get out of here *now*," Blitzen said.

"But we need to help the elves," I said.

True, with the exception of Hearthstone, I didn't think much of the elves I'd met. I liked the guppies in Andvari's pond more. But I also couldn't stand the idea of leaving four hundred people at the mercy of Mr. Alderman and his liquid nixie thugs. I pulled out my pendant and summoned Jack.

"Hey, guys!" Jack said. "What's going—ah, nøkks? Are you kidding me? There's nothing to cut with these guys."

"Just do what you can!" I yelled.

Too late, Hearthstone signed. *Violins!*

I wasn't sure if I'd read that last sign correctly. Then I looked downstairs. Half the nixies had stationed themselves around the room in humanoid form and were pulling out solid violins and bows from . . . well, somewhere inside their liquid selves. That seemed like a very bad place to store stringed instruments, but the nixies raised the wooden violins to their watery chins.

"Ears!" Blitz warned.

I clamped my hands to the sides of my head just as the nøkks began to play. It only helped a little. The dirge was so sad and dissonant my knees wobbled. Tears welled in my eyes. All around the room, more elves collapsed in fits of weeping— except Mr. Alderman, who seemed immune. He kept cackling and skipping around, occasionally kicking his VIP guests in the face.

From inside his terrycloth hood, Blitzen let out a muffled yell. "Make it stop or we'll die of broken hearts in a matter of minutes!"

I didn't think he was being metaphoric.

Thankfully, Hearthstone was not affected.

He snapped his fingers for attention then pointed at Jack: *Sword. Cut violins.*

"You heard him," I told Jack.

"No, I didn't!" Jack complained.

"Kill the violins!"

"Oh. That would be a pleasure."

Jack flew into action.

Meanwhile, Hearthstone fished out a runestone. He tossed it from the top of the stairs and it exploded in midair, making a giant glowing *H*-shape above the heads of the elves:

$$\mathsf{H}$$

Outside, the sky darkened. Rain hammered against the plate glass windows, drowning out the sound of the violins.

Follow me, Hearthstone ordered.

He clambered down the stairs as the storm intensified. Giant hailstones slammed into the windows, cracking the glass, causing the whole house to tremble. I pressed my hand to my waist, making sure the Skofnung Stone was still secure, then I ran after Hearth.

Jack flew from nøkk to nøkk, chopping up their violins and crushing the hopes and dreams of some very talented nixie musicians. The water creatures lashed out at Jack. They didn't seem capable of hurting the sword any more than Jack could hurt them, but Jack kept them occupied long enough for us to reach the bottom of the stairs.

Hearthstone paused and raised his arms. With a tremendous *BOOM!*, every window and glass door in the house shattered. Hail swept in, pummeling the elves, hulder, and nixies alike.

"Let's go!" I yelled to the crowd. "Come on!"

"Fools!" Alderman cried. "You are mine! You cannot escape!"

We did our best to herd everyone into the yard. Being outside felt like running through a hurricane of baseballs, but it was better than dying surrounded by nøkk fiddlers. I wished I'd had the good sense to cover myself in bath towels like Blitzen.

Elves scattered and fled. The nixies rushed after us, but the hail made them sluggish, slamming into them and forming icy froth until they looked like slushies escaped from their Big Gulp cups.

We were halfway across the lawn, heading for the wilderness, when I heard the sirens. Out of the corner of my eye, I saw emergency lights flashing as police cars and ambulances pulled into the main drive.

Above us, the dark clouds began to break up. The hail subsided. I caught Hearthstone as he stumbled. I almost thought we would make it to the woods when a voice behind us shouted, "Stop!"

Fifty yards away, our old friends Officers Wildflower and Sunspot had drawn their firearms and were preparing to shoot us for loitering, trespassing, or running away without permission.

"Jack!" I yelled.

My sword rocketed toward the cops and sliced off their utility belts. Their pants promptly fell around their ankles. Elves, I discovered, should never wear shorts. They have pale gangly legs that are not at all elegant or graceful.

While they tried to recover their dignity, we plunged into the woods. Hearthstone's strength was nearly gone. He leaned on me as we ran, but I'd had a lot of practice carrying him. Jack flew to my side.

"That was fun!" he announced. "Afraid I just slowed them down, though. I'm sensing a good place to make a cut just up ahead."

"Make a cut?" I asked.

"He means between worlds!" Blitzen said. "I don't know about you, but to me, any of the other eight would be preferable right about now!"

We staggered into the clearing where the old well had been.

Hearthstone shook his head weakly. He signed with one hand, pointing in different directions. *Anywhere but here.*

Blitzen turned to me. "What is this place?"

"It's where Hearth's brother . . . you know."

Blitzen seemed to shrink under his mound of towels. "Oh."

"It's the best spot, guys," Jack insisted. "There's a real thin portal between the worlds right on top of that cairn. I can—"

Behind us, a shot rang out. Everyone flinched except Hearthstone. Something buzzed past by my ear like an annoying insect.

"Do it, Jack!" I yelled.

He raced to the cairn. His blade sliced through the air, opening a rift into absolute darkness.

"I love darkness," Blitzen said. "Come on!"

Together we hauled Hearthstone toward Pees-in-Well's old lair and jumped into the space between the worlds.

THIRTY

Somewhere Over the Rainbow, There's Some Messed-Up Stuff Going On

WE TUMBLED down some steps to a concrete landing. The three of us lay there in a heap, gasping and stunned. We appeared to be in an emergency stairwell—exposed brick walls, industrial green handrail, fire extinguishers, and illuminated EXIT signs. Just above us, the nearest metal door was stenciled with the words FLOOR 6.

I patted frantically at my waist, but the Skofnung Stone was still lashed there securely, undamaged. Jack had returned to pendant form. He rested comfortably on my chain while all the energy he'd expended fighting the nixies drained out of my soul. My bones felt leaden. My vision swam. Who knew slicing up violins and cutting the pants off police officers took so much effort?

Hearthstone wasn't in much better shape. He clawed at the handrail to pull himself up, but his legs didn't seem to be working. I might have thought he was drunk, but I'd never seen him consume anything stronger than Diet Sergeant Pepper in Nidavellir.

Blitzen tugged off his bath-towel burka. "We're in Midgard," he announced. "I'd know that smell anywhere."

To me, the stairwell smelled only like wet elf, dwarf, and Magnus, but I took Blitz's word for it.

Hearth stumbled, a red stain soaking his shirt.

"Buddy!" Blitz rushed to his side. "What happened?"

"Whoa, Hearth." I made him sit down and examined the wound. "Gunshot. Our friendly elfish police officers gave him a parting gift."

Blitz pulled off his Frank Sinatra hat and punched right through it. "Can we *please* go twenty-four hours without one of us getting mortally wounded?"

"Relax," I said. "It just grazed his ribs. Hold him steady."

I signed to Hearth: *Not bad. I can heal.*

I pressed my hand to the wound. Warmth radiated through Hearthstone's side. He took a sharp inhale, then began to breathe more easily. The gouge in his skin closed up.

Until I took away my hand, I didn't realize how worried I'd been. My whole body was shaking. I hadn't tried my healing powers since Blitzen had been stabbed, and I guess I was afraid they wouldn't work anymore.

"See?" I tried for a confident smile, though it probably looked like I was having a stroke. "All better."

Thanks, Hearth signed.

"You're still weaker than I'd like," I said. "We'll rest here a minute. Tonight, you'll need a good meal, lots of fluid, and sleep."

"Dr. Chase has spoken." Blitz scowled at the elf. "And no more running into stray bullets, you hear me?"

The corner of Hearth's mouth twitched. *I can't hear you. I am deaf.*

"Humor," I noted. "That's a good sign."

We sat together and enjoyed the novelty of not being hunted, wounded, or terrified.

Well, okay, I was still pretty terrified, but one out of three wasn't bad.

The full suckage of our last thirty-something hours in Alfheim started to sink in. I wanted to believe we'd left that crazy place behind for good—no more trigger-happy cops, manicured estates, or eye-stabbing sunlight. No more Mr. Alderman. But I couldn't forget what Andvari had told us: Soon I would learn the price of stolen gifts, and Hearthstone was fated to return home again.

You've only delayed a much more dangerous reckoning.

The othala runestone still sat atop the cairn where Andiron had died. I had a feeling that someday Hearthstone would have to retrieve that missing letter of his cosmic alphabet, whether he wanted to or not.

I stared at Hearth as he flapped his shirt, trying to dry the blood on it. When he finally met my eyes, I signed: *I'm sorry about your dad.*

He half nodded, half shrugged.

"The curse of Fafnir," I said. "Can I ask . . . ?"

Blitzen cleared his throat. "Maybe we should wait on that until he's at full strength."

It's okay, Hearth signed.

He leaned against the wall, steadying himself so he could use both hands for signing. *Fafnir was a dwarf. Andvari's ring drove him crazy. He murdered his father, took his gold. Guarded the treasure in a cave. Eventually he turned into a dragon.*

I swallowed. "The ring can do that?"

Blitzen tugged at his beard. "The ring brings out the worst in people, kid. Maybe Mr. Alderman doesn't have that much evil inside him. Maybe he'll just . . . stay an unpleasant elf and win the lottery."

I remembered Hearth's father cackling as he kicked his guests, dancing around as his nixies attacked the crowd. Whatever Alderman had inside him, I doubted it was a fuzzy kitten.

I looked at the top of the stairwell, where a sign said ROOF ACCESS.

"We should find Sam," I said. "We're supposed to talk to the god Heimdall and get directions to some place in Jotunheim—"

"Ah, kid?" Blitzen's eye twitched. "I think Hearth might need a little more quiet time before we meet up with Samirah and go racing off to fight giants. I could use some rest, too."

"Right." I felt bad bringing up our to-do list. Too many people to meet, too many dangerous worlds to visit. Three days left to find Thor's hammer. So far we'd found a hot lady sword and a blue rock, barely managed not to get ourselves killed, and driven Hearthstone's father criminally insane. About par for the course.

"You want to crash at Valhalla for the night?" I asked.

Blitzen grunted. "The thanes don't like mortals mixing with the honored dead. You go ahead. I'll take Hearth to Nidavellir and let him rest at my place. His tanning bed is all set up."

"But . . . how will you get there?"

Blitz shrugged. "Like I told you before, there's tons of entrances to Dwarf World underneath Midgard. Probably one in the basement of this building. If not, we'll just find the nearest sewer."

Yes, Hearth signed. *We love sewers.*

"Don't you start with the sarcasm," Blitz said. "Kid, how about we meet tomorrow morning at the old rendezvous point?"

I couldn't help but smile at the memories of the good old days, hanging out with Hearth and Blitz, wondering where our next meal would come from and when we would next get mugged. The good old days really sucked, but they'd sucked in a less complicated way than the crazy new days.

"The old rendezvous point it is." I hugged them both. I didn't want Hearth or Blitz to leave, but neither of them was in any shape to face more danger tonight, and I wasn't sure what I would find up on the roof. I unfastened the Skofnung Stone from my belt and handed it to Blitz. "Hold on to that. Keep it safe."

"We will," Blitz promised. "And, kid . . . thanks."

They staggered down the stairwell arm in arm, leaning on each other for support. "Stop stepping on my toes," Blitz grumbled. "Have you put on weight? No, lead with your left foot, you silly elf. There you go."

I climbed to the top of the stairwell, wondering where in Midgard I had ended up.

Annoying fact about traveling between worlds: you often pop up exactly where you need to be, whether you *want* to be there or not.

Four people I knew already stood on the rooftop, though I had no idea why. Sam and Amir were having a hushed argument at the base of a huge illuminated billboard. And not just *any* billboard, I realized. Towering above us was the famous

Boston Citgo sign, a sixty-foot square of LEDs that washed the rooftop in white, orange, and blue.

Sitting on the edge of the roof, looking very bored, were Halfborn Gunderson and Alex Fierro.

Sam and Amir were too busy arguing to notice me, but Halfborn nodded in greeting. He didn't seem surprised.

I walked over to my fellow einherjar. "Uh . . . 'sup?"

Alex skipped a piece of gravel across the roof. "Oh, *so* much fun. Samirah wanted to bring Amir to see the Citgo sign. Something about rainbows. She needed a male relative as a chaperone."

I blinked. "So you . . . ?"

Alex gave me an exaggerated *at-your-service* bow. "I'm her male relative."

I had a moment of reality-flipping vertigo as I realized that, yes, indeed, Alex Fierro was presently a *he*. I'm not sure how I knew, other than the fact that he had told me so. His wardrobe wasn't gender specific. He wore his usual rose high-tops with skinny green jeans and a pink long-sleeved T-shirt. His hair, if anything, seemed a little longer, still green with black roots, now combed to one side in the shape of a wave.

"My pronouns are *he* and *him*," Alex confirmed. "And you can stop staring."

"I wasn't . . ." I caught myself. Arguing would've been pointless. "Halfborn, what are you doing here?"

The berserker grinned. He'd put on a Bruins T-shirt and jeans, maybe to blend in with the mortals, though the battle-ax strapped across his back was sort of a giveaway. "Oh, me? I'm chaperoning the chaperone. And my gender hasn't changed, thanks for asking."

Alex smacked him, which would've made Mallory Keen proud.

"Ow!" Halfborn complained. "You hit hard for an argr."

"What have I told you about that term?" Alex said. "*I* will decide what is manly, unmanly, womanly, or unwomanly for me. Don't make me kill you again."

Halfborn rolled his eyes. "You killed me *one time*. And it wasn't even a fair fight. I got you back at lunch."

"Whatever."

I stared at the two of them. It dawned on me that, over the last day and a half, they had become friends . . . in the sort of trash-talking, murdering-each-other way hallmates bonded on floor nineteen.

Alex slipped his garrote from his belt loops. "So, Magnus, did you manage to heal your dwarf?"

"Uh, yeah. You heard about that?"

"Sam filled us in." He started to make a cat's cradle with his wire, somehow managing not to cut off his own fingers in the process.

I wondered if it was a good sign that Samirah had shared information with Alex. Maybe they'd started to trust each other. Or maybe Sam's desperation to stop Loki had simply overridden her caution. I wanted to ask Alex about the dream I'd had of Loki in his suite, asking Alex for a *simple request* while Alex threw pots at him. I decided maybe this wasn't the time, especially with Fierro's garrote so close to my neck.

Alex pointed with his chin to Sam and Amir. "You should go on over. They've been waiting for you."

The happy couple was still arguing—Sam making imploring

gestures with her upraised palms, Amir tugging at his hair as if he wanted to pull his brain out.

I frowned at Halfborn. "How could they know I would be here? *I* didn't even know."

"Odin's ravens," Halfborn said, as if that was a perfectly logical explanation. "By all means, go over and interrupt. They're not getting anywhere with their argument, and I'm bored."

Halfborn's definition of boredom was *I am not killing anyone at the moment, nor am I watching someone get killed in an interesting way.* Therefore, I was not anxious to alleviate it. Nevertheless, I approached Sam and Amir.

Happily, Samirah did not impale me with her ax. She even looked relieved to see me. "Magnus, good." The light of the Citgo sign washed over her, turning her hijab the color of tree bark. "Is Blitzen okay?"

"He's better." I told her what had happened, though she seemed distracted. Her eyes kept drifting back to Amir, who was still trying to pull out his brain.

"So," I wrapped up, "what have you guys been up to?"

Amir barked a laugh. "Oh, you know. The usual."

The poor guy didn't sound like he was casting with a full bag of runes. I glanced at his hands to make sure he wasn't wearing a new cursed ring.

Sam steepled her fingers in front of her mouth. I hoped she didn't plan on piloting airplanes today, because she looked exhausted. "Magnus . . . Amir and I have been talking on and off since you left. I brought him here hoping to show him proof."

"Proof of what?" I asked.

Amir spread his arms. "Gods, apparently! The Nine Worlds! Proof that our whole life is a lie!"

"Amir, our life isn't a lie." Sam's voice quivered. "It's just . . . more complicated than you realized."

He shook his head, his hair now sticking up like an angry rooster's comb. "Sam, running restaurants is complicated. Pleasing my dad and my grandparents and your grandparents is complicated. Waiting another two years to marry you when all I want is to be with you—that is complicated. But this? Valkyries? Gods? Einher . . . I can't even pronounce that word!"

Samirah might have been blushing. It was hard to tell with the lights.

"I want to be with you, too." Her voice was quiet but filled with conviction. "And I'm trying to show you."

Being in the middle of their conversation, I felt about as awkward as an elf in swim trunks. I also felt guilty, because I'd encouraged Sam to be honest with Amir. I'd told her he was strong enough to handle the truth. I didn't want to be proven wrong.

My instinct was to back off and leave them alone, but I got the feeling Sam and Amir were only being this open with each other because they had three chaperones. I will never understand these betrothed teenagers nowadays.

"Sam," I said, "if you're just trying to show him proof of weirdness, bust out your blazing spear. Fly around the roof. You can do a million things—"

"None of which are *meant* to be seen by mortals," she said bitterly. "It's a paradox, Magnus. I'm not *supposed* to reveal my powers to a mortal, so if I try to do it on purpose, my powers won't work. I say, *Hey, look at me fly!* and suddenly I can't fly."

"That doesn't make any sense," I said.

"Thank you," Amir agreed.

Sam stomped her foot. "You try it, Magnus. Show Amir you're an einherji. Jump to the top of the Citgo sign."

I glanced up. Sixty feet . . . tough, but doable. Yet just thinking about it made my muscles feel wobbly. My strength abandoned me. I suspected that if I tried, I'd hop six inches and make a fool out of myself, which would no doubt be very entertaining to Halfborn and Alex.

"I see your point," I admitted. "But what about Hearthstone and me disappearing from the plane?" I turned to Amir. "You noticed that, right?"

Amir looked lost. "I—I think so. Sam keeps reminding me about it, but it's getting fuzzier. Were you *on* that flight?"

Sam sighed. "His mind is trying to compensate. Amir's more flexible than Barry, who forgot about you guys as soon as we landed. But still . . ."

I met Sam's eyes, and I realized why she was so worried. By explaining her life to Amir, she was doing more than just being honest. She was literally trying to reconfigure her boyfriend's mind. If she succeeded, she might open up his perception. He would see the Nine Worlds as we did. If she failed . . . best case, Amir might eventually forget it all. His mind would gloss over everything that had happened. Worst-case scenario, the experience would leave permanent scars. He might never fully recover. Either way, how could he look at Samirah in the same way again? He would always have a nagging doubt that something was *off*, not quite right.

"Okay," I said, "so why did you bring him here?"

"Because," Sam started, like she'd already explained this twenty times tonight, "the easiest supernatural thing for mortals to see is the Bifrost Bridge. We need to find Heimdall anyway, right? I thought if I could teach Amir to see the Bifrost, that might permanently expand his senses."

"The Bifrost," I said. "The Rainbow Bridge to Asgard."

"Yes."

I looked up at the Citgo sign, New England's largest illuminated billboard, which had been advertising gasoline over Kenmore Square for about a century. "You're telling me—"

"It *is* the brightest stationary point in Boston," Sam said. "The Rainbow Bridge doesn't *always* anchor here, but most of the time—"

"Guys," Amir interrupted. "Really, you don't have to prove anything to me. I'll just . . . I'll take your word for it!" He let out a nervous laugh. "I love you, Sam. I believe you. I may be having a nervous breakdown, but that's fine! That's fine. Let's go do something else!"

I understood why Amir wanted to walk away. I'd seen some crazy stuff—talking swords, knitting zombies, the world's wealthiest freshwater grouper. But even *I* had trouble believing that the Citgo sign was the gateway to Asgard.

"Listen, man." I grabbed his shoulders. I figured physical contact was my biggest advantage. Samirah was prohibited from touching him until they were married, but there was nothing quite as convincing as shaking some sense into a friend. "You have to try, okay? I know you're a Muslim and you don't believe in a bunch of gods."

"They're not gods," Sam volunteered. "They're just powerful entities."

"Whatever," I said. "Dude, I'm an atheist. I don't believe in *anything*. And yet . . . this stuff is real. It's some messed-up stuff, but it's real."

Amir bit his lip. "I—I don't know, Magnus. This makes me very uncomfortable."

"I know, man." I could tell he was trying to listen, but I felt like I was yelling at him while he was wearing noise-canceling headphones. "It makes me uncomfortable, too. Some of the stuff I've learned . . ." I stopped. I decided this wasn't the time to bring up my cousin Annabeth and the Greek gods. I didn't want to give Amir an aneurysm.

"Focus on me," I ordered. "Look in my eyes. Can you do that?"

A bead of sweat trickled down the side of his face. With the effort of somebody lifting three hundred pounds, he managed to meet my gaze.

"Okay, now listen," I said. "Repeat after me: We are going to look up together."

"We are g-going to look up together."

"We are going to see a Rainbow Bridge," I said.

"We are going to"—his voice cracked—"see a Rainbow Bridge."

"And our brains will not explode."

". . . not explode."

"One, two, three."

We looked.

And crud . . . there it was.

The perspective of the world seemed to shift, so we were looking at the Citgo sign from a forty-five-degree angle rather than a perpendicular one. From the top of the sign, a burning sheet of colors arced into the night sky.

"Amir," I said, "are you seeing this?"

"I don't believe it," he muttered, in a tone that made it clear he saw.

"Thank Allah," Sam said, smiling brighter than I'd ever seen, "most merciful, most compassionate."

Then from the heavens spoke a voice both squeaky and un-divine: *"HEY, GUYS! COME ON UP!"*

THIRTY-ONE

Heimdall Takes a Selfie
with Literally Everyone

AMIR ALMOST pulled an einherji move. He would've jumped sixty feet if I hadn't been holding on to him.

"What was that?" he demanded.

Samirah beamed. "You heard him? That's fantastic! It's just Heimdall inviting us up."

"Up, like—*up*?" Amir inched away from the Citgo sign. "How is that fantastic?"

Halfborn and Alex strolled over to join us.

"Will you look at that." Alex didn't sound particularly impressed by the cosmic bridge arcing into the sky. "Is it safe?"

Halfborn tilted his head. "Probably, if Heimdall invited them. Otherwise they'll burn to ash as soon as they set foot on the rainbow."

"*What?*" Amir yelped.

"We're *not* going to burn." Sam glared at Halfborn. "We'll be just fine."

"I'm in," Alex announced. "You two crazy kids still need an escort so you don't do anything irresponsible."

"*Irresponsible?*" Amir's voice went up another half octave. "Like climbing into the sky on a burning rainbow?"

"It's okay, man," I said, though I realized my definition of *okay* had become flexible over the last few months.

Halfborn crossed his arms. "You all have fun. I'm staying right here."

"Why?" Alex asked. "Scared?"

The berserker laughed. "I've met Heimdall before. It's an honor I only need once."

I didn't like the sound of that. "Why? What's he like?"

"You'll see." Halfborn smirked. "I'll meet you back in Valhalla. Have fun exploring inter-dimensional space!"

Sam grinned. "Amir, I can't *wait* to show you. Come on!"

She stepped toward the Citgo sign and vaporized in a smear of multicolored light.

"Sam?" Amir yelled.

"Oh, cool!" Alex leaped forward and also disappeared.

I clapped Amir's shoulder. "They're fine. Stay strong, man. Now I get to pay you back for all those falafel plates you spotted me when I was homeless. I get to show you the Nine Worlds!"

Amir took a deep breath. To his credit, he didn't collapse, curl into a ball, or cry, all of which would have been perfectly acceptable responses to finding out there were squeaky-voiced beings in the sky who would invite you up their rainbow.

"Magnus?" he said.

"Yeah?"

"Remind me not to give you any more falafel."

Together we stepped into the orange glow.

Nothing to see here. Just four teenagers hiking up a nuclear rainbow.

Radiance surrounded us, fuzzy and hot. Rather than walking across a slick, solid surface, I felt like we were wading through a waist-high field of wheat . . . if that wheat were made of highly radioactive light.

Somehow, I'd lost my sunglasses from Alfheim. I doubted they would've helped, though. This light was intense in a different way. The colors made my eyes throb like twin hearts. The heat seemed to swirl a millimeter from my skin. Under our feet, the bridge made a low-pitched rumble like the recording of an explosion played on a loop. I supposed Halfborn Gunderson was right: without Heimdall's blessing, we would have been vaporized the moment we set foot on the Bifrost.

Behind us, the cityscape of Boston became an indistinct blur. The sky turned black and full of stars like I used to see on my old hiking trips with my mom. The memory caught in my throat. I thought about the smell of campfires and toasting marshmallows, Mom and I telling each other stories, making up new constellations like the Twinkie and the Wombat and laughing ourselves silly.

We walked for so long, I began to wonder if there was anything at the other end of the rainbow. Forget pots of gold and leprechauns. Forget Asgard. Maybe this was a practical joke. Heimdall might just cause the Bifrost to disappear and leave us floating in the void. *YOU'RE RIGHT*, his squeaky voice would announce. *WE DON'T EXIST. LOL!*

Gradually the darkness grayed. On the horizon rose the skyline of another city: gleaming walls, golden gates, and behind them, the spires and domes of the gods' palaces. I'd only seen Asgard once before, from the inside, looking out a window in Valhalla. From a distance, it was even more impressive. I imagined charging up this bridge with an invading army of giants. I was pretty sure I'd lose hope when I saw that vast fortress.

And standing on the bridge in front of us, his legs planted wide, was a tall warrior with a huge sword.

I'd imagined a god who was suave and cool—a movie-star type. Real-life Heimdall was kind of a disappointment. He wore a padded cloth tunic and woolly leggings, all beige so he picked up the colors of the Bifrost. It was camouflage, I realized—the perfect way to blend into a rainbow. His hair was white-blond and fuzzy like ram's wool. His grinning face was darkly tanned, which might have been the result of standing on a radioactive bridge for thousands of years. I hoped he didn't plan on having kids someday.

In general, he looked like that goofy guy you didn't want to sit next to on the school bus, except for two things: his unsheathed sword, which was almost as tall as he was, and the huge curled ram's horn slung over his left shoulder. The horn and sword looked imposing, though they were both so large they kept knocking into one another. I got the feeling that if Heimdall killed you, it would only be because he got clumsy and tripped.

As we approached, he waved enthusiastically, making his sword and horn bang into one another: *clink, donk, clink, donk.* "What's up, guys?"

The four of us stopped. Sam bowed. "Lord Heimdall."

Alex looked at her like, *Lord?*

Next to me, Amir pinched the bridge of his nose. "I cannot believe what I'm seeing."

Heimdall arched his fluffy eyebrows. His irises were rings of pure alabaster. "Ooh, what are you seeing?" He gazed past us into the void. "You mean the guy in Cincinnati with the gun? No, he's okay. He's just going to the firing range. Or do you mean that fire giant in Muspellheim? He *is* coming this way . . . No, hold on. He tripped! That was hilarious! I wish I'd Vined that."

I tried to follow Heimdall's gaze, but I saw nothing but empty space and stars. "What are you—?"

"My eyesight is really good," explained the god. "I can see into all of the Nine Worlds. And my hearing! I was listening to you guys argue on that rooftop from all the way up here. That's why I decided to throw you a rainbow."

Samirah gulped. "You, ah, heard us arguing?"

Heimdall smiled. "The whole thing. You two are just *too* cute. In fact, could I get a selfie with you before we talk business?"

Amir said, "Uh—"

"Great!" Heimdall fumbled with his horn and his sword.

"Do you need some help?" I asked.

"No, no, I got it."

Alex Fierro sidled up next to me. "Besides, that wouldn't be nearly as funny."

"I can hear you, Alex," the god warned. "I can hear corn growing five hundred miles away. I can hear frost giants belching in their castles in Jotunheim. I can *definitely* hear you. But not to worry, I take selfies all the time. Now let's see . . ."

He fiddled with his massive ram's horn as if looking for a button. Meanwhile, his sword rested at a precarious angle in the crook of his arm, the six-foot-long blade leaning toward us. I wondered what Jack would think of that sword, whether it was a hot lady or a professional linebacker or maybe both.

"Aha!" Heimdall must have found the right button. His horn shrank into the largest smartphone I'd ever seen, its screen the size of a Sicilian pizza square, its case made of shiny ram's horn.

"Your horn is a phone?" Amir asked.

"I think technically it's a phablet," Heimdall said. "But yes, this is Gjallar, the Horn and/or Phablet of Doomsday! I blow this baby once, the gods know there's trouble in Asgard and they come running. I blow it *twice*, then it's Ragnarok, baby!" He seemed delighted by the idea that he could signal the start of the final battle that destroyed the Nine Worlds. "Most of the time, I just use it for photos and texting and whatnot."

"That's not scary at all," Alex said.

Heimdall laughed. "You have no idea. Once, I butt-dialed the apocalypse? *So* embarrassing. I had to text everybody on my contacts list, like, *False alarm!* A lot of gods came running anyway. I made this GIF of them charging up the Bifrost and then realizing there was no battle. Priceless."

Amir blinked repeatedly, perhaps because Heimdall was a moist talker. "You are in charge of Doomsday. You're really a—a—"

"An Aesir?" Heimdall said. "Yep, I'm one of Odin's sons! But between us, Amir, I think Samirah is right." He leaned in so the people in the cornfields five hundred miles away couldn't hear him. "Frankly, I don't think of us as *gods*, either. I mean, once you've seen Thor passed out on the floor, or Odin in his bathrobe, yelling at Frigg because she used his toothbrush . . . it's hard to see much divinity in my family. Like my moms used to say—"

"*Moms*, plural?" Amir asked.

"Yeah. I was born of nine mothers."

"How—?"

"Don't ask. It's a pain on Mother's Day. Nine different phone calls. Nine flower bouquets. When I was a kid, trying to cook nine breakfasts-in-beds . . . oh, man! Anyway, let's get this picture."

He corralled Sam and Amir, who looked stunned to have the grinning face of a god wedged between them. Heimdall held out his phablet, but his arm wasn't long enough.

I cleared my throat. "You sure you don't want me to—?"

"No, no! No one can hold the mighty phablet Gjallar except me. But it's fine! Time-out for a second, guys." Heimdall stepped back and fumbled with his phone and sword some more, apparently trying to attach them to each other. After a bit of awkward maneuvering (and probably several butt calls to the apocalypse), he held out the sword in triumph, the phablet now hooked on the point. "Ta-da! My best invention yet!"

"You invented the selfie stick," Alex said. "I was wondering who to blame for that."

"It's a selfie *sword*, actually." Heimdall wedged his face between Sam and Amir. "Say *gamalost*!" Gjallar flashed.

More fumbling as Heimdall retrieved his phone from the tip of his sword and inspected the picture. "Perfect!"

He proudly showed us the shot, as if we hadn't been there when it was taken three seconds ago.

"Has anyone ever told you you're crazy?" Alex asked.

"Crazy *fun*!" Heimdall said. "Come on, check out some of these other shots."

He gathered the four of us around his phablet and started

flipping through his photo stream, though I was pretty distracted by how much Heimdall smelled like wet sheep.

He showed us a majestic picture of the Taj Mahal with Heimdall's face looming large in the foreground. Then Valhalla's dining hall, fuzzy and indistinct, with Heimdall's total eclipse of a nose in perfect focus. Then the president of the United States giving a State of the Union address with Heimdall photo-bombing.

Pictures of all the Nine Worlds, all selfies.

"Wow," I said. "Those are . . . consistent."

"I don't like my shirt in this picture." He showed us a shot of elfish police beating a hulder with nightsticks, Heimdall grinning in front, wearing a blue striped polo. "But, oh, somewhere in here I've got this amazing photo of Asgard, with me making this angry face and pretending to eat Odin's palace!"

"Heimdall," Samirah interrupted, "those are really interesting, but we were hoping for your help."

"Hmm? Oh, you want a picture with all five of us? Maybe with Asgard in the background? Sure!"

"Actually," Sam said, "we're looking for Thor's hammer."

All the excitement went out of Heimdall's alabaster eyes. "Oh, not that again. I *told* Thor I couldn't see anything. Every day he calls me, texts me, sends me unsolicited pictures of his goats. 'Look harder! Look harder!' I'm telling you, it's *nowhere*. See for yourself."

He flipped through more shots. "No hammer. No hammer. There's me with Beyoncé, but no hammer. Hmm, I should probably make that my profile picture."

"You know what?" Alex stretched. "I'm just going to lie down over here and not kill anybody annoying, okay?" He lay on his back on the Bifrost, stuck out his arms, and leisurely waved them through the light, making rainbow angels.

"Uh, yeah," I said. "Heimdall, I know it's a drag, but do you think you could take another look for us? We think Mjolnir is hidden underground, so—"

"Well, that would explain it! I can only see through solid rock for, like, a *mile* at most. If it's deeper than that—"

"Right," Sam jumped in. "The thing is, we kind of know who took it. A giant named Thrym."

"Thrym!" Heimdall looked offended, as if that was someone he would *never* deign to take a selfie with. "That horrid, ugly—"

"He wants to marry Sam," Amir said.

"But he won't," Sam said.

Heimdall leaned on his sword. "Well, now. That's a dilemma. I can tell you where Thrym is easy enough. But he wouldn't be stupid enough to keep the hammer in his fortress."

"We know." I figured we were close to the end of Heimdall's attention span, but I told him about Loki's nefarious wedding plans, the Skofnung Sword and Stone, the deadline of three more days, and Goat-Killer, who might or might not be on our side, telling us to find Heimdall and ask for directions. Every so often I randomly tossed in the word *selfie* to keep the god's interest.

"Hmm," said Heimdall. "In that case, I'd be happy to scan the Nine Worlds again and find this Goat-Killer person. Let me set up my selfie sword again."

"Perhaps," Amir suggested, "if you simply looked without using your phone?"

Heimdall stared at our mortal friend. Amir had said what

we'd all been thinking, which was a pretty brave thing to do his first time in Norse outer space, but I was afraid Heimdall might decide to use his sword for something other than wide-angle shots.

Fortunately, Heimdall just patted Amir's shoulder. "It's all right, Amir. I know you're confused about the Nine Worlds and whatnot. But I'm afraid you're saying words that don't make any sense."

"Please, Heimdall," Sam said. "I know it seems . . . strange, but gazing *directly* at the Nine Worlds might give you a fresh perspective."

The god looked unconvinced. "Surely there's another way to find your goat-killer. Maybe I could blow Gjallar and get the gods up here. We could ask them if they've seen—"

"No!" we all screamed at once. Alex came in a little late, as he was still lying down making light angels. He may have added a few colorful modifiers to his *no*.

"Hmph." Heimdall scowled. "Well, this is highly unorthodox. But I don't want to see a big ugly giant come between a cute couple like you two." Heimdall wagged his finger between me and Sam.

"Uh, actually it's *those* two," I corrected, pointing to Amir.

Over in the rainbow, Alex snorted.

"Right, of course," Heimdall said. "Sorry. You guys look very different when you're not in the camera app. Perhaps you have a point about a fresh perspective! Let's see what we can find in the Nine Worlds!"

THIRTY-TWO

Godzilla Sends Me
an Important Message

HEIMDALL GAZED into the distance and immediately stumbled backward. "Nine Mothers of Me!"

Alex Fierro sat up, suddenly interested. "What is it?"

"Uh . . ." Heimdall's cheeks were turning the same sheeplike color as his hair. "Giants. A *lot* of them. They—they appear to be massing on the borders of Midgard."

I wondered what other threats Heimdall had missed while he was photo-bombing the president. Between this guy and hammerless Thor, it was no wonder the safety of Asgard depended on unprepared, undertrained people like . . . well, us.

Sam managed to keep her voice level. "We know about the giants, Lord Heimdall. They suspect Thor's hammer is missing. Unless we get it back soon—"

"Yes." Heimdall licked his lips. "I—I suppose you did say something like that." He cupped his ear and listened. "They're talking about . . . a wedding. Thrym's wedding. One of the giant generals . . . he's grumbling because they have to wait until it is over before they can invade. Apparently Thrym has promised them some good news after the ceremony, something that will make their invasion much easier."

"An alliance with Loki?" I guessed, though something about that didn't seem quite right. There had to be more.

"Also," Heimdall continued, "Thrym has said . . . yes, his own forces won't join the invasion until after the wedding. He's warned the other armies it would be rude to start the war without him. I—I don't think the giants are scared of Thrym, but from what I'm overhearing, they're terrified of his sister."

I remembered my dream: the harsh voice of the giantess who had swatted my pickle jar off the bar. "Heimdall," I asked, "can you see Thrym? What's he up to?"

The god squinted and looked deeper into the void. "Yes, there he is, just at the edge of my vision, under a mile or so of rock. Sitting in that horrid fortress of his. Why he wants to live in a cave decorated like a bar, I have no idea. Oh, he is *so* ugly! I pity the person who marries him."

"Great," Sam muttered. "What's he doing?"

"Drinking," Heimdall said. "Now he's belching. Now he's drinking again. His sister, Thrynga—oh, her voice is like oars scraping on ice! She's berating him for being a fool. Something about his wedding being a stupid idea and they should just kill the bride as soon as she arrives!"

Heimdall paused, maybe remembering that Samirah was the poor girl in question. "Uh . . . sorry. As I thought, though, there's no hammer anywhere. That's not surprising. These earth giants, they can bury things—"

"Let me guess," I said. "In the earth?"

"Exactly!" Heimdall looked impressed with my knowledge of earth giants. "They can retrieve those items simply by calling them back to hand. I imagine Thrym will wait until the wedding is finished. Once he has his bride and his bride-price, he'll summon the hammer . . . if he feels like keeping his part of the bargain, that is."

Amir looked more nauseated than I'd felt aboard the Cessna Citation. "Sam, you can't do this! It's too dangerous."

"I won't." She balled her fists. "Lord Heimdall, you're the guardian of the sacred marriage bed, aren't you? The old stories say you traveled among humankind advising couples, blessing their offspring, and creating the various classes of Viking society?"

"I did?" Heimdall glanced at his phone as if tempted to look up this information. "Um, I mean, yes. Of course!"

"Then hear my sacred vow," Sam said. "I swear upon the Bifrost and all the Nine Worlds that I will never marry *anyone* except this man, Amir Fadlan." (Thankfully, she pointed in the correct direction and did not implicate me. Otherwise things might have been awkward.) "I will not even *pretend* to marry this giant, Thrym. It will not happen."

Alex Fierro rose, his mouth set in a frown. "Uh . . . Sam?"

I figured Alex was thinking the same thing I was: that if Loki could control Sam's actions, she might not be able to keep this vow.

Sam gave Alex a warning look. Surprisingly, Alex shut up.

"I have made my vow," Sam announced. "Inshallah, I will keep it and marry Amir Fadlan in accordance with the teachings of the Quran and the Prophet Muhammad, peace be upon him."

I wondered if the Bifrost Bridge would collapse under the heavy-duty Muslim sacred vow Sam was laying down, but nothing seemed different except for Amir, who looked like he'd been hit between the eyes with a phablet.

"P-peace be upon him," he stammered.

Heimdall sniffled. "That was *so* sweet." A tear as white as plant sap slid down his cheek. "I hope you crazy kids make a go of it. I really do. I wish . . ." He tilted head, listening to the distant murmurings of the universe. "Nope, I'm not on the guest list for your wedding with Thrym, darn it."

Sam looked at me like, *Did I just imagine the last few minutes?* "Lord Heimdall, you mean . . . the wedding I just swore not to go through with?"

"Yes," he confirmed. "I'm sure it will be lovely, but that soon-to-be sister-in-law of yours, Thrynga, is going on and on—'No Aesir, no Vanir.' They apparently have some first-rate security in place for screening the guests."

"They don't want Thor getting in," Alex guessed, "and stealing back his hammer."

"That would make sense." Heimdall kept his eyes on the horizon. "The thing is, this underground fortress-bar of theirs . . . I've seen how it works. There's only one way in, and the entrance tunnel keeps shifting around, opening in a different place every day. Sometimes it turns up behind a waterfall, or in a Midgard cave, or under the roots of a tree. Even if Thor wanted to plan an assault, he'd have no idea where to start on any given day. I don't see *how* you could arrange an ambush to steal the hammer." He frowned. "Thrym and Thrynga are still talking about the guest list. Only family and giants are invited, and . . . Who is Randolph?"

I felt as if somebody had turned up the thermostat on the Bifrost. My face itched like a hand-shaped burn mark was forming across my cheek.

"Randolph is my uncle," I said. "Can you see him?"

Heimdall shook his head. "Not in Jotunheim, but Thrym and Thrynga are very annoyed about him being on the list. Thrym is saying, 'Loki insists.' Thrynga is throwing bottles." Heimdall winced. "Sorry, I had to look away. Without the camera, everything seems so three-D!"

Amir watched me with concern. "Magnus, you have an uncle who's involved in all this?"

I didn't want to get into it. The scene from the zombies' barrow kept replaying in my mind: Randolph crying as he drove the Skofnung Sword into Blitzen's gut.

Thankfully, Alex Fierro changed the subject.

"Hey, Lord Selfie," he said, "what about the goat-killer? That's who we need to find right now."

"Ah, yes." Heimdall raised his sword blade over his eyes like a visor, nearly decapitating me in the process. "You said a figure in black clothes, with a metal helmet, and a faceplate like a snarling wolf?"

"That's him," I said.

"I don't see him. But there is something strange. I know I said no camera, but . . . ah, I'm not sure how to describe this." He raised his phablet and snapped a picture. "What do you make of this?"

The four of us gathered around the screen.

It was hard to judge the scale, since the shot had been taken from inter-dimensional space, but at the top of a cliff sat a massive warehouse-looking building. Across the roof stretched glittery neon letters almost as eye-catching as the Citgo sign: UTGARD LANES.

Behind that, even larger and more awe-inspiring, was an inflatable Godzilla, like you might see advertising a sale at a car dealership. In Godzilla's hands was a cardboard sign that read:

'SUP, MAGNUS.

COME VISIT!

GOT INFO 4 U. BRING UR FRIENDS!

ONLY WAY 2 BEAT THRYM + GOOD BOWLING.

XOX BIG BOY

I let out a few Norse cuss words. I was tempted to throw the Phablet of Doomsday off the Bifrost Bridge.

"Big Boy," I said. "I should have known."

"This is bad," Sam muttered. "He *told* you that someday you would need his help. But if *he's* our only hope, we're doomed."

"Why?" Amir asked.

"Yeah," Alex demanded. "Who is this Big Boy who communicates through inflatable Godzillas?"

"I know this one!" Heimdall said cheerfully. "He's the most dangerous, powerful giant sorcerer of all time! His real name is Utgard-Loki."

THIRTY-THREE

Falafel Break? Yes, Thank You

ANOTHER VIKING pro tip: If Heimdall offers to drop you somewhere, say NO!

Heimdall's idea of sending us back to Midgard was making the Bifrost dissolve around our feet and literally dropping us through infinity. Once we stopped screaming (or it may have been just me again; don't judge), we found ourselves at the corner of Charles and Boylston, standing in front of the Edgar Allan Poe statue. By that point, I definitely had a telltale heart. My pulse was going so fast you could've heard that sucker through a brick wall.

We were all exhausted, but we were also hungry and buzzing with post-rainbow adrenaline. Most importantly, we were a block from the Transportation Building food court, where the Fadlans had a restaurant.

"You know . . ." Amir flexed his fingers as if making sure they were still there. "I could make us some dinner."

"You don't have to, man," I said, which I thought was pretty noble considering how much I loved his family's falafel recipe. (I know he asked me to remind him not to give me any more falafel, but I had decided to interpret that request as temporary insanity.)

Amir shook his head. "No, I—I want to."

I understood what he meant. The guy's world had just been cracked open. He needed to do something familiar to steady his nerves. He craved the comfort of deep-frying chick-pea patties, and really, who was I to argue?

The Transportation Building was closed for the night, but Amir had the keys. He let us in, opened Fadlan's Falafel, and prepped the kitchen to make us a late dinner/really early breakfast of amazingness.

Meanwhile, Alex, Sam, and I sat at a table in the darkened food court, listening to the clanging of pots and fryer cages echo through the vast space like metallic bird cries.

Sam looked dazed. She tipped over a saltshaker and wrote letters in the white grains—whether Norse or Arabic, I couldn't tell.

Alex kicked up his rose high-tops on the opposite chair. He twiddled his thumbs, his two-toned eyes scanning the room. "So, this sorcerer giant . . ."

"Utgard-Loki," I said.

A lot of folks in the Norse cosmos had warned me that names had power. You weren't supposed to utter them unless you had to. Me, I preferred to wear names out like hand-me-down clothes. That seemed the best way to drain the power from them.

"He's not my favorite giant." I glanced around the floor, making sure there were no talking pigeons nearby. "A few months ago, he showed up right here. Tricked me into giving him my falafel. Then he turned into an eagle and dragged me across the rooftops of Boston."

Alex drummed his fingers on the table. "And now he wants you to come visit his bowling alley."

"You know the really messed-up part? That's the *least* crazy thing that has happened to me this week."

Alex snorted. "So why is he called Loki?" He looked at Sam. "Any relation to us?"

Sam shook her head. "His name means Loki of the Outlands. No connection to . . . our dad."

Not since the Great Alderman Disaster of that afternoon had the word *dad* invoked such negative feelings in a conversation. Looking at Alex and Sam sitting across from each other, I couldn't imagine two people more different. Yet they both wore exactly the same expression: sour resignation that they shared the god of trickery as their pop.

"On the bright side," I said, "Utgard-Loki didn't strike me as a big fan of the other Loki. I can't see the two of them working together."

"They're both giants," Alex pointed out.

"Giants fight among each other just like humans," Sam said. "And, judging by what we learned from Heimdall, getting the hammer back from Thrym will *not* be easy. We need all the advice we can get. Utgard-Loki is crafty. He might be the right person to figure out a way to foil Dad's plans."

"Fight Loki with Loki," I said.

Alex ran his hand through his shock of green hair. "I don't care how tricky and clever your giant friend is. In the end, we're going to have to go to that wedding and get the hammer. Which means we'll have to face Loki ourselves."

"*We?*" I asked.

"I'm going with you," Alex said. "Obviously."

I remembered my dream of Loki in Alex's apartment: *It's such a simple request.* Having two children of Loki at the wedding, both of whom could be controlled by Loki's slightest whim . . . that was not my definition of a joyous occasion.

Samirah drew another design in the salt. "Alex, I can't ask you to go."

"You're not asking," Alex said, "I'm telling. You brought me into the afterlife. This is my chance to make it count. You *know* what we need to do."

Sam shook her head. "I—I still don't think that's a good idea."

Alex threw his hands in the air. "Are you even related to me? Where's your sense of recklessness? Of *course* it's not a good idea, but it's the only way."

"What idea?" I asked. "What way?"

Clearly I had missed a conversation between the two of them, but neither looked anxious to fill me in. Just then, Amir came back with the food. He set down a heaping platter of lamb kebab, dolma, falafel, kibbeh, and other heavenly yummies, and I remembered my priorities.

"You, sir," I said, "are a powerful entity."

He almost smiled. He started to sit next to Sam, but Alex snapped his fingers. "Uh-uh, lover boy. Chaperone says no."

Amir looked mortified. He moved to sit between Alex and me.

We dug in. (Actually, I may have done most of the digging in.)

Amir bit off the corner of a pita-bread triangle. "It doesn't seem possible . . . food tastes the same. The fryer fries at the same temperature. My keys work in the same locks. And yet . . . the whole universe has changed."

"Not everything has changed," Sam promised.

Amir's expression was wistful, as if remembering a good experience from childhood that couldn't be recaptured.

"I appreciate it, Sam," he said. "And I *do* see what you mean about the Norse deities. They aren't gods. Anyone who can take so many selfies with a sword and a ram's horn . . ." He shook his head. "Allah may have ninety-nine names, but Heimdall isn't one of them."

Alex grinned. "I like this guy."

Amir blinked, apparently unsure what to do with the compliment. "So . . . what now? How do you top a trip across the Bifrost?"

Sam gave him a faint smile. "Well, tonight, I have to have a conversation with Jid and Bibi to explain why I've been out so late."

Amir nodded. "Will you . . . try to show them the Nine Worlds, as you did for me?"

"She can't," Alex said. "They're too old. Their brains aren't as flexible."

"Hey," I said. "No need to be rude."

"Just being honest." Alex chewed on a piece of lamb. "The older you are, the harder it is to accept that the world might not be the way you thought it was. It's a miracle that Amir managed to see through all the mist and the glamour without going insane." He kept his eyes on me a moment longer than seemed necessary.

"Yes," Amir muttered. "I feel very fortunate not to be insane."

"Alex is right, though," Sam said. "When I talked to my grandparents this morning, the conversation they'd had with Loki was already fading from their memory. They knew they were supposed to be angry at me. They remembered that you and I had been arguing. But the details . . ." She made a *poof* gesture with her fingertips.

Amir rubbed his chin. "My dad was the same. He only asked if you and I had patched up our differences. I suspect . . . we could tell them anything about where we were tonight, couldn't we? Any mundane excuse, and they would believe it more readily than the truth."

Alex elbowed him. "Don't get any ideas, lover boy. I'm still your chaperone."

"No! I only meant . . . I would never—"

"Relax," Alex said. "I'm messing with you."

"Ah." Amir did not seem to relax. "And after tonight? What then?"

"We go to Jotunheim," Sam said. "We have a giant to interrogate."

"You're traveling to another world." Amir shook his head in amazement. "You know, when I arranged those flying lessons with Barry, I . . . I thought I was expanding your horizons." He laughed mirthlessly. "Foolish of me."

"Amir, that was the kindest gift—"

"It's all right. I'm not complaining. I just . . ." He let out a sharp exhale. "What can I do to help you?"

Sam put her hand flat on the table, her fingers stretched toward Amir like an air version of holding hands. "Just trust me. Believe what I promised."

"I do," he said. "But there must be something else. Now that I can see everything . . ." He waved a plastic fork at the ceiling. "I want to support you."

"You are," Sam assured him. "You've seen me as a Valkyrie,

and you haven't run away screaming. You don't *know* how much that helps. Just stay safe for me, please, until we get back. Be my anchor."

"Happily. Although . . ." He gave her a grin so sheepish it smelled like Heimdall. "I haven't actually *seen* you as a Valkyrie. Do you think . . . ?"

Sam got to her feet. "Alex, Magnus, I'll meet you in the morning?"

"The statue in the park," I said. "See you there."

She nodded. "Amir, two days hence, this will all be over. I promise." She rose into the air and disappeared in a golden flash.

The plastic fork fell out of Amir's hand. "It's true," he said. "I can't believe it."

Alex grinned. "Well, it's getting late. There is one more thing you could do for us, Amir, buddy."

"Of course. Anything."

"How about a doggie bag for this falafel?"

THIRTY-FOUR

We Visit My Favorite Mausoleum

THE NEXT MORNING, I woke in my own bed in Valhalla, unrefreshed and definitely not ready to go. I packed a duffel with camping supplies and leftover falafel. I checked in across the hall with T.J.—who handed me the Skofnung Sword and promised to remain on standby in case I needed cavalry reinforcements or help charging enemy fortifications. Then I met up with Alex Fierro in the lobby and we headed out to Midgard.

Alex agreed to make one stop with me before we rendezvoused with the others. I didn't really *want* to, but I felt obliged to break into Randolph's Back Bay mansion and check in on my murderous, traitorous uncle. Because, you know, that's what family is for.

I wasn't sure what I would do if I found him. Maybe I'd figure out a way to free him from Loki's clutches. Maybe I'd smack him in the face with a bag of kibbeh, though that would be a waste of good kibbeh.

Fortunately for Randolph and my leftovers, he wasn't home. I jimmied the back door as usual—Randolph had not gotten the message about upgrading his locks—then Alex and I wandered through the mansion, stealing Randolph's various stashes of chocolate (because that was a necessity), making fun of his fussy draperies and knickknacks, and finally ending up in the old man's office.

Nothing there had changed since my last visit. Maps lay on the desk. The big Viking tombstone thing stood in the corner, its figure of a wolf still snarling at me. Medieval weapons and trinkets lined the shelves along with leather-bound books and photographs of Randolph at dig sites in Scandinavia.

On the chain around my neck, Jack's pendant buzzed with tension. I had never brought him to Randolph's house before. I guess he didn't like the place. Or maybe he was just excited because the Skofnung Sword was strapped across my back.

I turned to Alex. "Hey, are you female today?"

The question slipped out before I had a chance to think about whether it was weird, whether it was rude, or whether it would get me decapitated.

Alex smiled with what I hoped was amusement and not homicidal glee. "Why do you ask?"

"The Skofnung Sword. It can't be drawn in the presence of women. I kind of like it better when it can't be drawn."

"Ah. Hold on." Alex's face scrunched up in intense concentration. "There! Now I'm female."

My expression must have been priceless.

Alex burst out laughing. "I'm kidding. Yes, I'm female today. *She* and *her*."

"But you didn't just—"

"Change gender by force of will? No, Magnus. It doesn't work that way." She ran her fingers across Randolph's desk. The stained glass transom window cast multicolored light across her face.

"So can I ask . . . ?" I waved my hands vaguely. I didn't have the words.

"How it *does* work?" She smirked. "As long as you don't ask me to represent every gender-fluid person for you, okay? I'm not an ambassador. I'm not a teacher or a poster child. I'm just"—she mimicked my hand-waving—"*me*. Trying to be me as best I can."

That sounded fair. At least it was better than her punching me, garroting me, or turning into a cheetah and mauling me. "But you're a shape-shifter," I said. "Can't you just . . . you know, be whatever you want?"

Her darker eye twitched, as if I'd poked a sore spot.

"That's the irony." She picked up a letter opener and turned it in the stained-glass light. "I can *look* like whatever or whoever I want. But my actual gender? No. I can't change it at will. It's truly fluid, in the sense that I don't control it. Most of the time, I identify as female, but sometimes I have very *male* days. And please don't ask me how I know which I am on which day."

That had, in fact, been my next question. "So why not call yourself, like, *they* and *them*? Wouldn't that be less confusing than switching back and forth with the pronouns?"

"Less confusing for who? You?"

My mouth must've been hanging open, because she rolled her eyes at me like, *You dork.* I hoped Heimdall wasn't recording the conversation to put on Vine.

"Look, some people prefer *they*," Alex said. "They're non-binary or mid-spectrum or whatever. If they want you to use *they*, then that's what you should do. But for me, personally, I don't want to use the same pronouns all the time, because that's not me. I change a lot. That's sort of the point. When I'm she, I'm *she*. When I'm he, I'm *he*. I'm not *they*. Get it?"

"If I say *no*, will you hurt me?"

"No."

"Then no, not really."

She shrugged. "You don't have to get it. Just, you know, a little respect."

"For the girl with the very sharp wire? No problem."

She must have liked that answer. There was nothing confusing about the smile she gave me. It warmed the office about five degrees.

I cleared my throat. "Anyway, we're looking for anything that might tell us what's going on with my uncle."

I started checking the bookshelves as if I had a clue about what I was doing. I didn't find any secret messages or levers that opened hidden rooms. It always looked so easy on *Scooby-Doo*.

Alex rummaged through Randolph's desk drawers. "So you used to live in this big mausoleum?"

"Thankfully, no. My mom and I had an apartment in Allston . . . before she died. Then I was on the streets."

"But your family had money."

"Randolph did." I picked up an old photo of him with Caroline, Aubrey, and Emma. It was too painful to look at. I turned it around. "You're going to ask why I didn't come to live with him instead of being homeless?"

Alex scoffed. "Gods, no. I would never ask that."

Her voice had turned bitter, as if rich-jerk relatives were something she knew about.

"You come from . . . somewhere like this?" I asked.

Alex closed the desk drawer. "My family had a lot of things, just not the things that mattered . . . like a son and heir, for instance. Or, you know, *feelings*."

I tried to imagine Alex living in a mansion like this, or mingling at an elegant party like Mr. Alderman's in Alfheim. "Did your folks know you were a child of Loki?"

"Oh, Loki made sure of that. My mortal parents blamed him for the way I was, for being fluid. They said he corrupted me, put ideas in my head, blah, blah, blah."

"And your parents didn't just . . . conveniently forget Loki, like Sam's grandparents did?"

"I wish. Loki made sure they remembered. He—he opened their eyes permanently, I guess you could say. Like what you did for Amir, except my dad's motives weren't as good."

"I didn't do anything for Amir."

Alex walked over to me and crossed her arms. She was wearing pink-and-green flannel today over regular blue jeans. Her hiking boots were boringly practical, except the laces glittered pink metallic.

Her different-colored eyes seemed to pull my thoughts in two directions at once. "You really believe you didn't do anything?" she asked. "When you grabbed Amir's shoulders? When your hands started to glow?"

"I . . . glowed?" I didn't have any recollection of calling on the power of Frey. It hadn't even occurred to me that Amir needed healing.

"You saved him, Magnus," Alex said. "Even *I* could see that. He would've cracked under the strain. You gave him the resilience to stretch his mind without breaking. The only reason he's in one piece, mentally, is because of you."

I felt like I was back on the Bifrost Bridge, superheated

colors burning through me. I didn't know what to do with the look of approval Alex was giving me, or the idea that I might have healed Amir's mind without even knowing it.

She punched me in the chest, just hard enough to hurt. "How about we finish up? I'm starting to suffocate in this place."

"Yeah. Yeah, sure."

I was having trouble breathing, too, but it wasn't because of the house. The way Alex spoke so approvingly of me . . . that had made something click. I realized who she reminded me of—her restless energy, her petite size and choppy haircut, her flannel shirt and jeans and boots, her disregard for what other people thought of her, even her laugh—on those rare occasions she laughed. She reminded me weirdly of my mom.

I decided not to dwell on that. Pretty soon I'd be psychoanalyzing myself more than Otis the goat.

I scanned the shelves one last time. My eyes fixed on the only framed photo without Randolph in it: a shot of a frozen waterfall in the wilderness, sheets of ice hanging over the ledges of a gray cliff. It could have been just a pretty nature picture from anywhere, but it looked familiar. The colors in it were more vibrant than in the other photos, as if this shot had been taken more recently. I picked it up. There was no dust on the shelf where the frame had been. But there was something else—a green wedding invitation.

Alex studied the photo. "I know that place."

"Bridal Veil Falls," I said. "New Hampshire. I've gone hiking there."

"Same."

Under different circumstances, we might've traded hiking

stories. It was another weird similarity between her and my mom, and maybe the reason why Alex had an open atrium in the middle of her hotel suite just like mine.

But at the moment my mind was racing in a different direction. I remembered what Heimdall had said about the fortress of Thrym, how its entrance was always changing, so it would be impossible to predict where it might be on the day of the wedding. *Sometimes it turns up behind a waterfall,* he'd said.

I scanned the wedding invitation, an exact duplicate of the one Sam had thrown away. The *when* column now said: TWO DAYS HENCE. In other words, the day after tomorrow. The *where* column still said: WE'LL GET BACK TO YOU.

The picture of Bridal Veil Falls might just be a random photo. The name of the location might be a coincidence. Or maybe Uncle Randolph wasn't completely under Loki's control. Maybe he'd left me a clue worthy of *Scooby-Doo.*

"That's Sam's wedding invitation," Alex said. "You think it means something that it was tucked behind this photo?"

"Could be nothing," I said. "Or it could be a point of entry for some wedding crashers."

THIRTY-FIVE

We Have a Tiny Problem

RENDEZVOUS SPOT: the George Washington statue in the Public Garden. Hearthstone, Blitzen, and Samirah were already there, along with another old friend who happened to be an eight-legged horse.

"Stanley!" I said.

The stallion whinnied and nuzzled me. He nodded toward the statue of George Washington on his charger as if to say, *Can you believe this dude? He ain't so great. His horse only has four legs.*

The first time I'd met Stanley, we'd hurtled off a Jotunheim cliff together, heading for a giant's fortress. I was glad to see the horse again, but I had a bad feeling we were about to take part in the sequel—*Cliff Hurtling II: The Rise of Big Boy.*

I stroked Stanley's muzzle, wishing I had a carrot for him. All I had was chocolate and kibbeh, and I didn't think either would be good for an eight-legged horse.

"Did you summon him?" I asked Hearthstone. "How are you still conscious?"

The first time Hearth used *ehwaz*, the transportation rune-stone, he'd collapsed and giggled about washing machines for half an hour.

Hearth shrugged, though I detected a little pride in his expression. He looked better today, after spending a night in the tanning bed. His black jeans and jacket were freshly cleaned, and he had his familiar candy-striped scarf around his neck.

Easier now, he signed. *I can do two, maybe three runes in a row before I collapse.*

"Wow."

"What did he say?" Alex asked.

I translated.

"Just two or three?" Alex asked. "I mean, no offense, but that doesn't sound like a lot."

"It is," I said. "Using one rune is like the hardest workout you've ever done. Imagine an hour of nonstop sprinting."

"Yeah, I don't really work out, so—"

Blitzen cleared his throat. "Ah, Magnus? Who's your friend?"

"Sorry. This is Alex Fierro. Blitzen, Hearthstone, Alex is our newest einherji."

Blitzen was wearing his pith helmet, so it was difficult to see his expression through the gauze netting. However, I was pretty sure he wasn't grinning in delight.

"You're the other child of Loki," he said.

"Yep," Alex said. "I promise I won't kill you."

For Alex, that was a pretty big concession, but Hearth and Blitz didn't seem to know what to make of her.

Samirah gave me a dry smile.

"What?" I demanded.

"Nothing." She was wearing her school uniform, which I thought was pretty optimistic, like, *I'll just zip over to Jotunheim and be back in time for third-period Government.* "Where have you two been? You didn't come from the direction of Valhalla."

I explained about our excursion to Randolph's, and the photo and wedding invitation that were now in my backpack.

Sam frowned. "You think this waterfall is the way into Thrym's fortress?"

"Maybe," I said. "Or at least it might be two days from now. If we know that in advance, we might be able to use the info."

How? Hearth signed.

"Um, I'm not sure yet."

Blitzen grunted. "I suppose it's possible. Earth giants can manipulate solid rock even better than dwarves can. They can definitely shift their front doors around. Also"—he shook his head in disgust—"their fortresses are almost impossible to break into. Tunneling, explosives, blasts of godly power—none of that will work. Believe me, D.I.C.E. has tried."

"Dice?" I asked.

He looked at me like I was a moron. "The Dwarven Infantry Corps of Engineers. What *else* would it stand for? Anyway, with earth giants you *have* to use the main entrance. But even if your uncle knew where it would be on the wedding day, why would he share that information? This is the man who stabbed me in the gut."

I didn't need the reminder. I saw that scene every time I closed my eyes. I also didn't have a good answer for him, but Alex intervened. "Shouldn't we get going?"

Sam nodded. "You're right. Stanley will only stay summoned for a few minutes. He prefers no more than three passengers, so I figured I would fly and carry Hearthstone. Magnus, how about you, Alex, and Blitz take our horse friend?"

Blitzen shifted uneasily in his navy three-piece suit. Maybe he was thinking how badly he and Alex would clash sitting next to each other on the horse.

It's okay, Hearthstone signed to him. *Be safe.*

"Hmph. All right." Blitz glanced at me. "But I've got dibs on the front. Is that called *shotgun* on a horse?"

Stanley whinnied and stomped. I don't think he liked *shotgun* and *horse* being used in the same sentence.

I handed Sam the Skofnung Sword. Blitzen gave her the Skofnung Stone. We figured, since they were her supposed bride-price, she should have the right to carry them. She wouldn't be able to draw the sword because of its enchantments, but at least she could brain people with the stone if the need arose.

Stanley allowed us to climb aboard—Blitzen first, Alex in the middle, and me in the back, or as I liked to think of it: *the seat from which you will fall off and die in case of rapid ascent.*

I was afraid that if I held on to Alex she might cut off my head or turn into a giant lizard and bite me or something, but she grabbed my wrists and put them around her waist. "I'm not fragile. And I'm not contagious."

"I didn't say anything—"

"Shut up."

"Shutting up."

She smelled of clay, like the pottery studio in her suite. She also had a tiny tattoo I hadn't noticed before on the nape of her neck—the curled double serpents of Loki. When I realized what I was looking at, my stomach took a preemptive drop off a cliff, but I didn't have much time to process the tattoo's significance.

Sam said, "See you in Jotunheim." She grabbed Hearthstone's arm and the two of them vanished in a flash of golden light.

Stanley wasn't quite so understated. He galloped toward Arlington Street, jumped the park fence, and charged straight toward the Taj Hotel. A moment before we would've hit the wall, Stanley went airborne. The hotel's marble facade dissolved into a bank of fog and Stanley did a three-sixty barrel roll right through it, somehow managing not to lose us. His hooves touched the ground again, and we were charging through a forested ravine, mountains looming on either side.

Snow-covered pines towered above us. Gunmetal gray clouds hung low and heavy. My breath turned to steam.

I had time to think, *Hey, we're in Jotunheim,* before Blitzen yelled, "Duck!"

The next millisecond demonstrated how much faster I could think than react. First I thought Blitz had spotted an actual duck. Blitzen likes ducks. Then I realized he was telling me to get down, which is hard to do when you're the last in a line of three people on horseback.

Then I saw the large tree branch hanging directly in our path. I realized Stanley was going to run right under it at full speed. Even if the branch had been properly labeled low clearance, Stanley couldn't read.

SMACK!

I found myself flat on my back in the snow. Above me, pine branches swayed in fuzzy Technicolor. My teeth ached.

I managed to sit up. My vision cleared, and I spotted Alex a few feet away, curled up and groaning in a pile of pine needles. Blitzen staggered around looking for his pith helmet.

Fortunately, Jotunheim light wasn't strong enough to petrify dwarves or he would've already turned to stone.

As for our intrepid ride, Stanley, he was gone. A trail of hoofprints continued under the tree branch and into the woods as far as I could see. Maybe he'd reached the end of his summoning time and vanished. Or maybe he'd gotten caught up in the joy of running and wouldn't realize he'd left us behind for another twenty miles.

Blitzen snatched his pith helmet out of the snow. "Stupid horse. That was rude!"

I helped Alex to her feet. A nasty-looking cut zigzagged across her forehead like a squiggly red mouth.

"You're bleeding," I said. "I can fix that."

She swatted away my hand. "I'm fine, Dr. House, but thanks for the diagnosis." She turned unsteadily, scanning the forest. "Where are we?"

"More importantly," Blitz said, "where are the others?"

Sam and Hearthstone were nowhere to be seen. I only hoped Sam was better at avoiding obstacles than Stanley was.

I scowled at the tree branch we'd run into. I wondered if I could get Jack to chop it down before the next group of poor schmucks rode through here. But there was something strange about its texture. Instead of the usual bark pattern, it consisted of crosshatched gray fiber. It didn't taper to a point, but instead curved down to the ground, where it snaked across the snow. Not a branch, then . . . more like a huge cable. The top of the cable wound into the trees and disappeared into the clouds.

"What is this thing?" I asked. "It's not a tree."

To our left, a dark, looming shape I'd taken for a mountain

shifted and rumbled. I realized with bladder-twisting certainty that it wasn't a mountain. The largest giant I'd ever seen was sitting next to us.

"No, indeed!" his voice boomed. "That's my shoestring!"

How could I not notice a giant that big? Well, if you didn't know what you were looking at, he was simply too large to understand. His hiking boots were foothills. His bent knees were mountain peaks. His dark gray bowling shirt blended in with the sky, and his fluffy white beard looked like a bank of snow clouds. Even sitting down, the giant's gleaming eyes were so far up they could have been blimps or moons.

"Hello, little ones!" The giant's voice was deep enough to liquefy soft substances—like my eyeballs, for instance. "You should watch where you are going!"

He tucked in his right foot. The tree branch/shoelace we'd smacked into slithered through the pines, uprooting bushes, snapping branches, and scattering terrified woodland creatures. A twelve-point buck leaped out of nowhere and almost ran over Blitzen.

The giant leaned over, blocking out the gray light. He tied his shoe, humming as he worked, looping one massive cable over the other, the laces flailing and laying waste to whole swaths of forest.

Once the giant had done a proper double knot, the earth stopped shaking.

Alex yelled, "Who are you? And why haven't you ever heard of Velcro straps?"

I'm not sure where she found the courage to speak. Maybe it was her head injury talking. Me, I was trying to decide if Jack had the power to kill a giant this big. Even if Jack managed to fly up the giant's nose, I doubted his blade would do much more than cause a sneeze. And we didn't want that.

The giant straightened and laughed. I wondered if his ears popped when he got that high in the stratosphere. "Hoo-hoo! The green-haired gnat is feisty! My name is Tiny!"

Now that I looked, I could see the name TINY embroidered on his bowling shirt like the distant letters of the Hollywood sign.

"Tiny," I said.

I didn't think he could possibly hear me any more than I could hear ants having an argument, but he grinned and nodded. "Yes, puny one. The other giants like to tease me, because, compared to most at Utgard-Loki's palace, I am small."

Blitzen dusted twigs from his blue jacket. "It's got to be an illusion," he muttered to us. "He can't really be that big."

Alex touched her bloody forehead. "*This* isn't an illusion. That shoelace felt plenty real."

The giant stretched. "Well, it's a good thing you woke me from my nap. I suppose I should get going!"

"Hold on," I yelled. "You said you were from Utgard-Loki's palace?"

"Hmm? Oh, yes. Utgard Lanes! Would you be heading that way?"

"Uh, yeah!" I said. "We need to see the king!"

I was hoping Tiny might scoop us up and give us a ride. That seemed like the proper thing to do for travelers who'd just had a hit-and-run with your shoestring.

Tiny chuckled. "I don't know how you'd fare at Utgard Lanes. We're a little busy getting ready for the bowling tournament tomorrow. If you can't even navigate around our shoestrings, you might get accidentally crushed."

"We'll do fine!" Alex said—again, with a lot more confidence than I could've mustered. "Where is the palace?"

"Just over yonder." Tiny waved to his left, causing a new low-pressure front. "Easy two-minute walk."

I tried to translate that from Giantese. I figured that meant the palace was about seven billion miles away.

"You couldn't give us a lift, maybe?" I tried not to sound too pitiful.

"Well, now," Tiny said, "I don't really owe you any favors, do I? You'd have to make it over the threshold of the fortress to claim guest privileges. *Then* we'll have to treat you right."

"Here we go," Blitzen grumbled.

I remembered how guest rights worked from our last time in Jotunheim. If you made it inside the house and claimed you were a guest, supposedly the host couldn't kill you. Of course, when we'd tried that before, we ended up slaughtering an entire giant family after they attempted to squash us like bugs, but it had all been done with the utmost courtesy.

"Besides," Tiny continued, "if you can't make it to Utgard Lanes yourself, you really shouldn't be there! Most giants are not as easygoing as I am. You need to be careful, little ones. My larger kin might take you for trespassers or termites or something! Really, I would stay away."

I had a terrible vision of Sam and Hearthstone flying into the bowling alley and getting caught in the world's largest bug zapper.

"We have to get there!" I shouted. "We're meeting two friends."

"Hmm." Tiny raised his forearm, revealing a Mount Rushmore–size tattoo of Elvis Presley. The giant scratched his beard, and a single white whisker twirled down like an Apache helicopter and crashed nearby, sending up a mushroom cloud of snow. "Tell you what, then. You carry my bowling bag. That way everyone will know you're a friend. Do me this small service, and I'll vouch for you with Utgard-Loki. Try to keep up! But if you do fall behind, make sure you reach the castle by tomorrow morning. That's when the tournament begins!"

He got to his feet and turned to leave. I had time to admire his scraggly gray man bun and read the giant yellow words embroidered across the back of his shirt: TINY'S TURKEY BOWLERS. I wondered if that was the name of his team or maybe his business. I pictured turkeys the size of cathedrals, and I knew they would be haunting my nightmares forever.

Then, in two steps, Tiny disappeared over the horizon.

I looked at my friends. "What did we just get ourselves into?"

"Well, good news," Blitzen said. "I found the bag. Bad news . . . I found the bag."

He pointed to a nearby mountain: a sheer dark cliff that rose five hundred feet to a wide plateau at the summit. But of course it wasn't a mountain. It was a brown leather bowling bag.

THIRTY-SIX

Solving Problems
with Extreme Fashion

AT THIS POINT, most people would have thrown themselves down on the ground and given up hope. And by most people, I mean me.

I sat in the snow and stared up at the towering cliffs of Mount Bowling Bag. TINY'S TURKEY BOWLERS was etched across the brown leather in black letters so faded they looked like random fault lines.

"There's no way," I said.

Alex's forehead had stopped bleeding, but the skin around the cut had turned as green as her hair, which wasn't a good sign. "I hate to agree with you, Maggie, but yeah. It's impossible."

"Please don't call me Maggie," I said. "Even Beantown is better than that."

Alex looked like she was mentally filing away that information for later use. "What do you want to bet there's a bowling ball in that bag? Probably weighs as much as an aircraft carrier."

"Does it matter?" I asked. "Even empty, the bag is too big to move."

Only Blitzen didn't look defeated. He paced around the foot of the bag, running his fingers across the leather, muttering to himself as if running calculations.

"It has to be an illusion," he said. "No bowling bag could be this big. No giant is that big."

"They *are* called giants," I noted. "Maybe if we had Hearthstone here he could do some rune magic, but—"

"Kid, work with me," Blitz said. "I'm trying to problem-solve. This is a fashion accessory. It's a *bag.* This is my specialty."

I wanted to argue that bowling bags were about as far from fashion as Boston was from China. I didn't see how one dwarf, no matter how talented, could solve this mountain of a problem with a few clever style choices. But I didn't want to seem negative.

"What are you thinking?" I asked.

"Well, we can't dispel the illusion outright," Blitz murmured. "We have to work with what we have, not against it. I wonder . . ."

He put his ear to the leather as if listening. Then he began to grin.

"Uh, Blitz?" I said. "You make me nervous when you smile like that."

"This bag was never finished. It has no name."

"A name," Alex said. "Like *Hi, Bag. My name is Alex. What's yours?*"

Blitzen nodded. "Exactly. Dwarves always name their creations. No item is fully crafted until it has a name."

"Yeah, but, Blitz," I said, "this is a *giant's* bag. Not a dwarf's bag."

"Ah, but it *could* be. Don't you see? I could finish crafting it."

Alex and I both stared at him.

He sighed. "Look, while I was hanging out with Hearthstone in the safe house, I got bored. I started thinking up new projects. One of them . . . well, you know Hearthstone's personal rune, right? *Perthro?*"

"The empty cup," I said. "Yeah, I remember."

"The what?" Alex asked.

I drew the rune sign in the dirt:

"It means a cup waiting to be filled," I said. "Or a person who's been hollowed out, waiting for something to make his life meaningful."

Alex frowned. "Gods, that is depressing."

"The point is," Blitz said, "I've been considering a perthro bag—a bag that can never be filled. The bag would always feel empty and light. Most importantly, it would be any size you wanted."

I looked at Mount Bowling Bag. Its side rose so high that birds wheeled against it in dismay. Or maybe they were just admiring its fine craftsmanship.

"Blitz," I said, "I like your optimism. But I have to point out that this bag is roughly the size of Nantucket."

"Yes, yes. It's not ideal. I was hoping to make a prototype first. But if I can finish the bowling bag by naming it, stitching a little stylish embroidery into the leather, and giving it a command word, I might be able to channel its magic." He patted his pockets until he found his sewing kit. "Hmm, I'll need better tools."

"Yeah," Alex said. "That leather is probably five feet thick."

"Ah," Blitz said, "but we have the best sewing needle in the world!"

"Jack," I guessed.

Blitz's eyes sparkled. I hadn't seen him this excited since he created the chain mail cummerbund.

"I'll also require some magic ingredients," he said. "You guys will have to pitch in. I'll need to weave thread from special filaments—something with power, resilience, and magical growth properties. For instance, the hair of a son of Frey!"

I felt like he'd smacked me in the face with a shoestring. "Say what now?"

Alex laughed. "I love this plan. His hair needs a good cut. Like, what *is* this, 1993?"

"Hold up now," I protested.

"Also . . ." Blitz scrutinized Alex. "The bag needs to change sizes, which means I'll need to dye the thread with the blood of a shape-shifter."

Alex's smile melted. "How much blood are we talking about?"

"Just a little."

She hesitated, maybe wondering if she should bust out her garrote and substitute the blood of a dwarf and an einherji.

Finally, she sighed and rolled up her flannel sleeve. "All right, dwarf. Let's make a magic bowling bag."

THIRTY-SEVEN

Meat S'mores Roasting on an Open Fire

NOTHING BEATS camping out in a dreary Jotunheim forest while your friend stitches runes on a giant bowling bag!

"All *day*?" Alex complained when Blitz estimated his time until completion. Granted, she was a little grumpy after being smacked down by a giant shoelace, getting cut with a knife, and having her blood drained into a thermos cap. "We're on the clock here, dwarf!"

"I know that." Blitz spoke calmly, like he was addressing a Nidavellir kindergarten class. "I also know that we're completely exposed here in the middle of giant territory and Sam and Hearth are missing, which is *killing* me. But our best chance of finding them and getting the information we need is by reaching Utgard-Loki's palace. The best way to do that without *dying* is to enchant this bag. So, unless you know a faster way, yes, it will take me all day. I may have to work through the night as well."

Alex scowled, but arguing with Blitzen's logic was as pointless as arguing with his fashion sense. "What are *we* supposed do, then?"

"Bring me meals and water," Blitz said. "Keep watch, especially at night, so I don't get eaten by trolls. Cross your fingers that Sam and Hearth show up in the meantime. And Magnus, let me borrow your sword."

I summoned Jack, who was happy to help.

"Oh, sewing?" His blade runes glowed with excitement. "This reminds me of the Great Icelandic Sew-Off of 886 C.E.! Frey and I *destroyed* the competition. A lot of warriors went home weeping, we shamed their stitching and darning skills so bad."

I decided not to ask. The less I knew about my father's sewing victories, the better.

While Jack and Blitz talked strategy, Alex and I made camp. She'd brought supplies, too, so in no time we had set up a nice level spot with a couple of pup tents and a stone-ringed fire pit.

"You must have camped a lot," I noted.

She shrugged, arranging twigs for kindling. "I love the outdoors. Me and some kids at my pottery studio in Brookline Village, we used to go up to the mountains just to get away."

She packed a lot of emotion in those last two words: *get away.*

"A pottery studio?" I asked.

She scowled as if trying to detect sarcasm. Maybe she'd fielded dumb questions from people, like: *Oh, you make pottery? How cute! I used to like Play-Doh when I was young!*

"The studio was the only consistent place for me," she said. "They let me crash there when things were bad at home."

From her pack, she dug out a box of wooden matches. Her fingers seemed to fumble when she took a few sticks from the box. The cut on her forehead had turned a darker shade of green, but she still refused to let me heal it.

"The thing about clay," she said, "it can turn into any shape. I get to decide what's best for each piece. I just sort of . . . listen to what the clay wants. I know that sounds stupid."

"You're saying this to a guy with a talking sword."

She snorted. "I suppose, but . . ." The matches fell out of her hand. She sat down hard, her face suddenly chalky.

"Whoa." I scooted over to her. "You're going to *have* to let me heal that head wound. Gods only know what kind of bacteria was on Tiny's shoestring, and you donating blood to Blitz's arts and crafts project didn't help."

"No, I don't want—" She faltered. "There's a first aid kit in my bag. I'll just—"

"A first aid kit isn't going to do it. What were you about to say?"

Alex touched her forehead and winced. "Nothing."

"You said 'I don't want—' "

"This!" she snapped. "You nosing around in my business! Samirah told me that when you heal people—like the elf, Hearthstone—you get inside their heads, you see stuff. I don't want that!"

I looked away, my hands turning numb. In the fire pit, Alex's kindling pyramid fell apart. Her matches had scattered in a rune-like pattern, but if it meant anything, I couldn't read it.

I thought about something Halfborn Gunderson had once told me about wolf packs: each wolf pushes the limits within its pack. They are constantly testing where they stand in the hierarchy—where they can sleep, how much they can eat of a fresh kill. They continue to push until the alpha wolf snaps at them and reminds them of their place. I hadn't realized I was pushing, but I'd just gotten a first-rate alpha-snapping.

"I . . . don't really control what happens when I heal." I was surprised that my voice still worked. "With Hearth, I had to use a lot of power. He was almost dead. I don't think I could read much from you while just fixing an infected cut. I'll try not to, anyway. But if you don't get some healing . . ."

She stared at the bandage on the spot where Blitzen had taken blood from her arm.

"Yeah. Yeah, okay. Just . . . forehead only. Nothing *inside* the head."

I touched her brow. She was burning up with fever. I summoned the power of Frey, and Alex let out a gasp. Instantly, her wound closed. Her skin cooled. Her color returned to normal.

My hands were hardly glowing at all. Something about being out in the wilderness, surrounded by nature, seemed to make the healing easier.

"I didn't learn a thing," I promised Alex. "You are still a mystery wrapped in a question mark wrapped in flannel."

She exhaled, making a sound between a laugh and a sigh of relief. "Thanks, Magnus. Now maybe we can actually get this fire started?"

She didn't call me Maggie or Beantown. I chose to take that as a peace offering.

Once we had a good blaze going, we tried to figure out the best way to repurpose Fadlan's Falafel over an open flame. We learned an important lesson: one cannot make s'mores out of lamb meat and chickpea patties. Mostly we ate the chocolate from Uncle Randolph's house.

Blitz took the better part of the morning spinning his magic thread on his collapsible travel spindle. (Of course he had one of those in his kit bag. Why wouldn't he?) Meanwhile, Jack flew up and down the side of the bowling bag, perforating the pattern Blitz wanted him to sew.

Alex and I kept watch, but nothing much happened. Sam and Hearthstone didn't appear. No giants eclipsed the sun or destroyed the forest with their untied shoelaces. The most dangerous thing we spotted was a red squirrel in a branch above our campfire. It probably wasn't a threat, but since meeting Ratatosk I took no chances. I kept an eye on it until it leaped to another tree.

In the afternoon, things got more exciting. After we fed Blitz some lunch, he and Jack got to work on the actual stitching. Somehow—uh, perhaps *with magic?*—Blitz had made a whole pile of shimmering red yarn from my hair, Alex Fierro's blood, and threads from his own vest. Blitz tied one end of it to Jack's pommel, and Jack flew back and forth across the side of the bag, diving in and out of the leather like a dolphin, leaving a shimmering trail of stitches. Watching him reminded me of how we'd tied up Fenris Wolf . . . which was a memory I didn't really care to have.

Blitzen called out directions. "Your left, Jack! Drop that stitch! Okay, give me a backstitch! Bunny-punch me a hole on the end there!"

Alex nibbled her chocolate bar. "Bunny-punch?"

"I have no idea," I admitted.

Maybe inspired by the sewing display, Alex unthreaded her garrote from her belt loops. She ran the metal wire across the soles of her boots, scraping off icy mud.

"Why that weapon?" I asked. "Or you can just tell me to shut up again."

Alex gave me a sideways smile. "You're fine. It started out as my clay-cutter."

"Clay-cutter. Like the wire you run through a slab of clay."

"You figured that out all on your own?"

"Ha, ha. I'm guessing most clay-cutters don't have combat applications?"

"Not so much. My m—" She hesitated. "Loki visited me one day at the studio. He was trying to impress me, show me how much he could do for me. He taught me an enchantment I could use to make a magical weapon. I didn't want to give him the satisfaction of helping me. So I tried his spell on the stupidest, most innocuous thing I could think of. I didn't figure a wire with dowel handles could ever be a weapon."

"And yet . . ."

Alex pointed to a nearby boulder—a rough chunk of granite about the size of a piano. She lashed out with her garrote, holding one end like a whip. The wire lengthened as it flew. The far end wrapped around the boulder and held fast. Alex yanked it toward her. The top half of the boulder slid off the bottom half with a grinding sound like a lid being removed from a porcelain cookie jar.

The wire flew back to Alex's hand.

"Pretty good." I tried not to let my eyes pop out of their sockets. "But does it make french fries?"

Alex muttered something about stupid boys, which I'm sure had nothing to do with me.

The afternoon light faded quickly. Over at the bowling bag, Blitz and Jack kept working on their entry in the Great Jotunheim Sew-Off. The shadows got longer. The temperature plunged. I noticed this because Blitz had recently given me a drastic haircut and my exposed neck was cold. I was just grateful there were no mirrors around to show me the horrors Blitz had worked upon my head.

Alex threw another tree branch into the fire. "You might as well ask."

I stirred. "Sorry?"

"You want to ask me about Loki," Alex prompted. "Why I put his symbol on my pottery, why I have a tattoo. You want to know if I'm working for him."

Those questions *had* been lurking in the back of my mind, but I didn't understand how Alex could know that. I wondered if my healing touch had backfired somehow. Maybe I'd given Alex a look inside *my* head.

"I guess it worries me," I admitted. "You act as if you don't like Loki—"

"I don't."

"Then why his symbol?"

Alex cupped her hands around the back of her neck. "That design, the two entwined snakes? It's usually called the Urnes snakes, named after some place in Norway. Anyway, it's not necessarily a symbol of Loki." She laced her fingers and wiggled them around. "The snakes signify change and flexibility. Being versatile. People started using the snakes to represent Loki, and Loki was fine with that. But I decided . . . why does Loki get to take over that cool symbol? I like it. I'm making it mine. He doesn't get to own the symbol for change any more than he owns me. To Helheim with what people think."

I watched the flames break down another piece of wood; a swarm of orange sparks rose from the pit. I remembered my dream of Alex's suite, Loki turning into a woman with red hair. I thought about the hesitation in Alex's voice when she talked about Loki as her parent.

"You're like the eight-legged horse," I realized.

Alex frowned. "Stanley?"

"No, the *original* eight-legged horse. What's his name? Sleipnir. Mallory Keen told me the story, something about Loki turning into a beautiful mare so he could lure a giant's stallion away. And then . . . Loki got pregnant. He—*she* gave birth to Sleipnir." I glanced at Alex, very aware of the garrote now lying across her thigh. "Loki's not your father, is he? He's your mom."

Alex just stared at me.

I thought, *Well, here comes the wire. Good-bye, limbs! Good-bye, head!*

She surprised me with a sour laugh. "I think that haircut improved your brainpower."

I resisted the urge to pat my hacked locks. "So I'm right?"

"Yes." She tugged at her glittery pink bootlaces. "I wish I could've seen the look on my dad's face when he found out. From what I gather, Loki shape-shifted into the sort of woman my dad liked. My dad was already married, but that never stopped him. He was used to getting what he wanted. He had an affair with this voluptuous redhead. Nine months later, Loki showed up at my dad's doorstep with a little baby as a present."

I tried to imagine Loki in his usual dashing form, maybe wearing a green tuxedo, ringing the doorbell of some upscale house in the suburbs. *Hi, I was that lady you had a fling with. Here's our kid.*

"How did your mortal mom react?" I asked. "I mean, your dad's wife . . . I mean, your stepmother . . ."

"It's confusing, huh?" Alex tossed another stick into the fire. "My stepmom wasn't happy about it. I grew up with *two* parents who resented me and found me embarrassing. Then there was Loki, who kept showing up at random times, trying to *parent* me."

"Man," I said.

"*Woman*, today," Alex corrected.

"No, I mean . . ." I stopped, realizing she was teasing me. "What happened? When did you finally leave home?"

"Two years ago, more or less. As for what happened? A lot."

This time I recognized the warning tone in her voice. I was not welcome to ask for more details.

Still . . . Alex had become homeless around the same time my mom died, the same time I'd ended up on the streets. That coincidence didn't sit well with me.

Before I could chicken out, I blurted, "Did Loki ask you to come with us?"

She locked eyes with me. "What do you mean?"

I told her about my dream: her throwing pots at her father (mother), Loki saying: *It's such a simple request.*

It was fully dark now, though I wasn't sure when that had happened. In the firelight, Alex's face seemed to shift and jump. I tried to tell myself it wasn't the Loki part of her revealing itself. It was just change, flexibility. Those twisting snakes on her neck were completely innocent.

"You've got it wrong," Alex said. "He told me *not* to come."

A strange pulsing sound filled in my ears. I realized it was my own heartbeat. "Why would Loki tell you that? And . . . what were you and Sam talking about last night—some plan?"

She curled her garrote around her hands. "Maybe you'll find out, Magnus. And by the way, if you ever spy on me in your dreams again—"

"Guys!" Blitzen yelled from Mount Bowling Bag. "Come take a look!"

THIRTY-EIGHT

You Will Never, Ever
Guess Blitzen's Password

JACK HOVERED proudly next to his handiwork.

Can you have handiwork if you don't have hands?

Stitched into the bag's side were several new lines of glowing red runic script.

"What does it say?" Alex asked.

"Oh, a few technical runes." Blitz's eyes crinkled with satisfaction. "Magic nuts and bolts, terms and conditions, the end-user agreement. But there at the bottom, it says: 'EMPTYLEATHER, a bag completed by Blitzen, son of Freya. Jack helped.'"

"I wrote that!" Jack said proudly. "I helped!"

"Good job, buddy," I said. "So . . . does it work?"

"We're about to find out!" Blitzen rubbed his hands eagerly. "I'm going to speak the secret word of command. Then this bag will either shrink to an easy carrying size, or—well, I'm sure it will shrink."

"Rewind to the *or*," Alex said. "What *else* might happen?"

Blitzen shrugged. "Well . . . there's a slight chance the bag could expand and cover most of this continent. No, no. I'm sure I got it right. Jack was very careful about backstitching the runes where I told him to."

"I was supposed to backstitch?" Jack glowed yellow. "Just kidding. Yeah, I backstitched."

I wasn't feeling so confident. On the other hand, if the bag expanded to continental size, I wouldn't live long enough to care.

"Okay," I said. "What's the password?"

"Don't!" Blitzen shrieked.

The bowling bag shuddered. The entire forest trembled. The bag collapsed so fast I got nauseated from the change in perspective. The mountain of leather was gone. Sitting at Blitzen's feet was a regular-size bowling bag.

"YES!" Blitz picked it up and peeked inside. "There's a bowling ball inside, but the bag feels completely empty. Jack, we did it!"

They gave each other a high five—or a high just-one, since Jack's blade had no fingers.

"Hold on," Alex said. "I mean . . . good job and all. But did you seriously make the password *password?*"

"DON'T!" Blitz threw the bowling bag like a grenade into the woods. Instantly it grew back to the size of a mountain, causing a tidal wave of crushed trees and terrified animals. I almost felt sorry for the untrustworthy squirrels.

"I was in a rush!" Blitzen huffed. "I can reset the p—the *word of command* later on, but that would take more thread and more time. For now, can you *please* avoid saying . . . you know, *that* word?"

He proceeded to say *that word.* The bag shrank back to small size.

"You did great, man," I said. "And hey, Jack, nice stitching."

"Thanks, *señor!* I love your sawed-off haircut, too. You don't look like that Nirvana guy anymore. More like, I dunno . . . Johnny Rotten? Or a blond Joan Jett?"

Alex cracked up. "How do you even know those people? T.J. told me you were you at the bottom of a river for a thousand years."

"I was, but I've been studying up!"

Alex snickered. "Joan Jett."

"Just shut up, both of you," I grumbled. "Who's ready to go bowling?"

No one was ready to go bowling.

Blitzen crawled into a pup tent and collapsed from exhaustion. Then I made the mistake of letting Jack return to pendant form and *I* collapsed from exhaustion, feeling like I'd spent all day climbing cliffs.

Alex promised to keep watch. At least I think that's what she said. She could have announced *I'll invite Loki into camp and kill you all in your sleep! HAHAHAHA!* and I still would've passed out.

I dreamed of nothing except dolphins happily leaping through a sea of leather.

I woke as the sky was turning from black to charcoal. I insisted Alex get a few hours of shut-eye. By the time all three of us had gotten up, eaten, and broken camp, the sky was a thick blanket of dirty gray.

Almost twenty-four hours lost. Samirah and Hearthstone were still missing. I tried to imagine them safe by the fire in Utgard-Loki's home, sharing stories and eating well. Instead, I imagined a bunch of giants by the fire, sharing stories about the tasty mortals they'd eaten the night before.

Stop that, I told my brain.

Also, the wedding is tomorrow, said my brain.

Get out of my head.

My brain refused to get out of my head. Inconsiderate brain.

We hiked through the ravine, trying to keep to the direction Tiny had indicated. You'd think we could've just followed his footprints, but it was difficult to tell them apart from the natural valleys and canyons.

After about an hour, we spotted our destination. On a massive cliff in the distance rose a boxy warehouse-type structure. The inflatable Godzilla was gone (the daily rental for something like that must have been exorbitant), but the neon sign still blazed: UTGARD LANES. The letters flashed one at a time, then all together, then with sparkles around the edges— just so you didn't miss the only neon sign on the biggest cliff in Jotunheim.

We trudged up a winding trail that was perfect for colossal donkeys, but not so much for small mortals. The cold wind pushed us around. My feet ached. Thank goodness for Blitzen's magic bowling bag, because dragging the full-size version up that cliff would have been impossible and also not fun.

Once we reached the top, I realized just how big Utgard Lanes really was. The building itself could have housed most of downtown Boston. The maroon upholstered double doors were studded with brass tacks each as big as your average three-bedroom house. In the grimy windows glowed neon ads for Jotun Juice, Big Small Ale, and Mega Mead. Tethered to posts outside were colossal riding animals: horses, rams, yaks, and, yes, donkeys—each roughly the size of Kilimanjaro.

"No need to fear," Blitz muttered to himself. "It's just like a dwarven bar. Only . . . bigger."

"So how do we do this?" Alex asked. "Direct frontal assault?"

"Ha, ha," I said. "Sam and Hearth might be in there, so we play by the rules. Walk in. Ask for guest rights. Try to negotiate."

"And when that doesn't work," Blitz said, "we improvise."

Alex, being all about change and versatility, said, "I hate this idea." Then she frowned at me. "Also, you owe me a drink for dreaming about me."

She marched toward the entrance.

Blitzen raised his eyebrows. "Do I want to ask?"

"No," I said. "You really don't."

Getting past the front doors was no problem. We walked right under them without even having to crouch.

Inside was the largest, most crowded bowling alley I'd ever seen.

To the left, twenty or thirty Statue-of-Liberty-size giants lined the bar, sitting on stools that would have made fine high-rise condominiums. The giants were dressed in neon-colored bowling shirts they must have stolen from a disco-era Salvation Army. Around their waists hung an assortment of knives, axes, and spiked clubs. They laughed and insulted each other and threw back mugs of mead that each could have watered all the crops in California for a year.

It seemed a little early in the morning for mead, but for all I knew these guys had been partying since 1999. That was the song blasting from the overhead speakers, anyway.

To our right stood an arcade where more giants played pinball and *Ms. Very Large Pac-Man*. In the back of the room,

about as far away as, oh, Boston is from New Hampshire, still
more giants gathered at the bowling lanes in groups of four or
five with matching Day-Glo outfits and suede bowling shoes. A
banner across the back wall read: UTGARD BOWLING ULTIMATE
TOURNAMENT! WELCOME, U.B.U.T. CONTESTANTS!!

One of the giants threw a ball. Thunder boomed as it
rolled down the lane. The floor vibrated, shaking me up and
down like a wind-up hoppy toy.

I scanned the place for Tiny in his gray Turkey Bowler
shirt. I couldn't spot him. Tiny should have been easy to see,
but from our vantage point on the floor, there were just too
many other enormous obstacles in the way.

Then the crowd shifted. Across the room, looking right
at me, was a giant I wanted to see even less than Tiny. He
sat in a tall leather chair on a dais overlooking the lanes like
he was the referee or the MC. His bowling shirt was made of
eagle feathers. His slacks were brown polyester. His iron-shod
boots looked like they'd been made from recycled World War
II destroyers. Clasped around his forearm was a thane's gold
ring studded with bloodstones.

His face was angular and handsome in a cruel sort of way.
Straight coal-black hair swept his shoulders. His eyes glittered
with amusement and malice. He definitely would've made the
list for *10 Most Attractive Murderers of Jotunheim*. He was about
ninety feet taller than the last time I'd seen him, but I recognized him.

"Big Boy," I said.

I'm not sure how he heard my pipsqueak voice through all
the chaos, but he nodded in acknowledgment.

"Magnus Chase!" he called out. "So glad you could make it!"

The music died. At the bar, giants turned to look at us. Big Boy raised his fist as if offering me a microphone. Clasped in his fingers like G.I. Joe figures were Samirah and Hearthstone.

THIRTY-NINE

Elvis Has Left the Bowling Bag

"WE CLAIM guest rights!" I yelled. "Utgard-Loki, let our friends go!"

I thought that was pretty brave of me, considering we were facing a heavily armed, badly-dressed Statue of Liberty convention.

The assembled giants laughed.

At the bar, one yelled, "What did you say? Speak up!"

"I said—"

The bartender turned "1999" back on and drowned me out. The giants howled with glee.

I frowned at Blitzen. "You told me Taylor Swift's songs were dwarf music . . . does this mean that Prince was a giant?"

"Eh?" Blitzen kept his eyes locked on Hearthstone, who was still trapped and struggling in Utgard-Loki's fist. "No, kid. This just means that giants have good taste in music. You think Jack could cut our friends out of the giant's hand?"

"Before Utgard-Loki crushes them? Unlikely."

Alex wrapped her garrote around her hand, though I didn't see what good it would do unless she intended to give the giants a good flossing. "What's the plan?"

"I'm working on it."

Finally, Utgard-Loki made a *cut it* gesture with his finger across his throat. (Not my favorite gesture.) The music shut off again. The giants settled down.

"Magnus Chase, we've been expecting you!" Utgard-Loki grinned. "As for your friends, they're not captives. I was merely lifting them up so they could see that you've arrived! I'm sure they are delighted!"

Sam did not look delighted. She twisted her shoulders, trying to break free. Her expression suggested she wanted to kill everyone wearing a bowling shirt and perhaps several people who were not.

As for Hearth, I knew how much he hated having his hands pinned down. He couldn't communicate, couldn't do magic. The cold fury in his eyes reminded me of his father, Mr. Alderman, and that was not a similarity I enjoyed seeing.

"Put them down now," I said, "if they're really not captives."

"As you wish!" Utgard-Loki set Sam and Hearth on the table, where they stood about as tall as the giant's mead cup. "We've made them quite comfortable while we waited for you to arrive. Tiny mentioned that you would bring his bowling bag no later than this morning. I was beginning to think you wouldn't make it!"

The way he phrased that made it seem like this was a hostage exchange. A cold heavy feeling settled in my gut. I wondered what would've happened to Sam and Hearth if we'd failed to show up with the bag. We'd kept them waiting, trapped here for twenty-four hours, probably wondering if we were even still alive.

"We've got the bag!" I said. "No worries."

I nudged Blitzen.

"Right!" Blitz stepped forward and raised his creation.

"Behold Emptyleather, soon to be famous among bowling bags, completed by Blitzen of Freya! And Jack helped!"

Our old friend Tiny muscled his way through the crowd. Mead stains speckled his gray shirt. His grizzled man bun had unraveled. Just like he'd warned us, compared to the other giants in the room, he actually *did* look tiny.

"What'd you do to my bag?" he cried. "Did you wash it on regular cycle? It's minuscule!"

"Like you!" another giant catcalled.

"Shut up, Hugo!" Tiny yelled.

"Not to fear!" Blitzen promised, his voice demonstrating what fear sounded like. "I can return the bag to its normal size! But first, I want assurances from your king that we have guest rights—the three of us, and our two friends on the table."

Utgard-Loki chuckled. "Well, Tiny, it seems like they did what you asked. They brought your bag."

Tiny gestured helplessly to his new extra-small carry case. "But . . ."

"Tiny . . ." the king said, his tone hardening.

Tiny glared at us. He did not look quite so easygoing now.

"Yes," he said through gritted teeth. "They have kept their part of their bargain. I vouch for them . . . in a very, very *small* way."

"There you have it!" Utgard-Loki beamed. "You are all officially guests in my bowling alley!" He plucked up Sam and Hearth and set them on the floor. Thankfully, the Skofnung Sword and Stone were still strapped across Sam's back.

The king turned to address the assembled giants. "My friends, if we entertain these guests in our present size, we'll get eye-strain trying to avoid stepping on them. We'll have to serve them food with tweezers and fill their teeny drinking glasses with eyedroppers. That's no fun! Let's take this party down a few notches, eh?"

The giants grumbled and muttered, but nobody seemed anxious to contradict the king. Utgard-Loki snapped his fingers. The room spun. My stomach churned from disorientation.

The bowling alley shrank from colossal to merely huge. The giants now averaged about seven feet tall. I could look at them without craning my neck or peering up their cavernous nostrils.

Samirah and Hearthstone hurried over to join us.

You okay? Blitz signed to Hearth.

Where were you? Hearth asked.

Samirah gave me a pained I-will-kill-you-later smile. "I thought you were dead. Also, what happened to your hair?"

"Long story," I told her.

"Yeah, sorry we're late," Alex said. Her apology surprised me more than anything so far today. "What did we miss?"

Sam stared at her like, *If I told you, you wouldn't believe me.*

I couldn't imagine that her story was any weirder than ours, but before we could compare notes, Tiny stumbled toward Blitzen. The giant grabbed his bowling bag, which was now just about the right size for him.

He zipped it open and breathed a sigh of relief. "Thank goodness! Elvis!"

He pulled out his bowling ball and examined it for damage. Airbrushed across the surface was a 1970s Elvis Presley in his white rhinestone jumpsuit. "Oh, did they hurt you, baby?" Tiny kissed the ball and hugged it to his chest. He scowled at Blitzen. "You're lucky you didn't harm Elvis, little dwarf."

"I have no interest in harming Elvis." Blitzen swiped the now-empty bag out of Tiny's hands. "But I'm keeping Emptyleather for insurance! You can have it back when we leave here unharmed. If you try anything, I should warn you, the bag only changes sizes with the word of command, and you'll never guess it on your own!"

"*What?*" Tiny shrieked. "Is it *Presley?*"

"No."

"Is it *Graceland?*"

"No."

"Friends, friends!" Utgard-Loki walked toward us with his arms extended. "This is tournament day! We have special guests! Let's not quibble. Let us feast and compete! Start the music! Drinks for everyone!"

"Little Red Corvette" blasted over the speakers. Most of the giants dispersed, going back to their mead-swilling or their bowling or their *Ms. Not-Quite-So-Large Pac-Man*. Some of the jotuns—especially those in gray shirts like Tiny's—looked like they wanted to kill us, guest rights or no, but I took comfort in knowing we had a doomsday option. If worse came to worst, we could always shout *password* and destroy the entire building in an avalanche of fine dwarven-embroidered leather.

Utgard-Loki patted Tiny on the back. "That's right! Go have a Jotun Juice!"

Tiny cradled Elvis and headed for the bar, glowering at us over his shoulder.

"Utgard-Loki," I said, "we need information—"

"Not now, you idiot." He maintained his grin, but his tone was a desperate snarl. "Look happy. Look like we're just joking around."

"What?"

"Good one!" shouted the giant king. "Ha, ha, ha!"

My friends tried to get into the act. "Yeah, ha, ha!" Sam said. Blitzen let out a good dwarvish belly laugh. "Hilarious!" Alex volunteered.

H-A, H-A, Hearth signed.

Utgard-Loki kept smiling at me, but his eyes were as sharp as daggers. "No giant here wants to help you except me," he said under his breath. "If you don't prove yourself worthy, you'll never leave this bowling alley alive."

"What?" Blitzen hissed. "You promised guest rights. You're the king!"

"And I've used every last bit of my influence and credibility trying to help you! Otherwise you wouldn't have made it this far alive!"

"*Help* us?" I said. "By killing our goat?"

"And infiltrating Valhalla?" Sam added. "And possessing an innocent flight instructor?"

"All to dissuade you bungling mortals from falling into Loki's trap. Which, so far, you've managed to do *anyway*." He turned his head and shouted for the onlookers, "Well boasted, little mortal! But you will never beat the giants!"

He lowered his voice again. "Not everyone here thinks Loki *needs* to be stopped. I'll tell you what you need to know to thwart him, but you'll have to play along. If you don't prove your worth and earn the respect of my followers, I'll be ousted and one of these morons will become the new king. Then we're *all* dead."

Alex scanned the crowd as if trying to decide which moron to garrote first. "Look, Your Feathery Majesty, you could've

just sent us this important information in a text or a phone
call days ago. Why all the cloak-and-dagger and the inflatable
Godzilla?"

Utgard-Loki wrinkled his nose at her. "I could not *text* you,
child of Loki, for several reasons. First and foremost, because
your father has ways of finding things out. Wouldn't you
agree?"

Alex's face mottled red, but she said nothing.

"Now," the king continued, "join the feast. I'll show you to
your table."

"And after that?" I asked. "How do we prove our worth?"

Utgard-Loki's eyes gleamed in a way I definitely didn't like.
"You entertain us with impressive feats. You best us in competition. Or you die trying."

FORTY

Little Billy Totally Deserved It

THE BOWLING alley breakfast of champions: peanuts, luke-warm hot dogs, and stale corn chips drizzled in orange goop that bore no resemblance to cheese. The mead was flat and tasted of Sweet'N Low. On the bright side, the portions were giant-size. I hadn't eaten much since yesterday except for left-over falafel and chocolate. I courageously managed to eat.

At each bowling lane, giants sat grouped by team—throwing food, cracking jokes, and boasting about their pin-destroying prowess.

Sam, Hearthstone, Blitz, Alex, and I sat together on a wraparound plastic bench, picking through our food for the most edible bits and nervously surveying the crowd.

Utgard-Loki had insisted we trade our regular footwear for bowling shoes—all of which were too big and Day-Glo orange and pink. When Blitzen saw his, I thought he was going to go into anaphylactic shock. Alex, however, seemed to like them. At least we didn't have to wear matching team shirts.

While we ate, we told Sam and Hearth what had happened to us in the woods.

Sam shook her head in disgust. "Magnus, you always get the easy stuff."

I almost choked on a peanut. "Easy?"

"Hearth and I have been here for a day trying to stay alive. We've almost died six times."

Hearth held up seven fingers.

"Oh, right," Sam said. "The thing with the toilets."

Blitzen tucked his feet under the bench, no doubt to avoid looking at his hideous shoes. "Didn't the giants give you guest rights?"

"That was the first thing we asked for," Sam said. "But these mountain jotuns . . . they'll try to twist your words and kill you with kindness."

"Like those sisters we met in January," I said. "The ones who offered to raise our seat to table height and then tried to smash us against the ceiling in it."

Sam nodded. "Yesterday I asked for a drink? The bartender dropped me in a full beer mug. First, I'm Muslim. I don't drink alcohol. Second, the sides were so slippery I couldn't get out. If Hearth hadn't cracked the glass with a rune . . ."

Had to watch everything we said, Hearth signed. *I asked for a place to sleep . . .* He shuddered. *Almost mangled to death in ball-return machine.*

Sam translated for Alex's sake.

"Ouch." Alex winced. "No wonder you guys look so bad. No offense."

"That's not the worst of it," Sam said. "Trying to do my prayers with Hearthstone keeping guard? Impossible. And the giants kept challenging us to rigged feats of skill."

Illusions, Hearthstone signed, circling his palms at us simultaneously to represent two shifting images. *Nothing here is what it seems.*

"Yep." Blitz nodded gravely. "Same with Tiny and his bowling bag. Utgard-Loki and his people are infamous for their powers of illusion."

I glanced around, wondering how big the giants actually were and what they looked like without magic. Maybe the hideous bowling outfits were mirages meant to disorient us. "So how do you know what's an illusion and what's real?"

"Most importantly . . ." Alex held up a tortilla chip soggy with orange goo. "Can I pretend this is really a burrito from Anna's Taqueria?"

"We have to stay sharp," Sam warned. "Last night, after we phrased the request very carefully, they finally gave us sleeping bags, but we had to 'prove our strength' by spreading them out ourselves. We tried for about an hour. The bags wouldn't budge. Utgard-Loki finally admitted they were made from curled shavings of titanium. The giants had a good laugh about that."

I shook my head. "How is that even funny?"

Hearth signed: *Tell about the cat.*

"Ugh," Sam agreed. "Then there was the cat. As a 'favor' before we got dinner, we were supposed to pick up Utgard-Loki's cat and put it outside."

I glanced around, but I saw no cat.

"It's around here somewhere," Sam assured me. "Except we couldn't move it, because the cat was actually a thirteen-thousand-pound African bush elephant. We weren't even aware until the giants told us later—after we'd tried for hours and missed dinner. They *love* to humiliate their guests by making them feel weak and puny."

"It's working," Blitz muttered.

I imagined trying to pick up an elephant and not realizing it was an elephant. That was usually the sort of thing I would notice.

"How do we combat something like that?" I asked. "We're supposed to impress them in a bunch of contests? Sorry, there's not much I can do with titanium sleeping bags and African bush elephants."

Sam leaned across the table. "Whatever you think is going on, just remember it's a ruse. Think outside the box. Do something unexpected. Break the rules."

"Oh," Alex said. "You mean like every other day in my life."

"Then your experience should come in handy," Sam said. "Also, that stuff Utgard-Loki told us about trying to help? I don't believe a word—"

"Hello, guests!"

For a big guy in a feather bowling shirt, the giant king was stealthy. Utgard-Loki leaned over the railing behind our table, peering down at us, a corn dog in his hand. "We only have a minute or so. Then the games must begin."

"The games," Sam said. "Like the ones we've been playing since *yesterday?*"

Utgard-Loki's eyes matched his eagle-feather shirt. He had that bird-of-prey gaze, like he was about to swoop down and grab a rodent—or perhaps a small human—for dinner. "Now, Samirah, you have to understand. My liege men are already upset that I invited you here. You must be good sports. Provide entertainment, give us a great show, prove that you're worthy. Don't expect any kindness from me during the contests. My men will turn on me if I show any preferential treatment."

"So you're not much of a king, then," I noted.

Utgard-Loki sneered. For the benefit of his followers, he shouted, "Is that all you can you eat, puny mortals? We have toddlers who can consume more nachos!" He pointed his corndog royal scepter at me and lowered his voice. "You know very little of leading, Magnus Chase. Kingship requires the right combination of iron and mead, fear and generosity. As great as I am at wielding magic, I cannot simply *force* my will upon my giants. They will always outnumber me. I must earn their respect every day. Now *you* must as well."

Alex leaned away from the king. "If it's so dangerous for you, why would you help us get back Mjolnir?"

"I care nothing about Thor's hammer one way or the other! The Aesir have always relied too much on the fear it inspires. It is a mighty weapon, yes, but when Ragnarok comes, Thor will be outnumbered. The gods will die anyway. The hammer is a bluff, an illusion of overwhelming force. And believe a master sorcerer"—the giant grinned—"even the best illusions have their limits. What I care about is not the hammer. I want to stop Loki's plan."

Blitzen scratched his beard. "To marry Sam and Thrym? You fear that alliance?"

Utgard-Loki went into acting mode again, shouting for his audience: "Bah! These are the mightiest corn dogs in Jotunheim! None are their equal!" He took a savage bite, then threw the empty stick over his shoulder. "Blitzen, son of Freya, use your head. Of course I fear an alliance. That ugly toad Thrym and his sister, Thrynga, would love to lead Jotunheim into war. With a marriage alliance to Loki *and* the hammer of Thor in his possession, Thrym would become Thane of Thanes."

Sam's eyes narrowed. " 'With Thor's hammer in his possession'? You mean, even if I went through with this wedding—which I won't—Thrym wouldn't give back Mjolnir?"

"Oh, wedding gifts will be exchanged! But perhaps not in the way you imagine." Utgard-Loki reached over and flicked the pommel of the Skofnung Sword, still slung across Sam's back. "Come, come, my friends. Before I can give you a solution, you must understand the problem. Do you truly not see Loki's goal?"

From across the room, one of the giants bellowed, "Our king, what of the contests? Why are you flirting with those mortals?"

More giants laughed and wolf-whistled at us.

Utgard-Loki stood tall, grinning at his subjects as if this was all good fun. "Yes, of course! Ladies and jotunmen, let us begin the entertainment!" He leered down at us. "Honored guests, with what amazing skills will you impress us?"

All the giants turned toward us, obviously anxious to hear what manner of embarrassing failure we would choose. My chief talents were running away and eating falafel, but after a heavy meal of hot dogs and chemically engineered nachos, I doubted I could win a gold medal in either of those categories.

"Don't be shy!" Utgard-Loki spread his arms. "Who wants to go first? We want to see what you champions of the mortal realms can do! Will you outdrink us? Outrace us? Outwrestle us?"

Samirah stood. I said a silent prayer of thanks for fearless Valkyries. Even when I was a regular mortal student, I hated going first. The teacher always promised to go easier on the first volunteer or give extra credit. No thanks. It wasn't worth the extra anxiety.

Sam took a deep breath and faced the crowd. "I am handy with the ax," she said. "Who would challenge me at ax-throwing?"

The giants cheered and catcalled.

"Well, now!" Utgard-Loki looked delighted. "That's a very small ax you have, Samirah al-Abbas, but I'm sure you throw it with skill. Hmm. Normally I would name Bjorn Cleaveskull as our champion ax-thrower, but I don't want you to feel *too* outmatched. How about you compete against Little Billy instead?"

From a knot of giants at the far end of the alley, a curly-haired kid giant stood. He looked about ten years old, his pudgy belly stuffed in a Where's Waldo striped shirt, yellow suspenders holding up his schoolboy knickers. He was also severely cross-eyed. As he walked toward us he kept running into tables and tripping over bowling bags, much to the amusement of the other giants.

"Billy is just learning to throw," Utgard-Loki said. "But he should be a good match for you."

Samirah clenched her jaw. "Fine. What are the targets?"

Utgard-Loki snapped his fingers. At the far end of lanes one and three, slots opened in the floor and flat wooden figures shot up, each painted with the likeness of Thor, with his wild red hair and flowing beard, and his face scrunched up the way he looked mid-fart.

"Three throws each!" Utgard-Loki announced. "Samirah, would you like to begin?"

"Oh, no," she said. "Children first."

Little Billy waddled toward the foul line. Next to him, another giant set down a leather bundle and opened it to reveal three tomahawks, each one almost as large as Billy.

Billy struggled to lift the first ax. He squinted at the distant target.

I had time to think, *Maybe Sam will be okay. Maybe Utgard-Loki is going easy on her after all.* Then Billy burst into action. He tossed one ax after another, so fast I could barely follow his movements. When he was done, one hatchet was embedded in Thor's forehead, another in his chest, and a third in the thunder god's mighty crotch.

The giants cheered.

"Not bad!" Utgard-Loki said. "Now, let us see if Samirah, pride of the Valkyries, can defeat a cross-eyed ten-year-old!"

Next to me, Alex muttered, "She's doomed."

"Do we step in?" Blitz worried. "Sam told us to think outside the box."

I remembered her advice: *Do something unexpected.*

I clasped my fingers around my pendant. I wondered if I should jump out of my seat, summon Jack, and cause a distraction by singing a duet of "Love Never Felt So Good." Hearthstone saved me from that embarrassment by raising his fingers: *Wait.*

Sam studied her opponent, Little Billy. She stared at the axes he'd planted in his target. Then she seemed to come to a conclusion. She stepped up to the foul line and raised her ax.

The room went respectfully quiet. Or maybe our hosts were just taking a deep breath so they could laugh really hard when Sam failed.

In one fluid movement, Sam turned and threw her ax right at Billy. The giants gasped.

Little Billy's eyes went even more cross-eyed as he stared at the hatchet now sprouting from his forehead. He fell backward and crashed to the floor.

The giants roared in outrage. Some rose and drew their weapons.

"Hold!" Utgard-Loki bellowed. He glared at Sam. "Explain yourself, Valkyrie! Why should we not kill you for what you just did?"

"Because," Sam said, "it was the only way to win this contest."

She sounded remarkably calm considering what she'd done, and considering the number of giants now ready to rip her apart. She pointed at the corpse of Little Billy. "This is no giant child!"

She announced it with all the authority of a TV detective, but I could see a bead of sweat trickling down from under the edge of her hijab. I could almost hear her thinking: *Please let me be right. Please let me be right.*

The crowd of giants stared at the corpse of Little Billy. He continued to look like a dead, badly-dressed giant child. I knew that at any moment the mob would charge Samirah and we'd all have to flee for our lives.

Then, slowly, the boy giant's form began to change.

His flesh withered until he looked like one of Prince Gellir's draugr. His leathery lips curled over his teeth. Yellow film covered his eyes. His fingernails lengthened into dirty scythes. Little Zombie Billy struggled to his feet and pulled the ax out of his forehead.

He hissed at Sam. A wave of pure terror swept through the room. Some giants dropped their drinks. Others fell to their knees and wept. My intestines tied themselves into a granny knot.

"Y-yes," Sam announced, her voice much smaller. "As you can see, this is not Little Billy. This is Fear, which strikes quickly and always hits its mark. The only way to conquer Fear is to attack it head-on. That's what I did. That's why I win the contest."

Fear threw down Sam's ax in disgust. With one final terrifying hiss, he dissolved into white smoke and was gone.

A collective sigh of relief spread through the room. Several giants hastened to the restrooms, probably to throw up or change their underpants.

I whispered to Blitzen, "How the heck did Sam know? How could that thing be Fear?"

Blitzen's own eyes looked a bit jaundiced. "I—I suppose she's met Fear before. I've heard rumors that the giants are on good terms with a lot of minor deities—Anger, Hunger, Disease. Supposedly, Old Age used to bowl with the Utgard Ultimates—though not well. But I never thought I'd meet Fear in person. . . ."

Alex shuddered. Hearthstone looked grim but not surprised. I wondered if he and Sam had encountered other minor deities during their twenty-four-hour ordeal.

I was glad Sam had gone first and not me. With my luck, I would've been pitted against Happiness and I would've had to whack it with my sword until it stopped smiling.

Utgard-Loki turned to Sam with a tiny glint of admiration in his eyes. "I suppose we will not kill you, then, Samirah al-Abbas, since you did what was necessary to win. This round goes to you!"

Sam's shoulders sagged with relief. "Then we have proven ourselves? The contest is over?"

"Oh, not yet!" The king's eyes widened. "What about our four other guests? We must see if they are as skilled as you!"

FORTY-ONE

When in Doubt, Turn Into a Biting Insect

I WAS STARTING to hate the Utgard Bowling Ultimate Tournament.

Hearthstone went next. He gestured to the arcade and, with me translating, challenged the giants to bring forth their highest scorer at any game of the contestants' choosing. Hugo's Jotun Jammers team nominated a guy named Kyle, who marched over to the skee-ball lane and scored a perfect thousand points. While the giants cheered, Hearthstone walked to the *Starsky and Hutch* pinball machine and put a red gold coin in the slot.

"Wait!" Hugo protested. "That's not even the same game!"

"It doesn't have to be," I said. "Hearth said 'any game of the contestants' choosing,' plural. Your guy chose skee-ball. Hearth chooses pinball."

The giants grumbled, but in the end they relented.

Blitzen grinned at me. "You're in for a treat, kid. Hearth is a wizard."

"I know that."

"No, I mean a pinball wizard."

Hearthstone fired up the first ball. I didn't see him use any magic, but he quickly destroyed Kyle's score—which, granted, wasn't fair, since pinball scores go *way* higher than a thousand points. Even after he'd passed five hundred million, Hearth kept playing. He nudged the machine and hit the flippers with such intensity I wondered if he was thinking of his father and all those coins he'd made Hearth collect for good deeds. On this machine, Hearth quickly became a make-believe billionaire.

"Enough!" Utgard-Loki yelled, pulling the plug on the machine. "You've proved your skill! I think we can all agree that this deaf elf sure plays a mean pinball. Who's next?"

Blitzen challenged the giants to a complete makeover. He promised he could turn *any* giant into someone more dashing and fashionable. The giants unanimously elected a jotun named Grum, who had apparently been sleeping under the bar—and collecting grime and lint there—for the past forty years. I was pretty sure he was the minor deity Bad Hygiene.

Blitzen was not deterred. He whipped out his sewing implements and got to work. It took him a few hours to slap together new clothes from odds and ends in the bowling alley's gift shop. Then he took Grum into the bathroom for a proper spa treatment. When they emerged, Grum's eyebrows had been waxed. His beard and hair were trimmed neater than the most metrosexual hipster's. He wore a shimmery gold bowling shirt with GRUM stitched across the front, along with silvery pants and matching bowling shoes. The giant ladies swooned. The giant dudes edged away from him, intimidated by his star power. Grum crawled back under the bar and started to snore.

"I can't fix bad habits!" Blitz said. "But you saw him. Did I beat the challenge or what?"

There was a lot of muttering, but no one dared to argue. Even magically enhanced ugliness was no match for a dwarven degree in fashion design.

Utgard-Loki leaned toward me and murmured, "You're doing very well! I'll have to make this last challenge really hard so you have a high chance of dying. That should solidify my liege men's respect."

"Wait, *what?*"

The helpful king raised his hands to the crowd. "Ladies and jotunmen! Truly we have some interesting guests, but never fear! We will have our revenge! Two guests remain. As fate would have it, that's the perfect number for a doubles bowling challenge. Since bowling is the reason we are here today, let's have our last two visitors face off against our defending champions from Tiny's Turkey Bowlers!"

The giants hollered and whooped. Tiny looked over at me and made the finger-across-the-throat sign—which I was getting really tired of seeing.

"The winners will take the usual prize," Utgard-Loki announced, "which is, of course, the losers' heads!"

I glanced at Alex Fierro and realized we were now a team.

"I suppose this is a bad time to tell you," Alex said, "I've never bowled."

Our opponents from Tiny's Turkey Bowlers were brothers with the delightful names of Herg and Blerg. It was difficult to tell them apart. In addition to being identical twins, they wore matching gray shirts and football helmets—the latter probably to keep us from throwing axes at their faces. The only differences I could see were their bowling balls. Herg's was airbrushed with the face of Prince. (Maybe he had provided the bar's playlist.) His brother Blerg had a red ball with Kurt Cobain's face on it. Blerg kept looking back and forth between me and the ball like he was trying to imagine me without the choppy haircut.

"All right, my friends!" Utgard-Loki announced. "We'll be playing an abbreviated game of three frames!"

Alex leaned toward me. "What's a frame?"

"*Shh,*" I told her. In fact, I was trying to remember the rules of bowling. It had been years since I'd played. There was an alley in Hotel Valhalla, but since the einherjar did most everything to the death, I hadn't been anxious to check it out.

"A very simple contest!" Utgard-Loki continued. "Highest score wins. First team up: the Insignificant Mortals!"

Nobody cheered as Alex and I walked to our ball return.

"What do you think?" Alex whispered.

"Basically," I said, "you're supposed to roll the ball down the lane and knock over the pins."

She glared at me, her pale eye twice as bright and angry as her dark one. "I know *that* much. But we're supposed to break the rules, right? What's the illusion here? You think Herg and Blerg are minor gods?"

I glanced back at Sam, Blitz, and Hearth, who'd been forced to watch from behind the railing. Their expressions told me nothing I didn't already know: we were in serious trouble.

I wrapped my fingers around my pendant and thought: *Hey, Jack, any advice?*

Jack hummed sleepily, as he tends to do in pendant form. *No.*

Thanks, I thought. *Huge assist from the magic sword.*

"Insignificant Mortals!" Utgard-Loki called. "Is there a problem? Do you wish to forfeit?"

"No!" I said. "No, we're good."

I took a deep breath. "Okay, Alex, we've got three frames. Uh, three rounds of play. Let's just see how the first frame goes. Maybe it'll give us some ideas. Watch how I bowl."

That's a statement I never thought I would utter. Bowling was *not* one of my superpowers. Nevertheless, I stepped into the approach with my pink fuzzy-dice-themed bowling ball. (Hey, it was the only one that fit my fingers.) I tried to remember the pointers my shop teacher, Mr. Gent, had given us when we had our middle school orientation party at the Lucky Strike Lanes. I reached the line, aimed, and threw with all my einherji might.

The ball rolled slowly, sluggishly, and stopped halfway down the lane.

The giants howled with laughter.

I retrieved the ball and walked back, my face burning. As I passed Alex, she grumbled, "Thanks, that was very instructive."

I returned to my seat. Behind the railing, Sam looked grim. Hearthstone signed his most helpful advice: *Do better.* Blitzen grinned and gave me two thumbs up, which made me wonder if he understood the rules of bowling.

Alex came to the line. She did a granny roll, hefting the ball between her legs and chucking it down the lane. The dark blue sphere bounced once, twice, then rolled a little farther than mine had before toppling into the gutter.

More laughter from the jotun crowd. A few high-fived each other. Gold coins exchanged hands.

"Time for the Turkey Bowlers!" Utgard-Loki shouted.

A roar of applause as Herg stepped to the next lane over.

"Hold up," I said. "Aren't they supposed to use the same lane as us?"

Tiny pushed through the crowd, his eyes wide with mock innocence. "Oh, but the king didn't say anything about that! He just said 'highest score wins.' Go ahead, boys!"

Herg threw Prince's head. It rolled straight down the middle at lightning speed and crashed into the pins with a sound like an exploding marimba.

Giants cheered and pumped their fists. Herg turned, grinning behind the face mask of his helmet. He patted Blerg on the shoulder and they exchanged a few words.

"I need to figure out what they're saying," Alex said. "I'll be back."

"But—"

"I NEED TO PEE!" Alex yelled.

Some of the giants frowned at this interruption, but generally when someone yells *I need to pee* in a crowd, people let them go pee. The other options are not great.

Alex disappeared into the little giant girls' room. Meanwhile, Blerg came to the approach. He hefted his Kurt Cobain ball and rolled it down the lane, Cobain's face flashing in and out of sight, saying *hello, hello, hello,* until it crashed into the pins and sent them flying with lots of rocker spirit.

"Another strike!" Tiny yelled.

Cheering and mead-drinking all around—except among me and my friends.

Blerg and Herg rendezvoused at the ball return, snickering and glancing in my direction. While the crowd was still celebrating and making new bets, Alex returned from the restroom.

"I HAVE FINISHED PEEING!" she announced.

She hurried over and grabbed my arm. "I just heard Herg and Blerg talking," she whispered.

"How?"

"I eavesdropped. I do this thing where I turn into a horsefly."

"Oh." I glanced at Sam, who was frowning severely. "I'm familiar with the horsefly thing."

"*Their* lane is a normal bowling lane," Alex reported. "But ours . . . I dunno. I heard Herg say, 'Good luck to them, hitting the White Mountains.'"

"The White Mountains," I repeated. "In New Hampshire?"

Alex shrugged. "Unless they have White Mountains in Jotunheim, too. Either way, those aren't bowling pins."

I squinted at the end of our lane, but the pins still looked like pins, not mountains. Then again, Little Billy hadn't looked like Fear . . . until he did.

I shook my head. "How is it possible . . . ?"

"No clue," Alex said. "But if our bowling balls are rolling toward a mountain range on a different world—"

"We'll never reach the end of the lane. We definitely won't be able to knock down any pins. How do we undo the hex?"

"Come on, Insignificant Mortals!" Tiny yelled. "Stop stalling!"

It was hard to think with a crowd of giants yelling at me. "I—I'm not sure," I told Alex. "I need more time. Right now, the best thing I can think of is to sabotage *their* lane."

It was impulsive, I'll admit. But I charged the foul line and threw my pink dice bowling ball overhand with all my strength, straight into Herg and Blerg's lane. The ball landed with such force it cracked the hardwood floor, ricocheted backward into the crowd, and felled one of the spectators, who squawked like a startled chicken.

"OHHHH!" the onlookers yelled.

"What was that?" Tiny bellowed. "You brained Eustis!"

Utgard-Loki scowled and rose from his throne. "Tiny is right, mortal. You can't cross-bowl. Once you've chosen a lane, you must stick to it."

"Nobody said that," I protested.

"Well, I'm saying it now! Continue the frame!"

A giant in the audience rolled my dice ball back to me.

I looked at Alex, but I had no advice to offer her. How do you bowl when your target is a distant mountain range?

Alex muttered something under her breath. As she made her approach, she changed into a full-size grizzly bear. She waddled on her back legs, the bowling ball clutched in her front paws. She reached the foul line and came down on all fours, hurling the ball forward with three hundred pounds of pure force. The ball almost made it to the first pin before stalling.

A collective sigh of relief went up from the giants.

"Now it's our turn!" Tiny rubbed his palms eagerly. "Go on, boys!"

"But, boss!" Herg said. "Our lane has a big dent in it."

"Just move over a lane," Tiny said.

"Oh, no," I said. "You heard the king: once you've chosen a lane, you must stick to it."

Tiny growled. Even the Elvis tattoo on his arm looked angry. "Fine! Herg, Blerg, just do your best. You already have an unbeatable lead!"

Herg and Blerg didn't look happy, but they bowled their second frame. They managed to avoid the dent in the lane, but both of them rolled gutter balls, adding no points to their score.

"That's all right!" Tiny assured them. He sneered at Alex and me. "I was tempted to step on you two in the forest, but now I'm glad I didn't. Unless you bowl a perfect last frame, you can't even *tie* their score. Let's see what you've got, mortals. I can't wait to cut off your heads!"

FORTY-TWO

Or You Could Just Glow a Lot.
That Works, Too

SOME PEOPLE like energy drinks. Me? I find that the threat of imminent beheading wakes me up just fine.

Panicked, I looked back at my friends. Hearthstone signed: *F-R-E-Y.*

Yes, Hearth, I thought, *he is my father.*

But how that helped me, I wasn't sure. It wasn't like the god of summer was going to appear in a blaze of glory and knock down the White Mountains for me. He was the god of the outdoors. He wouldn't be caught dead in a bowling alley. . . .

An idea started trickling through my brain like maple syrup. Outdoors. The White Mountains. Frey's power. Sumarbrander, Frey's sword, which could cut openings between the worlds. And something Utgard-Loki had said earlier: *Even the best illusions have their limits.*

"Insignificant Mortals!" Utgard-Loki called. "Do you forfeit?"

"No!" I yelled. "Just a second."

"Do you need to pee?"

"No! I just . . . I need to confer with my teammate before we are brutally decapitated."

Utgard-Loki shrugged. "That seems fair. Proceed."

Alex leaned in. "Please tell me you have an idea."

"You said you've been to Bridal Veil Falls. You've gone camping in the White Mountains a lot?"

"Yeah, sure."

"Is there any way those bowling pins could actually *be* the White Mountains?"

She frowned. "No. I can't believe anybody would be powerful enough to teleport an entire mountain range into a bowling alley."

"I agree. My theory is . . . those pins are just bowling pins. The giants couldn't bring a mountain range into a bowling alley, but they can send our bowling balls *out* of the alley. There's some kind of portal between the worlds right in the middle of our lane. It's hidden by illusions or whatever, but it's sending our bowling balls to New Hampshire."

Alex stared at the end of the lane. "Well if that's the case, why did my ball come back in the ball return?"

"I don't know! Maybe they loaded an identical ball into the ball return so you wouldn't notice."

Alex gritted her teeth. "Those cheating meinfretrs. What do we do about it?"

"You know the White Mountains," I said. "So do I. I want you to look down the lane and concentrate on seeing those mountains. If we both do it at the same time, we might be able to make the portal visible. And then, maybe, I can dispel it."

"You mean by changing our perception?" Alex asked. "Sort of like . . . the mind healing you did with Amir?"

"I guess. . . ." I wished I had more confidence in my own plan. The way Alex described it made me sound like a New Age guru. "But, look, it would work better if I held your hand.

And . . . I can't promise I won't, you know, sense stuff about your life."

I could see her wavering, weighing the options.

"So I can either lose my head or have you in my head," she grumbled. "Tough choice." She grabbed my hand. "Let's do it."

I studied the far end of the lane. I imagined a portal between us and the pins—a window looking out on the White Mountains. I remembered how excited I used to get on those weekend drives with my mom when she first spotted the mountains on the horizon: *Look, Magnus, we're getting close!*

I drew on the power of Frey. Warmth radiated through me. My hand in Alex Fierro's began to steam. A brilliant gold light surrounded us both—like the midsummer sun burning away fog and destroying shadows.

Out of the corner of my eye, I saw giants wincing and shielding their faces. "Stop that!" Tiny cried. "You're blinding us!"

I stayed focused on the bowling pins. The light grew brighter. Random thoughts from Alex Fierro whisked through my mind—her fatal fight with the wolves; a dark-haired man in tennis clothes towering over her, screaming that she should get out and stay out; a group of teenagers standing around ten-year-old Alex and kicking her, calling her a freak as she curled into a ball, trying to protect herself, too panicked and terrified to shape-shift.

Anger burned in my chest. I wasn't sure if it was my emotion or Alex's, but we'd both had enough of illusions and pretending.

"There," Alex said.

In the middle of the lane, a shimmering rift appeared, like the ones Jack cut between the worlds. On the other side, in the distance, was the snow-marbled summit of Mount Washington. Then the portal burned away. The golden light faded around us, leaving a regular lane with bowling pins at the end, just as it had looked before.

Alex pulled her hand away. She quickly wiped away a tear. "Did we do it?"

I wasn't sure what to say.

"Insignificant Mortals!" Utgard-Loki interrupted. "What was that? Do you always confer with each other by generating a blinding light?"

"Sorry!" I yelled to the crowd. "We're ready now!"

At least I *hoped* we were ready. Maybe we'd succeeded in burning away the illusion and closing the portal. Or maybe Utgard-Loki was just allowing me to *think* I'd dispelled his trick. It could be an illusion within an illusion. I decided there was no point overtaxing my brain in the last few minutes it might be on my neck.

I raised my bowling ball. I stepped to the foul line and rolled that stupid pink fuzzy-dice ball straight down the middle.

I have to tell you, the sound of the pins falling was the most beautiful thing I'd heard all day. (Sorry, Prince. You were a close second.)

Blitzen screamed, "Strike!"

Samirah and Hearthstone hugged each other, which wasn't something either of them tended to do.

Alex's eyes widened. "It worked? It worked!"

I grinned at her. "Now all you have to do is knock down all your pins and we tie. Do you have any shape-shifting form that could—?"

"Oh, don't worry." Her wicked smile was one hundred percent from her mother, Loki. "I've got it covered."

She grew to immense size, her arms morphing into thick forelegs, her skin turning wrinkled gray, her nose elongating into a twenty-foot trunk.

Alex was now an African bush elephant, though one confused giant in the back of the room screamed, "She's a cat!"

Alex picked up the bowling ball with her trunk. She stormed the foul line and hurled the ball, stomping with all her weight and shaking the entire alley. Not only did her bowling ball knock down the pins, the force of her stomping obliterated the pins in all twelve lanes, making Alex the first elephant in history, as far I knew, to score a perfect 300, twelve strikes, with only one throw.

I may have jumped up and down and clapped like a five-year-old girl who had just gotten a pony. (What did I say about not judging?) Sam, Hearth, and Blitz rushed us and tackled us in a big group hug while the crowd of giants looked on sourly.

Herg and Blerg threw down their football helmets.

"We can't beat that score!" Herg wailed. "Just take our heads!"

"The mortals are cheaters!" Tiny complained. "First they shrunk my bag and insulted Elvis! Now they've dishonored the Turkey Bowlers!"

The giants began to advance on us.

"Hold!" Utgard-Loki raised his arms. "This is my still bowling alley, and these competitors have won . . . uh, squarely, if not fairly." He turned to us. "The normal prize is yours. Would you like the severed heads of Herg and Blerg?"

Alex and I looked at each other. We tacitly agreed that severed heads really wouldn't go with the décor in our hotel rooms.

"Utgard-Loki," I said, "all we want is the information you promised."

The king faced the crowd. He spread his palms like *what ya gonna do?* "My friends, you must admit these mortals have spunk. As much as we tried to humiliate them, they humiliated us instead. And is there anything we mountain giants respect more than the ability to humiliate one's enemies?"

The other giants murmured in reluctant agreement.

"I wish to help them!" Utgard-Loki announced. "I believe they have proven their worth. How much time will you give me?"

I didn't quite understand the question, but the giants muttered among themselves. Tiny stepped forward. "I say five minutes. All in favor?"

"Aye!" shouted the crowd.

Utgard-Loki bowed. "More than fair. Come, my guests, let's talk outside."

As he steered us through the bar and out the front doors, I said, "Uh, what happens after five minutes?"

"Hmm?" Utgard-Loki smiled. "Oh, then my liege men are free to chase you down and kill you. You *did* humiliate them, after all."

FORTY-THREE

You Keep Using the Word *Help.* I Do Not Think It Means What You Think It Means

UTGARD-LOKI ESCORTED us around the back of the bowling alley. He led us down an icy path into a wide expanse of forest while I peppered him with questions like "Chase us? Kill us? What?" He just patted me on the shoulder and chuckled as if we were sharing a joke.

"You all did well!" he said as we walked. "Normally we have boring guests like Thor. I tell him, 'Thor, drink this mead.' He just tries and tries! It doesn't even occur to him that the mead cup is connected to the ocean and he can't possibly drain it."

"How do you connect a mead cup to the ocean?" Sam asked. "Wait, never mind. We have more important matters."

"Five *minutes*?" I demanded again.

The giant pounded me on the back like he was trying to dislodge something—perhaps my throat or my heart. "Ah, Magnus! I have to confess, when you threw that first frame, I got nervous. Then the second frame . . . well, sheer force never would have worked, but nice try. Alex, your ball almost reached the Taco Bell on I-93 south of Manchester."

"Thanks," said Alex. "That's what I was going for."

"But then you two broke the illusion!" Utgard-Loki beamed. "That was first-rate thinking. And of course, the elf's pinball skills, the dwarf's accessorizing, Sam hitting Fear in the face with an ax—well done, all around! It's going to be an honor slaughtering the four of you at Ragnarok."

Blitzen snorted. "The feeling is mutual. Now I think you owe us some information."

"Yes, of course." Utgard-Loki changed form. Suddenly the goat-killer stood before us in his black furs, soot-smeared chain mail, and iron helm, his face covered by a sneering wolf faceplate.

"Could you lose the mask?" I asked. "Please?"

Utgard-Loki flipped up his visor. Underneath, his face looked the same as before, his dark eyes gleaming murderously. "Tell me, my friends, have you figured out Loki's true goal?"

Hearthstone crossed one palm over the other, made his hands into fists, then pulled them apart as if ripping a sheet: *Destroy.*

Utgard-Loki chuckled. "Even *I* understood that sign. Yes, my pinball wizard, Loki wants to destroy his enemies. But that is not his primary concern at the moment." He turned to Sam and Alex. "You two are his children. Surely you know."

Samirah and Alex exchanged an uncomfortable look. They had a silent, very sibling-like conversation: *Do you know? No, I thought you knew! I don't know; I thought you knew!*

"He led you to the wight's barrow," Utgard-Loki prompted. "Despite my best efforts, you went there. And?"

"There was no hammer," Blitzen said. "Just a sword. A sword I hate very much."

"Exactly . . ." The giant waited for us to put the pieces together. I always hated it when teachers did that. I wanted to scream: *I don't like puzzles!*

Nevertheless, I saw where he was going. The idea had

been forming in my head for a long time, I guess, but my subconscious had been trying to suppress it. I remembered my vision of Loki lying in his cave, tied to pillars of rock with the hardened guts of his own murdered children. I remembered the serpent dripping poison in his face, and the way Loki had vowed: *Soon enough, Magnus!*

"Loki wants his freedom," I said.

Utgard-Loki threw back his head and laughed. "We have a winner! Of course, Magnus Chase. That's what Loki has wanted for a thousand years."

Samirah raised her palm to push the thought away. "No, that can't happen."

"And yet," Utgard-Loki said, "strapped to your back is the very weapon that could free him—the Skofnung Sword!"

My necklace started to choke me, the pendant tugging its way across my collarbone as if trying to get closer to Sam. Jack must have woken up when he heard *Skofnung.* I yanked him back, which probably made me look like I had a flea in my shirt.

"This has never been about Thor's hammer," I realized. "Loki is after the sword."

Utgard-Loki shrugged. "Well, the theft of the hammer was a good catalyst. I imagine Loki whispered in Thrym's ear, giving him the idea. After all, Thrym's grandfather once stole Thor's hammer and it didn't go so well. Thrym and his sister have been aching for revenge against the thunder god their entire lives."

"Thrym's grandfather?" I remembered the wording on the wedding invitation: *Thrym, son of Thrym, son of Thrym.*

Utgard-Loki waved aside my question. "You can ask Thor

about it when you see him, which I'm sure will be very soon. The point is, Loki advised Thrym on the theft and set up a scenario in which a group of champions such as yourselves would have no choice but to try retrieving the hammer . . . and in the process, you might bring Loki what he really wants."

"Wait." Alex cupped her hands as if wrestling a lump of clay on the wheel. "We're bringing the sword to give to Thrym. How does that—?"

"The bride-price." Sam suddenly looked sick. "Oh, I'm such a fool."

Blitz scowled. "Uh . . . granted, I'm a dwarf. I don't understand your patriarchal traditions, but isn't the bride-price something you give to the groom?"

Sam shook her head. "I was so busy denying that this wedding would ever happen, pushing it out of my head, I didn't think about . . . about the Old Norse wedding traditions."

"Which are also jotun traditions," Utgard-Loki agreed.

Hearthstone sniffed like he was dispelling something unpleasant from his nose. He spelled out: *m-u-n-d-r?*

"Yes, the mundr," Sam said, "the Old Norse term for bride-price. It doesn't go to the groom. It goes to the father of the bride."

We stopped in the middle of the woods. Behind us, Utgard Lanes was barely visible, its neon sign washing the trunks of the trees with red-and-gold light.

"You mean all this time," I said, "with the Skofnung Sword and the Skofnung Stone, we've been running around collecting gifts for *Loki?*"

The giant king chuckled. "It *is* pretty funny, except for the fact that Loki wants to get free so he can kill everyone."

Sam leaned against the nearest tree. "And the hammer . . . that's the morning gift?"

"Exactly!" the giant agreed. "The *morgen-gifu.*"

Alex tilted her head. "The *what*-tofu?"

Hearthstone signed: *Gift to bride from groom. Only given after wedding is* . . . His fingers failed him. *Complete. Morning after.*

"I'm going to throw up," Samirah said.

I translated Hearth's words for Alex.

"So, the hammer goes to you . . ." Alex pointed to Sam. "Hypothetically, if you were the bride, which you won't be. But only after the wedding night, and . . . Yeah, I'm going to be sick, too."

"Oh, it gets worse!" the giant said with a little too much glee. "The morning gift belongs to the bride, but it's held in trust by the groom's family. Therefore, even if you go through with the marriage and get Thor's hammer back—"

"It just stays with Thrym," I said. "The giants get a marriage alliance *and* the hammer."

"And Loki gets the Skofnung Sword." Sam swallowed hard. "No, this still doesn't make sense. Loki can't attend the wedding in the flesh. The best he can do is send a manifestation. His physical body will still be stuck in the cavern where he's imprisoned."

"Which is impossible to find," Blitzen said. "Impossible to access."

Utgard-Loki gave us a twisted smile. "Like the island of Lyngvi?"

Unfortunately, Utgard-Loki had a point, and that made me want to join Sam at the throw-up tree. Fenris Wolf's place of imprisonment was supposed to be a closely kept secret among the gods, but that hadn't stopped us from having a small convention there back in January.

"And the sword," Blitzen continued. "Why Skofnung? Why not Sumarbrander or some other magic weapon?"

"I'm not entirely sure," Utgard-Loki admitted. "Nor am I sure how Loki would get the sword to his true location or use it. But I've heard Loki's bonds are *quite* hard to break, being iron-hardened guts—strong, sticky, and corrosive. They will dull any sword, even the sharpest. You could perhaps cut one bond with Sumarbrander, but after that the blade would be useless."

Jack's pendant buzzed unhappily.

Calm down, buddy, I thought. *Nobody's going to make you cut iron-hardened guts.*

"Same with Skofnung . . ." Blitzen cursed. "Of course! The blade has a magical whetstone. It can be sharpened as many times as necessary. That's why Loki needed both sword and stone."

The giant king slow-clapped. "Ah, with only a *little* help, you put it together. Well done!"

Blitz and Hearth glanced at each other like, *Now that we've put it together, can we please take it apart again?*

"So we find another way to get the hammer," I said.

The giant snickered. "Good luck. It's buried somewhere eight miles under the earth, where even Thor can't reach it. The only way to retrieve it is to convince Thrym to do so."

Alex crossed her arms. "I've heard a lot of bad news from you, giant. I still haven't heard anything I would call *helpful.*"

"Knowledge is always helpful!" Utgard-Loki said. "But as

I see it, there are two options going forward to thwart Loki. First option: I kill you all and take the Skofnung Sword, thus preventing it from falling into Loki's hands."

Sam's hand crept to her ax. "I'm not liking option one."

The giant shrugged. "Well, it's simple, effective, and relatively foolproof. It doesn't get you the hammer back, but as I said, I don't care about that. My main concern is keeping Loki in captivity. If he gets free, he starts Ragnarok right *now*, and I, for one, am not ready. We have ladies' night at the bowling alley on Friday. Doomsday would completely mess that up."

"If you wanted to kill us," I said, "you could've done it already."

Utgard-Loki grinned. "I know! I've been on pins and needles! But, my tiny friends, there's a riskier option with a higher payoff. I was waiting to see if you were capable of pulling it off. After your performance in the contests, I think you are."

"All those challenges," Sam said. "You were testing us to see whether or not we were worth keeping alive?"

Hearthstone made a few hand signs I decided not to translate, though the meaning seemed clear enough to Utgard-Loki.

"Now, now, pinball wizard," the giant said. "No need to get testy. If I let you go, and if you can beat Loki at his own game, then I get the same rewards, plus the satisfaction of knowing the upstart god of mischief has been humiliated with my help. As I may have mentioned, we mountain giants *love* humiliating our enemies."

"And for engineering that humiliation," Alex said, "you gain respect from your followers."

Utgard-Loki bowed modestly. "Maybe in the process you get Thor's hammer back. Maybe you don't. I don't really care.

In my opinion, Thor's hammer is nothing but an Asgardian boondoggle, and you can tell Thor I said so."

"I wouldn't," I said, "even if I knew what that meant."

"Make me proud!" Utgard-Loki said. "Find a way to change the rules of Loki's game, the way you did today at our feast. Surely you can come up with a plan."

"*That's* option two?" Alex demanded. " 'Do it yourself'? That's the extent of your help?"

Utgard-Loki clasped his hands to his chest. "I'm hurt. I've given you *a lot*! Besides, our five minutes is up."

A *BOOM* reverberated through the woods—the sound of barroom doors being thrown open—followed by the roar of infuriated giants.

"Hurry along now, little ones!" Utgard-Loki urged. "Go find Thor and tell him what you've learned. If my liege men catch you . . . well, I'm afraid they are *big* fans of option one!"

FORTY-FOUR

We Are Honored with Runes and Coupons

I'D BEEN CHASED by Valkyries. I'd been chased by elves with firearms. I'd been chased by dwarves with a tank. Now, lucky me, I got to be chased by giants with giant bowling balls.

One of these days, I would love to exit a world without being pursued by an angry mob.

"Run!" Blitz yelled, like this idea hadn't occurred to us.

The five of us raced through the woods, jumping over fallen trees and tangled roots. Behind us, the giants grew with every step. One moment they were twelve feet tall. The next they were twenty feet tall.

I felt like I was being pursued by a tidal wave. Their shadows overtook us, and I realized there was no hope.

Blitzen bought us a few seconds. With a curse, he tossed the bag Emptyleather behind us and yelled, "Password!" The mob of giants abruptly found their path blocked by the appearance of Mount Bowling Bag, but they quickly grew tall enough to step right over it. Soon we would be trampled. Even Jack couldn't help against so many.

Hearthstone sprinted ahead, frantically gesturing *Come on!* He pointed to a tree with slender branches, clusters of red berries just ripening in their green foliage. The ground beneath was strewn with white flower petals. The tree definitely stood out among the huge pines of Jotunheim, but I didn't understand why Hearth was so anxious to die in that particular location.

Then the trunk of the tree opened like a door. A lady stepped out and called, "Here, my heroes!"

She had fine elfish features and long hair of red gold, rich and warm and lustrous. Her orange-red dress was clasped at the shoulder with a green-and-silver brooch.

My first thought: *It's a trap*. My experience with Yggdrasil had given me a healthy fear of jumping through doorways in trees. Second thought: The lady looked like one of the dryad tree spirits my cousin Annabeth had described, though I didn't know what one would be doing in Jotunheim.

Sam didn't hesitate. She sprinted after Hearthstone as the red-gold woman stretched out her hand and cried, "Hurry, hurry!"

That also seemed like pretty obvious advice to me.

The sky above turned midnight black. I glanced up and saw the yacht-size sole of a giant's bowling shoe ready to stomp us flat. The red-gold lady pulled Hearth inside the tree. Sam leaped through next, followed by Alex. Blitz was struggling with his shorter stride, so I grabbed him and jumped. Just as the giant's boot came down, the world was snuffed out in absolute, silent darkness.

I blinked. I seemed to be not dead. Blitzen was struggling to get out from under my arm, so I deduced he wasn't dead either.

Suddenly, I was blinded by a dazzling light. Blitz grunted in alarm. I got him to his feet as he scrambled to put on his pith helmet. Only when he was safely covered up did I scan our surroundings.

We stood in a lavish room that was *definitely* not a bowling alley. Above us, a nine-sided glass pyramid let in the daylight. Floor-to-ceiling windows surrounded the chamber, giving us a penthouse-level view over the rooftops of Asgard. In the distance, I could make out Valhalla's main dome. Hammered from a hundred thousand gold shields, it looked like the shell of the world's fanciest armadillo.

The chamber we were in seemed to be an interior atrium. Ringing the circumference were nine trees, each like the one we'd stepped through in Jotunheim. In the center, in front of a raised dais, a fire crackled cheerfully and smokelessly in the hearth. And on the dais was a chair elaborately carved from white wood.

The woman with the red-gold hair climbed the steps and seated herself on the throne.

Like her hair, everything about her was graceful, flowing, and bright. The movement of her dress reminded me of a field of red poppies swaying in a warm summer breeze.

"Welcome, heroes," said the goddess. (Oh, yeah. SPOILER ALERT. By this point, I was pretty sure she was a goddess.)

Hearthstone rushed forward. He knelt at the foot of the throne. I hadn't seen him so awestruck since . . . well, ever—not even when he was facing Odin himself.

He finger-spelled: *S-I-F.*

"Yes, my dear Hearthstone," said the goddess. "I am Sif."

Blitz scrambled to Hearth's side and also knelt. I wasn't much of a kneeler, but I gave the lady a bow and managed not

to fall over in the process. Alex and Sam just stood there looking mildly disgruntled.

"My lady," Sam said with obvious reluctance, "why have
you brought us to Asgard?"

Sif wrinkled her delicate nose. "Samirah al-Abbas, the
Valkyrie. And this one is Alex Fierro, the . . . new einherji."
Even Officers Sunspot and Wildflower would have approved
of her look of distaste. "I saved your lives. Is that not cause to
be grateful?"

Blitz cleared his throat. "My lady, Sam just meant—"

"I can speak for myself," Sam said. "Yes, I appreciate the
rescue, but it was awfully convenient timing. Have you been
watching us?"

The goddess's eyes flashed like coins underwater. "Of
course I have been watching you, Samirah. But obviously I
couldn't retrieve you until you had the information to help my
husband."

I looked around. "Your husband . . . is Thor?"

I couldn't imagine the thunder god living in a place so
clean and pretty, with an unbroken glass ceiling and windows.
Sif seemed so refined, so graceful, so unlikely to fart or belch
in public.

"Yes, Magnus Chase." Sif spread her arms. "Welcome to
our home, Bilskirnir—the renowned palace Bright Crack!"

All around us, a heavenly chorus sang *Ahhhhhhh!* then
shut off as abruptly as it had begun.

Blitzen helped Hearthstone to his feet. I didn't know godly
etiquette, but I guessed once the heavenly chorus sounded,
you were allowed to get up.

"The largest mansion in Asgard!" Blitzen marveled. "I have heard stories of this place. And such a fine name, Bilskirnir!"

Another chorus rang out. *Ahhhhhhhh!*

"Bright Crack?" Alex didn't even wait for the angels to finish before asking, "Do you live next door to Plumber's Crack?"

Sif frowned. "I do not like this one. I may send it back to Jotunheim."

"Call me *it* again," Alex snarled. "Just try."

I put my arm in front of her like a guardrail, though I knew I was risking amputation by clay-cutter. "Um, Sif, so maybe you could tell us why we're here?"

Sif's eyes settled on me. "Yes, of course, son of Frey. I've always liked Frey. He's quite handsome." She fluffed her hair.

Somehow I got the feeling that by *handsome* Sif meant *likely to make my husband jealous.*

"As I said," she continued, "I am Thor's wife. That's all most people know about me, sadly, but I am also a goddess of the earth. It was a simple matter for me to track your movements across the Nine Worlds whenever you passed through a forest, or tread on living grass or moss."

"Moss?" I said.

"Yes, my dear. There is even a moss called Sif's hair, named after my luxurious golden locks."

She looked smug, though I wasn't sure I would be so excited about having a moss named after me.

Hearth pointed at the trees around the courtyard and signed, *r-o-w-a-n.*

Sif brightened. "You know much, Hearthstone! The rowan is indeed my sacred tree. I can pass from one to another across the Nine Worlds, which is how I brought you to my palace. The rowan is the source of so many blessings. Did you know my son Uller made the first bow and the first skis from rowan wood? I was *so* proud."

"Oh, yeah." I recalled a conversation I'd once had with a goat in Jotunheim. (It's depressing I can even use that sentence.) "Otis mentioned something about Uller. I didn't know he was Thor's son."

Sif put a finger to her lips. "Actually, Uller is my son by my *first* husband. Thor's a little sensitive about that." This fact seemed to please her. "But speaking of rowan trees, I have a gift for our elfish sorcerer!"

From the sleeves of her elegant dress, she brought out a leather pouch.

Hearth almost fell over. He made some wild hand gestures that didn't really mean anything, but seemed to convey the idea *GASP!*

Blitzen grabbed his arm to steady him. "Is—is that a bag of runes, milady?"

Sif smiled. "That's correct, my well-dressed dwarven friend. Runes written on wood carry a very different power than runes written on stone. They are full of life, full of suppleness. Their magic is softer and more malleable. And rowan is the best wood for runes."

She beckoned Hearth forward. She pressed the leather pouch into his trembling hands.

"You will need these in the struggle to come," she told him. "But be warned—one rune is missing, just as with your other set. When any letter is absent, the entire language of magic is weakened. Someday you will have to reclaim that symbol to reach your full potential. When you do, come see me again."

I remembered the *inheritance* rune Hearthstone had left behind on his brother's cairn. If Sif could jump through trees and telepathically communicate with moss, I didn't understand why she couldn't just hand Hearthstone a new othala. Then again, I wasn't a graduate of Rune Magic with the All-Father: A Weekend Seminar.

Hearthstone bowed his head in gratitude. He stepped away from the dais, cradling his new pouch o' power like it was a swaddled baby.

Sam shifted, gripping her ax. She eyed Sif as if the goddess might be Little Billy in disguise. "Lady Sif, that's very kind. But you were going to tell us why you brought us here?"

"To help my husband!" Sif said. "I assume you now have the information necessary to find and retrieve his hammer?"

I glanced at my friends, wondering if anyone had a diplomatic way of saying *sort of, kind of, not really.*

Sif sighed with the slightest hint of disdain. "Oh, yes, I see. First you want to discuss the matter of payment."

"Um," I said, "that wasn't really—"

"Just a moment." Sif ran her fingers through her long hair like she was working a loom. Red-yellow strands fell into her lap and began weaving themselves into some sort of shape, like a 3-D printer spitting out solid gold.

I turned to Sam and whispered, "Is she like Rapunzel?"

Sam arched her eyebrow. "Where do you think that fairy tale came from?"

In moments, with no visible loss of integrity to Sif's hairdo, the goddess was holding a small golden trophy. She held it up proudly. "You'll each get one of these!"

At the top of the trophy was a tiny golden replica of the hammer Mjolnir. On the pedestal at the bottom was engraved: AWARD OF VALOR FOR RETRIEVING THOR'S HAMMER. And in smaller letters I had to squint to read: BEARER IS ENTITLED TO ONE FREE ENTRÉE WITH PURCHASE OF AN ENTRÉE OF EQUAL VALUE AT PARTICIPATING ASGARD RESTAURANTS.

Blitzen made a squeak sound. "That's amazing! Such workmanship! How . . . ?"

Sif smiled, obviously pleased. "Well, since my original hair was replaced with solid-gold magical hair after that *horrible* trick Loki played on me"—her smile soured as she glanced at Alex and Sam—"*one* benefit is that I can weave my extra hair into any number of solid-gold items. I am responsible for paying the house staff, including heroes such as yourselves, with tokens like this. Thor is so sweet. He appreciates my abilities *so* much he calls me his trophy wife."

I blinked. "Wow."

"I know!" Sif actually blushed. "At any rate, when your job is done, you'll each get a trophy."

Blitzen reached longingly for the sample. "A free entrée at—at any participating restaurant?" I was afraid he might weep for joy.

"Yes, dear," said the goddess. "Now, how do you plan to retrieve the hammer?"

Alex coughed. "Um, actually—"

"Never mind, don't tell me!" Sif raised her hand like she wanted to block out Alex's face. "I prefer to leave details to the help."

"The *help*," Alex said.

"Yes. Now, your first task will be tricky. Whatever news you have, you will need to deliver it to my husband. The elevator is just there. You'll find him in his—what does he call it?—his *man cave*. Just be warned, he has been in a very *bad* mood."

Sam drummed her fingers on the head of her ax. "I don't suppose you could just give him a message for us?"

Sif's smile hardened. "Why, no, I couldn't. Now run along. And try not to send Thor into a murderous rage. I don't have time to hire another group of heroes."

FORTY-FIVE

Pigtails Have Never Looked So Frightening

"SIF SUCKS," Alex muttered as soon as the elevator doors closed.

"Maybe this isn't the time to say that," I suggested, "when we're in her elevator."

"If the legends are true," Blitz added, "this mansion has over six hundred floors. I'd rather not fall all the way to the basement."

"Whatever," Alex grumbled. "Also, what kind of name is Bright Crack?"

A two-second chorus of heavenly bliss sounded from the overhead speakers.

"It's a kenning!" Blitzen said. "You know, like Blood River for the Skofnung Sword guy. Bright Crack—"

Ahhhhhhhh!

"—is just a poetic way of saying *lightning*, since Thor's the thunder god and all."

"Hmpf," said Alex. "There is *nothing* poetic about Bright Crack."

Ahhhhhhhh!

Since getting his new rune bag, Hearthstone had been even more withdrawn than usual. He leaned in the corner of the elevator, tugging at the string on the leather pouch. I tried to get his attention, to ask if he was okay, but he wouldn't meet my eyes.

As for Sam, she kept running her fingertips down the edge of her ax as if she anticipated using it soon.

"You don't like Sif, either," I noted.

Sam shrugged. "Why should I? She's a vain goddess. I don't often agree with my father's pranks, but cutting off Sif's original golden hair—that I understood. He was making a point. She cares about her appearance above everything else. The ability to weave things with her new precious-metal hair, the whole thing about her being a trophy wife? I'm sure my dad planned that, too. It's his idea of a joke. Sif and Thor are just too dense to pick up on it."

Hearthstone apparently caught that. He stuffed the rune bag into his pocket and signed, *Sif is wise and good. Goddess of growing things. You*– He pointed at Sam, then made two okay signs with his hands, flicking one across the other as if tearing a piece of paper—the sign for *unfair.*

"Hey, elf?" Alex said. "I'm guessing at your meaning, but if you're defending Sif, I gotta say I'm with Samirah on this one."

"*Thank* you," said Sam.

Hearthstone scowled and crossed his arms, the deaf equivalent of *I can't even talk to you right now.*

Blitz grunted. "Well, I think you're nuts to be bad-mouthing Thor's wife in Thor's own house when we're about to see—"

Ding.

The elevator doors slid open.

"Holy man cave," I said.

We stepped out of the elevator into a sort of garage area. Suspended on a hydraulic lift was Thor's chariot, the wheels off and what looked like a broken transaxle hanging from the undercarriage. Lining a Peg-Board against one wall were dozens of wrenches, saws, screwdrivers, and rubber mallets. I briefly considered picking up one of the mallets and yelling, *I found your hammer!* But I thought the joke might not go over well.

Past the garage area, the basement opened up into a fullfledged man cavern. Stalactites hung from the ceiling high above, filling the room with a Nidavellir-like glow. The back half of the cave was an IMAX theater with two full-size screens and a line of smaller plasma monitors across the bottom, so Thor could watch two feature films while keeping track of a dozen different sporting events. Because, you know, relaxing. The theater chairs were leather-and-fur recliners fitted with drink tables fashioned from moose antlers.

To our left was a galley kitchen: five stainless steel Sub-Zero refrigerators, an oven, three microwaves, a row of high-end blenders, and a butchering station that was probably *not* his goats' favorite place. At the end of a short hallway, a stuffed ram's head pointed the way to the restrooms with a placard hanging from either horn:

VALKYRIES →

← BERSERKERS

The right half of the cavern was mostly arcade games— pretty much the last thing I wanted to see after Utgard Lanes. Fortunately, there was no bowling alley. Judging from the oversize table that took place of honor in the middle of the cave, Thor was more of an air-hockey man.

The place was so huge I didn't even see Thor until

he marched out from behind the *Dance Dance Revolution* machine. He looked lost in thought, pacing and muttering while knocking two air-hockey paddles together, as if preparing to defibrillate someone's heart. Behind him trailed his goats, Otis and Marvin, but they weren't very nimble on their hooves. Every time Thor turned, he collided with them and had to shove them out of the way.

"Hammers," he was grumbling. "Stupid, stupid hammers. Hammers."

Finally, he noticed us. "Aha!"

He stormed over, his eyes bloodshot and furious, his face as red as his bushy beard. His battle armor consisted of a ragged Metallica T-shirt and gym shorts that showed off his pale hairy legs. His bare feet were in dire need of a gentlemen's pedicure. For some reason, his scraggly scarlet hair was in pigtails, but on Thor the look was more terrifying than funny. It was almost as if he wanted us to know *I can wear my hair like a six-year-old girl and still murder you!*

"What news?" he demanded.

"Hey, Thor," I said, in a voice about as manly as his pigtails. "Uh, Sumarbrander has something to tell you."

I pulled off my pendant and summoned Jack. Was it cowardly of me to hide behind a magical talking sword? I prefer to think of it as strategically wise. I wouldn't be able to do Thor any favors if he smashed my face in with an air-hockey paddle.

"Hi, Thor!" Jack glowed cheerfully. "Hi, goats! Ooh, air hockey! Sweet chill pad, Thunder Man!"

Thor scratched his beard with a paddle. The name of his son Modi was tattooed in blue across his knuckles. I really hoped I didn't get a closer look at that name.

"Yes, yes, hello, Sumarbrander," Thor grumbled. "But where is my hammer? Where is Mjolnir?"

"Oh." Jack glowed a darker shade of orange. He wasn't able to glare, but he definitely turned a sharp edge in my direction. "So . . . good news on that front. We know who has the hammer, and we know where he is keeping it."

"Excellent!"

Jack hovered back a few inches. "But there is some bad news . . ."

Otis sighed to his brother Marvin. "I have a feeling we're about to be killed."

"Stop that!" Marvin snapped. "Don't give the boss ideas!"

"The hammer was stolen by a giant named Thrym," Jack continued. "He's buried it eight miles under the earth."

"Not excellent!" Thor smashed his air-hockey paddles together. Thunder rolled through the room. Plasma-screen TVs toppled. Microwaves flickered. The goats stumbled back and forth like they were on the deck of a ship.

"I hate Thrym!" the god roared. "I hate earth giants!"

"So do we!" Jack agreed. "And here's Magnus to tell you about our brilliant plan to get the hammer back!"

Jack flew behind me and hovered there with great strategic wisdom. Otis and Marvin backed away from their master and hid behind the *Dance Dance Revolution* machine.

At least Alex, Sam, Blitz, and Hearth didn't hide, but Alex gave me a look like, *Hey, he's* your *thunder god.*

So I told Thor the whole story: how we'd been tricked into going to the wight's tomb for the Skofnung Sword, then we'd rushed to Alfheim for the Skofnung Stone, we'd climbed the

Bifrost for a selfie with Heimdall, and we'd gone bowling for information with Utgard-Loki. I explained about Thrym's demands for a marriage alliance with Loki.

Every so often I had to pause so Thor could process the news by storming around, throwing power tools, and punching the walls.

He needed a lot of processing time.

When I was done, Thor announced his well-reasoned conclusion. "We must kill them all!"

Blitz raised his hand. "Ah, Mr. Thor, even if we could get you close enough to Thrym, killing him wouldn't help. He's the only one who knows exactly where the hammer is."

"So we torture him for the information and *then* kill him! Then I will retrieve the hammer myself!"

Alex muttered, "Nice guy."

"Sir," Sam said, "even if we did that—and torture isn't very effective, or, you know, ethical—even if Thrym told you exactly where the hammer was, how would you get it back from eight miles under the earth?"

"I would break through the earth! With my hammer!"

We waited for Thor's mental gears to turn.

"Oh," said the god. "I see the problem. Curses! Follow me!"

He marched into the garage, tossed aside his hockey paddles, and started rummaging through his tools. "There must be something in here that can drill through eight miles of solid rock."

He considered a hand drill, a tape measure, a corkscrew, and the iron staff we'd almost died retrieving from Geirrod's fortress. He threw them all to the floor.

"Nothing!" he said in disgust. "Useless junk!"

Perhaps you could use your head, Hearthstone signed. *That is very hard.*

"Oh, don't try to console me, Mr. Elf," said Thor. "It's hopeless, isn't it? You have to *have* hammers to *get* hammers. And this . . ." He picked up a rubber mallet and sighed. "This won't do. I'm ruined! All the giants will soon know I'm defenseless. They'll invade Midgard, destroy the television industry, and I will *never* be able to watch my shows again!"

"There might be a way to get the hammer." The words came out of my mouth before I considered what I was saying.

Thor's eyes lit up. "You have a large bomb?"

"Uh, no. But Thrym is expecting to marry someone tomorrow, right? We can pretend to go along with it and—"

"Forget it," Thor growled. "I know what you're going to suggest. There's no way! Thrym's grandfather humiliated me enough when *he* stole my hammer. I will not do *that* again!"

"Do what?" I asked.

"Wear a wedding dress!" Thor said. "Pretend to be the giant's bride, Freya, who refused to marry Thrym. Selfish woman! I was disgraced, humiliated, and— What are *you* smirking about?"

This last comment was directed at Alex, who quickly put on her serious face.

"Nothing," she said. "Just . . . you in a wedding dress."

Hovering behind my shoulder, Jack whispered, "He looked a-MAZ-ing."

Thor grunted. "It was all Loki's idea, of course. It worked. I infiltrated the wedding, got my hammer back, and killed the giants—well, except for those little kids, Thrym the Third and

Thrynga. But when I got back to Asgard, Loki told the story so many times he made me a laughingstock. No one took me seriously for *ages!*" Thor frowned as if he'd just had a thought, which must have been a painful experience. "You know, I bet that was Loki's plan all along. I bet he arranged the theft *and* the solution to make me look bad!"

"That's terrible," Alex said. "What was your bridal dress like?"

"Oh, it was white with a high lace appliqué neckline and these lovely scalloped—" Thor's beard sparked with electricity. "THAT'S NOT IMPORTANT!"

"Anyway . . ." I stepped in. "This Thrym—Thrym the Third or whatever—he's expecting you to try that trick again. He's got some kind of security precautions in place. No gods are getting through the front door unnoticed. We'll need a different bride."

"Well, that's a relief!" He grinned at Samirah. "And I do thank you for stepping up, girl! I'm glad you're not as selfish as Freya. I owe you a gift. I'll have Sif make you a trophy. Or perhaps you'd like a Hot Pocket? I have some in the freezer—"

"No, Lord Thor," Sam said. "I'm not marrying a giant for you."

Thor winked slyly. "Right. . . . You're only pretending to marry him. Then once he brings out the hammer—"

"I'm not even pretending," Sam said.

"*I* am," Alex said.

FORTY-SIX

Here Comes the Bride
and/or the Assassin

ALEX KNEW how to get our attention. Hearth and Blitz gawped at her. Jack gasped and glowed bright yellow. Thor's eyebrows furrowed, sparking like jumper cables. Even the goats trotted over to get a closer look at the crazy girl.

"What?" Alex demanded. "Sam and I discussed it. She vowed to Amir that she wouldn't even *fake*-marry this giant, right? The charade doesn't bother me at all. I'll dress up, say the vows, kill my new husband, whatever. Sam and I are close to the same size. We're both children of Loki. She can pose as my maid of honor. It's our best option."

I stared at Sam. "That's what you and Alex have been talking about?"

Samirah fingered the keys on her belt ring. "Alex thinks she can resist Loki . . . unlike what happened to me in Provincetown."

It was the first time she'd talked about the incident so openly. I remembered Loki snapping his fingers, Sam collapsing in a heap, all the air expelled from her lungs. Sam was a Valkyrie. She had the strongest willpower and discipline of anyone I knew. If *she* couldn't resist Loki's control . . .

"Alex, are you sure?" I tried not to let doubt creep into my voice. "I mean, have you ever tried to resist Loki before?"

Alex's expression hardened. "What is *that* supposed to mean?"

"No," I said hastily. "I just—"

"The larger point," Thor butted in, "is that you're not even a proper girl! You're an argr!"

The air became still, like the moment before a thunderclap. I wasn't sure which possibility scared me more, Thor attacking Alex, or Alex attacking Thor. The look in her eyes made me wonder if we shouldn't just put her on the borders of Jotunheim to scare away the giants rather than bothering with Thor and his hammer.

"I'm a child of Loki," she said in an even tone. "That's what Thrym is expecting. Like my parent, I'm gender fluid. And when I'm female, I *am* female. I can definitely pull off a lace appliqué wedding gown better than you!"

Thor fumed. "Well, there's no need to be mean about it."

"Besides," Alex said, "I will *not* let Loki control me. I never have. I never will. I also don't see anyone *else* volunteering for this suicidal bridal mission."

"*Suicidal bridal,*" Jack said. "Hey, that rhymes!"

Otis clopped forward and sighed. "Well, if you need a volunteer to die, I suppose I can do it. I've always loved weddings—"

"Shut up, dummy!" Marvin said. "You're a goat!"

Thor picked up his iron staff. He leaned against it thoughtfully, tapping his fingers and making different images flicker across the surface—a soccer match, the Home Shopping Network, *Gilligan's Island.*

"Well," he said at last, "I still don't trust an argr to do this job—"

"*A gender-fluid person,*" Alex corrected.

"A gender . . . whatever you said," Thor amended. "But I suppose, respect-wise, you have the least to lose."

Alex bared her teeth. "I get now why Loki loves you so much."

"Guys," I said. "We have other problems to discuss, and not much time. Thrym is expecting his bride to arrive tomorrow."

Alex folded her arms. "It's decided, then. I get to marry the big ugly guy."

Yes, you marry him, Hearthstone signed. *Many happy years and fine children.*

Alex narrowed her eyes. "I can see I'm going to have to learn sign language. In the meantime, I will assume you said, *Yes, Alex. Thank you, Alex, for being so brave and heroic.*"

Close enough, Hearth signed.

I still wasn't loving the idea of Alex as a decoy bride, but I figured I'd better move things along. Keeping this group focused was like driving a chariot with no goats and a broken transaxle.

"So anyway," I said, "we have to assume we can't sneak Thor in with the wedding party."

"And he can't simply bust into an earth giant's lair," Blitz added.

Thor harrumphed. "I've tried, believe me. The stupid giants are buried too deep in rock too dense."

"You're an expert on density," Alex guessed.

I gave her a *shut up* look. "So we have to use the front door. I'm guessing they won't tell us where that is until the last minute to avoid an ambush or unwelcome tagalongs."

"What does the invitation say?" Sam asked.

I took it out and showed them. The time slot now read: TOMORROW MORNING!!! The location slot still said: WE'LL GET BACK TO YOU.

"That's okay," I said. "I think I may know where the entrance will appear."

I explained to Thor about the photo of Bridal Veil Falls.

The thunder god did not look overjoyed. "So either you're wrong and this is a random photograph, or you're right and you're choosing to believe information from your treacherous uncle?"

"Well . . . yeah. But if it *is* the entrance—"

"I could scout it out," Thor said. "I could have a team of gods in place, undercover, ready to follow the wedding party inside all stealthy-like."

"A team of gods sounds excellent," I agreed.

"Depending on the gods," Blitz murmured.

"We also have some einherjar standing by," Sam suggested. "Good warriors. Trustworthy."

She said *trustworthy* like it was a word Thor might not have heard before.

"Hmm." Thor twirled one of his pigtails. "I suppose this could work. And once Thrym summons the hammer—"

"*If* he summons it," Alex said. "He's using it as the, er, *morning after* gift."

Thor looked aghast. "Regardless, he *must* summon it for the ceremony! The bride has the right to insist. The symbol of my hammer is always used to bless a wedding. If Thrym has the real thing, he *must* use it if you request it. And once he does, we'll move in and kill everyone!"

Except us, Hearthstone said.

"Exactly, Mr. Elf! It will be a glorious bloodbath!"

"Lord Thor," Sam said, "how will you know when the time is right to charge in?"

"That's easy." He turned and patted Marvin's and Otis's heads. "You'll ride my chariot into the wedding hall. That's a common enough practice for lords and ladies. With a little concentration, I can see and hear what my goats see and hear."

"Yes," Otis said. "It gives me a tingling feeling right behind my eyeballs."

"Be quiet," Marvin said. "Nobody wants to hear about your tingling eyeballs."

"When the hammer appears"—Thor grinned evilly—"we move in, gods and einherjar. We slaughter the giants, and all will be well. I feel better already!"

"Yay!" Jack cheered, clinking against Thor's staff in a high five . . . or a high just-one.

Samirah raised her index finger like, *one moment*. "There's something else. Loki wants the Skofnung Sword so he can cut himself free. How do we make sure he doesn't get it?"

"That will never happen!" Thor said. "Loki's place of punishment is in a completely different location, sealed long ago by the gods. Loki is bound even better than Fenris Wolf."

And we saw how well that worked out, Hearth signed.

"The elf speaks wisely," Thor agreed. "There is nothing to worry about. Loki can't be at the wedding in the flesh. Even if Thrym gets hold of the Skofnung Sword, he won't have time to find Loki or free him—not before we swoop in and kill the big oaf!"

Thor swung his iron staff to demonstrate his ninja moves.

His left pigtail came loose in the process, which only added to the intimidating effect.

A cold feeling spread through my gut. "I don't know about this plan. It still feels like we're missing something important."

"My hammer!" Thor said. "But we'll get that back soon enough. Mr. Elf and Mr. Dwarf, why don't you go to Valhalla and alert the einherjar?"

"Sir, we would . . ." Blitz adjusted his pith helmet. "But we're not technically allowed in Valhalla, not being, you know, dead."

"I can fix that!"

"Don't kill us!" Blitz yelped.

Thor just rummaged around his worktable until he found a two-by-four with a key attached to one end. Burned into the side of the plank were the words THOR'S HALL PASS.

"This will get you into Valhalla," he promised. "Just return it. I'm going to fix this chariot so our gender argr bride can use it tomorrow. Then I'll gather my assault squad and scout out this location, Bridal Veil Falls."

"And the rest of us?" I asked reluctantly.

"You and the two children of Loki will be our guests tonight!" Thor announced. "Go see Sif upstairs, and she will get you settled. In the morning, you will ride forth to a glorious matrimonial massacre!"

"Oh," Otis said with a sigh. "I do love weddings."

FORTY-SEVEN

I Prepare for Funkytown Combat

THE NIGHT before a big massacre, you might think I would toss and turn.

Nope. I slept like a rock giant.

Sif gave each of us a guest room in the upper levels of Bright Crack. I collapsed on my rowan-wood bed with its sheets of woven gold and didn't stir until the next morning when I heard the alarm clock—a small gold Mjolnir trophy that wouldn't stop singing a divine chorus of *Ahhhhhhhh! Ahhhhhhhh! Ahhhhhhhh!* until I grabbed it off the nightstand and threw it against the wall. I have to admit, that was a satisfying way to wake up.

I don't think Sam and Alex slept quite as well. When I met them in Sif's atrium, they both looked bleary-eyed. In Alex's lap was a plate of what used to be doughnuts. She had broken them into pieces to make a frowny face. Her fingers were caked in powdered sugar.

Sam held a cup of coffee to her lips as if she liked the smell but couldn't remember how to drink. The Skofnung Sword was slung across her back.

She looked up at me and asked, "Where?"

At first, I didn't understand the question. Then I realized she was asking if I knew where we were going today.

I fumbled through my pockets for the wedding invitation. The *when* space now read: TODAY! AT 10 A.M. ARE YOU EXCITED?!? The *where* space read: PROCEED TO THE TACO BELL ON I-93 SOUTH OF MANCHESTER, NH. AWAIT FURTHER INSTRUCTIONS. NO AESIR, OR THE HAMMER GETS IT!

I showed this to Alex and Sam.

"Taco Bell?" Alex grumbled. "Those monsters."

"Something's not right." Sam took a sip of coffee. The cup trembled in her hands. "Magnus, all night I was thinking about what you said. We are missing something important, and I don't mean the hammer."

"Perhaps," said the voice of our hostess, "you're missing the appropriate clothes."

Before us stood Sif, having appeared out nowhere, as goddesses tend to do. She wore the same red-orange dress, the same green-and-silver brooch, and the same pained smile that said, *I think you're my house servants, but I don't remember your names.*

"My husband tells me you want to play dress-up." She gave Alex an up-and-down look. "I suppose it will be easier than putting Thor in a wedding dress, but we have a lot of work to do. Come along."

She strolled toward a hallway at the back of the atrium, crooking a finger over her shoulder for Alex to follow.

"If I'm not back in an hour," Alex said, "it means I have strangled Sif and am hiding the body."

Her expression gave absolutely no indication she was kidding. She sashayed off, doing such a good imitation of Sif's walk that I would've given her a trophy.

Sam rose. Coffee cup in hand, she walked to the nearest

window. She stared across the rooftops of Asgard. Her eyes seemed to fix on the shield-thatched golden dome of Valhalla.

"Alex isn't ready," she said.

I joined her at the window. A wisp of dark hair had escaped the edge of her hijab by her left temple. I had a protective urge to tuck it back in. Since I valued my hand, I didn't.

"Do you think she's right?" I asked. "Can she . . . you know, resist your dad?"

"She *thinks* she's right," Sam said. "She has some theory about claiming her own powers, not letting Loki possess her. She even volunteered to teach me. But I don't think she's ever tested herself against our father. Not really."

I thought about my conversation with Alex in the woods of Jotunheim, how confidently she had talked about using the image of the Urnes snakes for herself, stepping out of her parent's poisonous shadow. It was a nice idea. Unfortunately, I'd seen how easily Loki could manipulate people. I'd seen what he'd done to my Uncle Randolph.

"At least we won't be alone." I gazed at Valhalla in the distance. For the first time, I felt a twinge of homesickness for the place. I hoped Blitz and Hearth had gotten there safely. I imagined them with the gang from floor nineteen, preparing their weapons and suiting up in wedding attire for a daring raid that would save our butts.

As for Thor . . . I didn't have much faith in him. But with luck he and a bunch of other Aesir would be dug in around Bridal Veil Falls, dressed in camouflage with high-powered hand catapults or rocket spears or whatever other weapons god commandos were wielding these days.

Sam shook her head. "Help or no . . . Alex doesn't know

what it was like in that wight's tomb. She's not fully aware of what Loki is capable of, how easily he can just . . ." She snapped her fingers.

I wasn't sure what to say. *It's okay, you couldn't help it* didn't seem useful.

Sam sipped her coffee. "I should be the one in the wedding dress. I'm a Valkyrie. I have powers Alex doesn't have. I have more experience fighting. I—"

"You made a promise to Amir. You have lines you can't cross. That's not a weakness. It's one of your strengths."

She studied my face, maybe judging how serious I was. "Sometimes it doesn't feel like a strength."

"After what happened in that tomb in Provincetown?" I said. "Knowing what Loki can do and not knowing whether you can resist him, you're *still* going right back in to fight him. You ask me, that's *way* above Valhalla-level courage."

She set down her cup on the windowsill. "Thanks, Magnus. But today, if you have to choose . . . If Loki tries to use Alex and me as hostages, or—"

"Sam, no."

"Whatever he is planning, Magnus, you *have* to stop him. If we're incapacitated, you may be the only one who can." She shrugged off the Skofnung Sword and handed it to me. "Keep this. Don't let it out of your sight."

Even in the morning light of Asgard, in the warmth of Sif's atrium, the sword's leather sheath felt as cold as a freezer door. The Skofnung Stone was now strapped to the pommel. When I slung the sword across my back, the stone dug against my shoulder blade.

"Sam, it won't come down to a choice. I'm not letting Loki

kill my friends. I'm definitely not letting him near this sword. Unless he wants to eat the blade. I'm fine with that."

The corner of Sam's mouth twitched. "I'm glad you'll be at my side for this, Magnus. I hope someday, when I have my *actual* wedding, you'll be there, too."

That was the nicest thing anybody had said to me in a while. Of course, given how messed up my last few days had been, maybe that wasn't a surprise. "I will be there," I promised. "And it won't just be for the awesome catering from Fadlan's Falafel."

She swatted my shoulder, which I took as a compliment. Usually she avoided any sort of physical contact. I guess whacking a stupid friend occasionally was permissible.

For a while, we watched the sun rise over Asgard. We were a long way up, but as with the time I'd seen Asgard from Valhalla, I spotted no one stirring in the streets. I wondered about all the dark windows and silent courtyards, the untended gardens left to grow wild. Which gods had lived in those mansions? Where had they all gone? Maybe they'd gotten tired of the lax security and moved to a gated community where the guardian didn't spend all his time taking celestial selfies.

I'm not sure how long we waited for Alex. Long enough for me to drink some coffee and eat a frowny face of broken doughnuts. Long enough for me to wonder why Alex was taking so long hiding Sif's body.

Finally, the goddess and the bride-to-be emerged from the hall. All the moisture evaporated from my mouth. Electricity jumped from pore to pore across my scalp.

Alex's white silk gown glowed with gold embroidery, from the tassels on her sleeves to the serpentine curls along the hem that swept her feet. A necklace of golden arcs curved at the base of her neck like an inverted rainbow. Pinned to her black-and-green ringlets was a white veil, pushed back to show her face: her two-toned eyes lined with delicate mascara, her lips colored a warm shade of red.

"Sister," Sam said. "You look amazing."

I was glad *she* said it. My tongue was curled up like a titanium sleeping bag.

Alex scowled at me. "Magnus, could you please stop staring at me as if I'm going to murder you?"

"I wasn't—"

"Because if you don't, I *will* murder you."

"Right." It was difficult to look elsewhere, but I tried.

Sif had a smug glint in her eyes. "Judging from the reaction of our male test subject, I think my work here is done. Except for one thing . . ." From around her own waist, the goddess pulled a long strand of gold so thin and delicate I could hardly see it. On each end was a golden handle in the shape of an *S*. A garrote, I realized, like Alex's, except in gold. Sif fastened it around Alex's waist, buckling the *S*'s together so they formed the Urnes snakes.

"There," Sif said. "This weapon, fashioned from my own hair, has the same properties as your other garrote, except that it goes with your outfit, and it is *not* from Loki. May it serve you well, Alex Fierro."

Alex looked like she'd been offered a trophy entitling the bearer to pretty much everything. "I—I don't know how to thank you, Sif."

The goddess inclined her head. "Perhaps we can both try harder not to judge based on first impressions, eh?"

"That . . . yeah. Agreed."

"And if you get a chance," Sif added, "strangling your father with a garrote made from my magical hair would seem quite appropriate."

Alex curtseyed.

The goddess turned to Sam. "Now, my dear, let us see what we can do for the maid of honor."

After Sif had escorted Samirah down the Hall of Magical Makeovers, I turned to Alex, trying my best not to gawk.

"I, um . . ." My tongue started to roll up again. "What did you say to Sif? She seems to like you now."

"I can be very charming," Alex said. "And don't worry. It'll be your turn soon."

"To . . . be charming?"

"That would be impossible." Alex wrinkled her nose in a very Sif-like way. "But at least you can get cleaned up. I need my chaperone to look *much* spiffier."

I'm not sure I managed spiffy. More like iffy.

While Samirah was still getting dressed, Sif came back and guided me to the gentlemen's fitting room. Why the goddess even had a gentlemen's fitting room, I wasn't sure, but I guessed Thor didn't spend a lot of time there. It was completely devoid of gym shorts and Metallica T-shirts.

Sif outfitted me with a gold-and-white tuxedo, the inside lining made from chain mail à la Blitzen. Jack hovered nearby, humming with excitement. He especially liked the woven gold Sif-hair bow tie and the frilly shirt.

"Aw, yeah!" he exclaimed. "All you need now is the right runestone on this studly outfit!"

I'd never seen him so eager to turn into a silent pendant. The rune of Frey took its place just below my bow tie, nestled in the frills like a stone Easter egg. With the Skofnung Sword strapped to my back, I looked like I was ready to boogie down while stabbing my closest relatives. Sadly, that was probably accurate.

As soon as I got back to the atrium, Alex doubled over with laughter. There was something deeply humiliating about being laughed at by a girl in a wedding dress, especially a girl who was *rocking* that wedding dress.

"Oh my gods." She snorted. "You look like you're on your way to a Vegas wedding in 1987."

"In your own words," I said, "shut up."

She walked over and straightened my tie. Her eyes danced with amusement. She smelled like woodsmoke. Why did she still smell like a campfire?

She backed away and snorted again. "Yep. All better. Now we just need Sam— Oh, wow."

I followed her gaze.

Samirah had emerged from the hallway. She wore a green formal dress with black embroidery that was the mirror image of Alex's—serpentine swirls from the sleeves all the way down to the hem. In place of her usual hijab, she wore a green silk hood with a bandit sort of veil across the bridge of her nose. Only her eyes were visible, and even those were deep in shadow.

"You look great," I told her. "Also, I loved you in *Assassin's Creed*."

"Ha, ha," Sam said. "I see you're ready for the prom. Alex, have you tried your veil yet?"

With Sam's help, Alex drew the curtain of white gauze

over her face. There was something ghostly about her in that veil, like she might start floating away at any moment. You could see that she *had* a face, but her features were completely obscured. If I didn't know better, I might have thought she was Sam. Only her hands gave her away. Alex's skin tone was a few shades lighter than Sam's. She fixed this by pulling on lace gloves. I really wished Blitzen were with us, because he would've loved all the fancy outfits.

"My heroes." Sif stood next to one of her rowan trees. "It is time."

The trunk of the tree split open, revealing a rift of purple light the exact color of a Taco Bell sign.

"Where's the chariot?" Alex asked.

"Waiting for you on the other side," Sif said. "Go forth, my friends, and kill many giants."

Friends, I noted. Not *hired help.*

Maybe we'd really made an impression on the goddess. Or maybe she figured we were about to die, so a little kindness wouldn't hurt.

Alex turned to me. "You first, Magnus. If there are any hostiles, your tux will blind them."

Sam laughed.

Mostly to get the embarrassment over with, I walked through the rowan tree into a different world.

FORTY-EIGHT

All Aboard the Cheesy Gordita Express

THE ONLY THING hostile in the Taco Bell parking lot was Marvin, who was giving his brother, Otis, a thorough scolding.

"Thanks a lot for getting us turned into Hot Pockets, you idiot!" Marvin shouted. "You know how badly you have to annoy Thor before he eats us in that form?"

"Oh, look." Otis pointed his horns in our direction. "It's our passengers."

He said the word *passengers* like *executioners*. I guess for Otis those two words were often synonyms.

Both goats were harnessed to their chariot, which was parallel parked next to the restaurant's drive-through lane. Their collars were decked with golden bells that jingled cheerfully when Otis and Marvin shook their heads. The chariot box itself was garlanded in yellow-and-white flowers that didn't quite mask the lingering smell of sweaty thunder god.

"Hey, guys." I told the goats, "You look festive."

"Yeah," Marvin grumbled. "I feel *real* festive. You know where we're going yet, human? The smell of Grande Scrambler Burritos is making me sick."

I checked the invitation. The *where* line now said: PROCEED TO BRIDAL VEIL FALLS. YOU ONLY HAVE FIVE MINUTES.

I read it twice just to make sure I wasn't imagining it. I'd guessed correctly. Uncle Randolph really might have been trying to help me. Now we had a chance at smuggling in some godly wedding crashers.

On the other hand, there was no avoiding the wedding now. I'd won a lottery in which the grand prize was a one-way trip into an evil earth giant's lair of pickle jars, beer bottles, and death. I doubted he would even honor Sif's coupon trophies.

I showed the invitation to the goats and the girls.

"So you were right," Sam said. "Maybe Thor—"

"*Shh,*" warned Alex. "From this point on, I think we should assume Loki is watching and listening."

That was another cheerful thought. The goats looked around as if Loki might be hiding nearby, possibly disguised as a grande burrito.

"Yeah," Marvin said, a little too loudly, "maybe Thor . . . would be sad, because there's no way he could make it to Bridal Veil Falls with an assault team in only five minutes, since we just got this information now and are at a huge disadvantage. Bummer!"

His subterfuge skills were almost as refined as Otis's. I wondered if the two goats had matching trench coats, hats, and sunglasses.

Otis gave his bells a jolly jingle. "We'd better hurry along to our deaths. Five minutes isn't much time, even for Thor's chariot. Hop aboard."

Hopping wasn't possible for Sam and Alex in their wedding dresses. I had to pull them up, which neither of them enjoyed, judging from the muttering and cursing behind their veils.

The goats took off at a full gallop . . . or whatever it is goats do. Canter? Trot? Strut? At the edge of the parking lot, the chariot went airborne. We jingled as we flew from the restaurant like Taco Claus's sleigh, bringing Cheesy Gordita Crunches to all the good little boys and girls and giants.

The goats picked up speed. We cut through a cloud bank at a thousand miles per hour, the cold mist slicking back my hair and wilting my shirt frills. I wished I had a veil like Sam and Alex, or at least some goggles. I wondered if Jack could make like a windshield wiper.

Then, just as quickly, we began to descend. Below us spread the White Mountains—rolling gray ridges with veins of white where the snow clung to life in the crevices.

Otis and Marvin dive-bombed one of the valleys, leaving my internal organs up in the clouds. Stanley the horse would have approved. Sam did not. She clutched the railing and muttered, "Minimums, guys. Watch your approach speed."

Alex snickered. "Don't be a backseat pilot."

We landed in a forested ravine. The goats trotted onward, snow churning around the chariot wheels like thickening ice cream. Otis and Marvin didn't seem to mind. They forged ahead, jingling and exhaling steam, pulling us deeper into the shadow of the mountains.

I kept watching the ridges above us, hoping to spot some Aesir and einherjar hidden in the brush, ready to help should something go wrong. I would have loved to see the glint of T.J.'s bayonet or Halfborn's painted berserker face, or hear a bit of Gaelic cursing from Mallory. But the woods seemed empty.

I remembered what Utgard-Loki had said—that killing us

and taking the Skofnung Sword would be much easier than letting us go through with the wedding plans.

"Hey, guys . . . how do we know Thrym isn't a fan of, uh, option one?"

"He wouldn't kill us," Sam said. "Not unless he has to. He *wants* this marriage alliance with Loki, which means he needs me—I mean her, Samirah." She pointed to Alex.

Marvin tossed his horns as if trying to dislodge his bells. "You guys worried about an ambush? Don't be. Wedding parties are guaranteed safe passage."

"True," Otis said. "Though the giants could always kill us after the ceremony, I hope."

"You mean you *guess*," Marvin said. "Not you *hope*."

"Hmm? Oh, right."

"Let's be quiet now," Marvin groused. "We don't want to cause an avalanche."

The possibility of a spring avalanche seemed unlikely. There wasn't that much snow on the sides of the mountains. Still, after all we'd been through, it would be pretty stupid to get buried under a ton of frozen debris in this snazzy tuxedo.

Finally, the chariot drew up to a cliff face about ten stories tall. Sheets of ice glazed the rocks like a curtain of sugar. Underneath, the waterfall was slowly coming back to life, gurgling and shifting and pulsing with light.

"Bridal Veil Falls," Alex said. "I went ice climbing here a couple of times."

"But not in a wedding dress," I guessed. (Or maybe I *hoped*. Otis had confused me.)

"What do we do now?" Sam wondered.

"Well, it's been four minutes," Marvin said. "We're not late."

"Be a shame if we missed the doorway," I said. (Pretty sure that was a *hope*.)

Right on cue, the ground rumbled. The waterfall seemed to stretch, waking up from its winter sleep, sloughing off icy sheets that splintered and crashed into the stream below. The cliff face split right down the middle, and the water sluiced to either side, revealing the mouth of a large cave.

From the darkness, a giantess emerged. She was about seven feet tall—petite for a giant. She wore a dress stitched entirely from white furs, which made me feel sad for the animals—polar bears, most likely—that had given their lives for it. The woman's stark white hair was braided on either side of her face, and I kind of wished she had a veil, because, *yikes*. Her bulging eyes were the size of navel oranges. Her nose looked like it had been broken several times. When she grinned, her lips and teeth were stained black.

"Hello, there!" She had the same gravelly voice I remembered from my dream. I involuntarily flinched, afraid she might swat my pickle jar.

"I am Thrynga," she continued, "princess of the earth giants, sister of Thrym, son of Thrym, son of Thrym! I am here to welcome my new sister-in-law."

Alex turned toward me. I couldn't see her face, but the small creaking sound in her throat seemed to mean *Abort! Abort!*

Sam curtseyed. She spoke in a higher-pitched tone than usual. "Thank you, Thrynga! My lady Samirah is delighted to be here. I am her maid of honor—"

"Prudence," I offered.

Sam looked at me, her eye twitching above her bandit scarf. "Yes . . . Prudence. And this is—"

Before she could take revenge by naming me Clarabelle or Horatio Q. Pantaloons, I said, "Magnus Chase! Son of Frey and carrier of the bride-price. Nice to meet you."

Thrynga licked her black-stained lips. Seriously, I wondered if she sucked on ballpoint pens in her spare time.

"Ah, yes," she said. "You are on the guest list, son of Frey. And that is the Skofnung Sword you bear? Very good. I will take that."

"Not until gifts are exchanged during the ceremony," I said. "We want to observe tradition, don't we?"

Thrynga's eyes flashed dangerously—and hungrily. "Of course. Tradition. And speaking of that . . ." From her polar-bear-fur sleeves, she produced a large stone paddle. I had a brief moment of terror, wondering if giants traditionally paddled their wedding guests.

"You don't mind if I do a quick security sweep?" Thrynga waved the wand over the goats. Then she inspected the chariot, and finally, us. "Good," she said. "No Aesir in the vicinity."

"My therapist says Marvin has a god complex," Otis volunteered. "But I don't think that counts."

"Shut up, or I'll destroy you," Marvin grumbled.

Thrynga frowned as she studied our chariot. "This vehicle looks familiar. It even smells familiar."

"Well, you know," I said, "lords and ladies often ride chariots to their weddings. This is a rental."

"Hmmm." Thrynga pulled at the white whiskers on her chin. "I suppose . . ." She glanced again at the Skofnung Sword on my back, a greedy gleam in her eyes. She motioned toward the cave entrance. "This way, little humans."

I didn't think it was fair of her to call us *little*. She was just a petite seven-footer herself, after all. She loped into the cavern and our goats followed, pulling the chariot straight through the middle of the broken waterfall.

The tunnel was smooth-bored and barely wide enough for our wheels. Ice coated the floor, which sloped downward at such a perilous angle I was afraid Otis and Marvin would slip and drag us to oblivion. Thrynga, however, seemed to have no problem keeping her footing.

We were about fifty feet into the tunnel when I heard the cave entrance closing behind us.

"Hey, Thrynga," I said, "shouldn't we leave that waterfall open? How will we get out after the ceremony?"

The giantess gave me an inky grin. "Get out? Oh, I wouldn't worry about that. Besides, we have to keep the entrance closed and the tunnel moving around. We wouldn't want anyone interfering with the happy day, would we?"

Sweat soaked the collar of my tuxedo. How long had that tunnel entrance remained open after we passed through—a minute? Two minutes? Had Thor and his team been able to get inside? Had they been there at all? I heard nothing behind us, not even a discreet fart, so it was impossible to know.

My eyes felt jumpy in their sockets. My fingers twitched. I wanted to talk to Alex and Sam, to come up with some contingency plans in case things went wrong, but I couldn't do that with the white giantess Thrynga right in front of us.

As the giantess walked, she produced a chestnut from a pocket of her dress. She began absently tossing the nut into the air and catching it. This seemed like an odd lucky charm for a giant. Then again, I had a runestone that turned into a sword, so I shouldn't criticize.

The air got colder and thicker. The stone ceiling seemed to press down on us. I felt like we were sliding sideways, but I wasn't sure if that was the wheels on the ice, or the tunnel shifting through the earth, or my spleen banging on the side of my body, trying to get out.

"How far down does this tunnel go?" My voice echoed off the rock walls.

Thrynga chuckled, turning her chestnut in her fingers. "Scared of deep places, son of Frey? Not to worry. We're only going a bit farther. Of course, the road itself goes all the way to Helheim. Most subterranean passages do, eventually."

She paused to show me the bottom of her shoes, which were studded with iron spikes. "Giants and goats are best suited for such a road. You small ones would lose your footing and slide all the way to the Wall of Corpses. We can't have that."

For once, I agreed with the giantess.

The chariot rolled on. The smell of its flower garlands turned sweeter and cooler, reminding me of the funeral home where my mortal body had been displayed in a casket. I hoped I wouldn't have to have a second funeral. If I did, I wondered if I would be buried next to myself.

Thrynga's idea of "a bit farther" was four more hours of traveling. The goats didn't seem to mind, but I was going crazy with cold, anxiety, and boredom. I'd only had one cup of coffee and a few frowny pieces of doughnut at Sif's palace that morning. Now I felt hungry and strung out. I'd been reduced to an empty stomach, frayed nerves, and a full bladder. We saw no service stations or rest stops along the road. Not even a friendly bush. The girls must have also been suffering. They kept shifting from foot to foot and bouncing on their heels.

Finally, we reached a split in the tunnel. The main road continued down into the icy dark. But to the right, a short path dead-ended at a set of iron-studded oak doors with knockers fashioned like dragon heads.

The welcome mat read BLESS THIS CAVE!

Thrynga grinned. "We are here, little ones. I hope you're excited."

She pushed open the doors and our chariot rolled through . . . right into the barroom from *Cheers*.

FORTY-NINE

Thrym!

SUDDENLY, TAKING the road to Helheim didn't sound so bad.

No wonder Thrym's lair had seemed so familiar to me when I saw it through the pickle jar glass in my dream. The place was a near perfect replica of the Bull & Finch Pub, the inspiration for the old TV show *Cheers*.

Because it was across from the Public Garden, I'd been to the pub a few times when I was homeless—to get warm on a bitter winter's day or beg a hamburger from the patrons. The place was always full and rowdy, and somehow it made perfect sense to me that there would be an earth-giant equivalent.

As we rolled in, a dozen giants at the bar turned in our direction and raised their mead glasses. "Samirah!" they cried in unison.

More giants crowded the tables and booths, eating burgers and swilling down mead.

Most of the patrons were a bit larger than Thrynga. They were dressed in a riot of tuxedo pieces, fur, and armor that made my own outfit look positively understated.

I scanned the room but saw no sign of Loki or my Uncle Randolph. I wasn't sure whether to be relieved or worried. At the far end of the bar, on a simple wooden throne under the big-screen TV, sat the earth giant king himself: Thrym, son of Thrym, son of Thrym.

"At last!" he bellowed in his walrus voice.

The king rose unsteadily. He bore such an uncanny resemblance to Norm from the TV show I wondered if he got paid residuals. His body was perfectly round, stuffed into black polyester pants and a red T-shirt with a wide black tie. Fuzzy dark hair framed his moon face. He was the first giant I'd ever seen without facial hair, and I really wished he would grow some. His mouth was wet and pink. His chin was pretty much nonexistent. His voracious eyes fixed on Alex as if she were a luscious plate of cheeseburgers.

"My queen has arrived!" Thrym patted his ample belly. "We can begin the festivities!"

"Brother, you haven't even gotten changed yet!" yelled Thrynga. "And why is this place so filthy? I told you to clean up while I was gone!"

Thrym frowned. "What do you mean? We *did* clean up. We put on ties!"

"Ties!" yelled the crowd of giants.

"You worthless scoundrels!" Thrynga picked up the nearest stool and cracked it over the head of a random giant, who collapsed in a heap. "Turn off the television. Clean that counter! Sweep that floor! Wipe your faces!"

She wheeled on us. "Sorry about these idiots. I'll get them ready in no time."

"Yeah, that's fine," I said, dancing the I-need-to-pee dance. "Actually—restrooms?"

"Right down the hall there." Thrynga pointed. "Leave the chariot. I'll make sure no one eats your goats."

I helped Sam and Alex out of the chariot and we shuffled through the chaos, dodging mops and brooms and smelly giants while Thrynga moved through the crowd, shouting at her patrons to get ready for today's happy occasion quickly or she would rip their heads off.

The restrooms were located in the back, just where they would've been at Cheers. Fortunately, the area was empty except for one giant who was passed out and snoring in a corner booth, his face resting on a platter of nachos.

"I'm confused," Alex said. "Why is this Cheers?"

"A lot of elements bleed through from Boston to the other worlds," Sam said.

"Like Nidavellir looks like Southie," I said. "And Alfheim looks like Wellesley."

Alex shuddered. "Yeah, but I have to get married in Cheers?"

"Talk later," I said. "Pee now."

"Yep," the girls said in unison.

Being a guy and not burdened by a wedding dress, I finished first. A few minutes later the girls reappeared, a tail of toilet paper trailing from the hem of Alex's gown. I doubted any of the giants would've noticed or cared, but Sam removed it for her.

"You think our friends made it inside?" I asked.

"I hope so," Alex said. "I'm so nervous I—*URF!*"

That last syllable sounded like a bear choking on a Tootsie Roll. I checked the corner booth to make sure the giant hadn't heard it. He just muttered in his sleep and turned his head on his corn-chip pillow.

Sam patted Alex's shoulder. "It's okay." She faced me.

"Alex turned into a gorilla in the bathroom. She'll be fine."

"She *what*?"

"It happens," Sam said. "With shape-shifters, if you get nervous and lose focus—"

Alex belched. "I'm better. I think I'm back to human now. Wait . . ." She shimmied in her dress like she was trying to dislodge a pebble. "Yeah. All good."

I didn't know if she was being serious or not. I wasn't sure I *wanted* to know. "Alex, if you accidentally change shape while you're out there among the giants—"

"I won't," she promised.

"Just keep silent," Sam told her. "You're supposed to be the shy blushing bride. I'll do the talking. Follow my lead. We'll stall as long as possible, hopefully give Th—*our friends* enough time to get in position."

"But where is Loki?" I asked. "And my uncle?"

Sam got quiet. "Not sure. But we have to keep our eyes peeled. Once we see the ham—"

"There you are!" Thrynga emerged from the hallway. "We're ready for you now."

"Of course!" Sam said. "We were just, um, talking about how much we love ham. I hope there's ham at the feast!"

I winked at her like, *Smooth. Otis-level smooth.*

Thrynga ushered us back into the bar. Judging from the smell, someone had sprayed a copious amount of lemon Pledge. Most of the broken glass and food droppings had been swept from the floor. The TV was off, and all the giants were standing against the far wall in a line—their hair combed, their ties straightened, their shirts tucked in.

In unison, they chanted, "Good afternoon, Miss Samirah."

Alex curtseyed.

The real Samirah said, "Good afternoon, uh, class. My lady Samirah is too overwhelmed to speak, but she is very happy to be here."

Alex brayed like a donkey. The giants glanced uncertainly at Thrynga for etiquette tips.

King Thrym frowned. He'd put on a black tux jacket with a pink carnation pinned to the lapel, which made him look slightly more elegantly ugly. "Why does my bride sound like a donkey?"

"She is crying with joy," Sam said quickly, "because she has finally seen her handsome husband!"

"Hmm." Thrym ran a finger down his many chins. "That makes sense. Come, sweet Samirah! Sit by me, and we will begin the feast!"

Alex took the chair next to Thrym's throne. Thrynga flanked her brother like a bodyguard, so Sam and I stood on the other side of Alex and tried to look official. Our job seemed to consist mostly of not eating, swatting aside the occasional mead mug that accidentally flew in Alex's direction, and listening to our stomachs growl.

The first course was nachos. What was it with giants and nachos?

Thrynga kept grinning at me and eyeing the Skofnung Sword, which was still strapped to my back. It was clear that she coveted the blade. I wondered if anyone had told her it couldn't be drawn in the presence of women. I assumed giantesses counted as women. I didn't know what would happen if somebody tried to unsheathe Skofnung despite its restrictions, but I doubted it would be good.

Try it, Jack's voice hummed in my mind like he was having a pleasant dream. *Oh, man, she's so fine.*

Go back to sleep, Jack, I told him.

The giants laughed and shoveled down nachos, though they kept one eye on Thrynga as if making sure she wasn't going to smash them with a barstool for bad behavior. Otis and Marvin stood in their harnesses right where we'd left them. Occasionally a stray nacho flew in their direction, and one of the goats would snatch it out of the air.

Thrym did his best to chat up Alex. She shied away and said nothing. Just to be polite, she snuck an occasional tortilla chip under her veil.

"She eats so little!" Thrym worried. "Is she all right?"

"Oh, yes," Sam said. "She's too excited to have much of an appetite, Your Majesty."

"Hmm." Thrym shrugged. "Well, at least I know she isn't Thor!"

"Of course not!" Sam's voice went up an octave. "Why would you think that?"

"Ages ago, when Thor's hammer was first stolen by my grandfather—"

"*Our* grandfather," Thrynga corrected, examining the ridges on her lucky chestnut.

"—Thor came disguised in a wedding dress to get it back." Thrym's wet lips curled inward like he was trying to locate his back teeth. "I remember that day, though I was only a child. The false bride ate an entire ox and drank two cases of mead!"

"*Three* cases," Thrynga said.

"Thor could hide his body in a wedding dress," Thrym said, "but he could not hide his appetite." The giant smiled at

Alex. "But don't worry, Samirah, my love! I know you are not a god. I am smarter than my grandfather was!"

Thrynga rolled her huge eyes. "It's *my* security that keeps out the Aesir, brother. No god could pass through our doors without triggering the alarms!"

"Yes, yes," Thrym said. "At any rate, Samirah, you were all magically scanned the moment you came in. You are, as you should be, a child of Loki." He knit his eyebrows. "Although so is your maid of honor."

"We're related!" said the real Sam. "That's to be expected, isn't it? A close relative often serves as maid of honor."

Thrym nodded. "That's true. At any rate, when this wedding is concluded, the House of Thrym shall regain its former stature! My grandfather's failure will be put to rest. We will have a marriage alliance with the House of Loki." He pounded his chest, causing his large belly to ripple and no doubt drowning entire nations of bacteria in his gut. "I will finally have my revenge!"

Thrynga turned her head, muttering, "*I* will have my revenge."

"What's that, sister?" Thrym demanded.

"Nothing." She bared her black teeth. "Let's have the second course, shall we?"

The second course was burgers. That *really* wasn't fair. They smelled so good, my stomach rolled back and forth, throwing a temper tantrum.

I tried to distract myself by thinking of the fight to come. Thrym seemed dumb enough. Maybe we could actually beat him. Unfortunately, he was backed up by several dozen earth giants, and his sister worried me. I could tell Thrynga had her own agenda. Though she tried to conceal it, every once in a while she would glance at Alex with murderous hatred. I remembered something Heimdall had overheard her say . . . that they should just kill the bride as soon as she arrived. I wondered how long it would take the Aesir to get here once the hammer was revealed, and whether I could keep Alex alive for that long. I wondered where Loki was, and Uncle Randolph. . . .

Finally the giants finished their meals. Thrym belched loudly and turned to his bride-to-be.

"At last, it is time for the ceremony!" he said. "Shall we be on our way?"

My gut clenched. "On our way? What do you mean?"

Thrym chuckled. "Well, we're not doing the ceremony here. That would be rude! The entire wedding party is not present!"

The king rose and faced the wall opposite the bar. Giants scrambled out of the way, moving their tables and chairs.

Thrym thrust out his hand. The wall cracked opened and a new tunnel wormed its way through the earth. The sour, damp air from within reminded me of something I couldn't quite place . . . something bad.

"No." Sam sounded as if her throat were closing up. "No, we *can't* go there."

"But we can't have a wedding without the father of the bride!" Thrym announced cheerfully. "Come, my friends! My bride and I will say our vows in the cavern of Loki!"

FIFTY

A Little Refreshing Poison in Your Face, Sir?

I REALLY HATE jigsaw puzzles. Did I ever mention that?

I especially hate it when I stare at a piece for hours, wondering where it goes, then somebody else comes along, slaps it into place, and says, *There, stupid!*

That's what I felt like when I finally figured out Loki's plan.

I remembered the maps strewn across Uncle Randolph's desk when Alex and I had visited. Maybe, in the back of my mind, I'd realized how strange that was at the time. Randolph's quest to find the Sword of Summer was over. Why would he still be poring over maps? But I hadn't asked Alex—or myself—about it. I'd been too distracted.

Now I was willing to bet Randolph had been studying topographical maps of New England, comparing them with ancient Norse charts and legends. He'd been ordered to undertake a different search—to find the coordinates of Loki's cavern in relation to the fortress of Thrym. If anyone could do it, my uncle could. That's why Loki had kept him alive.

No wonder Loki and Randolph weren't at the bar. They were waiting for us at the other end of the tunnel.

"We need our goats!" I yelled.

I waded through the crowd until I reached our chariot. I grabbed Otis's face and pressed my forehead against his.

"Testing," I whispered. "Is this goat on? Thor, can you hear me?"

"You have beautiful eyes," Otis told me.

"Thor," I said, "red alert! We're on the move. They're taking us to Loki's cave. I—I don't know where that is. Tunnel is on the right-hand wall, angling down. Just—*find* us! Otis, did he get the message?"

"What message?" Otis asked dreamily.

"Magnus Chase!" the giant king yelled. "Are you ready?"

"Uh, yeah!" I called back. "We just have to ride in the chariot because . . . traditional wedding reasons."

The other giants shrugged and nodded as if this made perfect sense to them. Only Thrynga looked suspicious. I feared she was starting to doubt whether the chariot was a rental.

Suddenly the bar felt much too small, with all the giants putting on their coats, straightening their ties, swigging the last of their mead, and trying to figure out their places in the wedding procession.

Samirah and Alex made their way to the chariot.

"What do we do?" Alex hissed.

"I don't know!" Sam said. "Where's our backup?"

"We're going to be in the wrong place," I said. "How will they find us?"

That was all we had time to say to one another before Thrym came over and took the reins of our goats. He pulled our chariot into the tunnel, his sister by his side, the rest of the giants filing in two by two behind us.

As soon as the last giants were inside the tunnel, the entrance behind us sealed shut.

"Hey, Thrym?" My voice bore an unfortunate resemblance

to Mickey Mouse's, making me wonder what sort of strange gasses were in this tunnel. "You sure it's a good idea to trust Loki? I mean . . . wasn't it *his* idea to sneak Thor into your grandfather's wedding? Didn't he help Thor kill your family?"

The giant king stopped so abruptly Marvin ran into him. I knew I was asking an impolite question, especially on the guy's wedding day, but I was grasping for anything that might slow down the parade.

Thrym turned, his eyes like wet pink diamonds in the gloom. "Don't you think I know that, human? Loki is a trickster. It is his nature. But *Thor* is the one who killed my grandfather, my father, my mother, my entire family!"

"Except for me," Thrynga muttered. In the darkness, she glowed faintly—a seven-foot-tall apparition of ugliness. I hadn't noticed that earlier. Maybe it was an ability that earth giants could turn off and on.

Thrym ignored her. "This marriage alliance is Loki's way of *apologizing*; don't you see? He realizes now that the gods were always his enemies. He regrets betraying my grandfather. We will combine our forces, take over Midgard, and then storm the city of the gods itself!"

Behind us, the giants let loose a deafening cheer. "Kill the humans!"

"Shut it!" Thrynga yelled. "We have humans with us!"

The giants murmured. Someone in the back said, "Present company excepted."

"But, Great King Thrym," Sam said, "do you really trust Loki?"

Thrym laughed. For such a big guy, he had tiny teeth. "In his cave, Loki is a prisoner. Helpless! He is inviting me there.

He *gave* me the location. Why would he make such a gesture of trust?"

His sister snorted. "Gee, I don't know, brother. Maybe because he needs an earth giant to tunnel into his place of imprisonment? Because he wants to be free?"

I was kind of wishing Thrynga was on our side, except for the fact that she was a power-hungry giantess bent on revenge and murdering all humans.

"*We* hold the power," Thrym insisted. "Loki would not *dare* betray us. Besides, *I* am the one who will open his cave! He will be grateful! As long as he honors his part of the bargain, I will gladly let him go free. And the beautiful Samirah . . ." Thrym leered at Alex. "She is worth the risk."

Under her veil, Alex squawked like a parrot. The noise was so loud Thrynga almost hit the ceiling.

"What was *that?*" the giantess demanded. "Is the bride choking?"

"No, no!" Sam patted Alex's back. "That was just a nervous laugh. Samirah gets uncomfortable when people compliment her."

Thrym chuckled. "Then she will be uncomfortable often when she is my wife."

"Oh, Your Majesty!" Sam said. "Truer words have never been spoken!"

"Onward!" Thrym proceeded down the icy path.

I wondered if our delay had bought our backup troops any time. Assuming we even had backup troops. Could Thor still follow our progress through his goats' eyes and ears? Did he have some way to get a message to Blitz and Hearth and my einherji hallmates from floor nineteen?

The tunnel closed behind us as we descended. I had a horrible vision of Thor in the giants' barroom, trying to break through the wall with his corkscrew and hand drill.

After a few more minutes, the tunnel began to narrow. Thrym's progress slowed. I got the feeling that the earth itself was fighting him now, trying to push him back. Maybe the Aesir had placed some sort of magic barrier around Loki's tomb.

If so, it wasn't enough. We trudged onward and downward, though the chariot's axle now ground against the walls. Behind us, the giants walked single file. Next to me, Sam murmured softly—a chant in Arabic that I remembered from her prayers.

A foul smell wafted up from the depths—like sour milk, rotten eggs, and burned meat. I was afraid it was not Thor.

"I can sense him," Alex whispered, the first thing she'd said in almost an hour. "Oh, no, no, no . . ."

The tunnel widened suddenly, as if Thrym had finally burst through the earth's defenses. Our procession filed into the chamber of Loki.

I'd seen the place in my dream, but that didn't prepare me for the real thing. The cavern was about the size of a tennis court, with a high domed ceiling of cracked stone and broken stalactites, the remnants of which littered the floor. There were no other exits that I could see. The air was stale and sickly sweet with the stink of rot and burned flesh. Around the room, massive stalagmites rose from the floor. In other places, craters of viscous liquid bubbled and steamed, filling the cave with noxious gas. The temperature was about a hundred degrees, and all the earth giants tromping in didn't help with the heat or the smell.

In the center of the room, just as I'd seen in my dream, Loki lay prone on the floor, his ankles bound together and tied to one stalagmite, his arms spread wide and chained to two others.

Unlike the manifestations I'd seen of him before, the real Loki was neither handsome nor dashing. He wore nothing but a ragged loincloth. His body was emaciated, filthy, and covered with scars. His long stringy hair might once have been reddish brown, but it was now burned and bleached from centuries of being in this toxic cave. And his face—what was left of it—was a half-melted mask of scar tissue.

Coiled around the stalactite at Loki's head, a massive serpent stared down at the prisoner, its fangs dripping yellow venom.

At Loki's side knelt a woman in a white hooded robe. She was holding a metal bowl over Loki's face to catch the poison. The snake was a real producer, though. The venom dripped from its mouth like a partially turned-on showerhead. The woman's bowl was much too small.

As we watched, venom filled it to the brim and the woman turned to empty it, tossing the contents into one of the boiling pools behind her. She moved quickly, but poison still splattered Loki's face. He writhed and screamed. The cavern shook. I thought the ceiling would collapse on top of us, but somehow it held. Maybe the gods had fashioned this chamber to endure the shaking, just as they'd fashioned Loki's bonds never to break, the snake never to run dry, and the woman's cup never to be big enough.

I wasn't religious, but the whole scene reminded me of a crucifix in a Catholic church—a man in excruciating pain, his arms outstretched. Of course, Loki was nobody's idea of a savior. He wasn't good. He wasn't sacrificing himself for something noble. He was an evil immortal paying for his crimes. Still, seeing him here in person—broken, filthy, and in agony—I couldn't help feeling pity. No one deserved this kind of punishment, not even a murderer and a liar.

The woman in white lifted her cup again to shield his face. Loki shook the poison from his eyes. He took a ragged breath and glanced in our direction.

"Welcome, Magnus Chase!" He gave me a hideous grin. "I hope you'll excuse me if I don't get up."

"Gods," I muttered.

"Oh, no; no gods here!" Loki said. "They never visit. They sealed us in and left us. It's just me and my lovely wife, Sigyn. Say hello, Sigyn."

The woman in white looked up. Under her hood, her face was so emaciated she might have been a draugr. Her eyes were solid red, her expression blank. Bloodred tears streamed down her leathery face.

"Oh, that's right." Loki's voice was even more acidic than the air. "Sigyn hasn't spoken in a thousand years—ever since the Aesir, in their infinite wisdom, butchered our sons and abandoned us here to suffer for eternity. But where are my manners? This is a happy occasion! How are you, Thrym, son of Thrym, son of Thrym, son of Thrym?"

The king didn't look so well. He kept swallowing, like his nachos weren't staying down. "H-hello, Loki. It's—it's actually just *three* Thryms. And I am ready to seal our alliance with a marriage."

"Yes, of course! Magnus, you've brought the Skofnung Sword."

It was a statement, not a question. He spoke with such authority, I had to resist the urge to unsling the blade and show it to him.

"We have it," I said. "First things first. We want to see the hammer."

Loki laughed—a wet, gurgling sound. "First, let's make sure the bride is actually the bride. Come here, my dear Samirah. Let me see your face."

Both girls lurched toward him like they were being pulled with ropes.

My pulse throbbed against the collar of my tux shirt. I should have considered that Loki would check under the girls' veils. He was, after all, the god of deception. Despite Alex's assurances that she could resist Loki's orders, she staggered forward just like Samirah.

I wondered how fast I could get out my sword, how many giants I could kill. I wondered if Otis and Marvin would be any good in a fight. Probably too much to hope for that they were trained in goat fu.

"There we are," Loki said. "Now let's have the bride lift her veil, eh? Just to make sure everyone is playing fairly."

Alex's hands jerked upward like they were on marionette strings. She began to lift her veil. The cave was silent except for the bubbling of hot springs and the constant drip of poison into Sigyn's cup.

Alex pushed her veil back over her head, revealing . . .
Samirah's face.

For a second, I panicked. Had the girls somehow switched
places? Then I realized—I don't know how, maybe something
in her eyes—that Alex was still Alex. She'd shape-shifted to
look like Sam, but whether or not that would fool Loki . . .

I curled my fingers around my pendant. The silence was
long enough for me to begin mentally composing my will.

"Well . . ." Loki said at last. "I must admit I'm surprised.
You actually followed orders. Good girl! I suppose that means
your maid of honor is—"

Sigyn's cup slipped, sloshing poison into Loki's face. The
god screamed and writhed in his bonds. The girls quickly
retreated.

Sigyn righted her bowl. She tried to wipe the venom from
Loki's eyes with her sleeve, but that only made him scream
more. Her hem came away smoking and full of holes.

"Stupid woman!" Loki wailed.

For a moment, Sigyn seemed to meet my gaze, though it
was hard to be sure with those solid-red eyes. Her expression
didn't change. The tears kept flowing. But I wondered if she
had spilled that poison on purpose. I didn't know why she
would. As far as I knew, she'd been kneeling at her husband's
side faithfully for centuries. Still . . . it seemed an oddly timed
mistake.

Thrynga cleared her throat—a beautiful sound, like a
chain saw cutting through mud. "You asked about the maid of
honor, Lord Loki. She says her name is Prudence."

Loki cackled, still trying to blink the poison from his eyes.
"I'm sure she did. Her real name is Alex Fierro, and I told her

not to come today, but no matter! Let us proceed. Thrynga, have you brought the special guest I requested?"

The giantess curled her ink-stained lips. She brought out the chestnut she'd been tossing around earlier.

"Your special guest is a nut?" I asked.

Loki laughed hoarsely. "You could say that. Go on, Thrynga."

Thrynga stuck her thumbnail into the shell and cracked the nut open. She tossed it to the floor, and something small and dark rolled out—not the meat of a chestnut, but a tiny human form. It grew in size until a stout old man stood before me—his rumpled black tuxedo dusted with plant chaff, his cheek marked with a ghastly burn scar in the shape of a hand.

Whatever optimism I'd been holding on to shed faster than Sif's golden hair.

"Uncle Randolph."

"Hello, Magnus," he said, his face contorted with misery. "Please, my boy . . . give me the Skofnung blade."

FIFTY-ONE

Hello, Paranoia, My Old Friend

THIS IS WHY I HATE FAMILY REUNIONS.

You always have to face that one uncle you don't want to see—you know, the one who pops out of a nutshell and demands a sword.

Part of me was tempted to smack Randolph upside the head with the Skofnung Stone. Part of me wanted to shove him back into his chestnut, tuck him safely into my pocket, and get him away from Loki. None of me was tempted to give him the sword that could cut Loki free.

"I can't do that, Randolph," I said.

My uncle winced. His right hand was still bandaged from where I'd cut off two of his fingers. He pressed it against his chest and reached out with his left, his eyes desperate and heavy. A coppery taste spread over my tongue. I realized my rich uncle now looked more like a beggar than I ever had during my two years on the streets.

"Please," he said. "I was supposed to bring it today, until you took it. I—I *need* it."

That was his job, I realized. Along with finding the location of this cave, he had been charged with freeing Loki, wielding the Skofnung Sword as only one of noble blood could do.

"Loki won't give you what you want," I told him. "Your family is gone."

He blinked as if I'd thrown sand in his eyes. "Magnus, you don't understand—"

"No sword," I said. "Not until we see Thor's hammer."

The giant king scoffed. "The hammer is the morgen-gifu, silly human! It will not be given until after the wedding night!"

Next to me, Alex shuddered. The golden arcs of her necklace reminded me of the Rainbow Bridge, the way she had laid down so casual and relaxed on the Bifrost, making angels in the light. I couldn't allow her to be forced into marrying a giant. I just wished I knew how to stop it.

"We need the hammer to bless the wedding," I said. "That is the bride's right. Let us see it and use it in the ceremony. Then you can take it back until . . . until tomorrow."

Loki laughed. "I don't think so, Magnus Chase. Nice try, though! Now Skofnung—"

"Hold on." Thrynga fixed Loki with her I'm-about-to-hit-you-with-a-barstool glare. "The girl is within her rights. If she wants the blessing of the hammer, she should have it. Or does my brother wish to break our sacred tradition?"

Thrym flinched. His gaze flitted from his sister to his followers to Loki. "I . . . er . . . no. That is, yes. My bride, Samirah, may receive the blessing. At the proper time in the ceremony, I will bring forth Mjolnir. Shall we begin?"

Thrynga's eyes glittered wickedly. I didn't know what her game was, why she wanted to bring out the hammer early, but I wasn't going to argue.

Thrym clapped his hands. I hadn't noticed before, but a

few giants in the back of the procession had brought some pieces of furniture with them from the bar. Just to the left of Loki's binding place, they set down a plain wooden bench and covered the seat with furs. On either side of the bench, they placed a freestanding post like a totem pole, each one carved with fierce animal faces and runic inscriptions.

Thrym sat. The bench groaned under his weight. One of his giants placed a crown of stone on his head—a circlet carved from a single piece of dark granite.

"Girl, you stand there," the giantess told Alex, "between your father and your husband-to-be."

Alex hesitated.

Loki made a *tsk-tsk* sound. "Come now, daughter. Don't be shy. Stand next to me."

Alex did as she was told. I wanted to believe it was because she was playing the charade and not because she was being compelled, but I remembered the way she'd been yanked around as if by a rope earlier at Loki's command.

Sam stood to my right, her hands clasped anxiously. Randolph shuffled off to wait by Loki's feet. He hunched there like a guilty mastiff that had come back from the hunt with no dead animal for his master.

"The cup!" Thrym ordered.

One of his men placed a jewel-encrusted goblet in his fingers. Red liquid sloshed over the brim.

Thrym took a swig. Then he offered the cup to Alex. "Samirah al-Abbas bint Loki, I give you drink, and with it the binding promise of my love. By my troth, you shall be my wife."

Alex took the cup in her lace-covered fingers. She looked

around, as if for guidance. It occurred to me that she might not be able to imitate Sam's voice as well as her face.

"You need not speak, girl," Thrynga said. "Just drink!"

Me, I would have been concerned about backwash, but Alex lifted the bottom of her veil and took a sip.

"Excellent." Thrynga turned to me, her facial muscles twitching with impatience. "Now, at last, the mundr. Give me the sword, boy."

"Sister, no," Thrym rumbled. "It does not go to you."

Thrynga wheeled on her brother. "*What?* I am your only kin! The bride-price must pass through my hands!"

"I have an arrangement with Loki." Thrym looked more confident now, almost smug, with Alex so close at hand. I had a terrible feeling he was imagining the end of the ceremony, his chance to kiss the bride. "Boy, give the sword to your uncle. He will hold it."

Thrynga glared at me. Looking in her eyes, I realized what she wanted. She intended to claim Skofnung for herself, and probably Mjolnir, too. She had no interest in a marriage alliance with Loki. She saw this wedding as a chance to wrest the throne from her brother. She would kill anyone who stood in her way. Maybe she didn't know that the Skofnung Sword couldn't be unsheathed in the presence of a woman. Maybe she thought she could use it anyway. Or maybe she was happy wielding the power of a barstool, as long as the other two weapons were safely locked up and in her possession.

Under different circumstances, I might have wished her luck assassinating her brother. Heck, I would have even given her a trophy good for half-price entrées in Asgard.

Unfortunately, I got the feeling Thrynga's plan also included killing me, Sam, Alex, and probably Uncle Randolph.

I took a step back. "I told you, Thrym. No hammer, no sword."

Randolph shuffled toward me, his bandaged hand cradled against his cummerbund. "Magnus, you must," he said. "This is the order of the ceremony. Mundr must be given first, and each wedding *requires* an ancestral sword to put the rings on. The blessing of the hammer comes afterward."

Jack's pendant hummed against my collarbone. Maybe he was trying to warn me. Or maybe he just wanted to get another look at Skofnung, babe among swords. Or maybe he was jealous because *he* wanted to be the ceremonial sword.

"What is it, boy?" Thrym grumbled. "I have already promised that the traditional rights will be observed. Do you not trust us?"

I almost laughed out loud.

I looked at Sam. As discreetly as she could, she signed, *No choice. But watch him.*

Suddenly I felt stupid. This whole time, we could have been using sign language to give each other secret messages.

On the other hand, Loki might be controlling Sam, making her say that. Could he get inside her mind without even saying anything, without even snapping his fingers? I remembered what Sam had told me in Sif's atrium: *You have to stop him. If we're incapacitated, you may be the only one who can.* For all I knew, I was the only one in the room *not* under Loki's control.

Wow. Hello, paranoia.

Two dozen giants watched me. My uncle extended his good hand.

I happened to meet Sigyn's blank red eyes. The goddess inclined her head ever so slightly. I don't know why that convinced me, but I unslung the sword and put Skofnung in Randolph's hand, the stone hanging heavily from the pommel.

"You are still a Chase," I said quietly. "You still have *living* family."

Randolph's eye twitched. He took the sword mutely.

He knelt before the king's bench. With some fumbling due to his bandaged hand, he held the sheath horizontally like a serving tray. Thrym placed two gold wedding rings in the center and held his hand over them like a blessing.

"Ymir, ancestor of the gods and giants, hear my words," he said. "These rings signify our marriage."

He slipped one ring on his own finger and one on Alex's. Then he waved off Uncle Randolph. My uncle shuffled back with the sword, but Sam and I moved to intercept, blocking him from getting any closer to Loki.

I was about to insist on the hammer, but Thrynga beat me to it. "Brother, honor your promise."

"Yes, yes," Thrym agreed. "Samirah, my dear, please sit."

Alex stepped forward, trancelike, and sat at the giant's side. It was hard to tell under the veil, but she seemed to be staring at the ring on her hand as if it were a brown recluse spider.

"Giants, stand ready," Thrym said. "You will surround the hammer and bring it here. You will hold it over my bride, *very carefully,* while we say the blessing. Then I will immediately send it back into the earth . . ." He turned to Alex. "Until tomorrow morning, my sweet, when it will be officially your morgen-gifu. After that, I'll be sure to keep it safe for you." He patted Alex's knee, which she seemed to enjoy almost as much as the poisonous wedding ring.

Thrym extended his hand. He strained, his face turning the color of mulberry jam. The cavern rumbled. About twenty feet away, the floor cracked open, and gravel and mud pushed upward as if some huge insect were tunneling out. The hammer of Thor emerged and settled in a caldera of rubble.

It looked just as I'd seen it in my dream: a huge trapezoidal head of metal with swirling runic designs, and a thick short handle bound in leather. Its presence filled the room with a smell like thunderstorms. While the giants hurried to surround the hammer, I signed to Sam: *Watch Randolph.* Then I scooted in the other direction, toward our chariot.

I grabbed Otis's snout and pressed my face against his.

"We're a go," I whispered. "Hammer is in the cave. I repeat: hammer is in the cave. Red October. Eagle has landed. Defense Pattern Omega!"

I'm not sure where the military code stuff came from. I just figured it was the sort of thing Thor would respond to. And, hey, I was nervous.

"You have beautiful eyes," Otis murmured.

"Bring the hammer here!" Thrym told his giants. "Be quick about it!"

"Yes," Loki agreed, shaking the poison-soaked hair out of his eyes. "And while you're doing that . . . Randolph, cut me free."

That's when Alex snapped.

FIFTY-TWO

My Uncle Gets Some Backup Singers

ALEX RIPPED OFF her veil, whipped her new golden garrote from her waist, and looped it around Thrym's neck. The giant king rose, bellowing in outrage, as Alex scrambled onto his back and began choking him like she'd done with the lindworm in Valhalla.

"I want a divorce!" she yelled.

Thrym's face turned an even deeper purple. His eyes bulged. His throat should have been cut clean through, but the skin around the garrote seemed to be turning to gleaming gray rock—stupid earth giants and their stupid earth magic.

"Treachery!" Thrynga's eyes danced with excitement, as if she finally saw a chance to do some treachery of her own. "Bring me the hammer!" She lunged for Mjolnir, but Samirah's ax hurtled across the room and embedded itself in Thrynga's side. The giantess fell forward like she was stealing second base.

I summoned Jack. Uncle Randolph was almost at Loki's side. Before I could reach him, giants surrounded me.

Jack and I leaped into action, working together efficiently for once, cleaving through one earth giant after another. But we were badly outnumbered and the giants (OBVIOUS FACT

ALERT) were *really* big. Out of the corner of my eye I saw
Thrynga clawing across the floor, trying to reach the now-
unguarded hammer. Thrym was still staggering around the
room, slamming his back against the cave wall in an attempt
to dislodge Alex, but each time he tried, Alex changed into a
gorilla, which just made it easier for her to strangle Thrym.
The giant's tongue was the size and color of an unripe plan-
tain. He stretched his hand toward Thor's hammer, probably
trying to send it back into the earth, but Alex tightened her
garrote and broke his concentration.

Meanwhile, Sam ripped off her own veil. Her Valkyrie
spear appeared in her hand, flooding the room with white
radiance. Two more giants charged toward her, blocking my
line of vision.

Somewhere behind me, Loki screamed, "Now, you fool!"

"I—I can't!" Randolph wailed. "There are women present!"

The god snarled. I suppose he could've forced Alex and
Sam to pass out, but that wouldn't solve the problem of
Thrynga and Sigyn.

"Unsheathe it anyway," he ordered. "Curse the consequences!"

"But—"

"DO IT!"

I was too busy dodging clubs and stabbing giants to see
what happened, but I heard the Skofnung Sword being drawn.
It let loose an unearthly howl—an outraged chorus of twelve
berserker spirits unleashed against their will and in violation
of their ancient taboo.

The sound was so loud it gave me double vision. Several

giants stumbled. Unfortunately, Jack had also been affected. He turned heavy and inanimate in my hands just as one of the giants backhanded me, sending me flying across the cavern.

I slammed into a stalagmite. Something in my chest went *crack*. That probably wasn't good. I struggled to rise, trying to ignore the acid now sloshing around in my rib cage.

My vision swam. Uncle Randolph was screaming, his voice blending with the howl of the Skofnung spirits. Mist swirled around him, pluming from the blade as if it had turned to dry ice.

"Hurry, you fool!" Loki yelled. "Before the sword dissolves!"

Sobbing, Randolph struck the bonds at Loki's feet. With a sound like a high-tension wire snapping on a bridge, the ties broke.

"No!" Sam shouted. She lunged forward, but the damage had been done. Loki brought his knees to his chest for the first time in a thousand years. Sigyn retreated against the far wall, allowing the snake's venom to splash freely in her husband's face. Loki screamed and thrashed.

Sam thrust her spear at my uncle, but Loki still had enough presence of mind to yell, "Samirah, freeze!"

Sam did, her teeth clenched with effort. Her eyes burned with rage. She let loose a guttural howl almost worse than the Skofnung Sword's, but she couldn't seem to break Loki's command.

Randolph staggered, staring at his smoking sword. The edge was corroding, the black gunk from Loki's bindings chewing away at the magical blade.

"The stone, you idiot!" Loki kicked at him futilely, turning his face away from the trickle of venom. "Sharpen the blade and get on with it! You only have a few minutes!"

Smoke continued swirling around Randolph. His skin was starting to turn blue. I realized it wasn't just the sword that was dissolving. The enraged spirits of Skofnung, still howling, were taking out their anger on my uncle.

A giant charged me with a ceremonial totem pole. I managed to roll out of the way—my cracked ribs throbbing in protest—and cripple the giant by stabbing his ankles.

Alex was still throttling the giant king. Both of them looked pretty bad. Thrym stumbled, his hands clawing sluggishly at his bride. Blood trickled from Alex's ear, spattering her white dress. I hoped Sif didn't expect us to return it dry-cleaned.

Three of the giants had surrounded Thor's hammer again. Now they picked it up, staggering under its weight.

"What do we do with it?" one groaned. "Put it back in the earth?"

"Don't you dare!" Thrynga yelled. She was on her feet now, clutching the ax still embedded in her side. "That hammer is mine!"

Granted, I didn't know the rules of earth magic, but judging from the effort it had taken Thrym to retrieve the hammer, I doubted any of the giants would be able to sink it eight miles into the earth again right away—not in the middle of a battle with weapons flying and berserker spirits howling. I was more concerned about the sword.

Randolph had already re-sharpened the blade. As Sam screamed at him to stop, he moved toward Loki's right hand.

"Thrynga!" I yelled.

The white giantess glared at me, her inky lips curled into a snarl.

"You want the sword for yourself . . . ?" I said, pointing to my uncle. "You'd better hurry."

It seemed like a good idea, turning a murderous giantess on Loki.

Unfortunately, Thrynga also hated *me*. "That sword is finished," she said. "Already dissolving. But perhaps I'll take yours!"

She charged. I tried to raise Jack, but he was still dead weight in my hand. Thrynga plowed into me and we both skidded across the floor—straight into one of the bubbling pits.

News flash: Pits of boiling liquid are *hot*.

Had I been a regular mortal, I would have died in seconds. Being an einherji, I figured I had a minute or so before the heat killed me. Hooray.

My world was reduced to a boiling roar, a sulfurous yellow haze, and the white shape of the giantess, whose fingers were digging into my windpipe.

Jack was still in my grip, but that arm felt heavy and useless. With my free hand, I clawed blindly at Thrynga, trying to break her grip on my throat.

By chance, my fingers found the shaft of Sam's ax, still buried in Thrynga's side. I yanked it free and swung it in the general vicinity of the giantess's head.

The pressure on my throat abruptly loosened. I pushed the giantess away and flailed for the surface. Somehow I pulled myself, steaming and lobster red, out of the hot springs.

More sounds of battle: Blades clanging against blades.

Rocks shattering. Giants roaring. The Skofnung Sword's spirits continued their bitter howling. I tried to get up, but my skin felt like a cooked sausage casing. I was afraid that if I moved too fast, I might literally burst.

"Jack," I croaked, "go."

Jack left my grip, but he was moving slowly. Maybe he was still dazed by the howling of the spirits. Maybe my own condition was weakening him. It was all he could do to keep the giants from finishing me off.

My vision was cloudy white with yellow blobs, as though my eyeballs had turned into hard-boiled eggs. I saw Thrym stagger to the wedding bench, grab it in both hands, and with one final burst of strength, swing it over his head at Alex. It crashed against her scalp, and she dropped off the giant's back.

Nearby, I heard another high-tension *SNAP*. Loki's right hand was free.

"Yes!" the god cried. He rolled to one side, out of the snake's range. "The last one, Randolph, and your family will be returned to you!"

Sam was still frozen. She struggled against Loki's will so intensely that a capillary had burst across her forehead, making a dotted red line there. In the light of her spear, Randolph's face looked bluer than ever. His skin was turning translucent, the structure of his skull showing through as he hurried to sharpen the Skofnung blade for one last strike.

Three giants were still staggering around with Thor's hammer, not sure what to do with it. The giant king turned toward Alex, who now lay stunned on the floor. Another giant approached Sam warily, eyeing her glowing spear, obviously wondering if she was really as helpless as she looked.

"Jack," I murmured, my voice like wet sand. But I didn't know what to tell him. I was barely able to move. A dozen giants were still in fighting shape. Loki was almost free. I couldn't save Alex and Sam *and* stop my uncle all at the same time. It was over.

Then the cavern shook. A bulging rift split the ceiling like the opening claws of a grabber arm—spilling out a dwarf, an elf, and several einherjar.

Blitz struck first. Just as Thrym looked up, momentarily distracted from his desire to kill his bride, a dwarf in paisley chain mail landed on his face. Blitz wasn't heavy, but he had gravity and surprise on his side. The giant king crumpled beneath him like a pile of blocks.

Hearthstone hit the cavern floor with his usual elfish grace and immediately tossed a rune at Loki:

$$\mid$$

I guess the *I* stood for *ice*. Suddenly, the god of evil was encased in the stuff, his eyes wide with shock, his left arm still bound to the last stalagmite—making him the ugliest frozen treat I had ever seen.

My comrades from floor nineteen launched themselves into battle with glee.

"Death and glory!" Halfborn roared.

"Kill everyone!" Mallory said.

"Charge!" T.J. yelled.

T.J. bayonetted the nearest giant. Mallory's knives flashed as she took out two more with well-placed crotch strikes.

(Tip: Don't ever fight Mallory Keen without titanium crotch armor.) Halfborn Gunderson, our own version of a giant, waded into the battle—shirtless, as usual, with bloodred smiley faces painted all over his chest (I assumed Mallory had gotten bored on the tunneling trip down here). Laughing insanely, Halfborn grabbed a giant's head and introduced it to his left knee. Halfborn's knee won.

With Loki frozen, Samirah was able to shake herself free of his control. She immediately put her spear to work, impaling an advancing giant then threatening Uncle Randolph. "Back off!" she snarled.

For a moment, I thought the tide had turned. Giants fell one after another. I summoned Jack to my hand, and despite my overcooked condition, despite my exhaustion, I managed to get to my feet. The presence of my friends energized me. I staggered over to Alex and helped her up.

"I'm good," she muttered, though she looked disoriented and bloody. How she had survived being bashed with a bench was beyond me. I guess she *was* hardheaded. "He—he didn't control me. Loki didn't. I—I was pretending."

She gripped my hand, obviously concerned that I might not believe her.

"I know, Alex." I squeezed her hand. "You did great."

Meanwhile, Blitzen hit Thrym repeatedly in the face with his chain mail bow tie. As he did so, he looked up at me and grinned. "Thor got in touch with us, kid. Nice work! It was actually easier for *me* to tunnel here once I knew the location. The gods are still digging their way in from this idiot's lair. The rock is magically hardened, by this guy"—he punched Thrym in the face again—"but they'll get through it."

The bodies of fallen giants lay strewn across the cavern. The last three standing were the ones guarding Thor's hammer, but they'd been staggering around so much with Mjolnir, back and forth from Thrym to Thrynga like a moving crew with an oversize couch, that now they looked completely spent. Halfborn Gunderson made short work of them with his battle-ax. Then he stood triumphantly over them, rubbing his hands eagerly. "I've always wanted to try this!" He strained to lift Mjolnir, but the hammer stayed stubbornly in place.

Mallory snorted. "Like I keep telling you, you are *not* as strong as three giants. Now help me over here—"

"Look out!" Alex cried.

Halfborn's effort with the hammer had distracted us from Uncle Randolph and Loki. I turned just as the block of ice shattered, spraying us with frozen shards.

In the moment we were blinded, my uncle lunged forward with Skofnung. He struck the last restraint around Loki's left wrist, snapping the bonds.

The sword dissipated in a puff of smoke. The chorus of angry berserkers went silent. My uncle dropped to his knees, screaming, his arm beginning to dissolve into blue vapor.

In the back of the cave, Sigyn cringed as her husband rose to his feet.

"Free," Loki said, his emaciated body steaming, his face a wasteland of scarred flesh. "Now the fun begins."

FIFTY-THREE

It's Hammer Time!
(Someone Had to Say It)

TIMING.

The Aesir *really* needed to work on their timing.

We still had no godly backup. We had a hammer, but no one to wield it. And Loki stood unchained before us in all his mutilated glory, ice clinging to his hair, poison dripping from his face.

"Ah, yes." He smiled. "For my first act . . ."

He lashed out with more speed and strength than should have been possible for a guy who'd been chained up for a thousand years. He grabbed the snake that had been dripping venom on him, yanked it off its stalactite, and snapped it like a whip.

Its spine cracked with a sound like Bubble Wrap popping. Loki dropped it, as lifeless as a garden hose, and turned toward us.

"I really hated that snake," he said. "Who's next?"

Jack lay heavy in my hand. Alex could barely stand. Sam had her spear ready, but she seemed reluctant to charge, probably because she didn't want to be to be frozen by her father again . . . or worse.

My other friends closed ranks around me: three strong einherjar, Blitzen in his fashionable chain mail, Hearthstone with his rowan-wood runes clacking in their bag as his fingers shifted through them.

"We can take him," T.J. said, his bayonet wet with giant blood. "All at once. Ready?"

Loki spread his arms in a welcoming gesture. Randolph knelt at his feet, silent in agony as the blue vapor spread up his arm, eating away at his flesh. Against the far wall, Sigyn stood very still, her pure red eyes impossible to read, her empty poison bowl clasped to her chest.

"Come on, then, warriors of Odin," Loki taunted. "I'm unarmed and weak. You can do it!"

That's when I knew in my heart that we couldn't. We would charge in and die. We'd end up lying on the floor with our spines snapped, just like that snake.

But we had no choice. We had to try.

Then, from the wall behind us came a cracking sound, followed by a familiar voice. "We're through! Yes, Heimdall. I'm sure this time. Probably."

The end of an iron staff poked through the rock and wriggled around. The wall began to crumble.

Loki lowered his arms and sighed. He looked more annoyed than terrified.

"Ah, well." He winked at me, or maybe his face was just convulsing from centuries of poison damage. "Next time?"

The ground crumbled underneath him. The entire back half of the cavern fell away. Stalagmites and stalactites imploded. Pools of boiling liquid turned into steaming waterfalls before disappearing into the void. Loki and Sigyn fell into nothingness. My uncle, who had been kneeling at the edge of the break, also slipped into the chasm.

"Randolph!" I scrambled to the edge.

About fifty feet below, Randolph crouched on a wet and steaming slope of rock, trying to keep his balance. His right arm was gone, the blue vapor now crawling up his shoulder. He looked up at me, his skull grinning through his translucent face.

"Randolph, hold on!" I said.

"No, Magnus." He spoke softly, as if he didn't want to wake anyone. "My family—"

"I *am* your family, you old idiot!"

Maybe that wasn't the most endearing thing to say. Maybe I should've thought *good riddance* and let him fall. But Annabeth was right. Randolph *was* family. The whole Chase clan attracted the gods' attention, and Randolph had borne that curse more heavily than most of us. Despite everything, I still wanted to help him.

He shook his head, sadness and pain fighting for dominance in his eyes. "I'm sorry. I want to see them."

He slipped sideways into the darkness without a sound.

I had no time to grieve, no time even to process what had happened, before three gods in tactical armor burst into the cave.

They all wore helmets, infrared goggles, jackboots, and full Kevlar body armor with the letters GRRM across the chest. I might have mistaken them for a regular SWAT team except for the excessive facial hair and the non-standard-issue weapons.

Thor stormed in first, holding his iron staff like a rifle, pointing it in every direction.

"Check your corners!" he yelled.

The next god through was Heimdall, grinning like he was

having an excellent time. He also held his massive sword like a gun, his Phablet of Doomsday stuck to the end. He swept the room, taking pictures of himself from every angle.

The third guy I didn't recognize. He stepped into the cavern with a *CLANG* because his right foot was encased in the most grotesque oversize shoe I had ever seen. It was cobbled together from scraps of leather and metal, pieces of neon athletic shoes, Velcro straps, and old brass buckles. It even had half a dozen stiletto heels sticking up from the toe like porcupine quills.

The three gods scampered around looking for threats.

With incredibly bad timing, the giant king Thrym began to regain consciousness. The god with the weird shoe rushed over and raised his right foot. His boot grew to the size of a Lincoln Town Car—a junkyard wedge of old shoe parts and scrap metal all compacted together into a huge death-stomper. Thrym didn't even have time to scream before Shoe Man stepped on him.

SPLAT. No more threat.

"Good one, Vidar!" Heimdall called. "Could you do that again so I can snap a picture?"

Vidar frowned and pointed at the mess. In perfect ASL, he signed, *He is flat now.*

Across the room, Thor gasped. "My baby!"

He ran past his goats and snatched up the hammer Mjolnir. "At last! Are you okay, Mee-Mee? Did those nasty giants reprogram your channels?"

Marvin jingled the bells on his collar. "We're fine, boss," he muttered. "Thanks for asking."

I looked at Sam. "Did he just call his hammer Mee-Mee?"

Alex growled, "Hey, Aesir idiots!" She pointed to the newly formed abyss. "Loki went that way."

"Loki?" Thor turned. "Where?" Lightning flickered through his beard, which probably rendered his infrared goggles useless.

With even worse timing than Thrym, the giantess Thrynga chose that moment to show she was still alive. She launched herself from the nearest cesspool like a breaching whale and landed at Heimdall's feet, gasping and steaming.

"Kill you all!" she croaked, which wasn't the smartest thing to say when facing three gods in tactical armor.

Thor pointed his hammer at Thrynga as casually as if he were channel surfing. Tendrils of lightning shot from the runes engraved in the metal. The giantess burst into a million bits of rubble.

"Dude!" Heimdall complained. "What did I tell you about lightning so close to my phablet? You want to fry the motherboard?"

Thor grunted. "Well, mortals, it's a good thing we arrived when we did, or that giantess might have hurt someone! Now, what were you saying about Loki?"

The thing about gods is, you can't really slap them when they're acting stupid.

They'll just slap you back and kill you.

Besides, I was too exhausted, shocked, boiled, and grief-stricken to complain much, even though the Aesir had let Loki get away.

No, I corrected myself. We *let Loki get away.*

While Thor murmured sweet nothings to his hammer,

Heimdall stood at the edge of the chasm and peered into the darkness. "Goes all the way to Helheim. No sign of Loki."

"My uncle?" I asked.

Heimdall's white irises turned toward me. For once, he wasn't smiling. "You know, Magnus . . . sometimes it's best not to look as far as you're *able* to look, or to listen to everything you're able to hear."

He patted me on the shoulder and walked away, leaving me to wonder what the heck he meant.

Vidar, the god with the shoe, went around checking for wounded, but everybody seemed more or less okay—everybody aside from the giants, that is. All of them were now dead. Halfborn had pulled his groin trying to pick up Thor's hammer. Mallory had given herself a stomachache laughing at him, but both those problems were easily fixed. T.J. had come through without a scratch, though he was worried how to get earth-giant blood off the stock of his rifle.

Hearthstone was fine, though he kept signing othala, the name of his missing runestone. He signed to Blitz that he could have stopped Loki if he'd had it. I suspected he was just being too hard on himself, but I wasn't sure. As for Blitz, he leaned against the cave wall and sipped from a canteen, looking tired after stone-sculpting all the way into Loki's cavern.

As soon as the gods had arrived, Jack had turned back into a pendant, muttering something about not wanting to see Heimdall's diva sword. In truth, I think he mostly felt guilty that he hadn't been more help to us, and sorry that Skofnung had turned out not to be the blade of his dreams. Now Jack hung around my neck again, snoozing fitfully. Fortunately, he hadn't suffered any damage. And he'd been so stunned throughout most of the fight that I'd hardly absorbed any fatigue from him at all. He would live to fight (and sing top-forty songs) another day.

Sam, Alex, and I sat at the edge of the chasm, listening to the echoes in the darkness. Vidar wrapped my ribs, then dabbed some salve on my arms and face and told me in sign language that I wouldn't die. He also bandaged Alex's ear and signed, *Minor concussion. Stay awake.*

Sam herself had no major physical injuries, but I could sense the emotional pain radiating from her. She sat with her spear across her lap like a kayak paddle, looking as though she were ready to navigate straight to Helheim. I think Alex and I both knew instinctively that we shouldn't leave her alone.

"I was helpless again," she said miserably. "He just . . . he *controlled* me."

Alex patted her leg. "Not entirely true. You're alive."

I looked back and forth between them. "What do you mean?"

Alex's darker eye was more dilated than the lighter one—probably because of the concussion. It made her stare look even more hollow and shell-shocked.

"When things went bad during the fight," she said, "Loki just . . . willed us to die. He told my heart to stop beating, my lungs to stop breathing. I assume he did the same to Sam."

Samirah nodded, her knuckles whitening on the shaft of her spear.

"Gods." I didn't know what to do with all the anger inside me. My chest boiled at the same temperature as the cesspool. If I hadn't hated Loki enough already, now I was determined to follow him to the ends of the Nine Worlds and . . . and do something really bad to him.

Like tie him down with his children's guts? asked a little voice in my head. *Put a venomous snake over his face? How did that sort of justice work out for the Aesir?*

"So you *did* resist him," I told the girls. "That's good."

Alex shrugged. "I told you, he can't control me. Earlier, I was just acting so he wouldn't get suspicious. But, Sam, yeah . . . that was a good first start. You stayed alive. You can't expect complete resistance right away. We can work on it together—"

"He's *free*, Alex!" Sam snapped. "We failed. *I* failed. If I'd been faster, if I'd realized—"

"Failed?" The thunder god loomed over us. "Nonsense, girl! You retrieved my hammer! You are heroes and will all receive trophies!"

I could see Sam gritting her teeth, trying not to yell at Thor. I was afraid she'd bust another capillary from the strain.

"I appreciate that, Lord Thor," she said at last. "But Loki never cared about the hammer. It was all a smokescreen to get himself freed."

Thor frowned and raised Mjolnir. "Oh, don't you worry, lass. We'll put Loki back in chains. And I promise you, he *will* care about this hammer when I ram it down his throat!"

Brave words, but when I looked around at my friends, I could tell that no one was reassured.

I stared at the letters on Thor's Kevlar vest. "What is G-R-R-M, anyway?"

"It's pronounced *grrm*," Thor said. "An acronym for *God Rapid Response Mobilization*."

"Rapid?" Alex snarled. "Are you *kidding* me? You guys took forever to get here!"

"Now, now." Heimdall stepped in. "You were a moving target, weren't you? We got into the tunnel at Bridal Veil Falls just fine! But then the whole moving-to-Loki's-lair thing—that caught us off guard. We were sealed in at both ends with earth-giant-hardened stone. Digging after you . . . well, even with three gods, that was tough."

Especially when one takes pictures and does not help, Vidar signed.

The other two gods ignored him, but Hearthstone signed back: *They never listen, do they?*

I know, signed the god. *Hearing people. Silly.*

I decided I liked Vidar. "Excuse me," I asked him, signing as I spoke. "Are you the god of shoes? Or healing? Or . . . ?"

Vidar smirked. He crooked both of his index fingers. He placed one under his eye, then tapped that finger with the other hooked one. I hadn't seen that sign before, but I got it: *Eye for an eye. Talons and hooks.* "You're the god of vengeance."

That seemed odd to me, since he seemed so kind and was mute. Then again, he wore an expanding shoe that could stomp giant kings flat.

"Oh, Vidar is our go-to guy for emergencies!" Heimdall said. "That shoe of his is made from every shoe scrap that has ever been thrown away! It can . . . well, you saw what it can do. Hey, do you think we can get a group shot with everyone?"

"No," said everyone.

Thor glared at the bridge guardian. "Vidar is also called the Silent One, which means he doesn't talk. He also doesn't take selfies constantly, which makes him *good* company."

Mallory Keen sheathed her twin knives. "Well, that's fascinating, I'm sure. But shouldn't you Aesir be doing something productive now, like . . . oh, finding Loki and tying him up again?"

The girl is right, Vidar signed. *Time is wasting.*

"Listen to brave Vidar, girl," said Thor. "Loki's capture can wait for another day. Right now we should be celebrating the return of my hammer!"

That's not what I said, Vidar signed.

"Besides," Thor added, "I don't need to search for the scoundrel. I know exactly where he's going."

"You do?" I asked. "Where?"

Thor pounded me on the back—fortunately with his hand and not his hammer. "We'll talk all about it back at Valhalla. Dinner is on me!"

FIFTY-FOUR

Squirrels in the Window
May Be Larger Than They Appear

I LOVE IT when gods offer to pay for a dinner that's already free.

Almost as much as I love assault squads that show up after the assault.

I never got the chance to complain about it, though. Once we got back to Valhalla—thanks to Thor's very overcrowded chariot—we were given a celebration feast that was wild even by Viking standards. Thor paraded around the feast hall holding Mjolnir above his head, grinning and yelling "Death to our enemies!" and generally causing a commotion. Party horns were blown. Mead was guzzled. Piñatas were cracked open with the mighty Mjolnir and candy was eaten.

Only our little group sulked, clustered around our table and halfheartedly accepting the pats on the back and compliments from our fellow einherjar. They assured us we were heroes. Not only had we retrieved Thor's hammer, we had destroyed an entire wedding party of evil, badly-dressed earth giants!

Nobody complained about Blitz and Hearth's presence. Nobody paid much attention to our new friend Vidar, despite his strange footwear. The Silent One lived up to his name and sat with us silently, occasionally asking Hearthstone questions in a form of sign language I didn't recognize.

Heimdall left early to get back to the Bifrost Bridge. There were important selfies to be taken. Meanwhile, Thor partied like a madman, bodysurfing over crowds of einherjar and Valkyries. Whatever he had wanted to tell us about Loki's location, he seemed to have forgotten, and I wasn't going to get anywhere near him in that mob.

My only consolation: some of the lords at the thanes' table also looked uneasy. Every once in a while Helgi the manager would scowl at the crowd as if he wanted to scream what I was thinking: *STOP CELEBRATING, YOU IDIOTS! LOKI IS FREE!*

Maybe the einherjar were choosing not to worry about it. Maybe Thor had assured them, too, that it was a problem easily fixed. Or maybe they were celebrating *because* Ragnarok was near. That idea scared me the most.

As dinner ended, Thor rode off in his chariot without even acknowledging us. He bellowed to the assembled host that he had to hurry to the borders of Midgard and demonstrate his hammer's power by blasting some giant armies to sizzly bits. The einherjar cheered and then began streaming out of the feast hall, no doubt heading to smaller but even wilder parties.

Vidar said his good-byes after a short conversation with Hearthstone in that strange language. Whatever he said, the elf chose not to share it with us. My hallmates offered to stay with me, but they had been invited to an after-party afterparty, and I told them to go. They deserved some fun after the tedium of digging their way into Loki's cavern.

Sam, Alex, Blitz, and Hearth accompanied me to the elevators. Before we got there, Helgi appeared and grabbed my arm.

"You and your friends need to come with me."

The manager's voice was grim. I got the feeling we would not be receiving trophies and coupons for our brave deeds.

Helgi led us through passageways I'd never seen before, up staircases into the far reaches of the hotel. I knew Valhalla was big, but each time I went exploring, I was newly amazed. The place went on forever—like Costco or a chemistry lecture.

At last we arrived at a heavy oaken door with a brass plaque that read MANAGER.

Helgi pushed open the door and we followed him inside to an office.

Three of the walls and the ceiling were paneled in spears—polished oak shafts tipped with gleaming silver points. Behind Helgi's desk, the back wall was one huge plate glass window overlooking the endless swaying branches of the World Tree.

I'd seen a lot of different views from the windows of Valhalla. The hotel had access to each of the Nine Worlds. But I'd never seen a view straight into the tree. It made me feel disoriented, like we were floating in its branches—which, cosmically speaking, we were.

"Sit." Helgi waved to a semicircle of chairs on the visitors' side of the desk. Sam, Alex, Blitz, Hearth, and I got comfortable with lots of squeaking leather and creaking wood. Helgi plopped himself down behind his huge mahogany desk, which was empty except for one of those desk-toy thingies with the hanging silver ball bearings that you can knock back and forth.

Oh . . . and the ravens. At either front corner of the desk

perched one of Odin's twin ravens, both of them glaring at me as if trying to decide whether to assign me detention or feed me to the trolls.

Helgi leaned back and steepled his fingers. He would've looked intimidating if it weren't for his roadkill explosion of hair and the leftover bits of feast beast in his beard.

Sam fiddled nervously with her ring of keys. "Sir, what happened in Loki's cave . . . it wasn't my friends' fault. I take full responsibility—"

"The Helheim you do!" Alex snapped. "Sam did nothing wrong. If you're going to punish anyone—"

"Stop!" Helgi ordered. "No one is getting punished."

Blitzen exhaled with relief. "Well, that's good. Because we didn't have time to return this to Thor, but honestly we meant to." Hearthstone produced Thor's two-by-four hall-pass key and set it on the manager's desk.

Helgi frowned. He slipped the pass into his desk drawer, which made me wonder how many others he had in there.

"You are here," said the manager, "because Odin's ravens asked for you."

"Huginn and Muninn?" *Thought* and *Memory*, I recalled from the *Hotel Valhalla Guide*.

The birds made that weird croaking noise ravens love to make, as if regurgitating the souls of all the frogs they'd eaten over the centuries.

They were much larger than normal ravens—and creepier. Their eyes were like gateways into the void. Their feathers were a thousand different shades of ebony. When the light hit them, runes seemed to glisten in their plumage—dark words rising out of a sea of black ink.

Helgi tapped his desk toy. The balls started swinging and hitting each other with an annoying *click, click, click.*

"Odin would be here," said the manager, "but he is tending to other matters. Huginn and Muninn represent him. As a bonus"—Helgi leaned forward and lowered his voice—"the ravens don't show motivational PowerPoints."

The birds squawked in agreement.

"Now, down to business," Helgi said. "Loki has escaped, but we know where he is. Samirah al-Abbas . . . your next mission as Odin's Valkyrie in charge of special operations will be to find your father and put him back in chains."

Samirah lowered her head. She didn't look surprised—more like she'd lost the final appeal for a death sentence she'd been fighting her entire life.

"Sir," she said, "I will do as I'm ordered. But after what happened the last two times I faced my father, the ease with which he controlled me—"

"You can learn to fight it," Alex interrupted. "I can help—"

"I'm not you, Alex! I can't . . ." Sam gestured vaguely at her sister, as if to indicate all the things Alex was that Sam could never be.

Helgi brushed some food scraps out of his beard. "Samirah, I didn't say it would be easy. But the ravens say you can do it. You must do it. And so you shall."

Sam stared at the ball bearings bouncing back and forth. *Click, click, click.*

"This place where my father went . . ." she said. "Where is it?"

"The Eastern Shores," Helgi said. "Just as the old stories

say. Now that Loki is free, he has gone to the docks, where he hopes to complete construction of *Naglfar.*"

Hearthstone signed: *The Ship of Nails. That is not good.*

I felt cold . . . and seasick.

I remembered visiting that ship in a dream, standing on the deck of a Viking longboat the size of an aircraft carrier and made entirely from the toenails and fingernails of the dead. Loki had warned me that when Ragnarok began, he would sail the ship to Asgard, destroy the gods, steal their Pop-Tarts, and otherwise cause mass chaos.

"If Loki is free, is it already too late?" I asked. "Isn't his unbinding one of the things that signals the beginning of Ragnarok?"

"Yes and no," Helgi said.

I waited. "Am I supposed to pick one?"

"The unbinding of Loki *does* help start Ragnarok," Helgi said. "But nothing says *this* escape is his last and final escape. It's conceivable you could recapture him and put him back, thus postponing Doomsday."

"Like we did with Fenris Wolf," Blitz muttered. "That was a piece of cake."

"Exactly." Helgi nodded enthusiastically. "Cake."

"I was being sarcastic," Blitz said. "I suppose they don't have sarcasm in Valhalla any more than they have decent barbers."

Helgi reddened. "See here, dwarf—"

He was interrupted by a huge brown-and-orange shape slamming into his window.

Blitzen fell out of his chair. Alex leaped straight up and

clung to the ceiling in the form of a sugar glider. Sam rose with her ax in hand, ready for battle. I valiantly took cover down in front of Helgi's desk. Hearthstone just sat there, frowning at the giant squirrel.

Why? he signed.

"It's all right, everyone," Helgi assured us. "It's just Ratatosk."

The words *just Ratatosk* did not compute. I'd been chased through the World Tree by that monstrous rodent. I'd heard his soul-searing, scolding voice. It was *never* all right when he showed up.

"No, really," Helgi insisted. "The window is soundproof and squirrel-proof. The beast just likes to stop by and taunt me sometimes."

I peeked over the top of the desk. Ratatosk was barking and screeching, but only the faintest murmur came through the glass. He gnashed his teeth at us and pressed his cheek against the window.

The ravens didn't seem bothered. They glanced over as if to say, *Oh, it's you,* then went back to preening their feathers.

"How do you stand it?" Blitzen asked. "That—that thing is deadly!"

The squirrel puffed his mouth against the glass, showing us his teeth and gums, then licked the window.

"I'd rather know where he is than not," Helgi said. "Sometimes I can tell what's going on in the Nine Worlds just by observing the squirrel's level of agitation."

Judging from Ratatosk's current state, I guessed some serious stuff was going down in the Nine Worlds. To alleviate our anxiety, Helgi rose, lowered the blinds, and sat back down.

"Where were we?" he said. "Ah, yes, cake and sarcasm."

Alex dropped from the ceiling and returned to her regular form. She'd changed out of her wedding dress earlier and was back in her old diamond-pattern sweater-vest. She tugged at it casually as if to say, *Yes, I totally meant to turn into a sugar glider.*

Sam lowered her ax. "Helgi, about this mission . . . I wouldn't know where to start. Where the ship is docked? The Eastern Shores could be on any world."

The manager turned up his palms. "I don't have those answers, Samirah, but Huginn and Muninn will brief you privately. Go with them to the high places of Valhalla. Let them show you thoughts and memories."

To me, that sounded like some trippy vision quest with Darth Vader appearing in a foggy cave.

Sam didn't look too happy about it, either. "But, Helgi—"

"There can be no debate," the manager insisted. "Odin chose you. He has chosen this entire group because—" He paused abruptly and put a finger to his ear. I'd never realized Helgi wore an earpiece, but he was obviously listening to something.

He glanced up at us. "Apologies. Where was I? Ah, yes, all five of you were present when Loki escaped. Therefore, all five of you will have a part to play in recapturing the outlaw god."

"We broke it, we bought it," I muttered.

"Exactly!" Helgi grinned. "Now that that's settled, you'll have to excuse me. There's been a massacre in the yoga studio, and they need clean mats."

FIFTY-FIVE

Daisies in the Shape of an Elf

AS SOON AS we left the office, the ravens led Sam up another staircase. She glanced back at us uneasily, but Helgi had been pretty clear that the rest of us weren't invited.

Alex turned on her heel and marched off in the opposite direction.

"Hey," I called. "Where—?"

She looked back, her eyes so angry I couldn't finish my question.

"Later, Magnus," she said. "I have to . . ." She made a strangling gesture with her hands. "Just later."

That left me with Blitzen and Hearthstone, who were both swaying on their feet.

"You guys want to—?"

"Sleep," Blitzen said. "Please. Immediately."

I led them back to my room. The three of us camped in the grass in the middle of my atrium. It reminded me of the old days, sleeping in the Public Garden, but I'm not going to tell you I was nostalgic for being homeless. Homelessness is not something any sane person would ever be nostalgic about. Still, like I've said, it was a lot simpler than being an undead warrior who chased fugitive gods across the Nine Worlds and conducted serious conversations while a monstrous squirrel made faces at you in the window.

Hearthstone conked out first. He curled up, sighed gently, and went right to sleep. When he was still, despite his black clothes, he seemed to blend into the shadows of the grass. Maybe it was elf camouflage—a remnant of the time when they were one with nature.

Blitz wedged his back against a tree and stared at Hearth with concern.

"We're going to Blitzen's Best tomorrow," he told me. "Reopen the shop. Spend a few weeks trying to regroup and get back to . . . whatever *normal* is. Before we have to go and find . . ." The prospect of taking on Loki again was so daunting he couldn't even finish the thought.

I felt guilty that I hadn't considered Hearthstone's grief the past few days. I'd been too preoccupied with Thor's stupid TV hammer.

"That's a good idea," I said. "Alfheim was rough for him."

Blitz clasped his hands near where the Skofnung Sword had pierced him. "Yeah, I'm worried about Hearth's unfinished business there."

"I wish I'd been more help to him," I said. "To both of you."

"Nah, kid. Some kinds of help you have to do for yourself. Hearth . . . he's got a dad-shaped hole in his heart. You can't do anything about that."

"His dad will never be a nice guy."

"No kidding. But Hearth has to come to terms with that. Sooner or later, he'll have to go back and face him . . . get his inheritance rune back one way or another. When and how that will happen, though . . ." He shrugged helplessly.

I thought about my Uncle Randolph. How did you decide when someone was irretrievably lost—when they were so evil or toxic or just plain set in their ways that you had to face the fact they were never going to change? How long could you keep trying to save them, and when did you give up and grieve for them as though they were dead?

It was easy for me to advise Hearthstone on his father. The dude was way past horrible. But my own uncle, who had gotten me killed, stabbed my friend, and freed the god of evil . . . I still couldn't quite bring myself to write him off.

Blitzen patted my hand. "Whatever happens, kid, we'll be ready when you need us. We'll see this through and get Loki back in chains, even if I have to make those chains myself."

"Yours would be a lot more fashionable," I said.

Blitz's mouth twitched. "Yeah. Yeah, they would. And don't feel guilty, kid. You did good."

I wasn't so sure about that. What had I accomplished? I felt like I'd spent the last six days scrambling around doing damage control, trying to keep my friends alive, trying to minimize the fallout from Loki's plot.

I imagined what Samirah would say: *That's enough, Magnus.* She'd probably point out that I'd helped Amir. I'd managed to heal Blitzen. I'd gotten Thor's assault team into the giants' lair to retrieve the hammer. I'd bowled a really mean game of doubles with my partner the African bush elephant.

Still . . . Loki was free. He'd hurt Sam. He'd crushed her confidence *badly.* And then there was that little thing about all the Nine Worlds now at risk of being thrown into chaos.

"I feel terrible, Blitz," I admitted. "The more I train, the more powers I learn . . . It just seems like the problems get ten times bigger than what I can handle. Is that ever going to stop?"

Blitz didn't answer. His chin rested on his chest. He was quietly snoring.

I put a blanket over him. I sat for a long time watching the stars through the tree branches and thinking about holes in people's hearts.

I wondered what Loki was doing right now. If I were him, I would be planning the most massive revenge spree the Nine Worlds had ever seen. Maybe that's why Vidar, the god of vengeance, had seemed so gentle and quiet. He knew it didn't take much to start a chain reaction of violence and death. One insult. One theft. One severed chain. Thrym and Thrynga had nursed a grudge for generations. They'd been used by Loki not just once, but twice. And now they were dead.

I don't remember falling asleep. When I woke the next morning, Blitz and Hearth were gone. A bed of daisies bloomed where Hearthstone had slept—maybe it was his way of saying *good-bye, thank you, see you soon.* I still felt depressed.

I showered and got dressed. Just brushing my teeth felt ridiculously normal after the last few days. I was about to head to breakfast when I noticed a note slipped under my door, in Samirah's elegant cursive:

Some ideas. Thinking Cup? I'll be there all morning.

I stepped into the hallway. I liked the idea of getting out of Valhalla for a little while. I wanted to talk to Sam. I wanted good mortal coffee. I wanted to sit in the sunshine and eat a poppy seed muffin and pretend that I wasn't an einherji with a fugitive god to catch.

Then I looked across the hall.

First I needed to do one more difficult and dangerous thing. I needed to check on Alex Fierro.

Alex opened the door and greeted me with a cheerful "Get lost."

Wet clay spackled Alex's face and hands. I glanced inside and saw the project sitting on the potter's wheel. "Dude . . ."

I stepped inside. For some reason, Alex let me.

All the shattered pottery had been cleaned up. The racks were filled with new pots and cups, just drying and still unglazed. On the wheel stood a huge vase, about three feet tall, shaped like a trophy.

I grinned. "For Sif?"

Alex shrugged. "Yeah. If it turns out okay."

"Is this gift ironic, or serious?"

"You're going to make me choose? I dunno. It just . . . felt right to do. At first I hated her. She reminded me of my stepmother, all fussy and uptight. But . . . maybe I should cut her some slack."

Over on the bed lay the gold-and-white wedding dress, still spattered with blood, the hem caked in dust and spotted with acid stains. Nevertheless, Alex had smoothed it out very carefully, like it was something worth keeping.

"Ahem. Magnus, you had some reason to stop by?"

"Yeah . . ." I found it hard to concentrate. I stared at the rows of pots, all perfectly shaped. "You made all these last night?"

I picked one up.

Alex took it out of my hands. "No, you can't touch it, Magnus. Thanks for asking, Magnus. Yes, most of these were last night. I couldn't sleep. The pottery . . . it makes me feel better. Now you were about to say why you came over and then quickly get out of my hair?"

"I'm going to meet Sam in Boston. I thought—"

"That I'd want to come with? No, thanks. When Sam is ready to talk, she knows where to find me."

Alex marched back to the wheel, picked up a scraper, and started smoothing the sides of the trophy cup.

"You're angry with her."

Alex kept scraping.

"That's a pretty impressive vase," I offered. "I don't know how you can shape something that large without it falling apart. I tried to use a wheel in, like, fifth grade art class. The best I could manage was an off-center lump."

"A self-portrait, then?"

"Ha, ha. Just saying I wish I could do something this cool."

No immediate reply. Maybe because I hadn't left much room for a witty insult.

Finally, Alex glanced up warily. "You heal people, Magnus. Your dad is actually a *helpful* god. You've got this whole . . . sunshiny, warm, friendly thing going on. That's not enough cool stuff for you?"

"I've never been called *sunshiny* before."

"Oh, please. You pretend like you're all tough and sarcastic or whatever, but you're a big softie. And to answer your question, yes, I'm mad at Sam. Unless she changes her attitude, I'm not sure I can teach her."

"To . . . resist Loki."

Alex picked up a lump of clay and squeezed it. "The secret is, you have to be *comfortable* changing. All the time. You have to make Loki's power *your* power."

"Like your tattoo."

Alex shrugged. "Clay can be shaped and reshaped, over and over, but if it gets too dry, if it sets . . . then there's only so much you can do with it. When it gets to that point, you'd better be sure it's in the shape you want it to have forever."

"You're saying Sam can't change."

"I don't know if she can, or even if she wants to. But I do know this: if she won't let me teach her how I resist Loki, if she won't at least try—then the next time we face him, we're all dead."

I took a shaky breath. "Okay, good pep talk. I guess I'll see you at dinner tonight."

When I got to the door, Alex said, "How did you know?"

I turned. "Know what?"

"When you walked in, you said *dude*. How did you know I was male?"

I thought about it. At first I wondered if it had just been a throwaway comment—a non-gender-specific *dude*. The more I considered, though, the more I realized I'd genuinely picked up on the fact that Alex was male. Or rather, Alex *had* been male. Now, after we'd been talking for a few minutes, she definitely seemed like a she. But how I'd sensed that, I had no idea.

"Just my perceptive nature, I guess."

Alex snorted. "Right."

"But you're a girl now."

She hesitated. "Yeah."

"Interesting."

"You can leave now."

"Will you make me a trophy for my perceptiveness?"

She picked up a pottery shard and threw it at me.

I closed the door just as it shattered on the inside.

FIFTY-SIX

Let's Try This Whole "Meeting for Coffee" Thing Again

JUDGING FROM the line of empty cups, Sam was on her third espresso.

The idea of approaching an armed Valkyrie with three espressos in her system was usually not advisable, but I walked up slowly and sat across from her. She didn't look at me. Her attention was on the two raven feathers in front of her. It was a windy morning. Sam's green hijab rippled around her face like waves on a beach, but the two raven feathers didn't flutter.

"Hey," she said.

It was a lot friendlier than *get lost*. Sam was so different from Alex, but there was something similar in their eyes—a sense of urgency churning just below the surface. It wasn't easy thinking about Loki's inheritance battling inside my two friends, trying to take control.

"You got feathers," I noted.

She touched the one of the left. "A memory. And this one"—she tapped the right—"a thought. The ravens don't really speak. They stare at you and let you stroke their plumage until the right feathers drop out."

"So what do they mean?"

"This one, the memory . . ." Sam ran a finger down the barbs. "It's ancestral. From my distant forefather, Ahmad Ibn Fadlan Ibn al-Abbas."

"The guy who traveled among the Vikings."

Sam nodded. "When I took the feather, I could *see* his journey like I was there. I learned a lot of things he never wrote about—things he didn't think would go over well in the court of the caliph of Baghdad."

"He saw Norse gods?" I guessed. "Valkyries? Giants?"

"And more. He also heard legends about the ship *Naglfar.* The place where it's docked, the Eastern Shores, lies on the border between Jotunheim and Niflheim—the wildest, most remote part of either world. It's completely inaccessible, locked in ice except for one day of the year—Midsummer."

"So that's when Loki will plan to set sail."

"And that's when we'll have to be there to stop him."

I craved an espresso, but my heart was racing so fast I doubted I needed one. "So what now? We just wait until summer?"

"It's going to take time to find his location. And before we can leave, we'll need to prepare, train, make sure we can beat him."

I remembered what Alex had said: *I'm not sure I can teach her.*

"We'll make it happen." I tried to sound confident. "What did the second feather tell you?"

"That's a thought," Samirah said. "A plan to move forward. To reach the Eastern Shores, we'll need to sail through the farthest branches of the World Tree, through the old Viking lands. That's where giant magic is strongest, and where we'll find the sea passage to *Naglfar*'s dock."

"The old Viking lands." My fingers tingled. I wasn't sure whether it was with excitement or fear. "Scandinavia? I'm pretty sure there are flights from Logan."

Sam shook her head. "We'll have to go by sea, Magnus. The way the Vikings came *here*. Just as you can only enter Alfheim through the air, we can only reach the wild borderlands of the Eastern Shores through salt water and ice."

"Right," I said. "Because nothing is ever easy."

"No, it's not."

Her tone was distracted, wistful. It made me realize I was being kind of insensitive. Sam had a lot of other problems going on besides her evil father.

"How's Amir?" I asked.

She actually smiled. In the wind, her hijab seemed to shape-shift from waves to grassy fields to smooth glass.

"He's very good," she said. "He accepts me. He doesn't want to cancel our engagement. You were right, Magnus. He's a lot stronger than I gave him credit for."

"That's great. What about your grandparents, and his dad?"

Samirah laughed drily. "Well, we can't have everything. They remember nothing about Loki's visits. They know that Amir and I have made up. For now, all is well. I'm back to making excuses about why I have to rush off in the middle of class or after school. I'm doing a lot of 'tutoring.'" She put the word in air quotes.

I remembered how weary she'd looked when I met her here six days ago. If anything, she looked more tired now.

"Something's got to give, Sam," I told her. "You're running yourself ragged."

"I know." She put her hand over the feather of thought. "I've promised Amir—once we recapture Loki, once I am sure that Ragnarok has been averted, at least for the present, then I'm done."

"Done?"

"I'm retiring from the Valkyries. I'll devote myself to college, completing my pilot's training, and . . . marriage, of course. When I'm eighteen, as we've planned."

She was blushing like . . . well, like a bride.

I tried to ignore the hollow feeling in my chest. "And that's what you want?"

"It's entirely my choice. Amir supports it."

"Valkyries can resign?"

"Of course. It's not like being . . . ah . . ."

An einherji, she meant. I was one of the reborn. I could travel the worlds. I had amazing strength and stamina. But I would never again be a normal human. I would stay as I was, the same age forever—or until Ragnarok, whichever came first. (Certain restrictions may apply. Read your service agreement for full details.)

"Magnus, I know I brought you into this weird afterlife," she said. "It's not fair of me to leave you, but—"

"Hey." I touched her hand just briefly. I knew that wasn't Sam's thing, but she and my cousin Annabeth were the closest thing I would ever have to sisters. "Samirah, I just want you to be happy. And, you know, if we can keep the Nine Worlds from burning before you leave, that would be nice, too."

She laughed. "All right, then, Magnus. It's a deal. We'll need a ship. We'll need a lot of things, actually."

"Yeah." Salt and ice seemed to be making themselves at home in my throat already. I remembered our encounter in January with the sea goddess Ran—how she'd warned me that I would be in trouble if I ever tried to sail the seas again.

"First we need advice," I said. "About sailing across magical waters, fighting weird sea monsters, and not dying at the hands of a bunch of angry aquatic gods. Strangely enough, I know just the person to talk to."

"Your cousin," Sam guessed.

"Yeah," I said. "Annabeth."

FIFTY-SEVEN

I Call In Some Favors

TEXTING AND calling didn't work, so I sent a raven.

When I told T.J. that I was having trouble getting in touch with my cousin, he looked at me like I was dense. "Just send a bird, Magnus."

Stupid me, I'd spent months in Valhalla not realizing I could rent a raven, tie a message to its leg, and send it to find anybody in the Nine Worlds. The whole thing seemed a little too *Game-of-Thrones*-y to me, but whatever. It worked.

The raven came back promptly with Annabeth's reply.

We coordinated train rides and met halfway between Boston and Manhattan, in New London, Connecticut. Annabeth was there before me, standing on the platform in jeans and sandals and a long-sleeved purple shirt with a laurel-wreath design and the letters SPQR: UNR.

She hugged me until my eyeballs bugged out like Thrynga's. "I was so relieved," she said. "I never thought I'd be glad to see a raven at my window, but . . . Are you okay?"

"Yeah, yeah." I had to suppress a nervous laugh, because *okay* was a stupid word to describe how I felt. Also, it was obvious Annabeth was *not* okay, either. Her gray eyes seemed heavy and weary, less like storm clouds today, and more like fog banks that couldn't quite lift.

"A lot to talk about," I said. "Let's get some lunch."

We got a table on the deck of the Muddy Waters café. I supposed the place was named after the blues musician, but it seemed a little ominous considering the waters I was getting ready to sail through. Annabeth and I sat in the sunshine, ordered Cokes and cheeseburgers, and watched the sailboats heading out to Long Island Sound.

"It's been crazy in New York," Annabeth said. "I thought communications were only down among demigods . . . I mean *my* kind, the Greek and Roman, but then I realized I hadn't heard from you, either. I'm sorry that didn't dawn on me sooner."

"Wait, why are communications down?"

Annabeth poked at the table with her fork tines. Her blond hair was loose around her shoulders today. She seemed to be growing it out. It caught the sunlight in a way that reminded me of Sif . . . but I tried to shake that idea. I knew Annabeth would destroy anyone who dared call her a "trophy" anything.

"There's a crisis happening," Annabeth said. "A god fell to earth as a human. These evil Roman emperors are back, causing trouble."

"Oh, so just the usual, then."

She laughed. "Yeah. Somehow these evil Romans found a way to mess up communication among demigods. Not just the usual magical kinds of talking, but also cell phones, Wi-Fi, you name it. I'm surprised your raven made it to me. I would've come up to Boston to check on you sooner, but . . ." She shrugged helplessly. "I've had my hands full."

"I totally get it," I said. "I probably shouldn't be distracting you. You've got enough to deal with . . ."

She reached across the table and squeezed my hand. "Are you kidding? I want to help. What's going on?"

It felt so good to tell her everything. I remembered how weird it had been the first time we'd compared notes—her with the Greek gods, me with the Norse. We'd both left that day feeling like we'd overcharged our batteries and our brains were melting.

Now, at least, we had some kind of framework to build on. Sure, it was all still ridiculously crazy. If I stopped to think about it too long, I would start giggling like a lunatic. But I could tell Annabeth my problems without worrying that she wouldn't believe me. It made me realize how much Sam must appreciate being able to be totally truthful with Amir.

I told Annabeth about Loki's escape and Sam's idea for tracking him down—about an icy harbor at the farthest borders of Jotunheim and Niflheim (or Scandinavia, whichever came first).

"A boat trip," she said. "Oh, boy. That brings back painful memories."

"Yeah. I remembered what you said about sailing to Greece and . . . yeah." I didn't want to bring up all that horrible stuff again. She had cried when she told me about the things that had happened to her during their voyage, especially how she and her boyfriend, Percy, had fallen into some underworld place called Tartarus.

"Look," I said, "I don't want to put any pressure on you. I just thought . . . I don't know . . . maybe you'd have some ideas, some pointers."

A train rumbled through the station. My view of the bay

flickered between the rail cars like an old, out-of-alignment reel-to-reel movie.

"You say you have problems with sea gods," Annabeth said.

"Yeah, Ran . . . this bag lady with a net. And I guess her husband hates me too now. His name is Aegir."

Annabeth tapped her forehead. "I need more memory storage for all these names. Okay, I don't know how this works with multiple sea gods. Are the Norse ones just in the north and Poseidon is in the south, or do they do, like, a time-share program . . . ?"

I remembered an old cartoon with sheepdogs punching time clocks as they came in for different shifts to keep the wolves away from the flocks. I wondered if gods had punch cards like that, or maybe they all worked from home. Could sea gods telecommute?

"I don't know," I admitted. "But I'd like to avoid getting all my friends drowned in a tsunami as soon as we leave Boston."

"But you've got some time?"

"Until this summer," I said. "We can't leave while the seas are frozen or something."

"Good. We'll be done with school by then, finally graduated."

"I don't go to school. Oh . . . you mean *we* as in you and your boyfriend?"

"Exactly. Assuming he passes his semester and does okay on his standardized tests, assuming these evil Roman emperors don't kill us all and destroy the world. . . ."

"Yeah. Loki would be seriously ticked off if Roman emperors destroyed the world before he got to start Ragnarok."

"We should have enough time to help you, at least compare notes, maybe call in some favors."

"Um, what favors?"

Annabeth smiled. "I don't know the ocean very well, but my boyfriend does. I think it's time you met Percy."

GLOSSARY

AEGIR—lord of the waves

AESIR—gods of war, close to humans

ALICARL—Norse for *fatso*

ARGR—Norse for *unmanly*

AVENTAIL—a chain mail curtain around the base of a helmet, meant to protect the neck

BARROW—the tomb of a wight

BERSERKER—a Norse warrior frenzied in battle and considered invulnerable

BIFROST—the rainbow bridge leading from Asgard to Midgard

BILSKIRNIR—Bright Crack, Thor and Sif's palace

BINT—Arabic for *daughter*

BRUNNMIGI—a being who urinates into wells

DRAUGR—Norse zombies

EINHERJAR (EINHERJI, sing.)—great heroes who have died with bravery on Earth; soldiers in Odin's eternal army; they train in Valhalla for Ragnarok, when the bravest of them will join Odin against Loki and the giants in the battle at the end of the world

FENRIS WOLF—an invulnerable wolf born of Loki's affair with a giantess; his mighty strength strikes fear even in the gods, who keep him tied to a rock on an island. He is destined to break free on the day of Ragnarok.

FOLKVANGER—the Vanir afterlife for slain heroes, ruled by the goddess Freya

FREY—the god of spring and summer; the sun, the rain, and the harvest; abundance and fertility, growth and vitality. Frey is the twin brother of Freya and, like his sister, is associated with great beauty. He is lord of Alfheim.

FREYA—the goddess of love; twin sister of Frey; ruler of Folkvanger

FRIGG—goddess of marriage and motherhood; Odin's wife and the queen of Asgard; mother of Balder and Hod

GAMALOST—old cheese

GINNUNGAGAP—the primordial void; a mist that obscures appearances

GJALLAR—Heimdall's horn

HEIMDALL—god of vigilance and the guardian of Bifrost, the gateway to Asgard

HEL—goddess of the dishonorable dead; born of Loki's affair with a giantess

HELHEIM—the underworld, ruled by Hel and inhabited by those who died in wickedness, old age, or illness

HUGINN AND MUNINN—Odin's ravens, whose names mean *thought* and *memory*, respectively

HULDER—a domesticated forest sprite

HUSVAETTR—house wight

JORMUNGAND—the World Serpent, born of Loki's affair with a giantess; his body is so long it wraps around the Earth

JOTUN—giant

KENNING—a Viking nickname

LINDWORM—a fearsome dragon the size and length of an eighteen-wheeler, with just two front legs and leathery brown bat-type wings too small for effective flight

LOKI—god of mischief, magic, and artifice; the son of two giants; adept at magic and shape-shifting. He is alternately malicious and heroic to the Asgardian gods and to humankind. Because of his role in the death of Balder, Loki was chained by Odin to three giant boulders with a poisonous serpent coiled over his head. The venom of the snake occasionally irritates Loki's face, and his writhing can cause earthquakes.

MAGNI AND MODI—Thor's favorite sons, fated to survive Ragnarok

MEINFRETR—stinkfart

MIMIR—an Aesir god who, along with Honir, traded places with Vanir gods Frey and Njord at the end of the war between the Aesir and the Vanir. When the Vanir didn't like his counsel, they cut off his head and sent it to Odin. Odin placed the head in a magical well, where the water brought it back to life, and Mimir soaked up all the knowledge of the World Tree.

MJOLNIR—Thor's hammer

MORGEN-GIFU—*morning gift*; a gift from the groom to the bride, given on the morning after a marriage is consummated. It belongs to the bride, but it is held in trust by the groom's family.

MUNDR—*bride-price*; a gift from the groom to the father of the bride

MUSPELL—fire

NAGLFAR—the Ship of Nails

NØKK—a nixie, or water spirit

NORNS—three sisters who control the destinies of both gods and humans

ODIN—the "All-Father" and king of the gods; the god of war and death, but also poetry and wisdom. By trading one eye for a drink from the Well of Wisdom, Odin gained unparalleled knowledge. He has the ability to observe all the Nine Worlds from his throne in Asgard; in addition to his great hall, he also resides in Valhalla with the bravest of those slain in battle.

OSTARA—the first day of spring

OTHALA—inheritance

RAGNAROK—the Day of Doom or Judgment, when the bravest of the einherjar will join Odin against Loki and the giants in the battle at the end of the world

RAN—goddess of the sea; wife of Aegir

RATATOSK—an invulnerable squirrel that constantly runs up and down the World Tree carrying insults between the eagle that lives at the top and Nidhogg, a dragon that lives at the roots

RED GOLD—the currency of Asgard and Valhalla

SAEHRIMNIR—the magical beast of Valhalla; every day it is killed and cooked for dinner, and every morning it is resurrected; it tastes like whatever the diner wants

SIF—goddess of the earth; mother of Uller by her first husband; Thor is her second husband; the rowan is her sacred tree

SLEIPNIR—Odin's eight-legged steed; only Odin can summon him; one of Loki's children

SUMARBRANDER—the Sword of Summer

THANE—a lord of Valhalla

THINGVELLIR—field of the assembly

THOR—god of thunder; son of Odin. Thunderstorms are the earthly effects of Thor's mighty chariot rides across the sky, and lightning is caused by hurling his great hammer, Mjolnir.

THRYM—king of the jotun

TREE OF LAERADR—a tree in the center of the Feast Hall of the Slain in Valhalla containing immortal animals that have particular jobs

TYR—god of courage, law, and trial by combat; he lost a hand to Fenris's bite when the Wolf was restrained by the gods

ULLER—the god of snowshoes and archery

URNES—a symbol of two entwined snakes, which signifies change and flexibility; sometimes a symbol for Loki

UTGARD-LOKI—the most powerful sorcerer of Jotunheim; king of the mountain giants

VALA—a seer

VALHALLA—paradise for warriors in the service of Odin

VALKYRIE—Odin's handmaidens, who choose slain heroes to bring to Valhalla

VANIR—gods of nature; close to elves

VIDAR—the god of vengeance; also called the Silent One

WERGILD—blood debt

WIGHT—a powerful undead creature who likes to collect weapons

YGGDRASIL—the World Tree

ZUHR—Arabic for midday prayer

PRONUNCIATION GUIDE

AEGIR	*AY-gear*
AESIR	*AY-ser*
ALF SEIDR	*ALF SAY-der*
ALFHEIM	*ALF-haym*
ALICARL	*AL-ih-carrl*
ARGR	*ARR-ger*
ASGARD	*AZ-gahrrd*
BIFROST	*BEE-frrohst*
BILSKIRNIR	*BEEL-skeerr-neer*
DAGAZ	*DAH-gahz*
DRAUGR	*DRAW-ger*
EINHERJAR/EINHERJI	*in-HAIRR-yar/in-HAIRR-yee*
EHWAZ	*AY-wahz*
FEHU	*FAY-hoo*
FENRIS	*FEHN-rrihss*
FOLKVANGER	*FOHK-vahn-ger*
FREY	*FRRAY*
FREYA	*FRRAY-uh*
FRIGG	*FRRIHG*
GAMALOST	*GA-ma-lohst*
GEBO	*GIH-bo*
GEIRROD	*GAR-rod*
GERD	*GAIRRD*
GINNUNGAGAP	*GEENG-un-guh-gahp*
GJALLAR	*gee-YALL-ar*
HAGALAZ	*HA-ga-lahts*
HEIMDALL	*HAME-doll*
HEL	*HEHL*

HELGI	*HEL-ghee*
HELHEIM	*HEHL-haym*
HUGINN	*HOO-gihn*
HULDER	*HOOL-dihr*
HUNDING	*HOON-deeng*
HUSVAETTR	*HOOS-veht-tr*
ISA	*EES-ah*
JORMUNGAND	*YOHRR-mun-gand*
JOTUN	*YOH-toon*
JOTUNHEIM	*YOH-tuhn-haym*
LAERADR	*LAY-rrah-dur*
KENNING	*KEN-ning*
LINDWORM	*LIHND-wohrrm*
LOKI	*LOH-kee*
MEINFRETR	*MAYN-frih-ter*
MIDGARD	*MIHD-gahrrd*
MIMIR	*MEE-meer*
MJOLNIR	*MEE'OHL-neer*
MODI	*MOH-dee*
MORGEN-GIFU	*MORR-ghen-GIH-foo*
MUNDR	*MOON-der*
MUNINN	*MOON-in*
MUSPELL	*MOO-spel*
MUSPELLHEIM	*MOOS-pehl-haym*
NAGLFAR	*NAHG'L-fahr*
NIDAVELLIR	*Nee-duh-vehl-EER*
NIDHOGG	*NEED-hawg*
NIFLHEIM	*NIHF-uh-haym*
NØKK	*NAWK*
NORNS	*NOHRRNZ*
NORUMBEGA	*nohrr-uhm-BAY-guh*
ODIN	*OH-dihn*

OSTARA	*OH-starr-ah*
OTHALA	*OH-thal-ah*
PERTHRO	*PERR-thrroh*
RAGNAROK	*RAG-nuh-rrawk*
RAN	*RAN*
RATATOSK	*RAT-uh-tawsk*
SAEHRIMNIR	*SAY-h'rrihm-neer*
SAMIRAH AL-ABBAS	*sah-MEER-ah ahl-AH-bahss*
SIF	*SEEV*
SLEIPNIR	*SLAYP-neer*
SUMARBRANDER	*SOO-marr-brrand-der*
THINGVELLIR	*THING-vih-leer*
THURISAZ	*THOORR-ee-sahts*
THOR	*THORE*
THRYM	*THRRIMM*
THRYNGA	*THRRIN-gah*
TIWAZ	*TEE-vahz*
TYR	*TEAR*
ULLER	*OO-lir*
URNES	*OORR-nis*
URUZ	*OOR-oots*
UTGARD-LOKI	*OOT-gahrrd-LOH-kee*
VALA	*VAL-uh*
VALHALLA	*Val-HAHL-uh*
VALKYRIE	*VAL-kerr-ee*
VANAHEIM	*VAN-uh-haym*
VANIR	*Vah-NEER*
VIDAR	*VEE-dar*
WERGILD	*WIR-gild*
WIGHT	*WHITE*
YGGDRASIL	*IHG-druh-sihl*

THE NINE WORLDS

ASGARD—the home of the Aesir

VANAHEIM—the home of the Vanir

ALFHEIM—the home of the light elves

MIDGARD—the home of humans

JOTUNHEIM—the home of the giants

NIDAVELLIR—the home of the dwarves

NIFLHEIM—the world of ice, fog, and mist

MUSPELLHEIM—the home of the fire giants and demons

HELHEIM—the home of Hel and the dishonorable dead

RUNES (IN ORDER OF MENTION)

FEHU—the rune of Frey

OTHALA—inheritance

DAGAZ—new beginnings, transformations

URUZ—ox

GEBO—gift

PERTHRO—the empty cup

THURISAZ—the rune of Thor

HAGALAZ—hail

EHWAZ—horse, transportation

ISA—ice

COMING IN FALL 2017

RICK RIORDAN

MAGNUS CHASE

and the GODS of ASGARD

THE SHIP OF THE DEAD